Book Level 5.4

AR Points 17.0

SUPER EDITION
WARRIORS

BRAMBLESTAR'S STORM

WARRIORS

Book One: *Into the Wild*

Book Two: *Fire and Ice*

Book Three: *Forest of Secrets*

Book Four: *Rising Storm*

Book Five: *A Dangerous Path*

Book Six: *The Darkest Hour*

THE NEW PROPHECY

Book One: *Midnight*

Book Two: *Moonrise*

Book Three: *Dawn*

Book Four: *Starlight*

Book Five: *Twilight*

Book Six: *Sunset*

POWER OF THREE

Book One: *The Sight*

Book Two: *Dark River*

Book Three: *Outcast*

Book Four: *Eclipse*

Book Five: *Long Shadows*

Book Six: *Sunrise*

OMEN OF THE STARS

Book One: *The Fourth Apprentice*

Book Two: *Fading Echoes*

Book Three: *Night Whispers*

Book Four: *Sign of the Moon*

Book Five: *The Forgotten Warrior*

Book Six: *The Last Hope*

DAWN OF THE CLANS

Book One: The Sun Trail
Book Two: Thunder Rising
Book Three: The First Battle

εχpLORε τhε
WARRIORS
WORLD

Warriors Super Edition: Firestar's Quest
Warriors Super Edition: Bluestar's Prophecy
Warriors Super Edition: SkyClan's Destiny
Warriors Super Edition: Crookedstar's Promise
Warriors Super Edition: Yellowfang's Secret
Warriors Super Edition: Tallstar's Revenge
Warriors Field Guide: Secrets of the Clans
Warriors: Cats of the Clans
Warriors: Code of the Clans
Warriors: Battles of the Clans
Warriors: Enter the Clans
Warriors: The Ultimate Guide
Warriors: The Untold Stories

MANGA

The Lost Warrior
Warrior's Refuge
Warrior's Return
The Rise of Scourge
Tigerstar and Sasha #1: Into the Woods
Tigerstar and Sasha #2: Escape from the Forest
Tigerstar and Sasha #3: Return to the Clans

Ravenpaw's Path #1: Shattered Peace
Ravenpaw's Path #2: A Clan in Need
Ravenpaw's Path #3: The Heart of a Warrior
SkyClan and the Stranger #1: The Rescue
SkyClan and the Stranger #2: Beyond the Code
SkyClan and the Stranger #3: After the Flood

NOVELLAS
Hollyleaf's Story
Mistystar's Omen
Cloudstar's Journey
Tigerclaw's Fury
Leafpool's Wish

Also by Erin Hunter

SEEKERS

Book One: The Quest Begins
Book Two: Great Bear Lake
Book Three: Smoke Mountain
Book Four: The Last Wilderness
Book Five: Fire in the Sky
Book Six: Spirits in the Stars

RETURN TO THE WILD
Book One: Island of Shadows
Book Two: The Melting Sea
Book Three: River of Lost Bears
Book Four: Forest of Wolves

MANGA

Toklo's Story
Kallik's Adventure

SURVIVORS

Book One: The Empty City
Book Two: A Hidden Enemy
Book Three: Darkness Falls
Book Four: The Broken Path
Book Five: The Endless Lake

NOVELLAS

Alpha's Tale

SUPER EDITION
WARRIORS
BRAMBLESTAR'S STORM

ERIN HUNTER

HARPER
An Imprint of HarperCollinsPublishers

Special thanks to Cherith Baldry

Bramblestar's Storm
Copyright © 2014 by Working Partners Limited
Series created by Working Partners Limited
Manga text copyright © 2014 by Working Partners Limited
Manga art copyright © 2014 by HarperCollins Publishers
All rights reserved. Printed in the United States of America.
No part of this book may be used or reproduced in any manner
whatsoever without written permission except in the case of brief
quotations embodied in critical articles and reviews. For information
address HarperCollins Children's Books, a division of HarperCollins
Publishers, 195 Broadway, New York, NY 10007.
www.harpercollinschildrens.com

Library of Congress Cataloging-in-Publication Data
Hunter, Erin.
    Bramblestar's storm / Erin Hunter. — First edition.
        pages   cm. — (Warriors)
    "Warriors Super Edition."
    Summary: "As the new leader of ThunderClan, Bramblestar must
prepare to weather a storm the likes of which the warrior Clans have
never seen—and might not survive"— Provided by publisher.
    ISBN 978-0-06-229143-1 (hardback)
    ISBN 978-0-06-229144-8 (library)
    [1. Cats—Fiction. 2. Fantasy.] I. Title.
PZ7.H916625Brm   2014   2013047719
[Fic]—dc23   CIP
                                                     AC

14 15 16 17 18 CG/RRDH 10 9 8 7 6 5 4 3 2 1
❖
First Edition

*To Akbar: Be brave and live the dream,
and become the artist you always wanted to be.*

ALLEGIANCES

THUNDERCLAN

LEADER
    BRAMBLESTAR—dark brown tabby tom with amber eyes

DEPUTY
    SQUIRRELFLIGHT—dark ginger she-cat with green eyes

MEDICINE CATS
    JAYFEATHER—gray tabby tom with blind blue eyes

    LEAFPOOL—light brown tabby she-cat with amber eyes

WARRIORS
    (toms and she-cats without kits)

    GRAYSTRIPE—long-haired gray tom

    DUSTPELT—dark brown tabby tom

    SANDSTORM—pale ginger she-cat with green eyes

    BRACKENFUR—golden-brown tabby tom

    CLOUDTAIL—long-haired white tom with blue eyes

    BRIGHTHEART—white she-cat with ginger patches

    MILLIE—striped gray tabby she-cat with blue eyes

    THORNCLAW—golden-brown tabby tom

    SPIDERLEG—long-limbed black tom with brown underbelly and amber eyes
    APPRENTICE, AMBERPAW (pale ginger she-cat)

    BIRCHFALL—light brown tabby tom

    WHITEWING—white she-cat with green eyes
    APPRENTICE, DEWPAW (gray-and-white tom)

BERRYNOSE—cream-colored tom

MOUSEWHISKER—gray-and-white tom

CINDERHEART—gray tabby she-cat

IVYPOOL—silver-and-white tabby she-cat with dark blue eyes

APPRENTICE, SNOWPAW (white, fluffy tom)

LIONBLAZE—golden tabby tom with amber eyes

DOVEWING—pale gray she-cat with blue eyes

ROSEPETAL—dark cream she-cat

POPPYFROST—tortoiseshell she-cat

APPRENTICE, LILYPAW (tortoiseshell-and-white she-cat)

BRIARLIGHT—dark brown she-cat with sky-colored eyes, paralyzed in her hindquarters

BLOSSOMFALL—tortoiseshell-and-white she-cat

BUMBLESTRIPE—very pale gray tom with black stripes

APPRENTICE, SEEDPAW (golden-brown she-cat)

CHERRYFALL—ginger she-cat

MOLEWHISKER—brown-and-cream tom

QUEENS (she-cats expecting or nursing kits)

DAISY—cream, long-furred cat from the horseplace

ELDERS (former warriors and queens, now retired)

PURDY—plump tabby, former loner with a gray muzzle

SHADOWCLAN

LEADER   **BLACKSTAR**—large white tom with one jet-black forepaw

DEPUTY   **ROWANCLAW**—ginger tom

MEDICINE CAT   **LITTLECLOUD**—very small tabby tom

WARRIORS   **CROWFROST**—black-and-white tom

TAWNYPELT—tortoiseshell she-cat with green eyes
    APPRENTICE, GRASSPAW (pale brown tabby she-cat)

OWLCLAW—light brown tabby tom

SCORCHFUR—dark gray tom

TIGERHEART—dark brown tabby tom

FERRETCLAW—black-and-gray tom
    APPRENTICE, SPIKEPAW (dark brown tom)

PINENOSE—black she-cat

STOATFUR—tortoiseshell-and-white she-cat

POUNCETAIL—brown tabby tom

QUEENS   **SNOWBIRD**—pure-white she-cat

DAWNPELT—cream-furred she-cat

ELDERS   **SNAKETAIL**—dark brown tom with tabby-striped tail

WHITEWATER—white she-cat with long fur, blind in one eye

RATSCAR—brown tom with long scar across his back

OAKFUR—small brown tom

SMOKEFOOT—black tom

KINKFUR—tabby she-cat, with long fur that sticks out at all angles

IVYTAIL—black, white, and tortoiseshell she-cat

WINDCLAN

LEADER **ONESTAR**—brown tabby tom

DEPUTY **HARESPRING**—brown-and-white tom
APPRENTICE, SLIGHTPAW (black tom with flash of white on his chest)

MEDICINE CAT **KESTRELFLIGHT**—mottled gray tom

WARRIORS **CROWFEATHER**—dark gray tom
APPRENTICE, FEATHERPAW (gray tabby she-cat)

NIGHTCLOUD—black she-cat
APPRENTICE, HOOTPAW (dark gray tom)

GORSETAIL—very pale gray-and-white tom with blue eyes

WEASELFUR—ginger tom with white paws

LEAFTAIL—dark tabby tom, amber eyes
APPRENTICE, OATPAW (pale brown tabby tom)

EMBERFOOT—gray tom with two dark paws

HEATHERTAIL—light brown tabby she-cat with blue eyes

BREEZEPELT—black tom with amber eyes

FURZEPELT—gray-and-white she-cat

CROUCHFOOT—ginger tom

LARKWING—pale brown tabby she-cat

QUEENS
ELDERS

SEDGEWHISKER—light brown tabby she-cat

WHISKERNOSE—light brown tom

WHITETAIL—small white she-cat

RIVERCLAN

LEADER

MISTYSTAR—gray she-cat with blue eyes

DEPUTY

REEDWHISKER—black tom
APPRENTICE, LIZARDPAW (light brown tom)

MEDICINE CATS

MOTHWING—dappled golden she-cat

WILLOWSHINE—gray tabby she-cat

WARRIORS

MINTFUR—light gray tabby tom

MINNOWTAIL—dark gray she-cat

MALLOWNOSE—light brown tabby tom
APPRENTICE, HAVENPAW (black-and-white she-cat)

GRASSPELT—light brown tom

DUSKFUR—brown tabby she-cat

MOSSPELT—tortoiseshell she-cat with blue eyes
APPRENTICE, PERCHPAW (gray-and-white she-cat)

SHIMMERPELT—silver she-cat

LAKEHEART—gray tabby she-cat

HERONWING—dark gray-and-black tom

QUEENS

ICEWING—white she-cat with blue eyes

PETALFUR—gray-and-white she-cat

ELDERS

POUNCEFOOT—ginger-and-white tom

PEBBLEFOOT—mottled gray tom

RUSHTAIL—light brown tabby tom

CATS OUTSIDE CLANS

SMOKY—muscular gray-and-white tom who lives in a barn at the horseplace

CORIANDER—tortoiseshell-and-white she-cat who lives with smoky

TWOLEG NEST

GREENLEAF TWOLEGPLACE

CLEARING

TWOLEG PATH

TWOLEG PATH

SHADOWCLAN CAMP

HALFBRIDGE

SMALL THUNDERPATH

GREENLEAF TWOLEGPLACE

HALFBRIDGE

STREAM

ISLAND

RIVERCLAN CAMP

PROLOGUE

Firestar brushed through the long grass beneath the trees and drank in the warm scents of prey. Sunlight sliced between the branches, casting dapples onto his flame-colored pelt. For a moment he paused, unsure which of the tantalizing aromas he should follow. Then he picked out the scent of a squirrel; it had swarmed up the trunk of a nearby oak tree and was hiding somewhere in the branches above his head.

It's been a while since I tested my tree-climbing skills, he thought, remembering how he had taught his Clanmates to hunt aboveground. *Lionblaze really hated it at first.* With a purr of amusement Firestar recalled the golden-furred warrior standing at the foot of a tree, reluctant to set paw on the trunk. *Unlike Cinderheart, who seemed ready to sleep in a bird's nest once she learned how to climb.*

Firestar sprang up the tree, digging his claws into the rough bark, and spotted the squirrel on one of the outer branches. He leaped toward it, reveling in the strength in his haunches, pleased that he still kept his sense of balance. The squirrel fled, jumping from branch to branch, higher and higher. As Firestar crouched, ready to follow, he heard a voice calling him from below.

"Firestar! Firestar!"

He halted; the leaves around him rustled as the squirrel vanished into the dense foliage. Firestar allowed himself a single hiss of regret, then turned and scrambled down the trunk to the ground.

Bluestar, the former ThunderClan leader, was waiting for him at the foot of the tree. Her blue-gray fur shimmered in the sunlight. "Sorry to disturb you, Firestar," she meowed. Her eyes glinted. "I see you haven't lost any of your hunting skill. You looked pretty comfortable up there . . . but I'm happy to leave the tree hunting to others. Walk with me," she added, nodding deeper into the forest.

Firestar padded by her side, enjoying the sun's warmth soaking into his pelt. *StarClan has everything to make a cat content,* he thought. *But I still miss my old home and my Clanmates. Sometimes it seems like I left them when they needed me most.*

"ThunderClan has had a difficult time, hasn't it?" Bluestar commented, as if she had picked up Firestar's regrets. "Wounded cats had scarcely healed after the Great Battle when the greencough came."

Firestar hesitated before replying, swallowing the wail of grief that rose in his chest. *We were already weakened by the battle; we didn't stand a chance of fighting the greencough.*

He took a breath and let it out in a long sigh. "There has been so much loss, so much pain. But the sickness has gone, thanks to Leafpool and Jayfeather." He forced a note of optimism into his voice. "Brightheart and Cloudtail's kits have become apprentices. And Bramblestar is a fair and confident leader. ThunderClan will survive."

"Of course." Bluestar nodded. "Bramblestar had a good mentor. Do you walk in his dreams?"

"I don't need to," Firestar responded. "I trust him." He felt a familiar stab of anger in his belly. "I shouldn't have had to leave my Clan," he hissed. "I could have gone on serving them for many more seasons."

"Could you have saved them from the greencough? Healed their injuries more quickly?" Bluestar rested her tail on his shoulder. "You gave ThunderClan nine good lives. They could not ask for any more."

Ducking beneath some curling fronds of fern, they padded across a glade of bright green grass, circled by silver birch trees.

"All of the Clans have struggled this leaf-bare," Bluestar mewed. "ShadowClan has more elders than warriors, and WindClan lost most of its best hunters in the Great Battle. It is hard for every cat here to watch our Clanmates suffer." She paused to hold a bramble out of Firestar's way. "But there is always hope. Especially in StarClan."

"I know," Firestar meowed. "But I never realized how far I would be from my Clan. And I—I always thought Spottedleaf would be here to guide me." He pictured the beautiful tortoiseshell she-cat, ThunderClan's former medicine cat, who had given up her existence in StarClan fighting for her living Clanmates. Her amber eyes seemed to glow with sadness in his memory.

"Spottedleaf will be much missed," Bluestar agreed, a slight edge to her tone. "But one day Sandstorm will come here to be with you."

One day. Pain clawed once more at Firestar's heart as he thought of his mate. *How many seasons must I wait for her?*

Firestar had made a warm nest for himself at the bottom of a hollow tree. It seemed strange not to be sleeping in a camp with other cats, though if he listened carefully, he could hear the gentle murmurs of StarClan warriors settling around him, hidden in the ferns. As he closed his eyes, he hoped that he would dream himself into ThunderClan.

Instead it seemed only a heartbeat since he had slipped into sleep when he was roused by a paw prodding him in the shoulder. Firestar raised his head, blinking.

"Wake up, Firestar," a voice meowed.

A cat was standing in front of him: a muscular gray tom with patches of white on his fur.

"Cloudstar!" Firestar exclaimed.

The former SkyClan leader dipped his head. "Greetings, Firestar."

Firestar scrambled to his paws and shook scraps of moss from his pelt. He had last seen Cloudstar many, many seasons before, after the gray-and-white tom had led him upriver from the forest to restore his lost Clan. Once Leafstar, the new SkyClan leader, had received her nine lives, Firestar and Cloudstar had said farewell. Firestar had never expected to see him again.

"What are you doing here?" he asked. "The skies you walk are so far away."

"I was allowed to visit you," Cloudstar replied. "We must talk together. Come."

He padded ahead of Firestar down a grassy slope to the edge of the forest. A pool of water stretched before them, its silver surface reflecting the light of the full moon.

"I want to thank you again, for understanding why it was so important to rebuild SkyClan," Cloudstar meowed, halting at the water's edge and resting his calm blue gaze on Firestar. "Sometimes one Clan cannot survive without the help of others."

Firestar nodded. "We've certainly learned that recently, if we didn't know it before," he murmured. For a heartbeat the darkness of the Great Battle swirled around him once more, the stench of blood and the shrieks of dying cats.

"I saw your terrible battle," Cloudstar meowed. "And for the first time I was glad that I had to lead my Clan to find a new home, because we were spared the vengeance of the Dark Forest."

"It wasn't vengeance. It was slaughter." Firestar felt the fur rise along his spine. "I had to watch my Clanmates die. I gave my last life to save them . . . and it wasn't enough."

"The battle was won," Cloudstar pointed out quietly. "You did not lose your life for nothing." He padded alongside the pool, stepping delicately among the vegetation that grew by the edge of the water.

Firestar kept pace with him, their pelts brushing. "You haven't come all the way here to thank me for helping Leafstar, or to speak about the Great Battle. What is it, Cloudstar? Is there something wrong in SkyClan?"

Cloudstar stopped and sat down, looking across the pool. Suddenly he lifted his hind paw and sliced a foreclaw across his pad. A line of blood oozed out and dripped into the water, spreading in a scarlet cloud against the silver.

The violence of Cloudstar's response made Firestar wince. He stood with his mouth open, staring at the swirl of blood.

"I bring a message that you need to take to Bramblestar," Cloudstar meowed, still gazing at the water.

"A prophecy?" Firestar echoed. *My first prophecy! I am a true StarClan cat!*

"Yes. Listen well, Firestar. *When water meets blood, blood will rise.*"

Firestar blinked. *Is that it?* "What does it mean?"

"We do not need to know the meaning," Cloudstar told him, turning until his eyes burned into Firestar's like two small moons. "Bramblestar will find that out for himself."

"And when do I give this message to Bramblestar?" Firestar asked. He resisted the urge to demand more answers from the old cat. *Do all StarClan cats deliver prophecies that seem to mean nothing?*

"You will know when the time comes," Cloudstar replied.

Could you be any more vague? Firestar thought irritably. But he kept his voice steady. "Does this mean that more trouble is coming for my Clan?"

"The life of the warrior Clans is always storm-tossed," Cloudstar meowed. "It's our duty—the duty of all StarClan— to watch over them, whatever happens." His gaze softened. "I'm sorry, Firestar. I know this isn't what you want to hear.

But I promise, this message will help Bramblestar in the end. You have to trust me on that."

Firestar sighed. "I do trust you. But is it too much to ask that ThunderClan could have a few seasons of peace, after they've suffered so much?"

CHAPTER 1

Bramblestar stood near the entrance to the hollow and breathed deeply. The sky was milky-pale with dawn, and mist still drifted between the trees, but the air was full of the scents of fresh, growing things, announcing new life. Each twig was tipped with green, and tight fronds of ferns were starting to uncoil in the midst of the dead bracken.

It's been a long, harsh leaf-bare, Bramblestar thought. *The heavy snow made it harder, and we have so few warriors to hunt prey. Fewer still since the greencough . . .* Then he gave his pelt a shake. His Clan had made it through the bitter, grief-wracked leaf-bare, and the warmer weather was returning. "We've survived six moons since the Great Battle," he meowed aloud. "And now we'll start to build up our strength again. Nothing will destroy ThunderClan."

"That's right."

Bramblestar jumped at the sound of Berrynose's voice. He hadn't noticed the cream-colored warrior emerging from the barrier of thorns behind him.

"Berrynose, you nearly frightened me out of my fur!" he exclaimed.

"Nothing frightens you, Bramblestar," Berrynose responded. "I'm leading a border patrol. Do you want to come with us?"

As he spoke, Millie and Rosepetal pushed their way through the prickly wall, closely followed by one of the new apprentices, Amberpaw. Her mentor, Spiderleg, brought up the rear.

Amberpaw bounced up to Berrynose. "Where are we going today?" she chirped. "WindClan or ShadowClan? What will we do if we catch them trespassing? Will we need to fight? I learned a great move!"

Berrynose looked a little overwhelmed, and it was Spiderleg who replied. "Amberpaw, if you stop twittering like a blackbird and start listening, you might learn something."

His words were stern but not harsh, and Bramblestar was pleased to see that Amberpaw wasn't at all intimidated by her mentor. "Okay, Spiderleg," she mewed. "But—"

"We're going along the WindClan border," Berrynose interrupted. "And we're not expecting trouble." He strode downhill toward the lake.

Bramblestar waited until the rest of the patrol had passed, then fell in behind them. He noticed how thin the cats were, their ribs visible beneath sparse pelts. But their alertness showed in every twitch of their ears, and muscles bunched in their scrawny haunches as they moved. ThunderClan was not beaten yet.

Amberpaw skittered between the trees in a broad zigzag, and Spiderleg stretched out a black paw to halt her.

"If you go on like that," he warned, "you'll be exhausted

before the patrol is half over. And if there are any cats tres-passing on our territory, they'll hear you coming way before we spot them."

"Sorry, Spiderleg," Amberpaw mewed, flattening her ears.

"I want to see how quietly you can walk," Spiderleg told her. "Pretend you're stalking a mouse."

Bramblestar watched as the little ginger she-cat stalked forward, setting each paw down so lightly that she hardly disturbed the crumbled leaves.

"Not bad," Spiderleg commented. "Keep it up."

From Spiderleg, that was a considerable compliment, and Amberpaw puffed up her chest with pride.

It was a good decision to put those two together, Bramblestar thought. *In fact, all three apprentices are doing well.* They were the first apprentices he had made as Clan leader, and he had hesitated a long time over the choice of mentors. Now Dewpaw was paired with Whitewing, her sister from an earlier litter by Cloudtail and Brightheart, while Snowpaw was mentored by Ivypool.

They suffered so much hardship, so much grief as they were growing up, Bramblestar reflected. *I want their apprenticeship moons to be peaceful, so they can be reassured that life in the Clan is not always lived on the brink of death.*

As the patrol reached the edge of the trees above the lake, Bramblestar spotted Leafpool under an elderly beech tree. She was nipping off stems of early-flowering coltsfoot, the yellow buds glowing like tiny suns. Noticing the patrol, she waved her tail in greeting.

"You look busy," Bramblestar commented as he padded up to her.

"That's because I am." Leafpool gathered the coltsfoot stems into a neat bundle. "Jayfeather wants these gathered before the sun burns off the dew."

"Hi, Leafpool!" Millie bounded over to join them. "I just wanted to tell you that Briarlight's exercises are clearing her chest really well. I was so afraid she would never get over that bout of greencough."

Bramblestar felt a pang of relief shiver through his pelt. Millie was understandably anxious about her daughter, Briarlight, who had lost the use of her hind legs when she was trapped under a falling tree. It was hard to believe that the injured she-cat had recovered from a bout of greencough that had killed Toadstep, Icecloud, and Hazeltail.

Leafpool twitched her ears. "It's Jayfeather you ought to thank, Millie. He never stops figuring out different ways to help Briarlight. I'm collecting this coltsfoot for a new mixture of herbs to help her breathing, together with thyme and catmint."

"We still have catmint?" Millie asked.

"Oh, yes, there's new growth in the patch Jayfeather planted beside the old Twoleg den. I'm going to tend it as soon as I've taken these herbs back to camp."

Leafpool picked up her bundle and bounded off through the trees. Bramblestar watched her go, more glad than he could express that she was ThunderClan's medicine cat once more.

Berrynose led the patrol to the WindClan border. They paused for a moment on the bank of the stream where it spilled into the lake, then headed uphill, keeping close to the water's edge. Before they had gone more than a couple of fox-lengths, the sun crested the moor, bathing the tough grass in golden light. Bramblestar stopped to stretch his front legs, thankful for the warmth after so many cold moons.

As the cats trekked upward, the breeze blowing from beyond the stream carried WindClan scent markers strongly toward them.

"Those smell fresh," Berrynose muttered, wrinkling his nose. "Millie, Rosepetal, you'd better renew our markers as we go along. We don't want WindClan to think we're getting careless about boundaries."

"I want to set a scent marker!" Amberpaw piped up. "Can I, please?"

"Can she?" Spiderleg asked Berrynose. "She'll have to learn how sooner or later."

"I know how!" Amberpaw scampered up to the edge of the stream. "I watched—" She broke off with a squeal as the grass beneath her paws gave way and she slid out of sight. A heartbeat later, they heard a loud splash.

"Amberpaw!" Spiderleg yowled.

Every cat rushed to the edge of the stream where the apprentice had disappeared. Bramblestar couldn't remember whether the water was deep enough here to drown her.

Spiderleg plunged down the side of the bank into the swift-flowing water. Leaning over the edge, Bramblestar saw the black warrior boosting Amberpaw onto a ledge just above the surface of the stream. She was coughing up water while the current dragged at her tail.

"It's cold!" she gasped.

"Serves you right for being so idiotic," Spiderleg meowed as he scrambled up behind her, though Bramblestar noticed that he touched his nose comfortingly to the young cat's ear. "Come on, climb onto my shoulders and Bramblestar will help you out."

Before Amberpaw could move, Bramblestar spotted movement in the bushes at the other side of the stream, and a WindClan patrol emerged into the open, with Weaselfur in the lead.

"What's going on?" the WindClan warrior demanded. "Why are you in our stream?"

"It's not *your* stream," Spiderleg hissed, crouching lower on the ledge so that Amberpaw could reach his shoulders. "We haven't crossed the border."

"You'd better not," Weaselfur growled, his ginger fur starting to bristle. "We all know what ThunderClan thinks about boundaries."

Bramblestar reached down to sink his teeth into Amberpaw's scruff while she teetered wildly on Spiderleg's shoulders, and dragged her up to the safety of the bank. Before he had the chance to respond to Weaselfur, Rosepetal flashed past him, leaping the stream to stand nose to nose with the Wind-Clan warrior.

"How dare you!" she exclaimed. "Name one time

ThunderClan invaded your territory."

Weaselfur unsheathed his claws. His Clanmates Leaf-tail and Nightcloud sprang forward, hissing with fury, and trapped Rosepetal between them. Nightpelt lashed out, claw-ing at Rosepetal's ear.

Two soft-furred WindClan apprentices looked on with wide eyes, bouncing on their paws as if they were waiting for the signal to join in.

"Invading our territory? How about now?" Nightcloud mewed pointedly. She flicked her tail. "Get back on your own side of the stream."

"She's right," Bramblestar meowed, moving to the very edge of the bank. This wasn't a battle they needed to fight. "Rosepetal, get back here now."

Rosepetal jumped back across the stream, hanging her head as she halted in front of Bramblestar. Blood was trick-ling from a scratch on her ear. "Sorry," she muttered. "I lost my temper. But they started it."

"Never mind who started it," Bramblestar meowed. "Sorry," he called to Weaselfur and the rest of the WindClan cats. "Our apprentice fell into the stream. Spiderleg was just helping her out."

Weaselfur sniffed. "Then she should watch where she's putting her paws."

Bramblestar understood why the WindClan cats were so touchy. *We may have united to fight against the Dark Forest . . . but we're four Clans, not one, and borders need to be respected once more.*

To his relief, Weaselfur relaxed and waved his tail for the

rest of his patrol to take a step back. "Make sure it doesn't happen again," he growled. "And don't think you can jump across here any time you feel like it."

"She said sorry!" Berrynose spat at him.

"How's the prey running in WindClan?" Bramblestar asked with a glare at Berrynose, while Spiderleg clambered out of the stream and shook himself, spattering his Clanmates with icy drops.

"Fine," Weaselfur replied coolly. "More rabbits than we can count. What about ThunderClan?"

"Oh, prey is coming back now the cold weather is over," Bramblestar told him, sounding more optimistic than he felt. "We're looking forward to the warm seasons. And how is Onestar?" he added. "And Sedgewhisker? I haven't seen her at a Gathering for a couple of moons."

"Onestar is fine," Leaftail responded. "And Sedgewhisker is expecting Emberfoot's kits. She'll be in the nursery for a while yet."

"Congratulations," Bramblestar mewed, meaning it. "Well, we'd better be getting along."

He turned to the rest of the patrol. Millie was helping Amberpaw to groom her wet fur, while Berrynose stood close to Rosepetal, licking her scratched ear. At Bramblestar's signal he stopped and headed upstream again.

"Good-bye!" Bramblestar called to the WindClan patrol.

"You lot should try going for a swim!" Amberpaw added cheekily over her shoulder. "You need cooling down!"

Spiderleg instantly bounded to her side and gave her a cuff

over the ear, his claws sheathed. "Mouse-brain!" he muttered. "That was a lucky escape back there."

Once the patrol had left the WindClan cats behind, Berrynose dropped back to pad along beside Bramblestar. "Rosepetal seems okay," he mewed. "I was worried the Wind-Clan cats might have hurt her."

Bramblestar gave Berrynose a puzzled look. *Have I missed something?* he wondered. *Berrynose is still Poppyfrost's mate, right?*

"We've lost so many she-cats," Berrynose went on. "Holly-leaf, Sorreltail, and Ferncloud in the Great Battle, and Icecloud and Hazeltail from greencough. Now it's newleaf, and none of the survivors are expecting kits."

Bramblestar realized this was true. He felt guilty that he hadn't thought about this himself, and he was struck by how serious Berrynose sounded. *Maybe he's growing up at last,* he thought. *He used to be a real pain in the tail. . . .*

"We need to think about replacing the fallen warriors," Berrynose pointed out. "If we don't, we'll be weaker than the other Clans. We've just heard that kits are due in WindClan. We need to heal from the wounds of the Great Battle and make ourselves strong agin, but how can we do that if we have fewer cats than the other Clans?"

CHAPTER 2

Bramblestar pushed his way through the thorn barrier into the camp with the rest of the patrol behind him. The sun shone down into the hollow, casting long shadows across the ground. Above the cliffs, the trees rustled gently and a warm breeze stirred the dust on the ground.

Bramblestar could still see traces of the terrible conflict when the warriors of the Dark Forest had poured into the camp: fresh bramble tendrils entwined with the old in the walls of the nursery, and broken branches on the hazel bush that screened the elders' den. It was too easy to close his eyes and be plunged back into the storm of fighting and blood, with cats both dead and alive attacking from all sides. The Dark Forest cats had flung themselves into battle in a furious quest for power and vengeance, and it had taken all the strength of the living cats—and the strength of StarClan—to beat them back. Bramblestar gave his pelt a shake, trying to recall his earlier optimism. At least the dens were repaired, and the surviving cats had recovered from their wounds.

But the scars we can't see will be harder to heal.

When the battle was over, Jayfeather had propped a

bark-stripped branch against the cliff below the Highledge. He had scored claw marks across it, one for each life taken by the Dark Forest.

"It will remind us of the debts that we owe to our former Clanmates," he had explained.

Now Whitewing was standing in front of the branch with her apprentice, Dewpaw, beside her. Seedpaw and Lilypaw stood watching with their mentors, Bumblestripe and Poppyfrost.

"Can you remember all the names?" Whitewing asked her apprentice.

Dewpaw narrowed his eyes in concentration. "I think so. This one is for Mousefur. . . ." he began, touching the first claw mark. "She was an elder, but she fought so bravely! And this one is for Hollyleaf. She had been away for a while, but she came back in time to help us when the Dark Forest attacked. And this is for Foxleap, who died of his wounds afterward. . . ."

Bramblestar nodded as Dewpaw went on reciting the names. He had decided that all the apprentices had to learn the list as part of their training, so that their lost Clanmates would be remembered for season after season, as long as ThunderClan survived.

"This one is for Ferncloud," Dewpaw continued. "She was killed by Brokenstar when she was defending the kits in the nursery. And this is Sorreltail. She hid her wounds because she wanted to take care of the kits, but she died just when we thought we had won. She was the bravest of all."

"And the big mark right at the top?" Whitewing prompted.

"Do you know who that stands for?"

"That's our leader, Firestar," Dewpaw replied. "He was the best cat in the whole forest, and he gave up his last life to save us!"

Bramblestar felt a familiar stab of grief. *I wonder if he's watching us now? I hope he approves of what I have done.*

"I miss Firestar, too."

Bramblestar turned to see that Jayfeather had appeared at his side, the medicine cat's blue eyes fixed on him so intensely that it was hard to believe he was blind. "I didn't think you could tell what's in my mind anymore," Bramblestar mewed, surprised.

"No, those days are past," Jayfeather admitted, sounding a little wistful. "But it wasn't hard to figure out that you were thinking of Firestar. I heard Dewpaw run his paw over Firestar's mark and say his name, and then you sighed." He pressed himself briefly against Bramblestar's side. "I'm sure Firestar watches over us."

"Has he walked in your dreams yet?" Bramblestar asked.

Jayfeather shook his head. "No, but that's a good omen in itself. I've had enough warnings from StarClan to last me nine lifetimes." With a brisk nod to Bramblestar, he padded away to join Leafpool, who was sorting coltsfoot flowers and fresh-picked catmint outside their den.

"Come on, Snowpaw," Ivypool called to her apprentice. "Time for battle training!"

"Can we go too?" Dewpaw begged, as his sister scampered over to join her mentor.

"Sure we can," Whitewing meowed.

"And me!" Amberpaw raced across the camp and skidded to a halt beside her littermates.

"No, not you!" Spiderleg called from where he stood beside the fresh-kill pile with Cloudtail and Cherryfall. "You did the dawn patrol this morning. You need to rest."

Amberpaw's tail drooped. "But they'll be learning stuff when I'm not there!" she wailed. "I'll get behind, and then I'll never be a warrior!"

Spiderleg padded over to her and gave her ear a friendly flick with his tail. "Of course you'll be a warrior, mouse-brain! Once you've rested, I'll show you the move they're going to learn, I promise."

"Okay." Amberpaw still cast a regretful look after her littermates and their mentors as they left the hollow.

"What about us?" Lilypaw asked, exchanging a disappointed glance with Seedpaw. "Why can't we do battle training?"

"Because we're going hunting," Poppyfrost replied briskly. "Come on! Bumblestripe knows the best place to find mice."

"Great!" Seedpaw exclaimed with an excited little bounce. "Lilypaw, I bet I catch more mice than you."

"*I'm* going to catch enough for the whole Clan!" her sister retorted.

"It's not fair," Amberpaw muttered as she watched them go. "Why don't I get to do anything?"

"I told you," Spiderleg responded. "You did the dawn patrol. Now you rest. But before you do," he went on, "you can fetch some clean moss for Purdy's den."

Amberpaw brightened up. "Sure! And maybe he'll tell me a story!" She darted off and thrust her way into the barrier.

"I wonder if I ever had that much energy?" Bramblestar mewed aloud as he watched the young cat disappear.

Sandstorm popped her head out of the nearby nursery. "You still do!" she told him. She emerged into the open, pushing a ball of moss in front of her. "It's good to see the little ones being so lively. It gives me new hope for our Clan." She paused, her gaze clouding, and Bramblestar wondered if she was thinking about her former mate, Firestar, who wasn't here to watch this group of apprentices grow up. Then she lifted her head again. "Daisy and I are clearing out the nursery," she announced, giving the ball of moss a prod with one paw. "There might not be any kits now, but surely some of our young she-cats will be expecting soon."

"I hope so," Bramblestar replied, remembering his earlier conversation with Berrynose. *I really hope so.* "Surely there are other cats who could help Daisy?" he went on, thinking that Sandstorm didn't need to be struggling with bedding, covered in dust and scraps of moss.

Amusement sparked in Sandstorm's green eyes. "Are you trying to pack me off to the elders' den?" she teased.

"You've served your Clanmates long enough," Bramblestar responded. "Why not let them take care of you now?"

Sandstorm flicked her whiskers dismissively. "I've plenty of life in my paws yet," she insisted, retreating into the nursery to help Daisy wrestle with a huge clump of brittle, musty moss.

Bramblestar watched the she-cats for a moment longer before turning away. His deputy, Squirrelflight, stood near the elders' den, sorting out the hunting patrols with Graystripe; like Sandstorm, the former deputy was one of the oldest cats in the Clan now.

"We need the hunting patrols to go out early," Graystripe was explaining to Squirrelflight. "With the days getting hotter, it's best to avoid sunhigh for chasing around."

Squirrelflight nodded. "And the prey will be holed up by then, too. I've already sent out one patrol," she went on, "but I'll send out another. Brightheart would be a good cat to lead it." She glanced around. "Hey, Brightheart!"

The ginger-and-white she-cat slid out between the branches that sheltered the warriors' den. "Yes?"

"I want you to lead a hunting patrol," Squirrelflight told her. "But stick to one area, and come back before it gets too hot."

Brightheart dipped her head. "Any particular place?" she asked.

"You could try up by the ShadowClan border," Squirrelflight suggested. "Millie spotted a nest of squirrels there yesterday."

"Good idea," Brightheart mewed. "Which cats should I take with me?"

"Millie, obviously, since she knows where the nest is. Apart from her, any cat you like."

"I'm on my way." Brightheart bounded off to call Millie from the warriors' den. Then she rounded up Dovewing and Mousewhisker and headed out through the thorns.

The barrier was still trembling from their departure when Amberpaw reappeared with a huge bundle of moss in her jaws. As she staggered toward the elders' den, Bramblestar noticed that the moss was dripping with water, leaving a line of dark spots on the dusty floor of the clearing.

Squirrelflight stepped out to intercept the apprentice as she drew closer to the den. "You can't take that in there," she told Amberpaw sharply. "That moss is too wet. It'll soak all the other bedding and Purdy will claw your ears off for making his legs ache from the damp."

At the mention of his name Purdy ducked out of the shelter of the hazel bush. "There's nothin' wrong with my legs, or my ears," he snorted.

"How about your pelt?" Amberpaw asked, dropping the moss.

Bramblestar stifled a *mrrow* of amusement: Purdy's tabby pelt looked as if he had crawled backward through the thorns, the fur clumped and sticking up as if he hadn't groomed himself for a moon.

"Eh? Speak up!" Purdy complained. "Why are you mumblin'? Young cats these days always mumble," he added crossly.

"I was explaining to Amberpaw that she can't bring wet moss into your den," Squirrelflight meowed.

"What?" Purdy prodded the bundle of moss. "You're sure you weren't tryin' to bring me a drink instead?" he asked Amberpaw.

The apprentice looked crestfallen. "I was only trying to help."

"Sure you were, young 'un." Purdy stroked Amberpaw's

side with his tail. "Come on. You an' I will spread the moss out here, just outside the den, an' it'll soon dry in the sun. An' while it does that, I'll tell you how I once killed a whole nest o' rats."

"Yes!" Amberpaw bounced in delight and began spreading out the wet moss.

On the other side of the clearing, Sandstorm headed out of the camp, pushing a huge bundle of used bedding in front of her. Bramblestar slid into the nursery and began helping Daisy scratch together the next bundle.

"Have you heard anything about new kits?" he asked hopefully.

Daisy shook her head. "No, but I'm sure we'll need the nursery soon, now that newleaf is here." She paused, then added, "Come and look."

She led Bramblestar out of the nursery and pointed with her tail to where Lionblaze and Cinderheart were sharing tongues in a patch of sunlight. "That one will be expecting soon," Daisy mewed, twitching her ears at Cinderheart.

Bramblestar felt a flash of excitement. He remembered play fighting with Lionblaze as a kit outside the nursery, and how he had taught Lionblaze his first pounce. *In spite of all that's happened, I couldn't have loved those three kits more if I'd been their real father.*

Lionblaze looked up and noticed Bramblestar watching him. With a quick word to Cinderheart he got up and limped across the camp to join his leader.

"Did you want me?" he asked.

"No, but since you're here, you can tell me how things

are going. It looks as if we might have some new kits soon," Bramblestar meowed with an affectionate nudge.

"Great StarClan!" Lionblaze gave his chest fur a couple of embarrassed licks. "No pressure, then?"

"Are you sure you're okay?" Bramblestar went on more anxiously, spotting a scratch on Lionblaze's shoulder. *He's limping on that forepaw, too.*

Lionblaze sighed. "Yes, I'm fine. Leafpool and Jayfeather checked me out, and gave me a dock leaf for the sore pad. It's just hard to get used to the way I can be hurt now. All I did was trip over a stupid bramble!"

"Too bad," Bramblestar mewed. "You'll have to start watching where you tread!"

"That will make me very fearsome to our enemies. Not," Lionblaze muttered. He limped back to his mate and settled down beside her.

Movement at the entrance caught Bramblestar's eye as the first hunting patrol returned. Dustpelt was leading it; he carried a squirrel in his jaws. Behind him came Brackenfur, Blossomfall, and Poppyfrost, all laden with prey. Bramblestar watched approvingly while they carried their catch over to the fresh-kill pile.

He noticed that Dustpelt looked exhausted as he dropped his squirrel on the pile. The brown tabby tom was still haunted by the death of his mate, Ferncloud, in the Great Battle. Squirrelflight had told him that Dustpelt often woke yowling in the warriors' den, thrashing in his nest. In his dreams he still tried to save Ferncloud from the claws of Brokenstar, and every time he had to watch her die again.

A little more than a moon ago, Bramblestar had suggested that Dustpelt might like to retire and join the elders.

"Anything but that," Dustpelt had growled. "Let me keep busy. I need something to distract me, or the memories hurt too much."

"You'll meet Ferncloud again one day, in StarClan," Bramblestar meowed, trying to comfort the older warrior.

Dustpelt shook his head. "Sometimes I wonder if that's true." His voice shaking, he added, "I kept some of the moss from her nest. But I can't even smell her scent on it anymore."

Bramblestar hadn't known what he could do to help, except to do as Dustpelt asked and make sure he stayed busy.

Bramblestar headed across the camp, intending to praise Dustpelt's patrol for their good hunting, when he heard his name yowled from the other side of the barrier. Startled, he spun around to see Brightheart bursting out of the thorns with the rest of her patrol just behind.

"ShadowClan!" she gasped as she scrambled to a halt.

"Calm down," Bramblestar meowed. "Tell me what happened."

"Are they attacking?" Brackenfur called as the rest of the Clan gathered around, their whiskers quivering with curiosity.

"No, but it's almost as bad," Brightheart panted. "We picked up ShadowClan scent inside our borders."

"And it's not the first time it's happened," Millie added with a lash of her tail.

"Are they after that nest of squirrels?" Lionblaze asked.

More cats jumped in with urgent questions. Only Dovewing looked quiet and subdued. Bramblestar felt a stab of pity. Once she would have been able to look into ShadowClan without leaving the hollow, and listen to their conversations to find out why they were crossing the border, but those days were gone. *She feels blind and deaf without her powers,* he guessed.

Bumblestripe padded up to Dovewing and pressed his muzzle against her shoulder. "Are you okay?" he whispered.

Dovewing leaned into him. "I'm fine," she sighed.

Bramblestar raised his tail for silence. "Brightheart, where exactly—" he began.

"We should attack *now*!" Mousewhisker interrupted, his shoulder fur bristling with fury. "Those crow-food eaters have no right to set paw on our territory."

For a moment a cold trickle of suspicion passed through Bramblestar. Mousewhisker had been one of the cats who had trained in the Dark Forest, and although he had returned to his Clan, he seemed a bit too ready to attack their neighbors. Did he want to try out the skills he had learned from his Dark Forest mentors? Bramblestar thrust the suspicion away. *Mousewhisker is young, and young cats are hotheaded.*

"No cat will attack any of the Clans," he warned.

"Try telling that to WindClan," Rosepetal muttered, flicking the ear that Nightcloud had scratched that morning.

"So what are we going to do about ShadowClan?" Millie asked.

"We're not going to let ShadowClan get away with this, are

we?" Berrynose meowed. He sounded almost as belligerent as Mousewhisker.

"Not at all," Bramblestar replied. "I'm going to visit Blackstar, and find out why his warriors are crossing our border."

"Seriously?" Mousewhisker's eyes stretched wide, and his voice was even more indignant than before. "You're going to give them a chance to come up with a reason, when we all know what they're doing is wrong?"

"Mouse-brain!" Mousewhisker's sister Cherryfall gave him a hard nudge, almost unbalancing him. "That isn't what Bramblestar is doing. He's just going to tell Blackstar that he knows what's going on!"

Bramblestar was touched by the ginger she-cat's faith in him. *My Clanmates should be able to trust me to keep them safe. What would they say if they knew how much I doubt myself?*

CHAPTER 3

❧

"Squirrelflight, I'd like you to come with me," Bramblestar meowed. "And you, Brackenfur, and Cinderheart." He was careful not to choose any of the cats with Dark Forest associations, unwilling to risk any comments from ShadowClan. The Great Battle had revealed misplaced allegiances inside every Clan, and however much those cats had sworn loyalty to their living Clans since then, they would always be a source of mistrust for their rivals.

The cats Bramblestar had named started to head over to him. Cinderheart paused for a moment to touch noses with Lionblaze.

"Be careful," the golden tabby tom murmured.

Bramblestar led the patrol into the forest. By now it was almost sunhigh, warm and breezeless, and everything was still under the warm rays. But Bramblestar was too concerned about ShadowClan's trespass to enjoy the signs of life returning to his territory.

"I think we should double the patrols on the ShadowClan border," Squirrelflight suggested as they walked side by side through the trees. "And maybe hunt over there more regularly, too. Let ShadowClan know that our eyes and ears are open."

"Good idea," Bramblestar agreed.

As they trotted past the abandoned Twoleg den, Bramble-star spotted Leafpool tending to the herbs that she and Jayfeather had planted before leaf-bare. Tiny green shoots were beginning to sprout from the dark soil. Leafpool had her nose buried deep in a clump of catmint, and was unaware of the patrol.

"I'm glad Leafpool has found her place within the Clan again," Squirrelflight murmured with a warm glance at her sister. "I—I think she lost a bit of herself when she stopped being a medicine cat."

"We're lucky to have her," Bramblestar mewed. He was careful not to comment on Firestar's decision to send Leaf-pool to the warriors' den when the truth about Jayfeather, Lionblaze, and Hollyleaf came out. The fact that Leafpool had broken the medicine cats' code could not be ignored, and Bramblestar was relieved that he had not been forced to make the judgment.

Thinking of other cats whose lives had been transformed by the Great Battle, he fell back to walk beside Brackenfur, out of earshot of the she-cats.

"How are you doing?" Bramblestar asked. His fur felt hot with awkwardness, but he pictured Firestar gently making sure he knew how each of his Clanmates was coping with great change. "I know it's tough for you, facing the return of newleaf without Sorreltail." Somehow, grief had seemed eas-ier to bear when the skies were dark and a cold wind kept cats and prey inside their nests.

Brackenfur nodded, his eyes clouding. "I can't bear knowing that she needn't have died," he muttered. "If only she'd let Jayfeather treat her wounds straight after the battle . . . But she insisted on taking care of our kits first, and then it was too late."

"She was a great warrior, and a brilliant mother," Bramblestar meowed. "None of us will forget her."

"Every leaf and every blade of grass reminds me of her," Brackenfur told him, his voice steady. "I know she's watching over me and her kits from StarClan. One day we'll meet again." He paused, then added quietly, "I would wait forever to see her face once more."

Bramblestar nodded, too full of emotion to speak. He ran ahead to give Brackenfur a few moments alone with his memories.

As they approached the border, Bramblestar picked up the reek of ShadowClan scent. "This is well inside our territory," he remarked with a lash of his tail. "What was Blackstar thinking?"

"Who knows?" Squirrelflight let out a sigh of frustration. "I should have thought every cat in the forest has had a bellyful of trouble by now." Bramblestar watched her green eyes gleam. *Bellyful of trouble or not, she would run into battle today to protect her Clan. No leader could ask for a better deputy.*

The last few fox-lengths of their territory seemed full of ShadowClan scent, almost swamping the ThunderClan scent markers.

"Keep together," Bramblestar warned as the patrol crossed the open space where Twolegs brought their pelt-dens in greenleaf. This had been ShadowClan territory for a long time, until the battle in which Russetfur had died. "If we meet a ShadowClan patrol, remember we're here to talk, not fight."

"You mean we let them tear our pelts off?" Brackenfur asked. He sounded grim and focused, as if he had put aside his memories of Sorreltail.

"I mean that we should defend ourselves if we have to, but we won't strike the first blow," Bramblestar replied. "You know ShadowClan as well as I do. They'll do their best to provoke us, but we don't have to let them."

Brackenfur snorted as Bramblestar led the way across the border and into ShadowClan territory.

The bare trees of ThunderClan territory, with their swelling green buds, gave way to the gloomy ShadowClan pines, pierced by rare shafts of sunlight. The patrol's paw steps fell softly on the thick layer of needles that covered the ground. Here and there Bramblestar spotted places where the needles had been churned up to expose the soil below. Clots of earth lay scattered on the disturbed ground like forgotten pieces of fresh-kill.

"Cats fought there in the Great Battle," Cinderheart murmured, angling her ears toward a wide stretch of scarred earth. "Will the forest ever recover?"

"One day," Squirrelflight responded, sturdily optimistic. "We have to believe that."

Undergrowth was sparser here than in ThunderClan

territory, and Bramblestar felt more uneasy with each paw step. He kept glancing around, aware that they could be seen from some distance, and anxious not to let a ShadowClan patrol surprise them.

But he was still unprepared when a ShadowClan patrol raced around a nearby bramble thicket, moving almost silently over the ground. The warriors skidded to a halt with startled yowls as they came face-to-face with the ThunderClan cats.

Bramblestar's sister Tawnypelt, who was leading the patrol, bristled with a mixture of shock and anger. "What are you doing here?" she demanded. She glared at her brother, her claws working among the pine needles.

"We're on our way to see Blackstar," Bramblestar replied peaceably. "We're not looking for trouble."

"Chase them off!" A young brown tabby she-cat bounced excitedly up and down. "They can't trespass here!"

"Clan leaders are allowed to visit one another, Grasspaw," Tawnypelt meowed. "You don't have to react to everything by unsheathing your claws."

The apprentice looked disappointed; she took a step back but glared at Bramblestar from behind Tawnypelt, letting the tips of her claws peek out against the dark soil.

Tawnypelt looked wary as she faced Bramblestar. "We'll escort you to our camp," she meowed. "To make sure you don't run into any of the trouble you say you're not looking for."

"That's fine by us," Bramblestar told her.

The ThunderClan patrol drew closer together as they followed Tawnypelt through the trees. Owlclaw and Scorchfur, the other members of the ShadowClan patrol, flanked them on each side. Grasspaw brought up the rear, growling softly.

Bramblestar noticed more patches of torn earth, and in one place a clump of brambles that had been completely trampled down, as if fighting cats had rolled over it, oblivious to the sharp thorns. ShadowClan's territory had suffered more than ThunderClan's in the battle, it seemed.

The ShadowClan camp lay in a hollow, concealed by a tangle of brambles and the low-growing branches of the pine trees that clustered around it. Tawnypelt trotted ahead of them down a narrow tunnel through the brambles; Bramblestar felt the tendrils scraping his sides as he followed.

Blackstar was standing in the middle of the clearing when the ThunderClan patrol emerged from the tunnel. Rowanclaw, his deputy, stood at his shoulder, and more of the ShadowClan warriors had gathered around them. Littlecloud, the medicine cat, sat at one side of the open space, looking worried. Bramblestar was shocked to see how frail Blackstar looked. But then, the ShadowClan leader was much older than Graystripe and Dustpelt, and had led his Clan through the most terrible battle in their history, so perhaps it was no surprise that the seasons were showing in his patchy fur and gaunt frame.

"I found this ThunderClan patrol heading through our territory," Tawnypelt explained. "Bramblestar says he needs to speak to you."

"Well, I'm here." Blackstar's tone was mild. "What do you want?"

"Greetings, Blackstar." Bramblestar dipped his head to the old cat. "I've come to ask why my cats have found ShadowClan scent inside our borders."

"What?" Blackstar's eyes stretched wide, though Bramblestar had a suspicion that his astonishment was feigned. "Your cats must be dreaming, Bramblestar. No ShadowClan warrior has crossed your borders."

"Are you saying we don't know ShadowClan scent when we smell it?" Squirrelflight queried with a warning lash of her tail.

"I've smelled it myself," Bramblestar meowed. "And it's way inside our borders, beyond the clearing where Twolegs bring their pelt-dens."

"Then maybe you should strengthen your own scent marks," Blackstar retorted with a sideways glance at Rowan-claw. "If you can't be bothered to mark your borders, it's not our fault if we stray across by a few paw steps."

"A *few* paw steps?" Squirrelflight spat disbelievingly.

Bramblestar raised his tail to silence her. He could feel his own fur bristling, and all his instincts were telling him to leap at Blackstar and claw the smirk off his face. *Firestar wouldn't have started a fight,* he reminded himself. *He would have known what to say to keep things peaceful.*

"We know what you've done," he began. "What we don't know is why. What reason—"

He broke off as Ratscar, a skinny, brown elder, took a step forward. "What right do you have to question our leader?" he snarled. "Take yourself back to your own territory."

Bramblestar let out a hiss of anger, furious that a Shadow-Clan elder was trying to give him orders. Squirrelflight slid out her claws, and from behind him Bramblestar could hear low growls from Brackenfur and Cinderheart.

"Ratscar has one paw in the Dark Forest," Squirrelflight muttered into his ear.

"And we decided to give those cats another chance to prove their loyalty, remember?" Bramblestar muttered back, forcing his fur to lie flat.

Meanwhile Rowanclaw had shouldered Ratscar back into the group of ShadowClan cats. "That's enough!" the deputy snapped. To Bramblestar he added, "Maybe we should both agree to strengthen the scent marks along that stretch of the border. That way we can be sure that no cat will trespass accidentally."

Bramblestar guessed that he wouldn't get a full admission of guilt without unsheathing his claws. Reluctantly he nodded. "Very well," he meowed. "But be sure of this: ThunderClan will keep a *very* close watch on the border from now on."

"And so will ShadowClan," Blackstar responded. "Now it's time for you to go. Tawnypelt, escort them back to their own territory."

"We don't need an escort, thanks," Bramblestar told him.

"No, we don't," Squirrelflight agreed, just loud enough to be heard. "Do you think we'd stay one heartbeat more than we have to on your maggot-ridden territory?"

"That's enough!" Bramblestar hissed into her ear. Head and tail high, he turned and stalked out of the camp. Behind him he heard hostile snarls from the ShadowClan cats, and he took a deep breath to keep his fur flat and his claws sheathed.

But as he and his cats headed for the border, Bramblestar heard the pattering of paw steps behind him. He swung around, claws out, but the cat who was pursuing them was Littlecloud.

"Greetings, Bramblestar," he panted as he halted beside the patrol. "How are Leafpool and Jayfeather?"

"They're fine." It was Squirrelflight who replied. "They work together really well, and—"

"Squirrelflight, that's enough," Bramblestar interrupted. "We have to go. There's work to do back in camp."

"But I was only—" Squirrelflight protested, then broke off when she caught Bramblestar's eye. "Sorry, Littlecloud," she added as she turned to follow Bramblestar and her Clanmates.

Littlecloud watched them go with a disappointed expression.

"What did you do that for?" Squirrelflight demanded, trotting to catch up to Bramblestar. "Medicine cats don't take part in quarrels between the Clans. Littlecloud was asking a genuine question."

"Yes, but we aren't medicine cats," Bramblestar pointed out. Part of him sympathized with Squirrelflight, but since the Great Battle, obeying the code that kept the warriors of each Clan separate had never seemed more important. *We have to show that we can survive on our own. Being too friendly, too compassionate, is a sign of weakness to our enemies.*

"We may be forced to fight ShadowClan to make them stay

on their own side of the border," he continued. "This isn't the time to be gossiping with their medicine cat."

"We can't possibly start another battle now!" Squirrelflight protested.

Bramblestar halted, gazing into her eyes. "We might have to. ShadowClan might have been our ally when we faced the Dark Forest, but those cats are once again our rivals for every paw step of territory, every mouthful of prey. The Great Battle is over, but that doesn't mean the Clans are at peace with one another."

CHAPTER 4

By the time Bramblestar and his patrol returned to the hollow, the sun had climbed higher in the sky, casting unexpected heat for so early in newleaf. When Bramblestar pushed his way through the barrier of thorns, he saw that his Clanmates were basking in pools of sunlight, sharing tongues after completing the early patrols.

Most of the cats sprang to their paws as soon as they noticed the patrol had returned.

"What happened?" Poppyfrost called.

"Yes, what did those crow-food eaters have to say for themselves?" Thornclaw asked.

"And how are they coping after the Great Battle?" Cloudtail added.

Bramblestar didn't reply until he had padded into the center of the clearing and the Clan had gathered around him. "There's still a lot of damage inside their territory." He answered Cloudtail's question first. "But their camp looks more or less back to normal."

"The ones we saw are terribly thin," Brackenfur put in. "I'd guess prey's not running too well for them."

"Good," Spiderleg meowed, while Cloudtail gave a satisfied lash of his tail.

Bramblestar felt a claw-scratch of uneasiness at his cats' pleasure in the problems of a rival Clan.

"What about the trespassing?" Mousewhisker demanded. "What did Blackstar have to say for himself?"

"The ShadowClan cats insist that they crossed the border by accident," Bramblestar told him. "They advised us to renew our scent markers."

A chorus of indignation broke out. Whitewing's voice rose above the clamor. "That's mouse-brained! I renewed those scent markers myself yesterday!"

"We all know that," Squirrelflight assured her. "And ShadowClan knows perfectly well that there's nothing wrong with our scent markers. But they'll never admit that they trespassed."

"Then they need to be taught a lesson," Thornclaw growled.

Several of his Clanmates caterwauled their agreement.

Bramblestar shook his head. "No cat will set paw over the border to attack ShadowClan," he ordered, even though a prickling in his paws was urging him to disobey his own command. "Squirrelflight will organize extra patrols to refresh the markers, and that will make it clear to ShadowClan that we won't tolerate any more invasions."

Ignoring the mutters of protest, he turned away. On the other side of the hollow, the bramble screen that covered the entrance to the medicine cats' den was swept aside. Jayfeather padded out, followed a heartbeat later by Briarlight, who dragged herself forward with her front paws, her useless back legs trailing behind her.

Bramblestar winced when he saw how frail the young she-cat looked. It was clear that she hadn't fully recovered from the bout of greencough that every cat had expected would kill her. Her typical cheerfulness was muted, and she seemed to be using every scrap of her strength to keep her forepaws moving.

"Briarlight!" Cinderheart bounded across to her. "Come over here, into this patch of sunshine."

The rest of the Clan huddled around her, the trouble with ShadowClan temporarily forgotten. Briarlight was popular; every cat admired her courage and was glad to see her leaving the medicine cats' den after her long illness.

"Look here," Purdy meowed, padding over when Briarlight had flopped down in a sunny spot. A mouse dangled from his jaws. "Let's share this mouse, an' I'll tell you how I once chased a dog out of my Upwalker's garden."

"No thanks, Purdy," Briarlight mewed. "I'm not really hungry. But I'd love to hear the story," she added hastily, as the old cat looked disappointed.

"I've collected some thrush feathers for your nest," Snowpaw announced, bouncing up with the feathers in his jaws and one or two clinging to his pelt. "They're really soft. I'll go in now and make it all cozy for you."

"Thank you," Briarlight called hoarsely after the apprentice as he dashed away.

"You're doing brilliantly, little one," Millie praised her daughter, stroking the young cat's shoulders with her tail. "It won't be long before you're feeling in top form again."

"I guess." Briarlight sighed. She rested her chin on her paws and watched Millie walk over to the fresh-kill pile, where Graystripe was pulling feathers from a blackbird.

Bramblestar padded over to Briarlight. "Is something up?" he asked. "Can I help?"

Briarlight twitched her ears. "I doubt it." She lifted her head and looked at Bramblestar with sky-colored eyes. "I'm fed up with being treated as if I'm special!" she confessed. "I just want to be like every other cat."

"What?" Bramblestar tried to sound amused. "You want to be like Purdy? Are you going to tell me a story? Or maybe you want to be like Spiderleg, too shy to speak to Daisy even though she's been the mother of his kits? Or perhaps you want to be Dewpaw, and live in the apprentices' den with your fur smelling of mouse bile? We're all different," he reminded her briskly.

Briarlight let out a small *mrrow* of laughter. "I know," she mewed. "But sometimes it's really difficult to be Briarlight."

Bramblestar gazed down at her, feeling helpless. He turned at the sound of paw steps. Leafpool had returned to the camp. Her pelt was dusty and there was dirt wedged under her claws from tending the herbs by the Twoleg nest.

"Everything's tidy over there," she reported to Jayfeather. "A little rain would help the catmint to grow."

"Jayfeather, I'm tired!" Briarlight called. "I'd like to go back to the den, please."

"But you've only been outside for a couple of heartbeats," Jayfeather objected.

"It's not good for you to be shut up in there all by yourself," Leafpool added.

"I want to go back now," Briarlight insisted.

Jayfeather was opening his jaws to argue when Purdy, who had been sitting a tail-length away, nibbling at his mouse, brought the half-eaten prey over to Briarlight and dropped it at her paws.

"You were going to help me with this," he reminded her. "I can't finish it. An' I haven't told you my story yet."

"You've hardly eaten anything!" Briarlight scolded him. "Come on, share the rest with me, and I'll listen to the story."

Purdy flashed Bramblestar a knowing look as he tucked his paws underneath him and waited for Briarlight to take her first bite of mouse. "Well, there was this dog, see," he began. "Nasty, flea-bitten creature . . ." He paused as Briarlight swallowed her mouthful, and nudged the fresh-kill closer so she could take another bite.

You clever old cat! Bramblestar thought.

Beside him, Jayfeather was listening to Briarlight's movements with his head on one side. Grunting in satisfaction, he straightened up and turned to Bramblestar. "It's full moon tonight," the medicine cat announced. "We missed the last Gathering because the sky was covered with clouds. It will be interesting to hear how the other Clans have coped with these last two moons of cold and hunger."

Bramblestar looked around for Squirrelflight and spotted her chatting with Graystripe beside the fresh-kill pile. He beckoned her over with a wave of his tail. "Which cats should we take to the Gathering tonight?" he asked her.

His deputy thought for a moment. "Cloudtail and Cherry-fall haven't been for a while."

"True, and neither has Cinderheart," Bramblestar mewed. "I think we should take all the apprentices, too."

Squirrelflight's eyes stretched wide. *"All five?* You must be joking!"

"I'm not. Lilypaw and Seedpaw missed their chance last moon, and it wouldn't be fair not to take the other three as well. It's time they found out what goes on at a Gathering."

Squirrelflight let out a snort of amusement. "If they get across the tree-bridge without one of them falling in, I'll eat my fur!"

Bramblestar flicked her ear with his tail. "They'll be fine." Glancing around, he spotted Blossomfall and Thornclaw in the entrance to the warriors' den. He felt his pelt prick with suspicion when he saw them with their heads together, and with a pang of guilt he swiveled his ears so he could hear what they were saying.

"I hope I'm chosen to go to the Gathering," Blossomfall murmured.

"Me too," Thornclaw agreed. "It's been ages since we've seen the others."

Bramblestar's uneasiness intensified. "I hope those two aren't expecting to rekindle friendships they made in the Dark Forest," he muttered.

"We need to trust all our Clanmates equally." Lionblaze spoke up from behind Bramblestar, who turned to face him. "What's done is done, and can't be undone." His golden gaze was fixed on Bramblestar. "In the end, our Clanmates realized where their loyalties lay."

Bramblestar nodded, remembering that during the Great Battle, as soon as the ThunderClan cats had realized that the Dark Forest warriors were bent on death and destruction, they had all switched their allegiances and fought fiercely for their own Clan.

He saw Squirrelflight's gaze fixed on Thornclaw and Blossomfall, and knew that she struggled to forgive them. *She lost so much in the Great Battle,* Bramblestar thought. *Her father, Firestar . . . and Hollyleaf, who was like a daughter to her.*

"I understand how you feel," he whispered into Squirrelflight's ear. "But if we treat them like outsiders, won't that encourage them to start looking beyond the Clan again for support?"

"Leafpool has volunteered to stay behind," Jayfeather put in. "So I'll be able to come."

"And I presume I can join you?" Lionblaze meowed. He half released his claws so that they flashed in the sunlight. "Just in case ShadowClan causes more trouble."

Bramblestar looked around at the three cats: his deputy, his medicine cat, and one of the Clan's bravest warriors. But they meant far more than that to him. *They are my family,* he thought, *even though they're not my blood kin. These cats will always be the most precious parts of my life.* He felt a jolt of grief as he pictured a black-furred cat with sharp green eyes. *If Hollyleaf were still alive, my family would be whole once more.*

* * *

The sun had gone down when Bramblestar led his cats out of the hollow and down toward the lake. The horizon was still streaked with scarlet, and the surface of the water reflected the dying glow. Bramblestar looked up to see the moon, a huge silver circle, hanging above the trees in a clear indigo sky.

Amberpaw let out a yowl of excitement as the lake came into sight. She charged down the slope toward it, with her two littermates hard on her paws. Lilypaw and Seedpaw glanced at each other as if they were far too mature for such overexcited behavior, then squealed, "Wait for us!" and pelted after them.

"Hey, be careful!" Squirrelflight called after them.

Amberpaw and Dewpaw skidded to a halt at the water's edge in a shower of pebbles. But Snowpaw couldn't stop in time. He splashed into the lake; his squeal of alarm was cut off as his head went under the surface and he vanished.

"Fox dung!" Bramblestar spat.

With a lash of his tail he raced for the lake, with Cloudtail, Snowpaw's father, bounding along at his shoulder. As Bramblestar reached the edge of the water, he caught a brief glimpse of Snowpaw resurfacing with his paws flailing. Bramblestar plunged toward him and managed to grab Snowpaw by the scruff before he sank again.

Digging his paws into the pebbly lakebed, Bramblestar carried the apprentice back to the shore. Cloudtail leaned over Snowpaw as Bramblestar set him down on solid ground. The other apprentices gathered around anxiously.

"Are you completely flea-brained?" Cloudtail demanded. "If I were Clan leader, I'd send you straight back to camp!"

Snowpaw coughed up a mouthful of water and struggled to his paws. "I—I'm sorry!" he gasped. "I didn't mean to fall in. I think the lake is bigger than it used to be."

Bramblestar looked around. "He's right," he commented, noting how far up the shore the water had risen. *It's the end of leaf-bare, and we've had a lot of rain.*

"Look at the size of the moon," Brackenfur put in, joining them. "The lake is always fuller when the moon is extra big."

Bramblestar stepped back to give his pelt a shake without splattering his Clanmates. "I won't send you home," he told Snowpaw. "But let's have no more silliness, okay?"

"Okay," Snowpaw mewed. "Thank you, Bramblestar."

"You'd better run around to get dry," Cloudtail advised. "And remember, I'm keeping an eye on you."

Snowpaw ducked his head briefly before scampering off with the other apprentices.

"He's no worse for his wetting," Bramblestar observed. "I can't be too hard on him. I remember how excited I was about my first Gathering, back at Fourtrees."

"You?" Squirrelflight let out a snort of amusement. "You were cool as frost!"

Bramblestar gave her a friendly flick with his tail. "Not like you, then! You couldn't see a thornbush without getting stuck in it. I remember—"

"We don't have time for stories," Squirrelflight interrupted. "Are we going to the Gathering or not?"

The ThunderClan cats followed the shoreline until they reached the stream that marked the border with WindClan.

Bramblestar kept an eye on the five apprentices to make sure that they had no problems jumping across the steep-sided brook.

"Wow, we're on WindClan territory!" Dewpaw exclaimed when he landed.

"What happens if a WindClan patrol spots us?" Amberpaw asked. "Do we fight? I know a great move!"

"No, we don't fight," Cinderheart told her. "The ground three fox-lengths from the lake doesn't belong to any Clan, so we can travel safely as long as we don't take any prey."

"But what about the water level?" Dewpaw pointed out. "The safe ground has been swallowed up!"

Bramblestar realized the apprentice was right. Judging from what he recognized on the grassy slope—and it was difficult with so few markers here on the open moor—they were already standing above the three-fox-length boundary.

The five apprentices huddled together, darting scared glances up at the rest of WindClan's territory. "We can't go to the Gathering after all," Seedpaw mewed, her tail drooping with disappointment. "Lilypaw and I missed it last moon, too. It's not fair!"

"Of course we can go," Cinderheart reassured her. "We measure the safe ground from wherever the water starts." Unseen by the apprentices, she glanced questioningly at Bramblestar. He nodded, hoping that WindClan would agree.

There was no sign of other cats until the ThunderClan patrol drew close to the far border. Then the WindClan cats came pouring over the ridge, briefly outlined against the darkening sky. Their leader, Onestar, was a few paw steps ahead of the rest, with his new deputy, Harespring, just behind him.

Bramblestar saw the eyes of the WindClan warriors gleam with thinly veiled hostility when they saw the ThunderClan patrol. He guessed they were remembering the recent skirmish by the stream, and he felt himself bristling in response. He walked forward until he stood face-to-face with Onestar.

"Greetings, Onestar," he meowed. "A fine night for a Gathering."

Onestar gave him a curt nod. "Greetings to you, Bramblestar."

Suddenly aware of pushing and growls of anger behind him, Bramblestar whipped around to see the WindClan cats jostling his Clanmates. Cherryfall slipped on the wet pebbles and almost lost her balance. Bramblestar felt his neck fur rise and knew that truce or no truce, a fight was about to break out. *What is WindClan trying to prove?*

"Please, Onestar," he mewed, struggling to keep his voice steady, "take your warriors on ahead. With the water so high, we don't want any accidents."

Onestar dipped his head. "Thank you, Bramblestar." Waving his tail to his warriors, he added; "Follow me."

Muttered protests rose from the ThunderClan cats as the WindClan cats trotted along the lakeshore.

"If they want trouble, we can give it to them," Thornclaw snarled.

"Don't be a mouse-brain!" Squirrelflight hissed at him.

"Strike the first blow, and *we'd* be the Clan who broke the truce. Beside, respect costs nothing, and we are on their territory."

While he waited for the WindClan cats to draw ahead, Bramblestar spotted two sets of eyes gleaming from farther up the slope, on the other side of the border. He peered through the half light, but he couldn't make out who the eyes belonged to.

"Daisy!" he called, turning back to his cats.

The cream-furred she-cat slid between her Clanmates and padded up to him. She didn't often attend Gatherings, and now she looked startled to be called forward.

"Look up there," Bramblestar murmured, pointing with his tail to where the eyes still shone. "Do you know who that is?"

Daisy took a breath, tasting the air. "Smoky!" she exclaimed, naming the cat who had been her friend when they both lived at the horseplace. Bramblestar couldn't count the moons since she had last seen him, but she clearly hadn't forgotten him. "Hey, Smoky, it's me!" she yowled, raising her voice.

The eyes vanished abruptly.

Daisy's tail drooped. "I wonder why he didn't want to talk to me."

"I wouldn't let it worry you," Bramblestar responded, resting his tail on Daisy's shoulder. "Seeing a whole crowd of us has probably put him off."

"I guess so," Daisy agreed.

Since the WindClan cats had vanished into the twilight, Bramblestar led his cats across the marshy ground until they reached the tree-bridge that joined the lakeshore to the island. The water was so high that waves lapped the bottom of the trunk. Cherryfall trotted across first without even looking down at the lake, and the rest of the patrol streamed after her. Bramblestar kept a close eye on the apprentices, but after Snowpaw's dunking they all took great care in placing their paws in the center of the tree trunk, even though they were quivering with excitement again.

Bramblestar shouldered his way into the lead as they forced their way through the bushes into the clearing in the middle of the island. The wide-reaching branches of the Great Oak cast slender black shadows across the moonlit ground. The other three Clans had already arrived, circling like fish in the open space.

The WindClan cats huddled together at one side, casting hostile glances at the other Clans as if they didn't trust any cat to abide by the truce.

"At least it's not just us that they have problems with," Brackenfur murmured into Bramblestar's ear.

"I suppose that's some comfort," Bramblestar whispered back.

Glancing around the clearing, he realized that WindClan was not the only Clan looking ill at ease. ShadowClan seemed restless, and divided into little muttering groups rather than standing together. Bramblestar wondered if Blackstar was too old and frail to pull his Clan together after the Great Battle, and whether some cats were already looking forward to a younger, stronger leader.

"What's going on with RiverClan?" Squirrelflight muttered.

The usually sleek-furred cats looked nervous and ruffled as they clustered around their leader, Mistystar. Some of them were limping, or favoring paws with visibly ripped claws. *What in the name of StarClan have they been doing to end up so battered?* Bramblestar's curiosity grew as he realized that it was the strongest warriors who showed most signs of hard, physical effort.

"Something's wrong, that's for sure," he replied.

Mistystar left her Clanmates to thread her way across the clearing and jump into the branches of the Great Oak. Bramblestar realized it was time to begin the Gathering. He thrust a path through the crowd of cats and joined Mistystar in the tree.

Squirrelflight followed him to sit with the other deputies on the roots of the oak, while the medicine cats gathered nearby. Onestar jumped up into the tree beside Bramblestar, but Blackstar remained on the ground. Bramblestar tensed. Was the ShadowClan leader going to do this at every Gathering?

Blackstar waited until the other cats had found places to sit, and then announced, "Let us remember the fallen." An uneasy silence settled over the clearing as he continued. "From ShadowClan: Redwillow, Shredtail, Toadfoot, Shrewfoot, Starlingwing, Olivenose, Applefur, Cedarheart, Tallpoppy, and Weaselkit. From ThunderClan: Firestar, Hollyleaf, Mousefur, Ferncloud, Sorreltail, Foxleap. From WindClan:

Ashfoot, Owlwhisker, Swallowtail, Thistleheart . . ."

Bramblestar twitched his tail uncomfortably. *Shouldn't I be the one to speak the names from ThunderClan, and Onestar recall his WindClan Clanmates, if we have to do this at all?*

At the first Gathering after the Great Battle, Blackstar had offered to recite the names of the cats who had died. Back then it had seemed appropriate, but Bramblestar wasn't sure if they needed to begin every Gathering like this. He sensed that the other leaders shared his uneasiness, and when Blackstar began to announce the RiverClan names, Mistystar stood up and balanced gracefully on her branch.

"Blackstar," she interrupted with an edge to her voice, "none of us have forgotten the Clanmates that we lost to the Dark Forest. Let us remember our fallen in our own way. Since when have you spoken for all of us?"

CHAPTER 5

Blackstar looked up at the WindClan leader; Bramblestar could see shock and horror in his eyes.

"These cats are still with us, watching the Clanmates they died to save!" Blackstar protested. "We need to honor their memory!"

"But Blackstar," Mistystar mewed more gently, "life moves on, just like the seasons. We don't list every piece of prey we've eaten in the last moon, or remember every fallen leaf."

Blackstar looked even more outraged. "Our Clanmates are not prey and fallen leaves!" he gasped.

"I didn't mean . . ." Mistystar began, but she was drowned by a growing clamor from the cats in the clearing. ShadowClan supported their leader, but many of the others were obviously as unhappy as Bramblestar about the List of the Fallen.

"Why aren't we capable of honoring our own dead?" Cloudtail demanded.

"And why is *Blackstar* the only cat allowed to speak?" Crowfeather challenged from WindClan.

Bramblestar jumped to his paws, waving his tail for silence. This wasn't an issue to break the truce over. "I agree with

Mistystar," he meowed when he could make himself heard. "Each Clan should be allowed to remember the fallen in its own way."

Blackstar's neck fur bristled and he drew his lips back in a snarl. "You are too quick to forget that we fought as one Clan against the Dark Forest."

"But we are not one Clan now," Bramblestar reminded him. "We are four Clans, just as we were before."

Blackstar whirled around and began to stalk away from the Great Oak. "My Clan will not stay to hear our dead warriors scorned by the other Clans!" he hissed. "You all owe them a debt, just as we do."

Instantly his deputy, Rowanclaw, jumped up from his place on the oak roots and ran after his leader. "Come back, Blackstar," he urged. "No cat has shown any disrespect to us. Things are changing, that's all." As Blackstar halted, looking bewildered, Rowanclaw added, "Each Clan faces new challenges, and nothing stays the same forever. Look at ShadowClan: We're not weak and broken now as we were after the battle. No, we're a Clan you can be proud of. And we owe that to you, our leader."

After a long pause, Blackstar turned and scrambled up into the Great Oak to take his place with the other leaders. Bramblestar sought out his sister Tawnypelt and met her gaze, giving her a nod to acknowledge Rowanclaw's well-judged words. Tawnypelt's green eyes glowed with pride in her mate.

"Thank you, Blackstar," Mistystar meowed, dipping her head to the ShadowClan leader. "You can be sure that all the

Clans will remember their dead for as long as the forest lasts."
Raising her eyes to the stars, she went on, "Ancestors of all the
Clans, look down on us here and guide us through the hard
days to come. Welcome the new starry warriors among you,
and keep the memory of them fresh in our minds. We honor
them, and all of you, now and always."

A ripple swept through the clearing like wind through grass
as each cat bowed his or her head to hear Mistystar's prayer.

"Now," Mistystar continued more briskly, "moonlight is
passing, and we still haven't begun. I'll go first, shall I?" She
glanced briefly at the other leaders, then announced, "We
have had to move our camp a little farther back from the lake,
because the water level is so high. But all is well, and there's
still a good supply of fish."

Bramblestar caught Squirrelflight's eye below him. *That's
why the RiverClan warriors look so tired and pawsore, and why they seem
so unsettled.*

"And we have new kits in RiverClan," Mistystar reported,
with a satisfied swish of her tail. "Petalfur gave birth to a she-
cat and two toms."

Bramblestar spotted the brown tabby warrior Mallownose
looking very proud. *He must be the father.*

As the other cats murmured congratulations, Mistystar
stepped back. "Would you like to speak next, Blackstar?"

The ShadowClan leader rose to his paws. Bramblestar
thought that he looked older than ever, white as bone against
the dark branches. "ShadowClan is strong and thriving," he
announced. "Snowbird has had three kits, all she-cats."

He sank back down on his branch, while below in the clearing Scorchfur looked smug, licking one paw and passing it over his ear.

Onestar stood up. "There's excellent hunting in Wind-Clan," he reported. "Birds have been coming inland from the sun-drown-place, blown by the wind. They don't seem to be comfortable landing on grass, which makes them easy to catch. And although we have no new kits yet, we expect good news soon."

His gaze rested on Sedgewhisker, who gave her chest fur a couple of embarrassed licks, and leaned into her mate, Ember-foot.

Bramblestar's pads prickled with disquiet as he stepped to the end of his branch and looked out over the cats. *Why are the other leaders making such a big deal about new kits? It's barely newleaf; there's plenty of time to fill the nursery.* "We have been strengthening our boundaries," he announced, his tail-tip twitching. *Pay attention, ShadowClan and WindClan!* "And five new apprentices have begun their training: Lilypaw, Seedpaw, Amberpaw, Snowpaw, and Dewpaw. Lilypaw and Seedpaw have been apprentices for three moons, but this is their first Gathering. All are learning fast, and will make excellent warriors."

"Lilypaw!"

"Seedpaw!"

"Amberpaw!"

"Snowpaw!"

"Dewpaw!"

As their names were yowled to the star-filled sky, the five

young cats sat up straight, their eyes burning with pride. Bramblestar jumped as wind rattled the branches above him, and the Great Oak creaked in the cold blast. A scrap of cloud drifted across the moon, briefly dimming the silver light that bathed the island.

"The Gathering is over!" Onestar called out.

The cats on the ground began to break up into smaller groups. As he leaped down from the tree, Bramblestar spotted Squirrelflight staring at Tigerheart and Ratscar from ShadowClan, who were chatting with Cherryfall and Ivypool.

"You look like a hawk sizing up its prey," he meowed as he slipped through the crowd of cats to Squirrelflight's side. "Tigerheart and Ratscar are just being friendly."

"There are some cats I'll never be able to trust again," Squirrelflight growled.

"They're not your Clanmates; you don't have to trust them," Bramblestar murmured. "But you can't make them enemies because of a mistake they made in the past."

Squirrelflight let out a snort. "I bet I can."

Bramblestar didn't bother to argue. He knew it would take a long time for his deputy to put aside her mistrust of any cat who had been led astray by the warriors of the Dark Forest. He struggled himself with the knowledge of what a few of his Clanmates had done. *Some wounds are slow to heal.* Instead he looked around for his sister Tawnypelt, and spotted her squeezing through a group of her Clanmates as she made her way toward him.

"Hi," she purred, touching noses with him. "It's good to see you, Bramblestar."

"And you," Bramblestar replied. "Rowanclaw did a brilliant job with Blackstar."

Tawnypelt's purr deepened. "I know. Rowanclaw is great."

"And he'll make a good leader," Bramblestar went on. "It can't be long now. . . ."

Instantly Tawnypelt's neck fur bristled. "Are you suggesting that Blackstar is too old to lead us?" she growled. "Because you're wrong! Blackstar is fine."

"Okay, okay!" Bramblestar took a pace back. "Keep your pelt on!"

Tawnypelt lashed her tail once, then pressed her muzzle into her brother's shoulder. "Take care, you stupid furball," she meowed as she turned to rejoin her Clanmates.

Bramblestar noticed that Tigerheart was still talking to Ivypool, though Cherryfall and Ratscar had moved on. Faintly curious, he eased his way into earshot.

"Where's Dovewing?" Tigerheart was asking.

Ivypool had a guarded look, and her tone was distant as she replied. "She's in the camp."

"With Bumblestripe?" Tigerheart glanced around as if he was looking for the pale gray tom.

"I don't think that's any of your business," Ivypool retorted.

Bramblestar wondered why Tigerheart would want to see Dovewing. *Cats in other Clans never learned about the Three's special powers, so it can't be that he wants her to see something far away.*

The tiny incident reminded Bramblestar that the Clans needed to live separately now. He would always be proud of the cats for coming together to fight against the Dark Forest. *I'm honored to have fought alongside them, but that time has passed. We* need to reinforce the borders of our territories, and the boundaries that we can't see, the ones between cat and cat.

On his way across the clearing he paused to chat with Pouncetail, a RiverClan elder, who began telling him a long, complicated story about catching fish. *Maybe I should introduce him to Purdy,* Bramblestar thought. He was distracted from the tale by a sharp prod in his side, and turned to see Squirrelflight.

"You need to give the signal to leave," she hissed. "WindClan and ShadowClan have already gone."

Embarrassment stabbed through Bramblestar. *I forgot that's my job now!*

"You're the leader now," Pouncetail teased him gently. "You have to make all the hard decisions. You're lucky to have Squirrelflight to keep you in line!"

"I certainly am," Bramblestar agreed. Watching Squirrelflight as she began efficiently rounding up their Clanmates, he added to himself, *I'd be lost without her as my deputy.*

Bramblestar returned to camp with the dawn patrol just as the sun burned off the last of the early mist. *It's going to be another warm day,* he thought.

As he emerged from the thorns, Bramblestar was surprised to see Daisy pacing nervously in front of the nursery. As soon as she spotted him she came bounding over.

"Bramblestar, I'm so worried!" she burst out.

"What's the matter?" Bramblestar asked, resting his tail on the she-cat's shoulder.

"It's Smoky and Floss at the horseplace," Daisy replied. "I think Smoky was waiting for us when we were going to the Gathering, but he was too scared to come and talk to us."

Bramblestar wasn't convinced. "He might just have been watching—"

"No, why would he?" Daisy interrupted, working her paws anxiously into the earth. "Those cats stay out of the way of the Clans. Please, Bramblestar, let me go to the horseplace and make sure everything's okay."

Bramblestar hesitated for a moment, gazing into Daisy's eyes and seeing her fear for her friends. "Okay, but I'll go with you."

"You don't have to!" Daisy meowed. "You're the leader of ThunderClan. You must have more important things to do."

"This might be important too," Bramblestar insisted. "We'll go together, after sunhigh."

Daisy let out a long purr, blinking up at him gratefully. "Thank you, Bramblestar."

As she headed back to the nursery, Graystripe joined Bramblestar.

"What did Daisy want?" the gray warrior meowed. He looked surprised when Bramblestar explained. "She wants to go back to the horseplace? Do you think she's considering leaving ThunderClan?" He puffed out a brief sigh. "Maybe the Great Battle scared her too much."

"That was several moons ago," Bramblestar pointed out. "If Daisy was scared, she would have left right away."

"Then maybe it's because the nursery is empty," Graystripe

suggested, flicking his tail toward the deserted bramble-covered den. "Maybe Daisy feels there's no place for her here anymore, with no queens or kits to care for."

Bramblestar dug his claws into the ground. *Why is every cat always talking about kits?* "Wait until newleaf," he meowed. "The nursery will fill up then." He cast a hopeful glance at Millie, who was eating a sparrow beside the fresh-kill pile. "I don't suppose . . . ?"

Graystripe shook his head. "Our days of having kits are gone," he replied, sounding amused. "There are plenty of young cats around to do that duty."

But none of the she-cats are expecting kits, Bramblestar thought bleakly.

Sunhigh was just past when Bramblestar and Daisy set out toward the edge of the lake. Before they were halfway down the slope to the lake, Bramblestar noticed that Daisy was limping. *Her paws are sore after the long walk to the Gathering,* he thought. *She's not used to traveling far outside the hollow.*

"Are you sure you don't want to put this off to another day?" he asked.

"Oh, no, I'll be fine!" Daisy assured him. "I don't want to wait before I see Smoky and Floss again."

On the lakeshore, Bramblestar spotted Ivypool, Spiderleg, and Whitewing practicing battle moves with their apprentices. As he and Daisy drew closer, the three young cats dived into the undergrowth that edged the stones.

What are they up to? Bramblestar wondered.

Suddenly Amberpaw and Dewpaw exploded out of the ferns and hurled themselves on top of Daisy. She let out a startled yowl as her paws skidded out from under her, and lay shaking on the ground.

"Get off her, you stupid furballs!" Bramblestar growled, grabbing Amberpaw by the scruff and hauling her off. He gave Dewpaw a hard shove with his hind paws. "What do you think you're playing at?"

The three mentors came bounding up, while Snowpaw emerged from the bushes looking relieved that for once he wasn't the cat in trouble.

"We were practicing our stalking!" Amberpaw mewed.

"You didn't hear us coming, did you?" Dewpaw added.

"Are you mouse-brained?" Whitewing hissed. "You should be ashamed of yourselves, attacking an unprepared cat—and a cat who wasn't threatening you."

"Right," Spiderleg agreed, giving Amberpaw a hard cuff around the ear. "Learn to recognize a real enemy!"

"I'm so sorry," Whitewing mewed to Daisy, who was sitting up, looking flustered. "Are you okay?"

"I'm fine," Daisy replied, shaking her pelt to remove the dirt, then giving herself a quick groom to settle her ruffled fur.

Ivypool gave both apprentices a sharp prod. "Apologize . . . *now!*"

Both apprentices were looking dismayed. *Daisy helped raise them when they were in the nursery,* Bramblestar recalled. *She's the last cat they'd want to hurt.*

"We're very sorry," Dewpaw mewed, nuzzling Daisy's shoulder. "We'll make it up to you."

"I'll catch a vole and bring it to the nursery later," Amberpaw promised. "I know that's your favorite!"

"And I'll collect some thrush feathers and make your nest really soft," Dewpaw added.

Daisy gave both the young cats an affectionate lick around the ears. "It's okay," she mewed. "I know you were just practicing. I'll look forward to the vole and the feathers, though!"

"They didn't mean to give you a scare," Bramblestar meowed as he and Daisy continued toward the stream that marked the edge of their territory.

"Oh, I know," Daisy replied with a flip of her tail. "All apprentices get it wrong sometimes. And it was a pretty good attack move!"

Bramblestar purred in agreement, admiring Daisy for her quick recovery and her clear sympathy for the apprentices. *It's too easy to forget what she does for our kits in the nursery,* he thought. He remembered Ferncloud's words when she gave him one of his nine lives. She had warned him never to underestimate the cats who provided the Clan with its new members, and helped to raise them. *And she was right. Daisy deserves as much honor and respect as any warrior.*

With a surge of optimism, he sprang over the border stream and picked up the pace until he was running along the shore below the open stretch of moorland. Daisy followed him, though she soon dropped behind. Bramblestar halted and waited for her to catch up.

"Sorry!" she panted. "I'm not used to this. Maybe I should run a bit more often."

Bramblestar let her set the pace until they reached the marsh; then they followed the WindClan border up the slope until they reached the fence around the horseplace. Daisy flattened herself to the ground and slid underneath. As Bramblestar followed he felt the ground begin to shake, and looked up to see three enormous horses galloping across the field toward them. He crouched down with his tail curled around him, waiting for one of the huge feet to land on him and crush his bones as it stamped him into the ground.

"It's okay," Daisy meowed. "Even I can run faster than them. Come this way."

Bramblestar rose to his paws and gave his pelt a shake, feeling hot with embarrassment. He followed Daisy as she slipped along the fence toward a line of bushes. They looked too thick to find a way through, and Bramblestar was conscious of the horses drawing closer like rolls of thunder. But Daisy dived into a narrow gap between two gnarled stems and vanished out of sight. Bramblestar forced his way in after her, feeling thorns tug at his pelt as he scrambled through. A moment later he popped into the open on the other side; behind him the rumbling hoofbeats stopped and he heard the horses snorting in frustration.

He realized that his fur was bristling with terror and forced it to lie flat again. Daisy was watching him with a glint of amusement in her eyes. "There are different sorts of danger here," she commented. "Not so many Dark Forest cats, but a lot more living horses!"

"True," Bramblestar grunted. "Lead the way, Daisy."

As they headed toward the small wooden barn, Bramble-star spotted Smoky watching them from his perch on a fencepost. His eyes glowed with pleasure as he leaped down to touch noses with Daisy.

"It's great to see you!" he purred. He sounded more wary as he turned to Bramblestar. "I've met you before, haven't I?" he meowed. "Back when you were a young cat, I think."

"He's Clan leader now!" Daisy told the gray-and-white tom.

"Really?" Smoky didn't sound impressed.

"Where's Floss?" Daisy asked, looking around. "I can't wait to see her again."

Smoky bowed his head, and his voice was somber as he replied, "Floss is dead."

"No!" Daisy exclaimed. "How did it happen?"

"She caught greencough," Smoky explained. "The Twolegs tried to treat her, but it was no use."

For a few heartbeats Daisy was too upset to speak. She flexed her front claws, ripping up the turf. Smoky pressed himself to her side. "If you like, I'll show you where she's bur-ied," he mewed.

Daisy nodded mutely. Bramblestar followed a pace or two behind as Smoky led Daisy around the back of the barn to a small mound of fresh earth.

"Pip's buried here, too," Smoky told her. "You remember the dog? He was an annoying little flea-pelt, but now that he's gone, I kinda miss him."

Daisy turned a shocked look on the horseplace cat. "So much has happened!" she gasped. "And I'm only a moment's travel away. How could I not have known?"

Smoky shrugged. "I know I'm not welcome in the woods or on the moor. Besides, Daisy, you made the choice to leave us. We have to respect that."

For a heartbeat, Bramblestar thought Daisy looked as though she was regretting her decision. Movement at the corner of his eye distracted him. He turned to see a young she-cat appear around the side of the barn, her tortoiseshell-and-white pelt shining in the sunlight.

"You're new here," Daisy commented as the newcomer bounded up. There was an edge to her tone, and her fur began to fluff up. "Who are you?"

"This is Coriander," Smoky mewed, brushing his pelt against the tortoiseshell cat. "She replaced Floss. She's a great mouser!"

"Replaced Floss?" Daisy sounded even more upset. "How can any cat *replace* Floss?"

Bramblestar rested his tail-tip on her shoulder, trying to warn her silently that there was no point in getting agitated. Daisy seemed to understand, and took a deep breath. "Greetings," she meowed, dipping her head to Coriander.

The young she-cat didn't return the gesture. "You must be some of those weird cats from the woods," she mewed. "What are you doing here?"

"Just visiting," Daisy told her through gritted teeth. "Was that you watching us go to the island last night?" she asked Smoky.

Smoky nodded. "Yes, Coriander wanted to see these famous cats, and I know that you all go to the island on the night of the full moon, so we lay in wait."

"You should have come to talk to us," Daisy meowed.

"Well . . ." Smoky scuffled his paws awkwardly in the grass. "We didn't want to interrupt anything."

"Okay." Daisy's shoulders sagged, and Bramblestar could see that the visit wasn't turning out the way she had hoped. "I guess it's time we left."

"Don't you want to see inside the barn?" Smoky asked. "You can hunt if you want."

Daisy didn't look enthusiastic, but she followed Smoky and Coriander as they headed for the entrance to the barn. Bramblestar trotted just behind her. Inside, the wood-sided den was warm and musty. It was much smaller than the barn where Barley and Ravenpaw used to live near the old forest, but it smelled the same, of dust and dried grass and tempting scents of prey. Golden dust motes danced in shafts of sunlight that slanted in through holes just beneath the roof. Scuffling noises in the piles of hay showed the presence of mice, and Bramblestar's mouth watered.

"It's all changed," Daisy commented. "You used to have your nest over here."

"I know," Smoky responded. "But Coriander says it's less drafty over there." He indicated a deep hollow in the hay with a flick of his tail.

"Yes," Coriander agreed. "It's *so* comfortable!"

Bramblestar saw Daisy's claws slide out, and gave her a

hasty nudge. "We really should be getting back," he mewed.

Daisy nodded. "Yes, there's loads to do back in the camp."

"Good-bye, then." Smoky sounded quite cheerful to let Daisy go, and Bramblestar noticed he didn't invite her to drop in again.

"Do be careful on your way home," Coriander added with a gleam in her amber eyes. "The horses can be quite scary if you're not used to them."

"I'm fine with horses, thanks," Daisy snapped, whipping around and stalking out of the barn with her tail held high. Resisting a purr of amusement, Bramblestar followed her.

On the journey back through WindClan territory, Daisy was unusually quiet.

Bramblestar thought he should say something. "It's always hard to go back," he offered sympathetically.

Daisy halted and stared at him. "I didn't want to go back!" she protested. "Not forever. I know I belong in ThunderClan now, but I hadn't expected things to change so much. Why didn't I know that Floss had died? Has Smoky forgotten about her already because of Coriander? I thought he loved Floss!"

For a moment, an image of Squirrelflight flashed into Bramblestar's mind. She was standing in the hollow surrounded by three fluffed-up kits, trying to coax them to eat a piece of vole.

"We want milk!" squeaked the she-cat, as black as a yew branch.

"Not that nasty stuff," put in the golden tabby tom, prodding the vole with one stubby paw.

"It smells like the dirtplace," chirped the smallest kit, whose pale gray fur blended with the cliffs behind him.

"It does not smell like the dirtplace!" Squirrelflight scolded. She looked up and met Bramblestar's gaze. She looked ruffled, her pelt ungroomed and her eyes clouded with exhaustion, but he had never loved her more.

"Any cat would think I was trying to poison them!" she hissed to him.

He blinked at her. "You're a great mother," he assured her. "They'll know that one day."

A stone rolling out from beneath his paw jolted Bramblestar back to the present. Beside him, Daisy looked sad as she mourned the loss of her friends.

"Nothing stays the same," Bramblestar told her, brushing her ear with his muzzle. *However much you want it to.*

CHAPTER 6

On the day after the visit to the horseplace, the weather changed. A fierce wind lashed the trees and sent clouds scudding across the sky. The forest floor was littered with splintered branches, and Bramblestar warned all his cats to look out for signs of falling trees. He continued to keep a close watch on the ShadowClan border, but there were no more traces of trespassing.

"Maybe they've learned their lesson," he remarked as he led a patrol past the pelt-den clearing.

"And maybe they're just keeping quiet until we relax the watch," Molewhisker growled with a flick of his tail.

"Let's enjoy the peace while it lasts," Sandstorm suggested.

Bramblestar murmured agreement. He headed down the stream until the patrol emerged from the trees on the lakeshore.

Blossomfall ran ahead and sprang onto a rock at the water's edge. She studied the smooth gray stone beneath her paws. "The lake is still rising!" she announced. "I've been scratching marks on this rock, and—" She broke off with a yowl as a wave rose up and engulfed the rock. As the water rolled back, it carried Blossomfall with it and she plunged into the lake.

She flailed with her paws, managing to keep her head above water, but the waves buffeted her too much for her to make it back to the shore.

"Blossomfall!" Molewhisker wailed, dashing to the water's edge.

"Keep back!" Bramblestar warned him. "We don't want two of you in there."

"Bramblestar, over here!" Sandstorm's voice sounded behind him.

Turning, Bramblestar saw that she was trying to tug a tree branch out of the undergrowth at the edge of the forest, but the twigs were snagged among brambles, and she couldn't move it.

"Help me get this free!" she panted.

Bramblestar raced over and grabbed the branch in his jaws. Together they managed to wrench it free. Bramblestar dragged it across the pebbles until the lake water was lapping around his paws, and shoved it out into the waves. The branch bobbed madly, and Bramblestar braced his feet among the stones to hold it steady.

"Be careful!" Sandstorm called.

Blossomfall's head was still bobbing above the surface, but the end of the branch was just beyond her reach. Bramblestar could see that her long, thick fur was waterlogged and dragging her down. "Molewhisker, Sandstorm," he rasped. "Put your weight on this end. Don't let it move."

The warriors waded into the lake and gripped the branch with their front paws. Bramblestar pulled himself onto the narrow length of wood and began to work his way forward, balancing on his hind paws and digging his front claws into the branch after each step. Waves slapped against him and with every heartbeat he expected to be torn away into the swirling water. Blossomfall bobbed a tail-length beyond the end of the branch, spluttering and thrashing as she was dragged under by the weight of her fur.

When the branch narrowed too much to hold Bramblestar, he shuffled carefully around and held out his tail toward the drowning cat. "Blossomfall!" he yowled. "Here!"

Blossomfall shook her head to get water out of her eyes, then made a frantic lunge toward Bramblestar. He winced as she sank her teeth into the end of his tail. The she-cat's eyes bulged as she clamped her jaws shut. Bramblestar took a deep breath against the pain and pulled her toward him until she could grip the branch with her claws and release his tail. Drops of blood scattered into the lake and sank quickly.

"Hold on!" Bramblestar called.

Sandstorm and Molewhisker began to haul the branch in, dragging it up the shore until first Bramblestar and then Blossomfall managed to find a paw hold. They waded out of the lake and flopped down on the pebbles well above the waterline.

"Thank you, Bramblestar!" Blossomfall choked, coughing up several mouthfuls of water. "I thought I was going to drown!"

Bramblestar got up and gave his pelt a shake. "It's too dangerous down here," he meowed. "I'm going to order every cat to stay away from the lake until the water level goes down."

"Good idea!" Molewhisker agreed.

Turning to Sandstorm, Bramblestar continued, "Will you take Blossomfall back and have Jayfeather check her out? Molewhisker and I can finish the patrol on our own."

"No, I'm okay," Blossomfall objected, struggling to her paws. "I can keep going."

Bramblestar hesitated. *I wonder if she's trying to prove her loyalty.* Then he told himself to stop second-guessing the motives of every cat who had been connected with the Dark Forest. He gave a brisk nod. "Tell me if you want to stop," he warned her. "There's no shame in needing to rest after what you've been through."

"I'm fine," Blossomfall insisted. Her pelt was still wet, sticking up in spikes, but her eyes were bright and determined.

Bramblestar led his patrol a safe distance from the water's edge and turned inland to follow the stream at the WindClan border. He spotted a WindClan patrol racing across the moor after a couple of bulky, low-flying white birds. As he watched, two of the cats leaped into the air and almost clawed one of the birds out of the sky. At the last moment it gave a vigorous beat of its wings and lurched away, gaining height.

"I've never seen WindClan hunting like that before!" Sandstorm exclaimed.

"It's pretty brave of them." Molewhisker sounded impressed. "Those birds are *big*!"

"I wonder how hungry they must be to try learning how to fly after prey," Bramblestar mused. "The Tribe cats hunt birds like that, but it doesn't seem natural for us."

The wind was blowing strongly over the moor, bringing so much WindClan scent that it seemed to fill the forest.

"It's hopeless trying to tell if they've trespassed," Mole-whisker growled. "I can't smell anything *but* WindClan!"

The patrol renewed their own scent markers, but the wind whisked the scent away into the forest almost immediately. Battling through the gusts, the cats finally reached the ridge and gazed down at the churning gray lake. *It's definitely bigger than usual,* Bramblestar realized.

"It's hard to believe it was once empty," Sandstorm murmured.

"Was that in the Long Dry?" Molewhisker asked. "Purdy started telling me about it, but he never said how the water came back."

Purdy hardly ever gets to the end of his stories, Bramblestar thought, twitching his whiskers in amusement.

"Well," Blossomfall began, "all the Clans sent two cats to form a patrol, and they traveled up the dried-out stream until—"

"Which cats went from ThunderClan?" Molewhisker interrupted.

"Dovewing—she was Dovepaw then—and Lionblaze," Blossomfall replied.

The tortoiseshell she-cat broke off with a startled squeal as a huge white bird flew unsteadily over their heads. Bramble-star ducked to avoid its erratic wingbeats. A moment later it crashed into a holly bush and struggled in the branches, trapped.

Bramblestar raced over to it with Molewhisker beside him. Reaching the bush, he stood back to let the younger warrior make the easy kill.

Molewhisker dived into the bush and sank his teeth into the bird's neck. It stopped struggling and went limp; Molewhisker backed out of the bush, dragging his prey with him.

"Good job!" Bramblestar praised him.

Blossomfall let out a snort. "You've made a bit of a mess of its wings," she pointed out. "You should be more careful."

"I only bit its neck!" Molewhisker protested.

Looking more closely, Bramblestar saw claw marks on the wings, and a spattering of blood on the white feathers. "This must be the bird we saw the WindClan warriors attacking," he meowed. "They've wounded it badly enough to bring it down, but it managed to get onto our territory." He let out a satisfied purr. "It'll make a great addition to the fresh-kill pile," he added, "but it's so heavy we might need more warriors to carry it back, so we don't do any more damage."

"Hey—what are you doing?" An outraged yowl came from the other side of the stream.

Bramblestar turned to see Nightcloud at the head of a WindClan patrol. Her apprentice, Hootpaw, and gray-and-white Gorsetail were just behind her.

"That's our catch!" the black she-cat growled. "We should have it."

"It is not your catch," Molewhisker defended himself. "I killed it, so it's mine!"

"It was alive when it entered ThunderClan territory," Bramblestar pointed out, "and that makes it ours."

All three WindClan cats were bristling with fury. "Look at this," Nightcloud snarled, holding up one paw to show scraps of white feathers stuck between her claws. "That proves we wounded it. If we hadn't, you would never have caught it."

"And we need it more than you," Hootpaw put in. "Rabbits are scarcer than usual, so these white birds are all we have."

"Be quiet!" Nightcloud hissed, giving her apprentice a cuff around the ear.

Sandstorm spoke softly to Bramblestar. "We have plenty of prey. I think Firestar would have let WindClan have this bird."

"I'm not Firestar," Bramblestar retorted. "We caught this fairly, so it belongs to us."

"Absolutely right, you're not Firestar," Gorsetail muttered, overhearing.

Bramblestar felt a flash of anger. Snatching up the white bird, he stalked away with it, even though it was almost too heavy for him to carry and the trailing wings threatened to trip him. Sandstorm and Molewhisker hurried to help him, one on each side, while Blossomfall padded ahead to clear any twigs or bramble tendrils out of the way. As they headed into the trees, Bramblestar could hear the WindClan cats hissing behind him, but he paid no attention.

"You made the right decision," Sandstorm meowed after a moment. "You're the leader now, and you can't show weakness to another Clan."

Bramblestar shrugged. "Whatever," he mumbled around his mouthful of feathers. He was thinking about what Hootpaw had said: Rabbits were getting scarce in WindClan, and they were relying on birds that didn't usually come to the moor. *There's something very familiar about the scent of the white bird's wings. . . .*

The ThunderClan cats gathered around to stare at the white bird when the patrol returned to the hollow.

"Wow, it's huge!" Berrynose exclaimed.

"I never saw a bird like that before," Ivypool meowed. "It's enough to feed the whole Clan!"

"I caught it," Molewhisker announced, giving his shoulder a couple of proud licks.

His sister Cherryfall blinked at him. "Great catch! Those wings could really have hurt you."

"Oh, it wasn't that difficult," Molewhisker mewed.

No, because the bird was already wounded and trapped in a bush, Bramblestar thought, suppressing a *mrrow* of amusement. He said nothing. *Let Molewhisker have his moment of glory!*

"Squirrelflight!" he called, beckoning to his deputy with his tail. He led her up to the white bird and angled his ears toward it. "Smell it," he mewed. "What does it remind you of?"

Squirrelflight took a deep sniff, then looked up, puzzled. "Er . . . dead birds?" she guessed.

Bramblestar twitched the tip of his tail. "No, think of a place," he urged.

Squirrelflight sniffed again, and understanding began to dawn in her eyes. "Now I remember! There's a salt-tasting tang on the feathers, like the water in the sun-drown-place. Do you think that's where it came from?"

Bramblestar remembered that Onestar had mentioned at the Gathering that WindClan were hunting birds from the sun-drown-water. He hadn't paid much attention at the time, thinking that the WindClan leader must be imagining things. Now he wasn't so sure.

"The wind must be incredibly strong," he commented, "to blow these birds all the way here."

He gazed through the trees as though he could see all the way to the sun-drown-place. A shiver passed through him from ears to tail-tip as he remembered the surging mass of blue-green water.

Squirrelflight waited a few moments more to let all the Clan, especially the apprentices, get a good look at the white bird. Then she raised her voice to make herself heard throughout the clearing. "Come on, all of you! There's enough prey here for every cat!"

That night Bramblestar found it hard to rest. Wind blustering around the Highledge disturbed him, and when he did manage to snatch a few moments of sleep he was assaulted by strange dreams of salty water and falling down holes on top of badgers.

A paw prodding him in the side woke him. The faint light of dawn was trickling into his den, and he just managed to make out the features of Jayfeather. The medicine cat was wide-eyed and agitated.

"Wha . . . ?" Bramblestar muttered. "Did I call out in my sleep and wake you?"

Jayfeather shook his head. "No. I went out before dawn, because I was concerned about the new plants in the wind. And I found something . . . something awful. Come and see, Bramblestar!"

Shaking off the last remnants of sleep, Bramblestar followed Jayfeather out of his den and down the tumbled rocks to the floor of the hollow. Jayfeather led the way into the forest at a run, sure-pawed as always in spite of his blindness, while Bramblestar blundered after him in the near darkness.

The two cats followed the disused Thunderpath until they came to the abandoned nest. By now there was enough light for Bramblestar to see more clearly. He stopped, his fur bushing up in dismay. The plants that Leafpool and Jayfeather had tended so carefully had been destroyed by a branch from a nearby ash tree. Wind had blown it across the patch of earth, churning up the ground and flattening the young herbs. Torn leaves had blown everywhere.

"Well, it's bad, but it should be possible to repair it," Bramblestar meowed. "Some of the roots must have survived. I'll send you a patrol later today, to help clear up the mess and look for new plants in the forest."

"You don't understand," Jayfeather told him, his voice somber. "This is an omen. Something terrible is going to happen. Darkness and destruction and tragedy are closing in on our Clan once more."

Bramblestar felt an icy trickle of fear run down his spine. "Not the Dark Forest again?"

"No," Jayfeather replied, and his voice sounded far away, and somehow older. "Something different from the Great Battle. I don't know what it is, but I can feel it coming on the wind."

CHAPTER 7

❧

Dawn had scarcely broken by the time Bramblestar and Jayfeather returned to the hollow. But their Clanmates were already awake and restless, pacing around the clearing with their fur blown the wrong way and their ears turned inside out. The trees clattered overhead as the wind gusted through them.

"I don't like this," Squirrelflight muttered as she joined Bramblestar in the center of the camp. "It reminds me too much of the time the tree fell, when Longtail died and Briarlight was injured."

Bramblestar nodded, knowing that terrible day must be in the mind of every cat. A couple of fox-lengths away Dovewing was standing with her claws dug into the earth as if she were trying to take root. Her head was raised, and Bramblestar knew she was struggling to listen for falling trees.

Dovewing's mother, Whitewing, emerged from the warriors' den and padded up to her daughter. "This isn't doing any good," she murmured, giving Dovewing's ear a gentle lick. "Come and share a vole with me."

Dovewing hesitated, then allowed her mother to coax her over to the fresh-kill pile.

"I'm worried about Dovewing," Bramblestar confided to Squirrelflight.

"I know," Squirrelflight responded. "It was hard for all three cats to lose their powers."

"But Dovewing seems to be suffering most of all," Bramblestar mewed.

Lionblaze and Cinderheart pushed their way into the camp through the thorn barrier. Lionblaze looked ruffled, and was speaking over his shoulder to Cinderheart.

"It's mouse-brained, trying to hunt in this!" he complained. "That branch from the beech tree whacked me right on the head!"

"Honestly, Lionblaze," Cinderheart purred. "It was only a twig! You have to get used to being injured."

Bramblestar sent Squirrelflight to round up the senior warriors. "We still have to send out patrols," he began when they were gathered around him. He had to raise his voice to make himself heard above the blustering wind. "I don't want any cat injured by falling trees—"

"Right," Lionblaze muttered, rubbing the top of his head with one paw.

"But we need to restock the fresh-kill pile," Bramblestar went on. "And I wouldn't put it past ShadowClan or Wind-Clan to take advantage of all this noise and chaos to cross the border. Especially WindClan, chasing those storm-blown white birds."

Blossomfall nodded. "I'd bet a moon of dawn patrols that they'd have crossed our border after the bird we caught, if we hadn't been there."

"So who will lead a patrol?" Bramblestar asked.

"I will," Squirrelflight offered immediately.

"And me," Dustpelt and Ivypool added in chorus.

"I will, too," Bumblestripe meowed. "Except . . . Dovewing, will you be okay if I leave you?"

"I'll be fine," Dovewing replied, though she was working her claws agitatedly into the ground.

Bramblestar could see that she was in too much of a state to be sent out on patrol. She was still trying to use her far-senses, even though she had lost them right after the battle. *She feels like she's deaf and blind, and she can't bear it!*

"I'll keep an eye on her," Whitewing promised, leading her daughter back to the warriors' den.

"Four patrols, then," Bramblestar ordered. "Ivypool, take the WindClan border, and Dustpelt, take ShadowClan. Bumblestripe and Squirrelflight, your patrols can hunt. I'll go with Bumblestripe."

"Which cats should we take with us?" Dustpelt asked.

"Choose your own," Bramblestar responded. "Have one cat in each patrol to watch out for danger—wind-blown branches, creaking trees, whatever. And if that cat says run, *run!*"

As Bumblestripe began to look around for other cats, his apprentice, Seedpaw, scampered up. "Can I come?" she chirped.

Bumblestripe shook his head. "It's too dangerous out there for apprentices."

"But—"

"No *buts*," Bramblestar interrupted. "You and the others can help by clearing up any debris that gets blown into the camp. Tell your denmates I said so. You are responsible for keeping the camp tidy and safe, okay?"

Seedpaw lifted her head proudly. "We can do that, Bramblestar." She dashed off toward the apprentices' den.

The leaders of the patrols quickly found other cats to go with them and headed into the forest. Mousewhisker and Cherryfall had joined Bumblestripe's patrol. Both of them seemed spooked by the wind, darting uneasy glances around at every paw step, and starting at each unexpected noise.

Bramblestar took on the duty of keeping watch for danger. Though the trees were thrashing in the wind, none of them looked ready to fall. But the noise of the gusts and creaking branches was so loud that there was little chance of picking up tiny prey sounds, while the strong gusts scattered scents everywhere.

"I think we ought to hunt in places where prey might go to shelter," Bumblestripe suggested. "Like a bramble thicket, or maybe the abandoned Twoleg nest."

"Great idea!" Cherryfall agreed. "Let's go to the nest."

Anything to get out of this wind for a bit, Bramblestar thought.

He brought up the rear as Bumblestripe led the patrol along the old Thunderpath. Now they were battling into the wind, their eyes watering and their pelts pressed flat to their sides. Every paw step was a massive effort, as if the wind was trying to pluck them up and send them crashing into the trees.

When the Twoleg nest came in sight, Bumblestripe and the others halted, staring in dismay at the fallen branch and the damaged plants.

"Leafpool worked so hard over that!" Cherryfall gasped.

"And she and Jayfeather will put it right again as soon as this wind drops," Mousewhisker reassured her.

Bramblestar couldn't share Mousewhisker's optimism. His memory of Jayfeather's ominous omen was too strong, and he glanced around with his ears pricked. But all the trees within sight had their roots firmly fixed in the ground.

Bramblestar followed Bumblestripe and the others into the tumbledown den. Cherryfall puffed out a sigh of relief as she stepped inside. "Sheltered from the wind at last!" she mewed, smoothing her whiskers with one paw.

"Keep quiet and listen for prey," Bumblestripe ordered.

In a brief moment of silence when the wind dropped, Bramblestar picked up a strong scent of mouse and heard the patter of their tiny feet above his head, where strong, straight, Twoleg-crafted branches were supporting the roof.

Bumblestripe had heard it, too. "Up there," he whispered, pointing with his tail.

"I'll go!" Cherryfall lightly climbed the wooden slats that were fixed to the far wall. From the top she made a graceful leap onto one of the branches.

"Be careful!" Bramblestar warned.

The young she-cat stalked along the branch. Farther along, in the shadows, Bramblestar could just make out a flicker of movement that told him a mouse was there.

But as Cherryfall was readying herself to pounce, a powerful gust of wind hit the den. One of the flat stones that formed the roof was torn free and clattered away. Cherryfall jumped in shock and lost her balance. Yowling in terror, she fell, her body twisting in the air. She just managed to snag the bulky wood with one claw before she plummeted to the ground.

"Help!" she wailed.

"Can you climb back up?" Bramblestar yowled.

Cherryfall stretched up with her other forepaw, but she couldn't grasp the smooth surface. "I'm slipping!" she gasped.

"Mousewhisker, go after her," Bramblestar ordered. "And for StarClan's sake, watch where you're putting your paws."

Mousewhisker bounded up the wooden slats and leaped neatly onto the end of the branch. Balancing carefully in the center, he headed toward Cherryfall.

"Come on," Bramblestar meowed to Bumblestripe. "Let's collect dead leaves, debris, anything to break her fall if she loses her grip."

Together they scraped up the earthy litter that lay on the floor of the den, then darted outside to find more. Bumblestripe tore up moss from the side of the den, while Bramblestar scraped up a clump of yarrow that grew near the door. The pile was growing, but agonizingly slowly, while Cherryfall dangled above it.

Mousewhisker had reached the point on the branch where his Clanmate was hanging. He stretched down, trying to grab her scruff, but it was just out of reach. While he strained, he brushed against Cherryfall's leg, dislodging her precarious grip. She uttered a wild screech as she fell.

Bramblestar darted forward just in time to break her fall. She slammed into him, knocking him to the ground, and his head cracked against the stone floor. Darkness sparkled over Bramblestar's vision. Voices echoed around him, seeming to come from a long way off. *Am I losing a life?* he wondered.

Then the voices sounded more clearly and he recognized the tones of Cherryfall and Mousewhisker.

"Are you okay? I'm sorry I let you fall."

"Oof—all the breath's knocked out of me! But I'm fine, I think."

Then another voice, more distant, joined them. "What's going on in there?"

Bramblestar sat up groggily. His vision cleared and he saw Ivypool peering through the entrance to the den, with her patrol clustered anxiously behind her.

"Cherryfall fell off the branch up there," Bumblestripe explained. "Bramblestar was great—he broke her fall."

Ivypool's eyes stretched wide. "Are you hurt?" she mewed. "You should go straight back to camp and let Jayfeather check you out."

"There's no need," Bramblestar protested, rising to his paws. The walls of the den whirled around him.

"And hedgehogs can fly," Ivypool retorted. "You can barely stand. And don't try to hide your paw from me, Cherryfall. I can see the blood on it."

"It's only a ripped claw," Cherryfall muttered.

"It needs treating!" Ivypool hissed.

Bramblestar sighed. "Okay, Ivypool, keep your fur on. We'll go back. But I still want that mouse caught. Mouse-whisker and Bumblestripe, you can stay here and try again."

Bumblestripe nodded. "We'll get it, don't worry."

Bramblestar led the way out of the den with Cherryfall limping behind him. Ivypool and her patrol flanked them as they returned to the camp.

"Any sign of WindClan on the border?" Bramblestar asked Ivypool.

"Not a sniff," the silver-and-white tabby told him. "As far as we can scent anything in this wind. We didn't spot any more of those white birds, either."

Back in the hollow, Bramblestar sent Cherryfall to her nest, then headed for the medicine cats' den. Both Jayfeather and Leafpool were there, sorting piles of herbs.

"How am I supposed to keep my stocks tidy when the wind is this bad?" Jayfeather was grumbling as Bramblestar brushed past the bramble screen. "I no sooner put a stem down, when it's gone."

"We need to do this as fast as we can, and then shove everything down to the bottom of the cleft," Leafpool meowed.

Jayfeather snorted. "And what do *you* want?" he asked, looking up at Bramblestar with his intense blue gaze. "Not another skirmish with WindClan?"

"No," Bramblestar replied. He explained what had happened at the Twoleg nest. "Cherryfall has a ripped claw," he finished. "I sent her to rest in the warriors' den. Leafpool, I thought you could take a look at her there."

Jayfeather's eyes narrowed. "Are you the ThunderClan medicine cat, Bramblestar, or am I?" He sighed. "Okay, Leafpool. Better take some marigold, if it hasn't all blown away."

When Leafpool had slipped out carrying the herbs, Jayfeather faced Bramblestar again. "Go on, then," he meowed. "What do you want to talk about?"

"How do you know I—"

"You sent Leafpool away deliberately, right? Don't waste my time, Bramblestar."

"It's about the omen," Bramblestar began. "Was this the disaster we were warned about? I saved Cherryfall—does that mean I defeated the omen?"

Jayfeather looked thoughtful. "I don't know," he admitted. "With all this wind, it's impossible to think straight."

"Then you can't help?" Bramblestar asked.

"With the omen? No. But I can still help with your injuries. Sit still while I examine you."

Bramblestar's paws were itching to get back to his patrol, but he forced himself to wait while Jayfeather ran his paws expertly over him.

"You've got a bump on your head," the medicine cat mewed. "And does it hurt when I do this?" He gave Bramblestar a sharp prod in the shoulder.

"Ow! Yes, it does."

"Thought so," Jayfeather grunted. "You'll have some pain there for a day or two, but it's not serious. A poppy seed should ease it."

"No, thanks," Bramblestar meowed. "I'll put up with the pain so I can keep a clear head."

Jayfeather shrugged. "Suit yourself. Tell me if you change your mind."

Bramblestar thanked the medicine cat and padded out into the clearing again. Squirrelflight's hunting patrol had just returned, but their jaws were empty.

"It's hopeless!" Squirrelflight declared, her fur bristling. "I think the wind has blown all the prey out of the forest."

We'll go hungry tonight, Bramblestar thought. *I hope Bumble-stripe and Mousewhisker managed to catch that mouse.* Slipping into the warriors' den to check on Cherryfall, he found the young cat drowsy from poppy seed. Leafpool had put a poultice of marigold leaves on her injured paw and was stroking the warrior's fur while she went to sleep.

Bramblestar retreated quietly and crossed the clearing to the elders' den, where Purdy, his tabby pelt ruffled by the wind, was busy plugging the drafts with long tendrils of bramble.

"The apprentices should be helping you with that," Bramblestar meowed.

"I can manage fine," Purdy puffed. "I don't need no young cats runnin' around after me. They've better things to do."

But Bramblestar could see that the old tabby was looking tired, and the brambles were catching in his matted tabby fur. Backing out of the den, he beckoned with his tail to Lilypaw and Seedpaw, who were collecting sticks and dead leaves from the floor of the camp.

"Go and help Purdy, please," he meowed when they came bounding up. "His den needs wind-proofing, and then you could see if there's any fresh-kill left for him."

"Sure, Bramblestar," Lilypaw chirped.

Bramblestar let out a purr. *The two older apprentices are shaping up nicely.* Catching sight of Daisy in the entrance to the nursery, he padded over to her.

"This wind is terrible!" the cream-colored she-cat exclaimed as he approached. "It blows dust into my eyes and fur, and I can't hear myself think."

"It won't last long, I hope," Bramblestar mewed. "Daisy, I wonder if you could sleep in Purdy's den tonight? If anything happens, I don't want him to be alone."

Daisy twitched her whiskers. *She knows what I mean. Another falling tree would tear the heart out of this Clan.*

"I'll go," Daisy agreed, "but I probably won't get any sleep, what with the wind and the stench of mouse bile. Honestly, I think every tick in the forest heads straight for Purdy!"

Bramblestar looked around for Squirrelflight, wondering if it was too late to send out more patrols. Spotting her outside the warriors' den, he headed toward her, only to be intercepted by Millie.

"Briarlight is very worried about falling trees," the gray she-cat told him. "She won't be able to run away."

Looking at Millie's troubled eyes, and the way she was agitatedly working her claws into the ground, Bramblestar thought that Millie was more terrified than Briarlight for her daughter's safety. "Okay, I'll talk to her," he meowed.

Millie led him to the fresh-kill pile, where Briarlight was sharing a rather shriveled shrew with Molewhisker.

"Where would you feel most comfortable sleeping?" Bramblestar asked her.

Briarlight shivered. "Somewhere there are no trees," she replied.

Bramblestar figured that Briarlight might feel safest up on the Highledge, where the rock would shelter her. "You can sleep in my den," he told her. "Come on, I'll carry you up there."

Briarlight blinked at him in surprise. "Really? Wow!"

"Thank you, Bramblestar," purred Millie.

Feeling slightly embarrassed, Bramblestar crouched down so that Briarlight could haul herself onto his back. Mole-whisker gave her a boost, and Brackenfur saw what was going on and came to help too. With the toms steadying Briarlight on either side, Bramblestar struggled up the slope of rocks, wincing every time their paws dislodged small stones. Millie brought up the rear, and Bramblestar heard her gasp with alarm at each stone that pattered down into the clearing.

At last Bramblestar reached his den and settled Briarlight into his nest, pulling the moss and bracken closely around her to make her cozy. "You'd better stay with her, Millie," he meowed. "Call me if there are any problems. I'll be in the warriors' den."

"We'll be just fine here, Bramblestar," Millie responded. "Thank you so much."

Bramblestar headed down into the clearing and found Squirrelflight still sitting outside the warriors' den, her tail wrapped around her paws.

"Do you think we should take out another hunting patrol?" he meowed.

"In this?" Squirrelflight glanced up at the trees, still buffetted by the roaring wind. "No. We'll just have to go hungry tonight, and hope things are better in the morning."

Bramblestar was glad to agree with her. His head and his shoulder were aching, and he wanted nothing more than to curl up somewhere and go to sleep.

"That was very kind, what you did for Briarlight," Squirrelflight murmured as they slipped inside the warriors' den.

Bramblestar felt embarrassed all over again. "It was logical," he mewed with a shrug.

As the Clan settled down to sleep, Dustpelt and Brackenfur padded around to check each den, making sure that the branches were woven as securely as they could be, and plugging any new holes with moss and bramble.

"Don't stay awake too late," Bramblestar advised them. "You need your sleep too."

Dustpelt didn't reply. Bramblestar suppressed a sigh. He wondered if the tabby tom was deliberately working himself into exhaustion to have a chance of sleeping in his empty nest.

Though his mossy bed was comfortable, Bramblestar found it hard to sleep because of the noise of the wind. He couldn't stop listening out for the creaking sound that would warn of a tree about to fall. But at the same time he enjoyed hearing the breathing of his Clanmates and seeing their furry shapes in the dim light. He realized for the first time how much he missed their company when he was sleeping alone in his den on the Highledge.

If I had a mate, I wouldn't be alone, he thought, then gave himself a shake. *There's no point dwelling on that.*

Finally Bramblestar gave up his attempt to sleep and crept into the clearing. He staggered as the force of the wind hit him, with a slap of rain that probed his pelt with icy claws. Recovering himself, he began to pad around the camp.

Purdy's voice came from the elders' den. "So, I says to the dog, 'Listen, flea-pelt, this is *my* garden, so take your stench-ridden body out of here.'"

"Wow . . ." Daisy's voice sounded so drowsy that Bramblestar thought she was talking in her sleep. "How brave of you."

Moving on, Bramblestar paused underneath the High-ledge, but couldn't hear any sound coming from there. *I hope that means Briarlight and Millie are asleep.* He poked his head into the apprentices' den and made out five curled-up balls of fur deeply asleep in their thick nests of moss and bracken. All were silent except for Snowpaw, who was snoring loudly. As Bramblestar watched, Lilypaw shot out one hind leg and, without opening her eyes, prodded Snowpaw in the belly. Snowpaw grunted and was quiet.

Bramblestar sighed with relief. *The Clan is safe.*

He still felt restless, so he headed out of the camp with a nod to Thornclaw, who was on guard duty. Even in the shelter of the trees, wind swept cold raindrops into his face as he picked his way through the debris on the forest floor. Stars and the occasional glimmer of moonlight appeared through the racing clouds. Uneasiness stirred in Bramblestar's belly; in the flickering half light, something looked different.

Stumbling over fallen branches, Bramblestar made his way

closer to the lake. The creaking and clattering trees made him jump, his senses stretched to the edge of panic. *The air smells different, too. What's going on?*

He picked up the pace, desperate to find out if something was threatening his Clan. A tree stump loomed up in front of him; bunching his muscles, he leaped over it. A heartbeat later he landed up to his belly fur in icy water.

Bramblestar let out a startled screech. *But I'm only halfway to the lake!*

For a moment he floundered while the water dragged at him, surging around his legs. With a hiss he dug his claws into the ground and paw step by paw step hauled himself backward up the slope until he was clear of the water. Then he whirled around and raced for the hollow.

StarClan help us! The lake has flooded!

CHAPTER 8

Bramblestar scrambled through the long grass, heavy with rain, back up the slope to the hollow. Thornclaw was still crouched by the entrance; he leaped to his paws and stared in astonishment when he saw Bramblestar, drenched to his skin.

"What happened?" he demanded.

"The lake is flooding!" Bramblestar panted. "The water is coming up through the forest."

"What? It can't be!"

"Come and see."

Bramblestar whipped around and led Thornclaw at a run back down the hillside. This time he knew what to expect, and he halted beside the tree stump, right at the edge of the floodwater.

"Wow!" Thornclaw breathed. "That's some flood!"

In the darkness Bramblestar thought there was something sinister about the water, the surface ruffled by the wind and glinting in the light from the stars. Waves slapped against the tree trunks, sucking and gurgling around the roots.

"What should we do now?" Thornclaw asked.

"I'm not sure," Bramblestar admitted. "Let's get back to the camp and see what the others think."

The rain began lashing down more heavily, and by the time Bramblestar and Thornclaw reached the hollow, they were equally soaked through. While Thornclaw went back on watch, Bramblestar slipped inside the warriors' den and roused Squirrelflight and Brackenfur.

"What is it?" Squirrelflight muttered, struggling up out of her nest. "A fallen tree?"

"No, thank StarClan." Bramblestar gestured toward the entrance to the den. "Come over here where we can talk without waking the others."

Brackenfur picked his way among sleeping warriors to join them, disturbing Graystripe on the way. The gray warrior glanced up, and when Bramblestar beckoned to him, he hauled himself out of his nest and padded over to the little group by the entrance.

"What's the problem?" he asked with a massive yawn.

Bramblestar explained how the lake water had risen and flooded the forest. "It's still some way away," he meowed. "I don't think it will get this far."

"What do you want us to do?" Squirrelflight meowed.

Bramblestar gazed out across the camp. The clearing was covered with puddles that were starting to run together as the rain hissed down. "We need to decide what to do about hunting and border patrols," he mewed.

A screech from the elders' den interrupted him and Purdy stumbled into the open. "There's water all down my back!" he yowled.

Daisy emerged after the elder, her shoulders hunched against the downpour, and began chivvying him across to the nursery.

At the same moment Bramblestar heard cats stirring in the den behind him, and grunts of complaint as water seeped through the roof and showered the warriors. Cloudtail jumped up and shook himself with a disgusted look at the woven brambles above his head. Rosepetal tried to burrow deeper into the moss to get away from the cold trickles, while Berrynose snarled with annoyance as he squashed himself into a tiny, dry corner.

"We're going to be washed out of here," Bramblestar meowed. "Brackenfur, can you check the other dens, and see if anywhere is watertight?"

"Sure." Brackenfur slipped out into the storm and pelted across to the nursery.

"Do you think we need to leave the hollow?" Squirrelflight suggested.

Bramblestar glanced at Graystripe, wondering what he thought.

Graystripe shook his head. "It's just as wet out in the forest as it is here," he pointed out. "And it's too dark to see where we're putting our paws."

"There's more danger out there, too," Bramblestar agreed. "The wind is still strong enough to knock over trees. No, I think we'll stay put."

"What are you going to tell the others about the lake?" Squirrelflight asked.

Bramblestar hesitated for a moment. "Nothing," he decided. "They'll find out soon enough, and there's no point scaring them in the middle of the night."

Squirrelflight didn't look as if she agreed with him, but she just dipped her head and mewed, "Okay."

Behind them in the warriors' den, more cats were waking as the rain forced its way through the roof. Startled squeals sounded through the darkness.

"This is no good, Bramblestar," Cloudtail grumbled, squelching his way through the soaked moss and picking up each paw to shake it. "It's like trying to sleep under a waterfall!"

"We'll all die of greencough at this rate!" Spiderleg called out.

For a moment Bramblestar didn't know what to tell his Clanmates. *I can't make it stop raining!*

Just then Brackenfur returned, his pelt drenched and his legs splashed with mud. "The nursery is dry," he reported. "And so is the apprentices' den."

"Good." Bramblestar puffed out a breath of relief. "Jayfeather should be able to fit a couple of cats into his cave, and my den on the Highledge will be sheltered, too." He turned to face the shivering cats in the warriors' den, raising his voice so they could hear him above the clamor of wind and rain. "We have to move out of this den. Graystripe, take Blossomfall, Dustpelt, and Sandstorm to join Millie and Briarlight in my den. Mentors, you can bed down with your apprentices in their den. Brightheart and Cloudtail, go to Jayfeather. The rest of us will sleep in the nursery."

He stood with Squirrelflight at the entrance to the den, watching as his Clanmates darted out into the storm, hunched and miserable. Sandstorm and Dustpelt bounded toward the tumbled rocks, while Berrynose touched noses with Poppyfrost before she scurried off to join her apprentice. Whitewing seemed reluctant to leave Dovewing, who looked spooked by what was happening, as if she was straining to listen to all the forest at once.

"I'll keep an eye on her," Lionblaze promised.

Whitewing flashed him a grateful glance, then dashed through the teeming rain after Poppyfrost.

As the last of the warriors left the soaked den, another cat raced up to Bramblestar; peering through the darkness he made out Leafpool's pale tabby pelt.

"Jayfeather and I have spare dry bedding," she mewed. "Where do you need it?"

"Take some to the Highledge," Bramblestar ordered. "They'll be short up there. And check the apprentices' den. The nursery should have enough."

"Okay." Leafpool sped off again.

"Thanks, Leafpool!" Bramblestar called after her.

When all the cats had left, he and Squirrelflight headed for the nursery, but Bramblestar veered aside to check on the apprentices. When he stuck his head inside the den, he saw that all of them were awake now, squashed up tightly with their mentors.

"Are you all okay?" he asked.

"Fine," Whitewing replied. "We could do with a bit more bedding—"

"And a bit more space," Spiderleg added. "Lilypaw, take your tail out of my eye."

"This is exciting!" Amberpaw squeaked, her eyes gleaming in the dim light.

"No, it isn't!" Ivypool retorted. She was licking herself to dry off her pelt. "We're cold and wet, and StarClan knows what the camp will look like in the morning."

"Apprentices think everything is exciting," Bumblestripe pointed out as he burrowed into the dry moss.

"Except finding Purdy's ticks." Seedpaw yawned.

"I just thought of something!" Dewpaw exclaimed. "We must be warriors now, because we've got warriors sleeping here, so this is the warriors' den."

"Yay! No more ticks!" Snowpaw yowled.

"In your dreams!" Spiderleg meowed.

Poppyfrost rolled her eyes. "Very funny. Now be quiet and go to sleep."

Obediently the apprentices curled up, but Bramblestar could hear stifled snuffles of amusement, and see the glimmer of mischievous eyes peeping out over the tails that wrapped their noses. He drew back and spotted Leafpool scurrying across the clearing with a load of bedding. Jayfeather loomed up beside Bramblestar at the entrance to the apprentices' den, a bundle of moss wedged between his chin and his chest, with another bundle in his jaws.

When he shoved his burden through the ferns that

sheltered the den, Bumblestripe's voice called out, "Thanks!" and there was an outraged squeak from Lilypaw.

"Hey! You buried me!"

As Jayfeather turned away again, Bramblestar halted him with a touch of his tail, then drew him out of earshot of the apprentices' den. "Any more omens?" he meowed.

Jayfeather gestured with his tail to take in the whole camp. "Let's see . . . wind, rain, leaking dens . . . What exactly are you looking for, Bramblestar? You should thank StarClan that no cats have been injured."

Bramblestar twitched. Unpleasant as the storm was, he didn't feel it was bad enough to be the terrible doom that Jayfeather had prophesied. *Unless there's worse to come. Maybe the lake . . .*

"Is there something you're not telling me?" Jayfeather asked sharply.

"No," Bramblestar replied, still unwilling to reveal the encroaching lake. "We just need to make sure our Clanmates are okay. You'd better get back to your den."

When Jayfeather had gone, Bramblestar ran to the nursery and pushed his way in, thankful to be sheltered at last. The air inside felt still and welcoming after the chaos outside, in spite of the tang of wet fur. It was almost completely dark, but he could just make out the shapes of his Clanmates, and spotted Squirrelflight waving her tail at him.

"Over here, Bramblestar. I've kept a space for you."

Bramblestar headed toward her, weaving his way with difficulty between his Clanmates, who were packed in tightly from one end of the nursery to the other.

"Hey!" Molewhisker yelped. "That's my tail you're treading on."

"Sorry," Bramblestar muttered.

Cherryfall swiped her brother across the ear. "Careful,
Molewhisker. You don't talk to our Clan leader like that!"

"It's okay," Bramblestar meowed. "It's tough for all of us,
squashed together like this." He squeezed into the gap between
Squirrelflight and Birchfall and wriggled into the moss, trying to get comfortable. But his pelt was still wet, and it took a
while for the warmth of the nursery to penetrate through it.

Some of his Clanmates were already snoring, though the
younger warriors were whispering to one another with occasional *mrrows* of laughter.

It's an adventure for them, Bramblestar thought wearily. *I hope it
turns out to be no worse.*

From somewhere at the back of the nursery he heard Purdy's voice. "This is nothin' compared to the storms I remember
when I was a kit. . . ."

There was something soothing about the elder's words.
Nothing will stop Purdy telling his stories! The tale rumbled on as
Bramblestar closed his eyes, but sleep was a long time coming.
At last he fell into a doze, haunted by dreams of rising water
and drowning cats, their paws stretched out helplessly as the
waves swept them away.

"Bramblestar!" The voice jerked him awake, along with icy
drops spattering onto his pelt.

Bramblestar opened his eyes to see Thornclaw standing

over him. The warrior's golden-brown pelt was dripping, plastered to his sides, and he was shivering violently. The first gray light of a new day was seeping into the den, but the storm hadn't let up. Rain thundered down onto the roof of the den, and the wind still blustered through the camp.

"Bramblestar, there's something you need to see," Thornclaw mewed through chattering teeth.

Careful not to disturb his sleeping Clanmates, Bramblestar followed Thornclaw into the clearing, flinching as icy rain poured down on him. The floor of the hollow was awash with leaves and twigs floating on the water, while here and there a bigger branch rocked in the current with one end wedged in the mud. Up above, gaps had opened up in the line of trees, telling Bramblestar that some of them had fallen. Part of the thorn barrier had been torn away, leaving a ragged gap where the entrance had been.

"It's going to take a lot of work to put this right," Bramblestar meowed with a flick of his tail.

"It gets worse," Thornclaw warned.

He led the way right up to the thorns. Staring through the gap, Bramblestar saw water surging up the slope toward them, gray and menacing. The line of waves broke and swirled as they met swift-flowing streams that had burst their banks and now crisscrossed the forest, flattening the undergrowth.

"Great StarClan!" Bramblestar gasped. "The lake has reached the camp!"

There was a tang in the air that reminded him of the sundrown-water; the eerie sounds of lapping waves and trees groaning sent a shiver through him from ears to tail-tip.

"We need to leave," Thornclaw meowed urgently.

Bramblestar spun around and raced back to the center of the hollow. "Cats of ThunderClan!" he yowled. "Come out now!"

For a heartbeat no cat appeared, though he could hear startled murmurs from the dens. Then Squirrelflight rushed out of the nursery. "What's going on?"

"Go and look beyond the thorn barrier," Bramblestar told her.

Squirrelflight sped up to the camp entrance, then halted abruptly as she saw what was outside. When she returned her face was frozen in fear, her eyes stretched wide. But her voice was steady as she asked, "What are we going to do?"

By now, cats were spilling dazedly from their makeshift nests, staring around with a mixture of fright and anger. Bramblestar splashed his way across the hollow and climbed the rocks to the Highledge. He hoped that from up there he could make himself heard above the noise of the storm. Millie and Briarlight and the other cats who had been sheltering in his den were huddled at the top of the slope, and Bramblestar had to push his way through them.

"The lake has flooded the forest!" he yowled. "We need to leave the hollow right now!"

Screeches of disbelief came from his Clanmates. "It couldn't have!" Rosepetal gasped. "The lake is at the bottom of the hill!"

"Not anymore," Bramblestar meowed.

As he spoke, water began trickling through the gap in the thorns, mingling with the rainwater already there. At first it looked like nothing more than a shallow ripple, easy enough to wade through. Then there was a surge of gray-brown waves crested with yellowish foam, sloshing through the thorns. When the waves retreated, they swept most of the barrier away, leaving room for more water to rush in, deeper and swirling.

For a moment all the cats stared at it in horrified silence, broken by yelps of panic as they realized that the unthinkable was happening.

"Lilypaw! Seedpaw! Over here!" their father, Brackenfur, called, while Cloudtail and Brightheart rounded up the younger apprentices.

"Bramblestar!" Millie was staring at him, her eyes wide with terror and her claws raking frenziedly at the wet stone of the Highledge. "What about Briarlight? She won't be able to swim if the hollow floods!"

"No cat will have to swim," Bramblestar reassured her. "There are other ways out of the hollow."

Leafpool, who was standing outside the medicine cats' den, waved her tail to attract every cat's attention. "Follow me!" she ordered.

Bramblestar silently thanked StarClan for the steep, twisting path that led up the cliff from the bushes near the entrance to the medicine cats' den. It would be a hard climb, he knew, but it was their only escape route from the rising water. He turned to face the cats clustered on the ledge behind him.

"Graystripe," he ordered, "get the others to help you bring Briarlight down. I'll see you at the bottom of the path."

Graystripe crouched down while Dustpelt and Sandstorm began lifting Briarlight onto his back. Bramblestar left them to it and ran down the tumbled rocks to join Leafpool.

By now most of the Clan was clustered around the medicine cats' den, while Leafpool and Squirrelflight forced a way through the bushes, revealing the first few tail-lengths of the path. The cats crowded into the space behind the thorns, which was slightly sheltered from the force of the storm.

"Wow!" Snowpaw squeaked, tipping back her head to follow the path up the cliff. "How did Leafpool know about this?"

Brightheart gave her daughter a flick around the ear. "Medicine cats know a lot of things," she mewed.

Bramblestar swallowed hard as he gazed up at the path. It was a tricky scramble at the best of times, but it was going to be treacherous in this pouring rain and fierce wind. *What if a cat falls? They could break their neck, and it would be my fault.* He shook himself to clear his head. *I'm the leader of this Clan. It's my responsibility to protect these cats, and there's no other way to leave the hollow.*

"Brackenfur, Spiderleg," he meowed briskly. "You go up first. Make sure we can still get out that way. And for StarClan's sake, be careful."

With a grim nod, Brackenfur sprang up the path with Spiderleg hard on his paws. Bramblestar narrowed his eyes against the driving rain, trying to watch their progress. From time to time he lost sight of them as they vanished behind bushes or jutting rocks, but at last he made out Brackenfur's light brown pelt at the edge of the cliff top.

"It's okay!" Brackenfur yowled. "But the path is very slippery. . . . Don't try to rush it."

"Right, let's get moving," Bramblestar ordered. "Daisy, you next." He beckoned with his tail to the shivering she-cat, whose long, cream-colored pelt hung like rats' tails around her. "Lionblaze, follow her up and make sure she's okay."

"I'll be fine," Daisy mewed. "I've done it before."

Bramblestar remembered how Squirrelflight, Brightheart, and Cloudtail had climbed the path with Daisy and her kits to rescue them from the badger attack, so many moons ago. Now—in spite of how he had longed for a nursery full of kits— he was thankful that there were no tiny cats who had to be carried out of the hollow. *Moving Briarlight will be hard enough. . . .*

Once Lionblaze and Daisy were halfway up, Bramblestar sent the apprentices, each with their mentor to keep an eye on them. He sent Cloudtail with Amberpaw, since Spiderleg had already made the climb. The young cats showed no fear at all, sure-pawed and nimble as they followed the narrow path back and forth across the cliff face.

"Dovewing next!" Bramblestar called.

The pale gray she-cat splashed forward through the puddles, her ears twitching. "I'm not sure I can do this," she muttered. "I keep looking for stuff that isn't here, and I can't see what's right under my nose."

"Of course you can do it." Her father, Birchfall, padded up to her. "I'll be right behind you. I won't let you fall."

Taking a deep breath, Dovewing began to climb. At first she was slow and nervous, but gradually she seemed more sure of herself and her pace quickened.

"Take your time," Birchfall urged. "This isn't a race!"

"Now you, Thornclaw," Bramblestar meowed. "Once you get to the top, find a bush or something to take shelter. You've had a terrible night."

Thornclaw gave his Clan leader a brief nod. "I've had better."

By now the daylight had strengthened a little, but the sky was covered with heaving gray clouds. There would be no sunrise. The rain still pelted down, sweeping in waves across the hollow as it was buffeted by the wind.

Peering upward, Bramblestar could see a growing crowd of cats at the top of the cliff. None of them had lost their footing so far. *Maybe we'll all make it.* "Molewhisker and Cherryfall, off you go," he ordered.

Cherryfall set off first, scrambling confidently from one paw hold to the next, disappearing into the driving rain, but when Molewhisker tried to follow he halted a few tail-lengths above the ground, his ears flat and his eyes staring in terror.

"I can't do it!" he wailed. "I'm going to fall!"

Bramblestar's heart began to thud. "You'll be fine!" he called up to the panicking young tom. "All the other cats have done it."

"I'm slipping! Help!"

"Mouse dung!" Bramblestar muttered.

He was about to start climbing to give Molewhisker a boost

from below, when he spotted Lionblaze making his way carefully down from the top of the cliff.

"Hang on, Molewhisker!" the warrior yowled. "I'm coming! You see that rock just there . . . the flat one?" Lionblaze slithered to a halt, leaning into the cliff face with his hind paws gripping the loose stones. "Put your forepaw there. Now bring your hind paws up to that crack. That's right. . . ."

Very slowly Molewhisker started to move. The two cats climbed together until Bramblestar lost sight of them, and Lionblaze's reassuring tones were lost in the howl of the wind.

Brightheart and Cinderheart shuffled up to the end of the path. "We're ready, Bramblestar," Brightheart mewed.

"Wait a moment," Bramblestar warned. "I want to be sure Molewhisker gets up safely. If he falls, he could knock any cat below him off the path."

As he finished speaking, he heard Lionblaze again, yowling from the cliff top. "We made it!"

Thank StarClan, Bramblestar thought. *And thank Lionblaze!* "Okay, off you go," he told the two she-cats.

They set off well, taking small, cautious steps and keeping their bodies low and close to the rock. Then a gust of wind caught Brightheart, who was climbing a fox-length behind Cinderheart. She slipped and hung off the edge of the path, her paws scrabbling wildly, letting out a screech of terror. "Help!"

Bramblestar bunched his muscles to leap up to her, but before he could move Cinderheart had turned back, her claws clinging to the rock. She fastened her teeth in Brightheart's scruff and hauled her back onto the path.

Brightheart crouched, trembling. "Thanks, Cinderheart," she gasped.

"Are you okay?" Cinderheart mewed. "Can you keep going?"

Brightheart nodded. "Let's go."

As Bramblestar watched them struggling slowly up the cliff face, he felt water washing against his belly fur and he realized that the flood in the hollow was getting deeper. *Time is running out!* Glancing around at the cats who were left, he saw that Graystripe had arrived with Briarlight and the other cats who had spent the night in the den on the Highledge. Purdy had joined them. The two medicine cats were standing near their den, while Berrynose and Mousewhisker were closer to the bottom of the path, their claws working impatiently as they waited for their turn. Rosepetal was hanging farther back with Squirrelflight.

Bramblestar gave a nod to the two toms, who set off with quick, steady paw steps. For the first few tail-lengths he kept an eye on Berrynose, knowing that the cream-colored warrior tended to be overconfident, but both he and his brother vanished up the path with no trouble.

Squirrelflight stepped up to him. "Rosepetal's nervous," she murmured in Bramblestar's ear. "I'll go up with her, if that's okay."

Bramblestar gave his deputy a grateful nod. "Please. I know she'll be safe with you."

"Come on," Squirrelflight meowed, giving Rosepetal a

friendly shove. "You chase squirrels up trees all the time. This is no different."

Rosepetal nodded, but she clearly wasn't convinced. "I'll try," she whispered.

"I'll be right behind you," Squirrelflight promised. "I won't let you fall."

Just do it now, not tomorrow, Bramblestar thought, conscious of the rising water.

Squirrelflight nudged Rosepetal over to the path and they began to climb. To Bramblestar they seemed to be going agonizingly slow, but the she-cats steadily gained height, and to his relief Rosepetal didn't freeze with terror like Molewhisker. Bramblestar noticed that Lionblaze and Cinderheart were standing at the top of the path, helping their Clanmates up the last few paw steps. *Thank StarClan for them,* he thought. *And for all the cats who're helping. Where would we be without them?*

His gaze fixed on the cliff, he didn't see Millie until he felt her tail touch his shoulder, and turned to see her beside him, her whole body tense with worry.

"What about Briarlight?" she whimpered. "She'll never climb up there!"

Bramblestar felt a heavy weight in his belly. He had imagined that some cat would carry Briarlight up the path, but now that he had watched his Clanmates make the climb, he knew that would be impossible. Glancing past Millie, he saw Briarlight waiting quietly beside Sandstorm and Dustpelt. *She trusts me! Great StarClan, what am I going to do?*

"We'll get her out," he promised. "Let's send up as many

of the others as we can first. Graystripe, Blossomfall, you go next. Sandstorm, as soon as they're out of the way, can you help Purdy?"

"Sure, Bramblestar," Sandstorm responded.

Purdy frowned at the narrow, twisty path. "I'm not sure my old legs will get me up there," he grunted.

"Of course they will," Sandstorm reassured him. "And think what a great story you'll have to tell afterward!"

With a muffled curse, the old cat began to climb the cliff. Sandstorm followed, encouraging him every step, but his progress became slower and slower as he climbed higher. Purdy was less than halfway up when part of the cliff face flaked off beneath his paws and he plunged backward in a shower of stones. Sandstorm dived forward to grab him, but she was too late.

"Purdy!" she screeched.

As he fell, Purdy grabbed for a scrawny bush that was growing in a crack in the rock. His front claws sank into it, while his hind paws scrabbled against the cliff face.

"I'm stuck!" he yowled.

Sandstorm leaned over, gripped Purdy's shoulder fur in her teeth, and heaved, but she couldn't pull him up.

Bramblestar gave the waiting cats a swift glance. "I'll be back," he meowed, then began to climb.

When he reached Purdy, who still clung grimly to the bush, he realized the problem was worse than he thought. Just above them, the cliff face was starting to crumble away, probably eroded by the rain, and the weight of several cats was breaking it up even more.

"Sorry, Bramblestar!" Purdy gasped. "I'm too old and stiff for this. I can't get up or down, so I'd better live here, okay?"

Bramblestar could see that the elder was trying to be brave, but he was clearly scared and humiliated by his failure. "No, this is no good as a den," he responded, thinking quickly. "Sandstorm, go to the top and find a good, strong ivy stem, long enough to stretch down here. Get Lionblaze to help you."

"We'll never haul Purdy up on an ivy stem," Sandstorm objected. "He's too heavy."

"Too many voles," Purdy attempted to joke. "Not enough exercise."

"We might not be able to get him up," Bramblestar replied to Sandstorm. "But we can lower him down. Once his paws are on firm ground, we can think again."

"Firm ground?" Purdy scoffed. "It's a lake down there!"

Sandstorm gave her Clan leader a brisk nod, and headed up the path. Bramblestar thought she was moving too fast for safety, but he didn't call out to her, just appreciating her care for her Clanmate.

Bramblestar stayed with Purdy until a long tendril of ivy came snaking down from the cliff top. Several stems had been twined together, making it strong.

"We're ready!" Sandstorm called down.

"Okay, Purdy, grab the stem in your teeth," Bramblestar instructed, guiding it into the old cat's reach.

Once Purdy was biting down on the tendril, Bramblestar climbed down to the next curve of the path, so that he was directly underneath the old cat. "Let go of the bush!" he yowled.

Purdy hesitated, then pulled his claws out of the branch and clutched the ivy instead. He lurched down the cliff face, crashing and swinging from the tendril. Bramblestar fixed his hind claws into the gritty path and reached out with his front paws to take Purdy's weight, guiding him to where he could stand. Purdy was stiff with fear, his eyes staring, but he let out a little snort of satisfaction when he felt his paws touch the rock.

Bramblestar thought it was too risky to expect him to climb down the path on his own. Instead he made Purdy keep hold of the ivy tendril and yowled instructions up to Lionblaze and Sandstorm, who lowered the old cat stage by stage until he reached the bottom of the cliff.

"We're down!" Bramblestar called out to the cats at the top. *But what do we do now?*

"I'll be fine," Purdy meowed, shaking himself free from the ivy. "The hollow won't fill right up. I'll wait out the storm on the Highledge."

"I'll wait with him," Briarlight meowed.

Millie moved closer to her daughter. "In that case, I'm staying too."

Bramblestar looked at the water flowing into the camp through the thorn barrier. Already it was high enough to reach his flanks, and Briarlight was having to strain to keep her head above the surface. "No cat will be left behind," he growled.

"Then what are we going to do?" Millie hissed, her eyes wild with fear.

Bramblestar spotted a branch bobbing past in the flood-water, and a plan began to form in his mind. "To start with," he told Millie, "I want you and Leafpool to climb the cliff. Then I'll know you're safe."

Millie stared at him in disbelief. "Have you got bees in your brain? I'm not leaving Briarlight!"

Bramblestar clenched his teeth on a sharp reply. He understood Millie's anxiety for her daughter, but she wasn't helping. To his relief, Leafpool stepped forward and curled her tail around Millie's shoulder. "Come on," she urged kindly. "Briarlight will be fine. You can trust Bramblestar."

I hope she's right, Bramblestar thought.

"It's okay," Briarlight mewed. "Go with Leafpool. I'll see you at the top of the cliff."

Millie narrowed her eyes at Bramblestar. "If she dies, I'll never forgive you."

Bramblestar dipped his head to her. "Millie, I promise you that I'll get Briarlight out, or die trying."

Millie held his gaze for a moment longer, then turned away with Leafpool. The two she-cats vanished up the path.

"I can climb the cliff too," Jayfeather announced.

"No, I need you to help with Briarlight," Bramblestar replied. "No cat knows as much about her condition as you." *And I don't want a blind cat dangling off the cliff face.* "Dustpelt, I'll need your help too," he continued. "And it would be good to have Brackenfur."

He yowled the order to the top of the cliff, and a few moments later the golden-brown warrior appeared, treading sure-footedly along the path.

Squirrelflight scrambled down after him. "What's going on?" she called.

"We need to find a different way out of the hollow," Bramblestar explained. "I thought we might use some kind of branch to float Briarlight and Purdy and Jayfeather out on the floodwater."

"Great StarClan, that's risky!" Brackenfur exclaimed. "Do you want us to find a branch?"

"I have one in mind," Bramblestar told him. "The memorial branch with the claw marks for the cats who fell in the Great Battle."

Jayfeather let out an outraged yelp. "Can't you use a different one?"

"It's by far the longest and strongest piece of wood in the camp," Bramblestar pointed out. "Besides, if we use it, perhaps our fallen Clanmates will be able to help us. If ever we needed StarClan, it's now."

Dustpelt and Brackenfur exchanged a glance, as if they were wondering whether their mates were watching over them.

"We'll get it," Dustpelt meowed.

The memorial branch had fallen on its side, but it was still visible, poking up out of the water below the Highledge. Brackenfur and Dustpelt waded over to it and dragged it back to the bushes where the other cats waited.

"It's not floating very well," Brackenfur remarked dubiously.

"That's because the water's too shallow here," Bramblestar meowed. "We need to push it farther out."

Dustpelt and Brackenfur maneuvered the branch away from the cliff face, until they stood in water that lapped against their shoulders. "It's fine here!" Brackenfur called.

"Come on, then, this way," Squirrelflight urged the other cats.

"You don't have to do this," Bramblestar murmured to her as they guided Purdy, Jayfeather, and Briarlight toward the branch. "You should go back up the cliff to the others."

Squirrelflight turned a green glare on him. "You annoying furball, if you think you can send me—"

Bramblestar interrupted her by resting his tail on her shoulder. A spark of warmth woke inside him at his deputy's courage and bold spirit. "That's no way to talk to your Clan leader," he purred. "Come on, I won't argue."

Squirrelflight snorted. As they headed into deeper water, Briarlight was hardly able to keep her head above the surface. With her hind legs dragging behind her, she could only raise herself on her forelegs, and the floodwater washed around her muzzle.

Bramblestar pushed through the swirling water until he was alongside her. "Here, hang on to me." He tried to hide his wince of pain as Briarlight dug her claws into his shoulder. She managed to raise her head a mouse-length, but with her added weight Bramblestar could hardly make any headway through the water. His paws sank into mud, and the young she-cat's body dragged at him.

"Wait," Squirrelflight mewed. "I've got an idea."

She splashed over to the side of the hollow where Brackenfur and Dustpelt kept their den-building supplies, and came back with a bundle of twigs clamped in her jaws. "Here, Briarlight, shove these under your belly. They should hold you up a bit."

Briarlight let go of Bramblestar while Squirrelflight thrust the twigs into place. To Bramblestar's relief they boosted her a little way out of the water, enough for her to keep her muzzle clear and drag herself forward.

The other cats were waiting for them beside the memorial branch. Pushing it ahead of them, they waded toward the camp entrance. Water was gushing in from the flooded lake, the strong current threatening to sweep them off their paws. For a moment Bramblestar wondered if they had enough strength to push their way against it, and he kept an especially close eye on Briarlight.

There was a squawk from Jayfeather as he lost his balance, the cry cut off abruptly as his head went under. Bramblestar plunged toward him and dived below the surface, wondering if he would be able to find him in this chaos of water. Then a thrashing tail hit him in the ear. Bramblestar lashed out a paw and sank his claws into sodden fur. He dragged Jayfeather upward; the medicine cat's head broke the surface and he began coughing up mouthfuls of water.

"Thanks," he spluttered, managing to stand again. "I really *hate* water!"

The current swirled and bubbled around them as they forced their way through the gap. Outside the camp the flood stretched in all directions. All Bramblestar could see was tossing water with debris floating in it and trees looming out of it, their roots, trunks, and even some of the lower branches swallowed up by the rising lake.

"Okay," he meowed. "This is where you climb onto the branch."

"I don't think this is goin' to work," Purdy muttered, eyeing the branch.

"Come on," Squirrelflight encouraged him. "Twolegs do this all the time. We've seen them floating on the lake in those flat things with pelts sticking up to catch the wind. If they can do it, so can you! You're not telling me you're more stupid than a Twoleg, are you?"

Purdy grunted and began hauling himself onto the branch while Brackenfur and Dustpelt steadied it. To Bramblestar's surprise, once Purdy was crouching on top of the stick, he balanced quite easily, and turned his head to give Squirrelflight a smug look.

"Reckon I could teach Upwalkers a thing or two," he purred.

Jayfeather climbed quickly onto the branch once Bramblestar showed him where to put his paws, his light weight making it easier for him. But it was a struggle for Briarlight to haul herself up. She couldn't move her hind legs; when Bramblestar shoved them onto the branch they fell off again. The water tugged at them, threatening to sweep Briarlight away.

"What should I do?" she wailed.

For a horrible moment Bramblestar didn't have an answer. Then Squirrelflight exclaimed, "Wait!"

To Bramblestar's alarm she turned around and headed back into the camp, half wading and half swimming as the current swept her along.

"You can't go back in there!" Bramblestar yowled after her.

Squirrelflight's voice came faintly back through the wind and the rain. "I'll be fine!"

Bramblestar's heart thumped painfully as he waited for her return. He sagged with relief when he saw her battling her way back through the water. She was dragging something with her; as she drew closer he saw that it was the ivy tendril they had used to lower Purdy down the cliff.

"We can use this to tie Briarlight to the branch," Squirrelflight panted as she came up to the others. "Quick, lift up her hind legs."

Once Bramblestar was holding Briarlight's legs in position, Squirrelflight took the twisted ivy stems in her jaws and dived underneath the branch, coming up on the other side. Brackenfur grabbed the tendril and wrapped it around Briarlight, ready for Squirrelflight to carry it under the branch again.

"That feels secure," Briarlight meowed when they had repeated the move a few times. She looked tiny and fragile, her pelt slicked flat with water and her blue eyes huge as moons. Her front paws were wrapped around the branch, claws dug into the pale wood.

Squirrelflight resurfaced for the last time, water streaming from her dark ginger pelt, and tucked the end of the tendril underneath Briarlight's chest. "Tell me if you think it's coming loose."

With all three cats balanced on the branch, Squirrelflight and Dustpelt began to guide it through the water from the front while Bramblestar and Brackenfur pushed from behind. As soon as they began to move the branch wobbled violently. Jayfeather let out an apprehensive hiss, but all three dug their claws in hard and managed to cling on.

As soon as they were outside the hollow, the water grew deeper, so that Bramblestar and his Clanmates had to swim. Bramblestar fought his way through churning water, hissing when his legs kept getting caught on branches and foliage below the surface. Once his paw was trapped in what felt like brambles; he had to wrench it hard to free himself and keep swimming. Wind ruffled the water and dashed rain into his face, but all he could do was go on battling his way forward toward higher ground.

StarClan, save us! he prayed silently as his drenched pelt dragged at him. *We can't do this alone!*

The only way he could keep going was to grip the branch in his teeth while paddling furiously with all four legs. Water gushed into his mouth; he had to keep swallowing, making it almost impossible to breathe. *I won't let go!* Beside him, Brackenfur was having the same difficulties, and his breath rasped noisily over the sound of the wind. Bramblestar only caught glimpses of Squirrelflight and Dustpelt at the front of the branch, just enough to know that they were still afloat, still swimming.

Slowly the four cats maneuvered the branch around the side of the hollow toward the closest spot where the sloping ground emerged from the floodwater. Bramblestar gasped with relief when his paws thrashed against solid earth and he could walk under the water, pushing the branch forward with his chest and paws until it grounded. Purdy heaved himself up and stepped off, splashing through the last tail-length of floodwater until he was standing on the rain-soaked grass of the slope that led up to the cliff top. Jayfeather scrambled after him.

Squirrelflight waded to Briarlight's side and began tearing at the ivy tendril, but before she could free her Clanmate a huge brown wave swelled up and crashed against the branch. It knocked Squirrelflight off her paws and she vanished into the water. The branch flipped over, trapping Briarlight beneath the surface. Bramblestar plunged down, finding Squirrelflight almost at once and shoving her up into the air. Then he groped toward the branch and tore the ivy away with his teeth and claws. He knew Briarlight was free, but he could feel her body sinking helplessly down into the flood.

The water swirled again and Bramblestar spotted Dustpelt diving down beside him. Together they grabbed Briarlight's body and hauled her upward, thrusting her toward the slope where Brackenfur dragged her clear of the water. Gasping for breath, Bramblestar looked down at the she-cat. Briarlight lay unmoving, a trickle of water escaping from her mouth.

"She can't be dead!" Squirrelflight wailed.

I promised Millie, Bramblestar thought. *I said I would save her or die trying.*

"Get out of the way!" Jayfeather thrust Bramblestar aside and pounced on Briarlight, working feverishly as he pressed her chest down again and again. "I won't let her drown!"

There was agony in the medicine cat's voice. Bramblestar remembered how Jayfeather had struggled in the lake to rescue Flametail, how he had nearly drowned trying to bring the ShadowClan medicine cat back to the surface. *He failed then; StarClan, please don't let him fail now!*

Suddenly Briarlight's body jerked and she coughed up a mouthful of dirty water. Bramblestar saw her chest rise and fall as she took a breath. A moment later she raised her head. "Did we make it?" she asked feebly.

"We did," Bramblestar meowed. He felt dizzy with relief.

Squirrelflight gave Briarlight's ear a lick. "Come on, let's get you to the top of the cliff. Millie and Graystripe will be worried about you."

Bramblestar could see that Briarlight was too weak to walk. "I'll carry you," he told her, and added to the others, "Lift her onto my back."

He was about to begin the weary trudge up the hill when he noticed Jayfeather pacing beside the water. "What's the matter?" he asked.

"I can't find the memorial branch," the medicine cat replied.

Scanning the edge of the flood, Bramblestar guessed that the branch had been swept away by the wave that had knocked Squirrelflight and Briarlight underwater. He thought he could spot it floating several fox-lengths away, but there were so many pieces of debris tossing on the flood that he couldn't be certain it was the right one. "It's gone," he meowed. "Washed away."

"But it held the memory of our dead Clanmates!" Jayfeather wailed.

"No, our hearts and minds hold those memories," Bramblestar reminded him. "And the branch saved the cats who needed its help. Now we hold that memory as well." When Jayfeather did not reply, he added, "When all this is over, you can make another."

Jayfeather mumbled agreement and turned away.

Brackenfur took the lead as the little group of drenched cats plodded up the hill under the trees. His shoulders ached under Briarlight's weight, and his paws kept slipping on the muddy ground. Branches lashed at them, the trees almost bent double in the wind. Closer to the cliffs the ground was more open, and the going would be easier, but Bramblestar didn't dare go closer to the edge. *We could all be blown over, back into the hollow.*

"I'm going to fetch some of the others to help," Squirrelflight announced, breaking into a run.

Where does she get her energy? Bramblestar wondered, feeling as weary and battered as the oldest elder. He carried on toiling up the slope until he saw Squirrelflight coming back with a group of his Clanmates. Millie was racing ahead, stumbling and skidding in her haste to get to her daughter. Graystripe was close behind, with Lionblaze and Cinderheart.

"Briarlight!" Millie screeched as she reached Bramblestar and the others. "Are you okay?" She covered her daughter with frantic licks.

"I'm fine," Briarlight replied hoarsely. "My Clanmates looked after me."

Millie turned toward Bramblestar, blinking in gratitude. "Thank you," she meowed. "Thank you from the bottom of my heart."

Bramblestar felt hot with embarrassment. "Every cat helped," he mumbled.

Lionblaze stepped forward. "Here, let me carry her. You must be exhausted."

Bramblestar was only too willing to let the other cats transfer Briarlight from his back to Lionblaze's. As they set off up the slope again, Graystripe gave Bramblestar a boost under his shoulder, while Squirrelflight and Cinderheart helped Purdy. At the top of the slope Bramblestar saw that Sandstorm had gathered the rest of the cats under a beech tree. It didn't give much shelter, but although the branches lashed and groaned in the wind, they were sturdy enough not to snap. Soaked and scared, the cats huddled together in a mass of drenched fur.

Several pairs of eyes stared anxiously at Bramblestar as he reached them. "We'll stay here until the storm passes," he decided. "Try to get some rest if you can." He sank to the ground where he was, dazed with tiredness and only half-aware of Squirrelflight coming to lie next to him, warming him with her fur.

Bramblestar woke to a strange calm, and for a moment he wondered where he was. He should have been asleep in his den on the Highledge, not dozing uncomfortably on a thin layer of fallen leaves. Then he saw branches densely blocking out the sky above him, and heard his Clanmates stirring, and he remembered the desperate escape from the hollow in the middle of the night. The rain had stopped and the wind died down to a faint, whispering breeze. The sky was still covered with cloud, but it was much thinner, and a silver glow suggested that the sun had climbed almost to sunhigh. Bramblestar hauled himself stiffly to his paws and padded out of the shelter of the beech tree.

From up here, he could look out at the whole lake and the land beyond. For a moment he swayed on his paws. The forest was a wreck of swirling water and floating debris. Water reflecting the pale gray sky had risen up the sides of the hill and spilled over the far shore, swallowing up the fields as far as Bramblestar could see.

RiverClan has been completely flooded! he thought, every hair on his pelt rising in horror. *WindClan should be okay,* he added to himself as his gaze swept around to take in the moor. *Their camp is pretty high up.* His belly lurched when he turned to look out across ShadowClan territory. The flat area of pines was waterlogged, with only the top halves of the trees sticking up above the flood.

"This is terrible!" Birchfall gasped, padding up behind Bramblestar. "What has happened to the other Clans?"

"We need to worry about our own Clan first," Bramblestar replied. *We're in no state to help any other cats.*

More warriors emerged from the shelter of the tree and studied the devastation with looks of stunned disbelief. Bramblestar beckoned to some of them with his tail. "I want a patrol to come down with me and check out the hollow," he meowed. "Cloudtail, Brightheart, Cherryfall—and you too, Birchfall."

With the cats he had named squelching after him through the muddy grass, Bramblestar led the way down the slope to a point on the cliff top where they could get a good view of the whole camp. His heart lurched when he looked over the edge. All that was left of the ThunderClan camp was a pool of gray water that stretched halfway up the cliff. There was no sign of the clearing, or the dens, or even the Highledge. *Our home is gone!*

"Great StarClan!" Cloudtail whispered beside him. "What are we going to do now?"

CHAPTER 9
❧

"*We can't shelter under this tree* forever," Bramblestar announced. "We need to find somewhere to make a temporary camp."

When the patrol had returned from the flooded hollow, Bramblestar had called a Clan meeting. To his surprise, his Clan seemed undaunted by the challenge of finding a new home.

"What about the old Twoleg nest?" Blossomfall suggested.

Bramblestar shook his head. "It's lower than the hollow," he replied. "It'll be flooded."

"Why don't we use the tunnels?" Ivypool meowed.

Bramblestar heard a sharp intake of breath from Lionblaze, and remembered how the golden tabby warrior had once been trapped when the tunnels flooded. Other cats were exchanging nervous glances. But remembering his own vague knowledge of the tunnels from Hollyleaf's training and the battle with WindClan, Bramblestar thought the idea had possibilities. *It's probably the best we can do.*

"Good thinking, Ivypool," he meowed. "And no cat needs to worry about getting lost or trapped by rising water. We'll stay well away from the cavern where the underground river flows."

His Clanmates started talking to one another, raising their voices to be heard above the clashing of the branches overhead. To Bramblestar's dismay, the lull in the storm was over. The rain had started again and the wind was growing stronger. Heavy drops of rain penetrated the branches of the beech tree, soaking fur that had begun to dry out.

"I don't care where we go," Berrynose declared. "I just want somewhere out of the wet!"

Bramblestar ordered Lionblaze and Cinderheart to take the Clan to the tunnel entrance on the hillside above the cliffs.

Squirrelflight gathered the apprentices together and spoke in a low voice. "I want you all to look after Purdy," she told them. "He's had a tough time and he must be feeling sore and tired. But for StarClan's sake, don't let him know that you're helping him."

Lilypaw nodded, looking thoughtful. "I know! We'll ask him to help us." She pattered over to Purdy. "We're scared about going into the tunnels," she mewed to the old cat. "Will you stay with us?"

"Sure, young 'un." Purdy heaved himself to his paws. "Nothin' to be scared of when you're with me."

He stumbled off after Lionblaze and Cinderheart with all the apprentices clustered around him.

Squirrelflight glanced at Bramblestar with a smug flick of her whiskers. "Easy . . ." she murmured.

Bramblestar blinked gratefully at her, then turned to Dovewing. "Can you guide Jayfeather?" he asked her.

"Sure."

"I can guide myself, thanks," Jayfeather cut in with a snort.

"No, you *can't*." Bramblestar stood over the scrawny medicine cat. "Jayfeather, there may be a time when it helps for you to be an uncooperative furball, but this isn't it. The whole forest has changed because of the wind. There are fallen trees, branches scattered everywhere . . . Just let Dovewing help you, and put up with it."

Jayfeather sighed. "Yes, O great Clan leader."

Leaving Dovewing to cope with him, Bramblestar went to look for Briarlight. He found her near the trunk of the beech tree with Millie and Graystripe. "Up you come," he meowed, crouching down so that she could climb onto his back. "We'll soon have you somewhere dry."

"I'm giving you so much trouble," Briarlight murmured as Graystripe helped her onto Bramblestar's shoulders.

"No, you're not," Millie purred, though her eyes were worried. Bramblestar guessed that she was bothered by her daughter's depressed mood.

"You're doing me a favor, actually," he told Briarlight. "You'll keep the rain off my back while you're up there. And you're no heavier than a good-sized squirrel!"

That wasn't entirely true, he thought as he plodded up the hillside. Briarlight's weight pressed down on his shoulders, making it hard to force a way through the tangled undergrowth. The rest of the cats followed in a miserable line, their heads down and their tails trailing in the mud while the howling wind swept their fur backward.

When they reached the entrance to the tunnels, half-hidden

behind an outcrop of rocks, the cats clustered around, waiting for their turn to squeeze inside. Though the dark hole looked forbidding, they were all eager to get out of the storm.

"Wow, this is so weird!" Amberpaw exclaimed as she padded a couple of tail-lengths down the tunnel. "You said Hollyleaf *lived* down here? Did she really?" she asked Spiderleg.

Her mentor nodded. "She did, for several moons. None of us knew she was here."

"And you fought WindClan here?" Dewpaw added. "How did you see anything?"

"What happened if you got lost?" Snowpaw shuddered, though Bramblestar thought he was enjoying the adventure. "What if you never found your way out?"

"That's enough," Whitewing meowed. "You can't stand here chattering all day."

"Yes, you're blocking the tunnel," Ivypool hissed. "Cats are waiting out in the rain."

"Sorry," Seedpaw mewed, nudging the younger apprentices ahead of her. "They're still kits, really," she added to Ivypool.

"Kit yourself!" Amberpaw retorted.

"Let's explore," Dewpaw urged. "I want to see everything. Come on, Purdy."

"Don't go far!" Ivypool called after them.

Hoping that Purdy would stop the apprentices from doing anything too stupid, Bramblestar followed them down the tunnel. When he reached a place where it grew a little wider, just before the light from the entrance faded entirely, he let Briarlight slide from his shoulders. Millie rushed up to her daughter and began to groom her fur, licking it the wrong way to dry it and warm her up.

As the rest of the cats settled around them in pulpy mounds of wet fur, Bramblestar wondered what kind of life Hollyleaf had led in the darkness of the tunnels. He had a vivid memory of the starlit cat who had stood over Hollyleaf as she died in the Great Battle. *What was his name? Fallen Leaves. He wasn't a Clan cat, but he seemed to know Hollyleaf very well. I wonder if they met down here.*

"Bramblestar." Cinderheart's voice roused him from his thoughts.

Bramblestar twitched his ears. "Yes, what is it?"

"Do you think we should explore a bit farther?" the gray she-cat asked. "Should we check if there's any flooding below-ground? With all this rain . . ."

"Good thinking," Bramblestar responded, though inwardly he winced at the thought of having to get up and move again. "Find some other cats to go with us."

Cinderheart nodded and padded away, returning a moment later with Lionblaze and Ivypool. Bramblestar rose to his paws and led them down the tunnel. They had to pick their way through the rest of the ThunderClan cats, who bunched anxiously together, unhappy in the cold shadows. Purdy was farthest down the tunnel, with all five apprentices clustered around him.

"So we all climbed onto the branch," he was meowing. "Squirrelflight had to tie Briarlight on with a bit of ivy . . ."

The apprentices had their jaws open with excitement.

Even in his weary state, Bramblestar had to stifle a *mrrow* of amusement to think that their desperate struggle for safety had already become a thrilling story for Purdy to tell. Satisfied that his Clan was safe for the time being, he headed into the darkness. The damp underpaw owed nothing to the recent rain and everything to the absence of sunlight and fresh air down here. Bramblestar had always been uneasy in the tunnels, but this time something was different. Before he had always felt as if he was being watched, as if there was something just out of hearing or sight in the shadows. But now the passages felt silent and empty. Somehow this made them even bleaker and more unwelcoming, especially as the light faded behind the warriors until they walked in complete darkness.

Bramblestar could tell that Ivypool and Lionblaze felt the difference too: There was a wariness about them, a subtle change in their scent, as if they were expecting something to happen.

The tunnel led downward in a straight line, so narrow that Bramblestar could feel his pelt brushing the walls on both sides.

"We should come to a side tunnel soon," Lionblaze meowed after a while. "We ought to take it, and check out the main cave."

Before he had taken many more paw steps, Bramblestar felt a colder flow of air from one side, and turned into the new tunnel. This passage was narrower still, and twisted around sharp corners so that Bramblestar had to swallow down a fear of getting his shoulders wedged. A dull roar came up the tunnel to greet them, growing louder as they headed farther down. Gradually Bramblestar realized that he could see the walls ahead of him in a dim light.

"We're getting close to the cave," he reported.

A heartbeat later he halted with icy black water lapping against his paws. The cave was filled with a dark torrent, waves glinting in the light that came from the crack in the roof.

"Get back!" Bramblestar warned.

When he and his Clanmates had retreated several paw steps from the water's edge, Bramblestar stopped again, looking back. "We ought to make sure that the water isn't rising," he mewed.

Cautiously he crept back along the passage and scored his claws down the wall to mark the highest point of the water. Moments dragged by as he crouched there watching. After a while he realized that Lionblaze was peering over his shoulder.

"It's not getting any worse," the golden tabby warrior murmured.

Bramblestar nodded. "I think we can go back," he decided. "This is the lowest part of the caves, so we should be safe where we are."

He let Lionblaze take the lead back to where their Clanmates were waiting.

"It looks like we'll be okay here," Bramblestar announced. "But the big cave is flooded, so no cat is to go farther down." He turned around to give the apprentices a hard look. "Understood?"

The young cats nodded seriously, and Bramblestar hoped that their adventures so far had taught them how dangerous water could be.

Glancing around his Clan, Bramblestar was pleased to see that they seemed more relaxed than when he had left them to explore the tunnels. They had dried off and groomed themselves. One or two were sleeping, but most of them were watching him with bright, expectant eyes.

"So this is our new camp," he began. "We have to assume that we'll be here for several days."

"Then we'll need clean, fresh bedding," Daisy meowed. "I'll take charge of that, if you want, Bramblestar."

"That would be great, Daisy," Bramblestar replied. "Pick a few cats to go with you, and see if you can salvage any dry moss and leaves."

"We might find some inside hollow trees." Daisy rose to her paws and glanced around. "Rosepetal, Mousewhisker, will you come with me?"

The three cats slipped out together into the rain-drenched forest. Bramblestar realized with relief that while he had been down in the tunnels the storm had blown itself out again; only a light drizzle was falling. He noticed that Leafpool was leaving the tunnel too, hard on the paws of the other cats, without telling him where she was going. He felt a stab of annoyance, then reminded himself that medicine cats didn't have to answer to their Clan leader.

"What about prey?" Cloudtail called. "My belly thinks my throat's clawed out! I'll lead a hunting patrol if you like."

"So will I," Bumblestripe added.

"And me," Graystripe meowed. "Though what we'll find out there, I don't know."

Several cats joined in, offering to join the patrols. Cloudtail raised his voice above the clamor. "What about the fresh-kill pile, Bramblestar? Where do you want it?"

"It'll have to be in here," Bramblestar meowed.

"What?" Berrynose gave a snort of disgust. "Sleeping next to fresh-kill? Yuck!"

Bramblestar suppressed an irritated hiss. "If you have a better idea, share it with the rest of us," he mewed. "If we leave prey outside, it will get wet, or foxes will steal it."

As the warriors divided themselves into groups, Bramblestar began padding up the tunnel to join Cloudtail's patrol. He was stopped by Sandstorm, who blocked his path with her ginger tail.

"I think you should stay here, where your Clan can see you," she advised him in a quiet voice. "They need to know that you're safe and in control."

Bramblestar knew she was right, though his tail-tip twitched in frustration to see the hunting patrols going off without him. He was distracted by Leafpool, who reappeared just as the hunters were leaving.

"Where have you been?" Bramblestar asked her sharply. *Medicine cat or not, she shouldn't be wandering about on her own in the flooded forest.*

"Only down to the top of the hollow," Leafpool mewed. "When I looked down into the camp, I thought I could see some bundles of herbs floating in the water. Can I go fetch them?"

Bramblestar's first instinct was to refuse. "It's too risky," he began.

"No, I'll be fine, really," Leafpool assured him.

"Some cat needs to go," Jayfeather broke in from where he sat nearby. "We've lost so many herbs to this flood; we need to salvage as many as we can."

Bramblestar could see that the medicine cats had a point. *Any one of us could go down with greencough, or get injured on all the branches lying about the forest.* "Okay," he meowed to Leafpool. "But take a warrior with you. One who doesn't mind getting wet!"

"Thanks, Bramblestar." Leafpool went out, beckoning Cherryfall to follow her.

"I'll go into the forest and see if I can find any herbs that haven't been washed away," Jayfeather mewed, hauling himself to his paws.

"Not alone," Bramblestar ordered.

Jayfeather heaved a long sigh. "Okay, not alone. Brightheart, will you come with me?"

When they had gone, Bramblestar looked around. Most of the cats were out on patrol now, except for Millie and Briarlight, Purdy and the apprentices, and Thornclaw, who was deep in sleep, worn out after his tough night on watch. It had to be a good idea to keep to the Clan's daily routine as much as possible, if only to stop them from worrying.

In spite of Sandstorm's advice, Bramblestar was too restless to stay in the tunnel for long. He padded out and headed for the cliffs, his pelt soaked and muddy again as he tried to find a clear route through the undergrowth. By the time he reached the top of the hollow he saw that Leafpool and Cherryfall had made their way down the steep path and were swimming around in the flood, grasping at scraps of floating greenery. Their voices drifted up to him.

"Leafpool, is this anything useful?"

"No, it's just an oak twig. I found some tansy, though."

"Yuck! That's just slimy tree bark!"

Bramblestar turned at the sound of paw steps and saw Sandstorm padding up to him. He tensed, expecting a scolding for leaving the tunnel, but understanding shone in the she-cat's green eyes.

"Firestar always found it hardest when he had to let his Clanmates do something dangerous," she mewed. "He felt that because he had nine lives, he could spare a few!"

"He was right." Bramblestar felt a wave of guilt sweep over him. "I should be the one to hunt in the flooded forest, or go swimming in the hollow after herbs."

Sandstorm touched his ear with her nose. "You can't do everything," she murmured. "You have to trust your Clanmates."

"I know," Bramblestar sighed, but he felt a sharp pang of envy for his warriors, who were able to act on his orders.

He returned to the tunnel with Sandstorm to check on the cats who remained there. Briarlight was sleeping at last, with Millie drowsily licking her pelt. Purdy was asleep, too, while

Dustpelt had lined up the apprentices and was testing them on their knowledge of the warrior code. Bramblestar was pleased to see him keeping the young cats occupied and out of trouble.

Not long after, Cloudtail returned with his hunting party, dragging three rabbits with them.

"Good job!" Bramblestar exclaimed. "I didn't expect you to bring back as much as that."

"We didn't exactly catch it," Cloudtail admitted, dropping his rabbit near the entrance to start a new fresh-kill pile. "These rabbits drowned. The floodwater must have washed them out of their burrow."

"That's crow-food!" Snowpaw spat, his lips curling back and his white pelt beginning to fluff up. "I'm not eating that."

"Then you can go hungry," Dustpelt snapped, swiping the apprentice over the ear with his tail.

"It'll be okay," Bramblestar meowed. "Those rabbits can't have been dead long. We're all hungry and we need to eat. We'll find live prey soon."

But when the other hunting patrols returned, Graystripe was empty-pawed, while Bumblestripe's cats had only managed to kill one thrush.

The rabbits are starting to look a lot more appetizing, Bramblestar thought.

Sandstorm and Blossomfall began to dole out the prey, while Leafpool and Cherryfall returned with the few herbs they had managed to salvage. Leafpool found a hole in the tunnel wall to act as a store. Jayfeather and Brightheart weren't far behind, carrying yarrow and marigold.

"It's a start," Jayfeather commented as he placed his herbs in the hole beside Leafpool's. "But we've got no cobweb at all. I just hope no cats cut themselves."

"Bramblestar?" Cloudtail beckoned him aside with a wave of his tail. "I need to tell you something."

"Not more trouble?" Bramblestar asked, his belly starting to churn unpleasantly.

"I'm not sure. When I was leading the patrol along the floodwater, I drank some. The water tasted very odd. Do you think it could be poisoned?"

"Great StarClan, I hope not," Bramblestar meowed. Had something bad been washed into the flood? "Show me where you went. I'd like to taste it for myself."

He followed Cloudtail as the white warrior retraced his steps to the flood. It still felt very strange to see a huge lake lapping halfway up the hillside. *How are we going to survive in the middle of all this water?*

Cloudtail halted at the water's edge. "Just here," he meowed.

Reminding himself that a taste of the water hadn't killed Cloudtail, Bramblestar crouched down and lapped. Cloudtail was right: The water did taste different. But Bramblestar had encountered the sharp tang before.

"It's salty, like the water from the sun-drown-place," he told Cloudtail, straightening up again and flicking drops from his whiskers.

"How has that water reached all the way here?" Cloudtail asked, amazed. "Is the lake going to turn into a sun-drown-place?"

"I don't know," Bramblestar admitted. "But I can tell you one thing. It isn't poison. I swallowed enough of it when we traveled there and I fell in. But we still can't drink it. The few drops I tasted have just made me more thirsty."

"So what are we going to drink?" Cloudtail lashed his tail. "There are no streams up here. The closest is on the Wind-Clan border."

Bramblestar lapped up a few mouthfuls of rainwater from a puddle in the grass, to get the acrid tang off his tongue. *Going thirsty won't be a problem for us while it's still raining,* he thought. *But how long will we have to rely on that? It could take a while for the lake to shrink again.*

Returning to the tunnel, he called to Berrynose and Poppyfrost, who were sharing part of a rabbit at the entrance. "I want to take a patrol to the WindClan border," he meowed. "We need to find out how easy it is to get to the stream there, and whether the flood has affected it."

The two cats hurriedly swallowed their last mouthfuls and came to join him. Glancing at Sandstorm, Bramblestar added, "Is it okay for me to leave? Again?"

Amusement glimmered in Sandstorm's green eyes. "Oh, yes," she assured him. "No cat wants an idle leader!"

Bramblestar took the lead as the three cats trekked through the soaked forest. The rain had stopped and the wind died down, but the trees were still dripping, and the banks of fern and long grasses spilled their loads of water on the cats as they brushed past.

As they crossed the territory, Bramblestar felt his tension

rising. All the sights and scents of the forest had changed. His pads prickled with the knowledge that the edge of the lake was only a few fox-lengths below them. Apart from the sound of water lapping and drops falling from trees, the woods were silent. There were no faint scufflings to betray the presence of prey, no birdsong in the branches. *Where have they all gone?* Bramblestar wondered. *How long will it be before they come back?*

It took a long time to make their way around the flooded parts of the territory. At last they emerged into the stretch of sparse young trees that led up to the WindClan border. The sound of the stream, rushing and gurgling, reached their ears as they bounded through the thin woodland to the border. Just here the water usually flowed deep beneath overhanging banks. Now it was level with the top of the gully, a brown flood sweeping twigs and leaves in the fast current.

"Keep back, both of you," Bramblestar warned.

He crouched down at the edge of the water, stretching out his neck so that he could lap. He dug his claws hard into the ground, fighting the fear of being swept away like a loose twig. But the water he drank had a cold, clear taste that reminded him of the mountains.

"Thank StarClan, it's fine!" he meowed, rising and backing away.

As he spoke the patter of rapid paw steps came from farther upstream, along with angry yowls and hisses. To Bramblestar's astonishment a WindClan patrol raced into sight on the ThunderClan side of the stream.

Weaselfur, who was in the lead, let out a furious screech.

"Get away from there!"

Bramblestar faced him, his fur bristling. "What do you mean?" he demanded. "You're on our territory!"

Behind him, he was aware of Berrynose and Poppyfrost sliding out their claws. The two other WindClan cats, Leaftail and Furzepelt, hurtled toward them as if they were about to leap into battle.

But Weaselfur halted when he reached the ThunderClan cats, signaling to his patrol to do the same. "This is the only clean water we have," he mewed, glaring at Bramblestar. "We have reset the border markers to this side of the stream. It belongs to WindClan now."

"Don't be mouse-brained!" Bramblestar snapped. "Look at all that water! There's enough for every cat."

But the WindClan warriors were too wound up to listen. "Stay away from that water!" Furzepelt snarled.

Poppyfrost took a step forward. "Do you really want to fight for it?" she growled.

At once Leaftail hurled himself at her, knocking her over and clawing at her ears. Berrynose started forward to help her, but Bramblestar flung himself between them, pushing the cream-colored warrior back with a paw on his shoulder.

"Stop!" he growled. "Poppyfrost can cope. I don't want an all-out battle."

As the two cats rolled screeching on the ground, Bramblestar turned to Weaselfur. "This is madness," he meowed. "You can't shift an entire border because the lake has risen."

"Yes, we can," Weaselfur retorted, "and we have. If you

have a problem, you'll have to speak to Onestar. But know that ThunderClan cats will not be welcome in our territory."

For a moment all Bramblestar's instincts were to leap on the WindClan warrior and claw the stubborn look off his face. *We can beat these scrawny rabbit-chasers easily!* But fighting here wouldn't solve anything. Instead he stalked across to the two battling cats and hauled Poppyfrost away from Leaftail.

"That's enough," he ordered. "We're leaving."

Poppyfrost stood up, panting. There was a trickle of blood coming from one of her ears, and she was missing a few tufts of fur, but the scratches down Leaftail's side showed that it had been an equal fight.

"Is that it?" Berrynose hissed, coming to stand beside his mate. "You're going to let them get away with this?"

"No," Bramblestar replied. "But I'm going to think before I do anything."

"Think!" Berrynose echoed, turning to Poppyfrost and giving her injured ear a lick.

Bramblestar ignored the hostile glares from the WindClan cats as he led his patrol away from the stream. His mind was whirling.

ThunderClan can survive without this stream while the forest is full of rainwater. But what does the flooded lake mean for the rest of the Clans? If ThunderClan and WindClan are so badly affected, have ShadowClan and RiverClan survived at all?

CHAPTER 10

❧

Bramblestar returned to the tunnel to find the cats spreading out bedding for nests. He could tell at once that their optimistic mood had changed to irritation as the reality of their homelessness set in.

"That's not nearly enough bedding for Briarlight's nest," Millie complained.

"I'm sorry, but she'll have to make do for now," Daisy meowed, looking flustered. "We can get more later."

Millie huffed with annoyance as she took away the bundle of moss and leaves.

Daisy whirled around when she spotted Snowpaw and Dewpaw play fighting on top of the pile she was trying to distribute, scattering moss everywhere. "*What* do you think you're doing?" she snapped. "If that's how you treat the bedding, you don't deserve to have any."

"It's all wet and yucky anyway," Snowpaw whined.

Daisy took a deep breath, as if she was trying to hold on to her temper, then decided not to bother. "You ungrateful little furball!" she hissed. "If you're so miserable here, feel free to go back and sleep in your den!"

Snowpaw blinked up at her. He wasn't used to hearing that tone from Daisy. "Sorry," he muttered.

Purdy loomed out of the shadows with the other apprentices behind him. "Come on, young 'uns," he rumbled. "Let's get some moss, an' you can show me how to make a nest. Then we'll all bed down together."

"Will you tell us again how you escaped from the hollow?" Lilypaw begged.

"I sure will!"

"Thank StarClan for Purdy," Daisy sighed as the elder and the apprentices disappeared down the tunnel with their share of the bedding. "He's so good with those young cats."

"But he wouldn't take any fresh-kill," Blossomfall told Bramblestar, coming up to him with a worried look. "I did everything I could, short of shoving the rabbit down his throat, but it was no use. He told me to give it to the warriors instead."

"We can't have that," Bramblestar meowed. "Thanks for telling me, Blossomfall."

There were still some scraps of rabbit on the new fresh-kill pile. Picking up the biggest piece, Bramblestar padded down the tunnel until he found Purdy supervising the apprentices as they made their nests. Bramblestar dropped the rabbit at the elder's paws. "Eat."

Purdy refused to meet his gaze. "I'm not hungry."

"Purdy, I won't stand for any heroics," Bramblestar insisted. "We all need to keep our strength up."

The old cat turned away, gazing down into the darkness.

"I'm not worth the effort of hunting," he muttered.

"Never say that!" Bramblestar protested. "The warrior code is built on caring for our elders and kits."

Purdy turned back to him and met Bramblestar's gaze. His eyes were wide and distressed. "But I never served this Clan as a young cat," he rasped. "And now, with Mousefur gone, things aren't the same."

Bramblestar took a deep breath and looked at Purdy with his head on one side. "Purdy, you're being unfair. If you hadn't saved us from the dog the first time we met, we might not have reached the sun-drown-place, and the Clans might never have made the Great Journey. And what do you think would have happened in the Great Battle, if you hadn't saved Lionblaze when he was trapped with the dogs? ThunderClan owes you more than we can ever repay."

Purdy shrugged. "Maybe," he meowed with a flash of his old stubbornness, "but I still think you need to worry about the cats who need worrying about." But he did sit down, tucked in his paws, and began to eat the rabbit.

As Bramblestar returned up the tunnel, Squirrelflight stepped up to his side. "What's the matter? You look as if you bit into a vole and found it was crow-food."

She listened while Bramblestar told her about his conversation with Purdy. "Hmm . . ." she murmured when he had finished. "I think I know what the problem is. Sandstorm!" She beckoned to her mother, who was arranging her nest a tail-length away.

"What is it?" Sandstorm asked.

"Purdy needs company," Squirrelflight mewed. "And I don't just mean those pesky apprentices. I know you could run the Clan without us—and so could Purdy, for that matter—but could you at least pretend that you want to spend more time with him? Don't worry, we'll still find things for you to do."

Sandstorm's green eyes glimmered. "I'll do what I can," she promised. "But perhaps the answer isn't banishing more cats to the elders' den, but getting Purdy more involved in Clan life. Why not put him in charge of bedding distribution along with Daisy?"

"That's a great idea!" Bramblestar meowed. He headed farther up the tunnel to where Daisy was still struggling to share out the bedding she had collected. "You look as if you could do with another set of paws," he told her. "Why not get Purdy to help?"

Daisy's harassed expression brightened immediately. "Oh, I wonder if he would? I'll go ask him right away."

She headed down the tunnel and Bramblestar followed a few paces behind. Purdy looked taken aback when Daisy made her request. "Well . . . I've got my paws full keepin' an eye on these young 'uns," he meowed. "But I reckon if you really need me . . ."

"I do, Purdy!" Daisy assured him. "I'm so busy I don't know where to start."

"Well, then . . . you'd better show me what to do. You young cats behave now," he added to the apprentices, "an' I'll tell you the story when I come back."

Daisy padded back up the tunnel with Purdy at her flank, passing Bramblestar on their way to the heap of bedding. There was a proud gleam in Purdy's eyes, and Bramblestar guessed there wouldn't be any more fuss about taking his fair share of fresh-kill. *Sandstorm, you know Purdy so well!*

Hoping for a few moments alone, Bramblestar headed out of the tunnel and sharpened his claws on a nearby ash tree. They felt all clogged up with dirt and leaves, and he experienced a fierce satisfaction in seeing them gleaming again. *I wish every problem could be solved by good fighting skills and a dose of courage,* he thought, remembering how much simpler it had been to rip his claws through the pelt of a Dark Forest warrior. *Coping with all these different cats is more exhausting than going into battle!*

Night was beginning to fall by the time Bramblestar returned to the tunnel. His Clanmates were settling down among the sparse bedding, huddling together to share the precious moss. Before he went to his own nest, which Squirrelflight had prepared for him, Bramblestar set Cloudtail on watch at the entrance and Lionblaze farther down the tunnel beyond the last cats.

Now enemies can't sneak up on us, and neither can the flood!

But the makeshift nests weren't comfortable; the moss and leaves were damp in spite of Daisy's efforts, and there wasn't enough to go around. Even worse, a chilly draft whistled down the tunnel, lifting the cats' fur.

"Can't we go deeper into the tunnels?" Spiderleg asked Bramblestar. "That wind is freezing my ears off."

"No, we can't," Bramblestar told him. "We can't risk the river in the cave rising any higher."

Spiderleg twitched his tail-tip. He didn't argue, but Bramblestar heard him grumbling to himself as he curled up in his nest.

Eventually Bramblestar fell into an uneasy doze, and woke to see gray light flooding through the entrance. The Clan was rousing around him, looking tired and rumpled. *But at least they're all alive.*

Bramblestar stood up and arched his back in a long stretch, trying not to wince as his muscles protested. At the entrance he spotted Squirrelflight with a number of cats clustered around her.

"We need hunting patrols," she was meowing. "Sandstorm, will you lead one? And you, Mousewhisker . . . and Bright-heart."

Bramblestar relaxed from his stretch and stepped through the scattered bedding to join her. "We only need one border patrol," he meowed. "I'll lead it."

Squirrelflight dipped her head. "Sure, Bramblestar. Which cats do you want?"

Bramblestar thought quickly. "Dovewing, Graystripe, and Thornclaw," he decided. *All levelheaded cats who can cope with whatever we find.*

Venturing out at the head of his patrol, Bramblestar discovered that a light rain was falling, and a stiff breeze blew clouds across the sky, carrying the scent of the sun-drown-place from the lake. But the worst of the storm was over, and above his head he spotted an occasional glimpse of blue.

"We'll avoid the WindClan border for today," he meowed. "I need to think before we tackle that problem. Let's go the other way and see what we can find out about ShadowClan."

The patrol scrambled through the drenched forest toward the ShadowClan border. The water had risen to cover the old Thunderpath that led past the Twoleg den, leaving only a short stretch of the ShadowClan border still visible. Bramble-star ordered Thornclaw to renew the ThunderClan scent markers, but he couldn't detect any fresh ShadowClan scent.

"They haven't sent a patrol this way," he remarked. "We'd better cross the border and find out what's going on."

"I hope they're okay," Dovewing murmured.

Briefly Bramblestar wondered why the young she-cat should be so anxious about their neighbors, then dismissed the thought. *I'm anxious about them myself.*

"It all looks so different," Dovewing mewed as they took their first paw steps into ShadowClan territory. "I have no idea which way we should go."

"We can't get lost if we keep to the edge of the water," Graystripe pointed out. "And it's no use thinking we can keep to the safe ground three tail-lengths from the lakeshore." His mouth twisted in wry amusement. "The safe ground is right in the middle of ShadowClan territory now."

Looking around as he led the way along the waterline, Bramblestar tried to figure out where they were. On one side pine-covered slopes stretched upward. He could just make out the walls of the Twoleg den among the trees, and he wondered if the flood had reached the two hostile kittypets that gave ShadowClan so much trouble. On the other side stretched the floodwater, the gray surface interrupted by the dark pointed tops of pine trees. There was something familiar about the way the ground dipped toward the flood, and the shape of the bramble thicket ahead of them.

Bramblestar's belly lurched. *We're above the ShadowClan camp! The whole of their hollow is filled with water!*

The rest of his patrol had realized it too.

"So where are the cats?" Dovewing asked, working her claws in the soggy ground. "Something awful must have happened to them!"

As if they had heard her speaking, a ShadowClan patrol sprang out from behind a cluster of fir trees. Scorchfur was in the lead, with Pinenose and Ferretclaw just behind him. Ferretclaw's apprentice, Spikepaw, brought up the rear.

"What are you doing here?" Scorchfur demanded, racing up to the ThunderClan patrol. "Get out!"

Bramblestar dipped his head, keen to avoid a hostile confrontation like the one with WindClan the day before. "We're just making sure you survived the flood," he replied. "We got worried when there were no fresh scent marks along your border."

"ShadowClan doesn't need ThunderClan to worry about us!" Scorchfur hissed.

"And we're on our way to set the scent markers now," Pinenose added, her black fur bristling.

For all their brave words, Bramblestar thought that the

ShadowClan cats looked scared out of their fur, their eyes wide, their gazes darting from side to side as if they expected an enemy to pounce on them from out of the nearest cover. "I'm sorry about your camp," he mewed, waving his tail toward the swirling water that filled the dip. "We've lost our home, too."

"We don't want your sympathy," Scorchfur snarled. "We're fine. And if you think we're going to tell you where we're living now, think again!"

If you're fine, why do you look so distraught? Bramblestar wondered. Aloud he meowed, "I wouldn't dream of asking. Just tell me one thing: Is Tawnypelt okay?"

"And your other Clanmates?" Dovewing put in quickly.

After a moment's hesitation, Ferretclaw gave a reluctant nod. "We're *all* okay."

"And hedgehogs fly," Thornclaw muttered from behind Bramblestar, who gave him a warning flick of his ears.

"We want to cross your territory to check on RiverClan," Bramblestar meowed. "Do we have your permission, as long as we stay inside three fox-lengths from the edge of the water?"

"I suppose so," Scorchfur growled. "If it'll get you off our territory sooner."

With another respectful dip of his head Bramblestar turned to go, waving his tail for his patrol to follow.

"RiverClan won't thank you for interfering!" Ferretclaw called after them. "You've got no right to act like Thunder-Clan is here to save us all!"

Ignoring the parting shot, Bramblestar led his patrol

farther along the water's edge to where the Twoleg half bridge had once reached out into the lake—now covered now by many tail-lengths of water.

"You know something?" Graystripe meowed, padding along beside Bramblestar. "When you asked about Tawnypelt, Ferretclaw said that all the cats are okay, but none of them ever mentioned Blackstar. If you ask me, those are cats who are mourning their leader."

Bramblestar halted, staring at the gray warrior in alarm. "Great StarClan! Do you really think Blackstar lost his ninth life in the storm?" *If a Clan leader has died, the rest of us need to know!* But he was sure that he wouldn't be welcome if he tried to find the place where ShadowClan was sheltering. He would have to wait for them to bring him any news.

Still following the waterline, the patrol emerged from the trees some way inland from the half bridge. The small wooden Twoleg dens on the lakeshore were completely submerged except for the pointed tops of their roofs. Because the ground was flatter here, the floodwater had reached a long way up the narrow Thunderpath. The smooth silver surface stretched ahead of them, covering everything that had been there before. It was impossible to tell what was happening over in RiverClan territory.

"We need to get some height," Bramblestar muttered.

Clawing his way up a pine tree, he edged out along a branch until he could see to the farthest end of the lake. Where the RiverClan camp had stood between two streams, circled by bushes, there was nothing but shining gray water.

Graystripe scrambled up after Bramblestar and gazed over his shoulder. "StarClan help them!" he breathed. "Are they all dead?"

Bramblestar didn't know. Leaping down from the tree, he gathered his patrol around him. "There's no sign of River-Clan," he meowed. "We have to find out what happened to them."

Thornclaw looked doubtful. "That ShadowClan warrior was right. It's not up to ThunderClan to save every cat."

Bramblestar met his gaze. "If we can save one life, StarClan would want us to try," he insisted. "We've been lucky in the storm. RiverClan hasn't."

Thornclaw shrugged, though he still didn't look happy.

Bramblestar began looking for a way to cross the flooded Thunderpath. The water was too deep and swift moving to swim across close to where the RiverClan camp used to be. "We'll have to head farther away from the lake," he decided.

"That's going to bring us close to the Twoleg dens," Graystripe pointed out. "Are we prepared for that?"

"We have to be," Bramblestar replied. "And if you ask me, the Twolegs have more to worry about right now than a few cats."

The four warriors trekked along the line of the Thunderpath, as close as they could get without wetting their paws. When the Twoleg nests came into sight they were still and silent, with strange Twoleg things bobbing about in the water between them.

"This is weird," Dovewing mewed, shivering. "But at least

it doesn't look like there are any Twolegs around."

"Let's find a way across," Bramblestar announced, trying to sound more confident than he felt. The vast expanses of water all around them unnerved him, too.

"Do you think we should go back and get more cats?" Graystripe suggested.

Bramblestar shook his head. "We might not have time. We don't know what we're going to find in RiverClan."

"And I'm sure ShadowClan would be *so* pleased to see ThunderClan marching back and forth across their territory," Thornclaw added.

Bramblestar padded as close as he could get to the nearest Twoleg den. The water lapped at the wall, high enough that the den must be flooded inside, deeper than a cat could walk. The cats clearly weren't going to get across to RiverClan territory without getting wet, but could they avoid having to swim all the way? Bramblestar spotted a dark line that seemed to surround the nest just below the surface of the water. He realized that it must be a fence stretching around the square of grass and flowers, like the fences on the border with the old forest.

"Look," he mewed, pointing with his tail. "If we can reach that, we can walk along the top and get as far as the Thunderpath."

"And then?" Thornclaw meowed.

"Swim across, and hope there's another fence on the other side." Bramblestar looked at his patrol, knowing he was leading them into danger. *What if I lose one of them?* But he also knew that he couldn't turn around and go back to ThunderClan without finding out what had happened to the cats of River-Clan.

Not giving himself time to change his mind, Bramblestar waded into the water, then swam until he reached the barrier. As he had hoped, it was a wooden fence. He managed to claw his way up it; when he stood on the top, the water reached halfway up his legs.

"It's okay!" he called, waving his tail for the others to join him. But the top of the fence was narrow, and with the water lapping and sucking at his legs, it was hard to keep his balance. The fence shuddered as the next cat reached it; Bramblestar stifled a screech of shock as his hind paws slipped, and only just stopped himself from sliding back into the flood.

Behind him he heard Thornclaw hiss, "Fox dung!" but when Bramblestar looked back he realized that the tabby warrior was still upright on the fence, and the other cats were managing to follow him. The water distorted Bramblestar's view of the fence, but he figured out a way of putting his paws down in a straight line while he balanced with his tail. Step by step he made his way to the other end of the fence, overlooking the submerged Thunderpath.

When he reached it, he was puzzled by the sight of a flat red object under the water a mouse-length below where he was standing. Examining it more closely, he realized what it was.

"There's a drowned monster here!" he exclaimed.

Thornclaw, who was just behind him, peered over his

shoulder. "Creepy!" he commented.

Bramblestar looked down at the monster. If they jumped onto it, they could be several paw steps closer to RiverClan before they had to swim. *But what if it wakes up?* He studied the edges of the top of the monster carefully. There were no air bubbles, no signs of movement, nothing to suggest that it was still alive.

"Come on," he called to the others. "This way!"

"Are you mouse-brained?" Thornclaw asked. "Jump on top of a monster?"

"It's underwater, and I'm sure monsters can't swim like fishes," Bramblestar pointed out. Without giving Thornclaw time to argue, he launched himself onto the top of the monster. As he splashed down, the hard surface lurched beneath his paws, and panic stabbed through him as he fought for balance.

It's alive!

But then the rocking motion steadied. Bramblestar stood still for a moment while his heart stopped thumping. "It's fine," he meowed breathlessly. "Follow me."

Thornclaw, Dovewing, and Graystripe jumped onto the monster behind him, gasping as the creature swayed beneath their paws. It was impossible to sink in their claws and get a secure grip, so Bramblestar started moving as soon as Graystripe reached them, sliding his feet one by one across the slippery surface.

At the far end of the monster, it was clear they would have to swim across the deep water that covered the Thunderpath.

But Bramblestar could just make out another fence leading away on the other side, past a Twoleg den toward the fields beyond RiverClan's territory.

"Aim for that fence over there," he meowed, pointing with his tail. "Swim!"

"Oh, StarClan," Dovewing muttered, but she launched herself into the water and started paddling strongly.

Bramblestar reached the fence first and helped his Clanmates clamber onto it, water streaming from their pelts. The Twoleg dens here were joined together in a long line. The fence where they were clinging ran past the dens at one end, and by following it they could make their way around the back. Bramblestar led the way, finding it easier now to push his legs through the water and keep his footing on the narrow strip of submerged wood.

The cats sploshed their way past the Twoleg dens and stopped at the edge of the enclosed grass, looking out over a field to the place where RiverClan had once lived—but now it was just a stretch of shining water, with the top of a bush poking up here and there.

"It's gone!" Thornclaw whispered. "Their whole territory is underwater!"

"There's no way they could survive that much flooding," Graystripe meowed.

"Wait!" Dovewing mewed. "You were at the Gathering, weren't you? I wasn't there, but Ivypool told me about it. Didn't Mistystar say they'd already moved their dens away from the edge of the lake? She didn't say where, but is it possible they were far enough away to escape the flood?"

Bramblestar nodded. "You could be right. We have to find out!"

He looked down into the field. Long strands of grass drifted on top of the water, like weeds in a stream. Bramblestar was pretty sure the cats wouldn't be too far out of their depth now. The land had risen up slightly since the Thunderpath, and continued to rise until he could see a ridge of turf poking above the flood near the center of the field. He took a deep breath and leaped off the fence.

There was a mighty splash as he landed, but to his relief his paws struck a firm bed of grass, and when he straightened up the water only reached up to his belly fur. Without waiting for an order, the other cats jumped down beside him.

"Great StarClan!" Graystripe exclaimed. "It's good to have my paws on the ground again."

Bramblestar agreed, though it was still uncomfortable to wade through the flood and feel their paws sinking into sodden grass. He wasn't looking forward to licking himself clean after this was over.

A stream ran along the far side of the field, though it had spilled over its banks, covering everything with a gray sheen. Bramblestar headed for the ridge that was clear of the flood. The water rapidly grew shallower until they were wading out onto the grass with droplets streaming from their fur.

"At last!" Graystripe exclaimed. "I thought I was turning into a fish."

Thornclaw snorted. "You realize we've got to go through

all this again on the way back? You've still got a chance to grow fins and scales."

Farther up the ridge, as it curved toward the far corner of the field, there was a clump of low, leafless bushes. Bramble-star spotted a flash of movement underneath. He tensed, and stopped to taste the air. Beneath the now-familiar tang of the sun-drown-place, he thought he could detect RiverClan scent. Signaling with his tail for his patrol to keep close to him, Bramblestar crept forward. As they approached, two RiverClan cats rushed out of the thicket and halted in front of the ThunderClan patrol with fur bristling and eyes glaring. Bramblestar recognized the Clan deputy, Reedwhisker, and the black she-cat Shimmerpelt.

"Stop!" Reedwhisker growled. "What are—" He broke off, relaxing. "Oh, it's you! We thought you were rogues."

"Thank StarClan, you survived!" Dovewing gasped.

"Only just," Shimmerpelt mewed with a shudder.

Now that he was closer, Bramblestar realized the bushes were heaving with mews and scuffling sounds. The scent of RiverClan was much stronger here.

"I'll tell Mistystar you're here," Reedwhisker meowed, vanishing into the brambles.

A moment later the RiverClan leader emerged, with Moth-wing, the RiverClan medicine cat, just behind her. In spite of everything, Mistystar looked calm and sleek, her blue-gray fur neatly groomed.

She dipped her head. "Greetings, Bramblestar. It's good to see you. You must have had a struggle to get here."

"It wasn't easy," Bramblestar agreed. "But we were worried about you. Is RiverClan safe?"

"RiverClan is fine," Mistystar replied with a slight edge to her voice. "We knew the lake was rising, so when it reached our new dens we left and kept going until the water stopped chasing us." Her voice shook a little, and it was clear that she and all her cats had been more terrified than she wanted ThunderClan to know.

"And Petalfur's kits are okay?" Bramblestar pressed.

"Of course. Three warriors carried them. How are things in ThunderClan?" Mistystar asked.

"Not good," Bramblestar told her. "The hollow flooded, but all of us survived, and we've found a safe place to stay for now."

Perhaps it was Bramblestar's admission that ThunderClan had lost their home too, but Mistystar seemed to soften. She padded forward to stand beside Bramblestar, and together the two leaders looked out across the flooded landscape.

"I wonder if things will ever return to how they were," Miststar murmured. "The Great Battle, and now this . . . Doesn't StarClan have the power to protect us anymore?"

"We can protect ourselves," Bramblestar insisted. "The water won't stay like this forever."

"But what if it does?"

Bramblestar turned to face Mistystar. "Then we will all make new homes. We did it before; we can do it again."

He saw warmth in her blue eyes. "Thank you for coming," she purred. "It helps to know that we're not suffering alone."

Bramblestar touched his muzzle to the tip of Mistystar's ear. "None of the Clans are alone," he murmured. "Good luck, and may StarClan light your path."

The RiverClan cats said good-bye with more friendliness than before, and Bramblestar led his patrol back the way they had come. *There's no way of going through the marshes to reach Wind-Clan territory. It's just floodwater as far as I can see.*

They waded through the flooded field and with an effort, jumped back onto the fence. The water seemed even colder and murkier than before, whipped into splashy little waves by the breeze. None of the cats spoke; they just trudged along the submerged fence in concentrated silence.

Reaching the flooded Thunderpath, Bramblestar was bracing himself to swim for the drowned monster when a shriek split the air.

"Help! Oh, please help me!"

CHAPTER 11

Bramblestar froze. Behind him, his Clanmates bristled.

"What's that?" Thornclaw spat.

"It's coming from over there," Dovewing mewed, pointing with her tail farther up the flooded Thunderpath. At Bramblestar's startled look she hissed under her breath, "I can hear the same as you! I'm not deaf!"

"It's a she-cat, and she sounds terrified." Graystripe was staring in the direction of the sound. "We have to go help her."

"I don't know. . . ." Bramblestar stalled, anxiety rising inside him like a flood. "With all this water, it could be dangerous." He knew that he had to put his Clanmates' safety above rescuing a strange cat.

"We should at least see if we can spot the cat," Dovewing suggested. Her fur was fluffed up with anxiety and her blue eyes were huge.

The Twoleg fence where they were standing led right up to the wall of the den. Ivy covered the den wall.

"If we climb that," Graystripe meowed, angling his ears toward the densely growing green leaves, "we should get a better view."

Thornclaw heaved a sigh. "You mean, go right up to a Two-leg den that might be full of Twolegs, and risk falling into the flood, all for a cat we haven't even set eyes on?"

Graystripe looked at his Clanmate with a hint of scorn. "You could show a little compassion," he growled.

The fur on Thornclaw's neck began to rise, and Bramble-star meowed quickly, "We'll climb the ivy and see if we can find the cat, without putting ourselves in unnecessary danger. Come on."

He waded along the top of the fence until he could claw his way up the ivy. His belly churned as Thornclaw's words echoed in his mind. The golden-brown warrior was right. *We don't know for sure that all the Twolegs have gone.* But Twolegs were noisy creatures, and now their surroundings were so quiet that Bramblestar could hear every lap and gurgle of the water, every wail from the she-cat in trouble.

"Help! Is anyone there?"

Saving his breath for the climb, Bramblestar reached the upper level of the Twoleg den and scrambled along the ivy until he reached the corner. The cat's cries were even louder here. Bramblestar looked down and almost lost his grip in astonishment. Just around a bend in the flooded Thunder-path, a small white cat with black patches on her ears and belly was crouching in a round, hollow object made of wood. The object bobbed in the water, stuck in the branches of a sub-merged bush.

"Hi! Up here!" Bramblestar called.

The cat spun around, making her little sanctuary rock so

wildly that it almost tipped over. "You found me!" she gasped, tipping back her head to look up. "Please help! Did you get left behind, too?"

Bramblestar opened his jaws to reply, but before he could speak, the she-cat continued in a rush. "When the lake flooded, my housefolk took Brandy and Polly, but they couldn't find me." She glanced down for a moment, and her voice grew quieter. "I was asleep under their bed. I didn't hear them calling until it was too late." With a shake, she lifted her head again. "Then the water started coming into the house so fast! I climbed into this tub to keep dry. I didn't realize it would float away!"

"Calm down," Bramblestar meowed when the she-cat paused for breath. "We'll figure out a way to get to you."

Now that he had found the cat, there was no way he could leave her floating helplessly in the flood. But she was a long way out and surrounded by deep water. *Can we swim that far?* Bramblestar wondered. *And if we do reach her, how do we get her to safety?*

"I've got an idea," Thornclaw mewed, with a light touch of his tail on his leader's shoulder.

"Okay, spit it out," Bramblestar told him, tensing as he felt the ivy stem where he was clinging start to tear away from the wall of the den. "We can't stay here."

"See those little ledges on the den walls?" Thornclaw nodded toward them. "We might be able to use them to cross from den to den."

"Those are windowsills," Graystripe meowed unexpectedly.

Every cat stared at him. "Huh?" Thornclaw grunted.

"Don't forget that I once lived in a Twoleg den," Graystripe told them. "After I was captured when the Twolegs were cutting down the old forest. Twolegs sleep in nests on this upper level," he went on. "These gaps in the wall are called windows. The Twolegs look through them, but they don't go in and out of them."

"So what are they for?" Dovewing asked.

"Well, they let light into the den."

"And I expect the Twolegs use them to watch for predators," Thornclaw added. "That's a pretty neat idea, for Twolegs."

Bramblestar cleared his throat. "If you've all finished discussing Twoleg dens," he mewed, "we have a cat to rescue. Thornclaw," he continued, "I think your idea could work, but it's going to be tricky. Maybe you and I should try it alone."

"No way!" Dovewing exclaimed.

Graystripe lashed his tail. "Forget it, Bramblestar. We're coming with you."

Bramblestar was warmed by the loyalty of his Clanmates. "Okay," he purred. "But for StarClan's sake, be careful."

Taking the lead, he clambered through the ivy until he reached the first windowsill. He pulled himself onto it, gritting his teeth; even though the windowsill was wider than a tree branch, it was angled slightly downward, so he was afraid he was going to slip. He dug his claws hard into the wood and crept forward with his heart thudding.

At the end of the windowsill he had to leap across a gap of bare red stone to reach the next one. *It's just like chasing a squirrel in the trees,* he told himself, bunching his muscles and launching himself into the air. He landed awkwardly, one hind paw waving in the air, and took a moment to steady himself.

A glance over his shoulder told himself that the others were following safely. Confidence began to seep back into his paws, only to drain away again when he saw that the gap between this windowsill and the next was much wider.

That's because the next one belongs to the next den, Bramblestar realized. *But how else can we reach it? It looks like it's too far to leap, but we have to try.*

He pushed off with all his strength, reaching out with his forepaws. His belly hit the windowsill, and he had to scrabble frantically with his hind paws to pull himself up. *And we have to keep on doing this,* he thought with a tremor of fear in his belly. *Surely one of us will fall?* But his Clanmates followed him without any mishaps, even managing to speed up as they got used to the hazards.

When Bramblestar reached the fourth windowsill he was able to look down and get a clearer view of the cat in the tub. Her blue eyes stared up at him, filled with terror.

"Please hurry!" she begged. "There's water coming into the tub. I'm getting wetter!"

"We're coming!" Bramblestar called as he readied himself for the next jump.

"Bramblestar, stop!" Graystripe yowled.

Bramblestar froze. "What's the matter?"

"Look at the next windowsill. Can't you see that the wood is rotten? It won't bear our weight."

Following the gray warrior's gaze, Bramblestar saw that the end of the windowsill was jagged and loose as if it was crumbling away. "Just like a rotten branch . . ." he murmured. "So what do we do now?" he asked, not expecting an answer.

"We'll have to go into the den and find a way out on the lower level," Graystripe meowed.

Thornclaw flattened his ears. "I'm not setting paw in there!" he exclaimed. "Have you got bees in your brain?"

Dovewing's whiskers flickered. "Isn't there another way?"

Graystripe shook his head. "We don't have a choice if we want to help the she-cat," he insisted, keeping his voice low.

The she-cat was already beginning to panic. "What's happening?" she demanded. "Why have you stopped?"

Bramblestar glanced down at her. "It's okay!" he called.

But he wasn't sure that was true. The window where he and his Clanmates were crouching was blocked by hard, transparent stuff, and he couldn't see any way of getting past it. He pressed it with one paw, then butted his head against it, but it held fast.

"Are you trying to get in?" the she-cat asked. "It's easy! My friend Parsnip lives there, and the windows open if you press them at the top."

Bramblestar glanced at Graystripe. "Worth a try, I suppose."

Stretching his forepaws as high as they would go, he thrust at the slippery, transparent window. The bottom swung out toward him, catching him in the belly, and he let out a startled yowl as he felt his hind paws slipping. Dovewing sank her teeth into his scruff, steadying him until he could recover his balance.

"Thanks!" he gasped. Peering through the gap that had opened up at the bottom of the window, he added, "Graystripe, you'd better lead the way."

The gray warrior crawled through the gap, flattening his body as if he were creeping up on prey. There was another windowsill inside the nest; Graystripe hesitated there for a moment, then jumped down. Dovewing followed him, but Thornclaw took a pace back, his lips curling as if he had just smelled crow-food.

"I don't like it," he muttered.

"I'm not asking you to like it," Bramblestar mewed.

Thornclaw puffed out his breath. "I can't believe I'm doing this."

While his Clanmate was scrambling through the gap, Bramblestar looked back and called out to the she-cat in the tub. "We'll be with you in a few heartbeats!"

Inside the den, the scent of Twolegs wreathed around Bramblestar, and every hair on his pelt stood on end. All his instincts were telling him to run, but there was nowhere to run to. Solid white walls loomed all around, trapping him. Then he realized that all the scents were stale, and he managed to relax a little.

What a lot of stuff the Twolegs have in their dens! he thought as he glanced around. The floor was covered in a layer of dense green tufts that Bramblestar thought was grass, until he rubbed his paws against it and realized it was some kind of Twoleg pelt.

More soft pelts lay scattered on top of it, and on top of a large, flat object that stood against one wall. There were big structures made out of wood, with hard, straight lines, not the soft contours of real trees.

"This is a bedroom," Graystripe announced. Meeting blank stares from the other three cats, he added, "The nest where the Twolegs sleep."

"Fascinating," Thornclaw muttered.

"Yes. Graystripe, can we just keep going?" Bramblestar meowed.

Graystripe nodded and led the way toward a gap in the den wall. As Bramblestar padded after him he realized how soft the pelts were against his paws. *This would be a good place for cats to sleep too,* he thought, *provided there weren't any Twolegs.*

Following Graystripe out of the sleeping den, Bramblestar and his Clanmates slipped silently alongside the wall until they reached an uneven slope leading downward.

"This reminds me of the abandoned Twoleg den," Bramblestar remarked.

"They call it *stairs*," Graystripe informed him.

"You never told us any of this before," Dovewing mewed as they began to descend the slope. "It's really interesting."

Graystripe snorted. "We're Clan cats, not kittypets," he reminded her. "How they live has nothing to do with us."

Water was lapping at the bottom of the slope, and Bramblestar waved his tail for Graystripe to step back and let him go ahead. There were more gaps in the den walls, and at first he didn't know which one would lead to the outside. Then he sensed a flow of cooler air coming from one of the gaps, and heard the shriek of the she-cat from that direction. "Where have you gone?"

Cautiously Bramblestar stepped down into the water, wincing at the cold, wet touch on his fur. At first it was shallow enough to wade, but as he stepped through the gap the ground suddenly gave way beneath his paws, and he found himself floundering, thrashing his paws until he managed to climb onto something solid.

"There's another step just there, I think," Graystripe mewed helpfully.

"Whatever." Bramblestar gave his pelt a disgusted shake. "Jump from the top to this . . . thing I'm standing on," he instructed.

"It's a chair," Graystripe told him. "And that big, flat thing over there is a table. If you jump up there, Bramblestar, there'll be room for the next cat."

"Good idea," Bramblestar responded. "Thank StarClan you know a bit about these Twoleg places, Graystripe."

"I'll still be glad to get out of here," the gray warrior grumbled.

Soon all four cats were standing on the table. More chairs were scattered around, as if the flood had carried them from their proper places. One of them was wedged by the opening that led outside, holding back the piece of wood that the Twolegs had used to block the gap.

Two jumps brought Bramblestar to this chair, and at last he was able to see outside. A fence ran around the garden and joined onto the den not far from where Bramblestar was standing. A few fox-lengths away a monster was crouching, with water lapping halfway up its shiny blue sides. Between Bramblestar and the monster was the tub, floating very low in the water now. The black-and-white she-cat was peering anxiously over the side.

"Please hurry!" she wailed. "The tub is sinking!"

Bramblestar turned to his Clanmates. "We'll have to leap from here to the fence," he told them. "It's an awkward angle, but we should be able to manage it."

"How are we going to get the cat out of there?" Dovewing asked as she landed neatly on the chair beside him.

Bramblestar wasn't sure. *Maybe the tub will bump up against the fence, and she can climb out of it.* "Just go," he meowed.

Dovewing obeyed, reaching the fence with Graystripe and Thornclaw just behind her. But when Bramblestar tried to follow he misjudged the jump because he was trying to avoid his Clanmates, who were crowded together along the fence-top. His claws raked the wood of the fence, but he couldn't get a grip on it. A heartbeat later he plunged into icy water. His yowl of alarm was cut off as the flood closed over his head.

Bramblestar flailed his legs desperately, feeling the cold sink deep into his pelt. His chest ached with the need to breathe. It seemed like a whole season before his head broke the surface. Gasping for air, he glanced around, but at first he could see nothing but the tossing water.

"Over here!" the kittypet yowled. "Hurry!"

Bramblestar splashed in a circle until he caught sight of the tub, only a few tail-lengths away from him. It had floated away from the fence. *Great StarClan! I hope I can move it!*

Struggling to keep his head above the surface, Bramblestar thrashed his way over to the tub and started to push. It was sluggish, hard to move, because by now most of it was under the water. The black-and-white she-cat propped her forepaws on the rim, her terrified gaze fixed on Bramblestar. He didn't have enough breath or strength to reassure her.

The tub was closer to the monster than the fence, so Bramblestar headed that way. At last he felt the tub bump gently against the shiny blue side. "Climb out!" he choked.

The she-cat floundered through the water that by now was filling the tub, and clawed her way onto the top of the monster. Bramblestar followed her, managed to give her a boost upward, then hauled himself to safety and flopped down on the monster's back. Hearing a gurgle from below, he looked down to see the tub vanish under the surface of the water. The she-cat was watching it too.

"I could have been in that!" she gasped. "You saved me!"

"Not exactly," Bramblestar grunted, waving his tail to indicate the silver water all around them.

"But you did!" the she-cat insisted. "Thank you! My name's Minty. What's yours?"

"I'm Bramblestar." He angled his ears toward the other cats, who were approaching along the fence. "Those are Graystripe, Dovewing, and Thornclaw."

"What weird names!" Minty mewed, wrinkling her nose.

Bramblestar didn't comment. When his Clanmates jumped down onto the monster's back, he stood up and shook the water from his pelt. "What do we do with this kittypet now?" he asked quietly.

"I don't see why we have to do anything," Thornclaw meowed. "We've saved her life. What she does next is up to her."

"You can't leave me here!" Minty wailed. "My housefolk and my littermates have gone. What will I eat?"

Fish, with all this water, Bramblestar was strongly tempted to answer, but he stopped himself. *It's not her fault she's so helpless.*

"We can't leave her here," Dovewing whispered. "She'll starve or freeze. She's a kittypet; they can't look after themselves."

"Can I come home with you?" Minty begged, fixing a wide-eyed blue gaze on Bramblestar. "Where do your housefolk live? Did their houses escape the flood?"

Bramblestar exchanged a glance with Graystripe. "We don't live with Twolegs," he explained. "We're wild cats, from the Clans by the lake."

Minty's eyes stretched even wider. "Wow, I've heard of them!" she exclaimed. "I mean, you. But you're supposed to be dangerous. You eat bones and kill trespassers!"

Bramblestar sighed. "We really need to stop these rumors. We won't eat you, we promise," he continued. "We don't eat cats. Just mice and birds and squirrels, just like you."

Minty uttered a little shriek and looked as if she was going to pass out. "I don't eat those!" She gave her tail a flick. "I don't think I want to come with you after all."

Thornclaw shrugged, his whiskers twitching. "Okay. Stay put. Your choice."

Minty hesitated. "Why don't you stay here?" she suggested after a moment. "The house is really comfortable, and there must be some of my food in the kitchen."

"No, that's impossible," Bramblestar meowed. "Our Clanmates need us."

"There are more of you?" Minty squealed. Her tail drooped. "I don't know where my housefolk keep my food. It's probably ruined by the water anyway." She put her head on one side, thinking, then announced, "Okay, I'll come with you."

"You're not doing us any favors," Dovewing muttered. "Don't act like we're begging you to come."

If Minty heard the comment, she didn't react to it. She stared at Bramblestar. "You promise the other cats won't eat me?"

"Oh, no," meowed Thornclaw. "There's not enough meat on you to be a decent meal."

Minty squeaked, and Bramblestar tapped Thornclaw with his tail. "Don't torment her. Minty, you won't be eaten. But we've got a long way to go, so you need to be prepared for a difficult journey."

Minty shrugged. "It won't be difficult for me. I go outside every day."

Bramblestar blinked. *That's not exactly forest training, but I guess it will have to do.* He turned to the fence. "Leap up there," he encouraged Minty, "and we'll follow."

Minty peered up at the fence. "It's awfully high," she mewed.

"For StarClan's sake!" Thornclaw spat. "Have you never climbed a fence before?"

"Of course I have!" Minty retorted, stung. "It's just that . . . Well, I used to climb up by the creeper there." She pointed with her tail over to the other side of the enclosed space, where a plant with thick, glossy leaves was growing up the fence.

"Well, you can swim over to the creeper, or jump up here," Dovewing told her.

Minty blinked uncertainly. "You'll help me, won't you?" she asked Bramblestar.

"We'll all help," Bramblestar promised. "Dovewing, you hop onto the fence and grab Minty when she jumps."

"Okay." Dovewing bunched her hindquarters and propelled herself onto the fence in a graceful bound. Bramblestar suspected she was showing off.

"Come on," he mewed to Minty. "You can stand on me to get a bit nearer if you like." He crouched at the side of the monster nearest the fence and winced as the kittypet dug her claws into his back to heave herself onto his shoulders. Bramblestar forced himself to take her weight and stand straight, lifting her as high as he could. "Now jump!"

He felt Minty's paws scuffling for balance, then a vigorous shove as she sprang upward. Shaking his pelt, he looked up to see her clawing frantically at the wood, while Dovewing leaned down and grabbed her by the scruff. A moment later she stood beside Dovewing on the fence.

"Great," Thornclaw growled. "Now can we get moving?"

Bramblestar let Graystripe lead the way along the fence-top while he brought up the rear, just behind Minty. He wanted to be close enough to help her if she slipped. But to Bramblestar's surprise she trotted along more confidently than the Clan cats, not at all fazed by the narrowness of the fence. *Of course, she must have done this often, visiting her friends in the other dens.*

When they reached the corner of the fence and Graystripe turned toward the Thunderpath, Minty halted and stared at the vast stretch of flooded ground. "There's so much water!" she exclaimed. "Parsnip and his housefolk are gone, and my housefolk, and all the housefolk and the cats! I'm the only one left!" She sounded lost and small, as if she hadn't realized the extent of the disaster until now.

Graystripe glanced over his shoulder at her. "It'll be okay," he comforted her. "They'll come back and look for you when the flood goes down."

Minty nodded, but Bramblestar wasn't sure whether she believed him.

Finally they arrived at the end of the fence where they had first heard Minty's cries, opposite the drowned monster on the Thunderpath. Here the water still reached halfway up their legs, and Minty was starting to look scared again.

"We can't go any farther," she mewed.

"Yes, it's fine," Bramblestar told her. "We have to swim over to where you can see that drowned monster, then get onto the fence, and that takes us to dry ground."

Minty turned to him with her blue eyes wider than ever. "Swim?"

Thornclaw let out a hiss of annoyance. "Don't tell me you can't swim!"

"I don't know," Minty replied. "I've never tried."

Bramblestar took a deep breath. "Graystripe, you go first. Dovewing, swim on that side of Minty, and I'll swim on this side. Thornclaw, follow us. Minty, I promise we'll get you across, okay?"

"Okay . . . I guess."

Graystripe launched himself into the water, powering toward the monster with strong sweeps of his paws. Minty clung to the fence until Dovewing gave her a shove. She plopped into the water with a startled squeak. With Bramblestar on one side and Dovewing on the other, the kittypet splashed furiously, wasting far too much effort, but somehow she managed to propel herself forward.

"Hey, I can swi—" she squealed. The last word was cut off as water slopped into her mouth. She started spluttering, and Bramblestar steadied her with a shoulder underneath her until she caught her breath.

Bramblestar knew that he was getting tired, and guessed that his Clanmates felt the same. The swim to the drowned monster seemed twice as far as it had on the way out. *If we hadn't stopped to help Minty, we'd be back on our own territory by now.* He was exhausted by the time they stood safely on ShadowClan territory. It was an effort to make his paws move along the waterline, beside the drowned pines.

"Is this where you live?" Minty asked, and added politely, "It's ... er ... very nice."

"No, this is where ShadowClan lives," Graystripe told her. "We're ThunderClan." He waved his tail toward the other side of the lake. "We live over there."

"What?" Minty screeched. "I can't walk that far! My legs will fall off!"

Bramblestar looked at her. "You'd better hang on to them," he teased her. "Or Thornclaw might find he has a taste for kittypets after all."

Minty let out a yelp and raced ahead, glancing back over her shoulder at Thornclaw with a look of terror in her eyes.

"What did you say that for?" Thornclaw looked bemused. "When did I ever eat kittypets?"

"Just show your fangs," Dovewing muttered. "At least she's moving!"

Minty waited for them to catch up, though she stayed as far from Thornclaw as possible, and padded beside the Clan cats as they headed toward the open stretch of grass.

"How many cats live by the lake?" she asked. "Do you all live together? And do you really eat mice and squirrels and yucky stuff like that?"

"I don't know exactly how many cats there are," Bramblestar replied. "Lots. Each Clan has its own camp, where they live together. And yes, we catch our own prey and eat it. You will too, while you're staying with us."

Minty shuddered. "Never!"

Bramblestar exchanged a glance with Thornclaw, guessing

that the golden-brown warrior was thinking the same thing. *Wait until she gets hungry!*

"It's really dark under these trees, isn't it?" Minty chattered on. "I wouldn't like living here. Is it dark in your territory, too?"

Graystripe shook his head. "ThunderClan territory is more open than this."

"I can't wait to see it!" Minty mewed with an excited little skip. "Ooh, look, a squirrel! Are you going to catch it?"

"No," Bramblestar told her. "We're allowed to cross ShadowClan territory, but not to take prey here. The ShadowClan cats would be furious."

Minty watched the squirrel dart across the gap between two pines and scramble up into the branches. "Will we meet any ShadowClan cats?" she asked. "I wish we could. It'd be fun!"

Dovewing rolled her eyes. "Trust me, it wouldn't. Why don't you save your breath for walking?"

Minty gave her an injured look, but said nothing more.

Bramblestar was thankful that so far they hadn't met any ShadowClan patrols. His pelt was prickling with apprehension at the thought of bringing a kittypet into his Clan. *ThunderClan doesn't need more cats. It needs to strengthen and protect the ones it has.*

But Bramblestar couldn't have left Minty to starve. He padded over to the kittypet, who was nervously eyeing a fallen tree in her path.

"Just hop on top of it," he meowed, "and then jump down

on the other side. It's not that high."

He leaped up to show her, and grabbed her to help her up the last couple of mouse-lengths as her hind paws scuffled against the trunk.

I just hope my Clanmates understand why I've brought a stranger home with me.

All four ThunderClan cats let out a sigh of relief as they crossed the border into ThunderClan territory. Their scent marks were faint against the smell of mud and water, but there were no fresh ShadowClan scents. Following the edge of the flood, Thornclaw led them up the slope until they were just below the ridge. It was hard going, pushing through the soaking undergrowth on paws that were tired and heavy as stone.

"We're on ThunderClan territory now," Graystripe told Minty, "and we're just going past the flooded camp." He veered down the slope and vanished into a clump of thorns.

Bramblestar followed, nodding to Minty. "Come on, you can see where our home used to be."

He waited for her to join him at the edge of the cliff. Bramblestar felt his heart beat faster as he stared into the hollow. The sheer gray cliffs now encircled nothing but a pool of black, swirling water. He pictured the dens, the fresh-kill pile, the half stump where the apprentices liked to play. Were they all still there, under the water?

Or had every trace of ThunderClan been washed away?

CHAPTER 12

🍀

"It's even more flooded than my home!" Minty exclaimed. "Where do you live now?"

"You'll see," Bramblestar told her. "It's this way." He turned away from the cliff, feeling a stab of grief for the lost camp, and forced his way back through the thorns. It was a steep climb to the tunnel, and he heard Minty puffing behind him, though to her credit she didn't complain. Bramblestar wondered if she realized he and the others had traveled twice this distance in one day.

Several cats were outside the tunnel entrance. Daisy, Purdy, and Squirrelflight were spreading out bundles of wet moss and bracken to dry in the weak sun. A little farther off, the three younger apprentices and their mentors were watching closely while Ivypool and Spiderleg demonstrated a battle move.

As Bramblestar and his patrol trekked up the last few fox-lengths of the slope, every cat looked up.

Squirrelflight leaped to her paws. "Thank StarClan you're okay! Did you find out about the other Clans?"

More cats emerged from the tunnel and crowded around the patrol.

"Did RiverClan survive?"

"How far do the floods stretch?"

It was Spiderleg who first noticed Minty. "Who's this?" he demanded. "Bramblestar, why have you brought another cat here?"

"Another mouth to feed," Berrynose added with a disapproving twitch of his whiskers. "Haven't we got enough trouble, providing for our own cats?"

Minty stared around her with huge blue eyes, daunted by the number of cats and the hostility from the two toms.

"Her name is Minty," Bramblestar meowed, his tone cold as he raked his gaze over Spiderleg and Berrynose. "We rescued her from the flooded Twoleg dens near RiverClan territory."

"Twoleg dens?" Sandstorm's ears flicked up in surprise. "You mean this is a *kittypet*?" She stretched her neck forward and sniffed Minty's fur. "You don't smell like one," she commented.

"I—I've been swimming," Minty stammered.

"Her housefolk left her behind," Bramblestar explained. "She'd have drowned or starved if we hadn't helped her." Then he remembered that he was Clan leader. He didn't have to justify his decisions. "Take her inside, make a nest for her, and find her something to eat," he ordered.

"We'll do that," Amberpaw offered, pushing through the knot of warriors.

"Yeah, come on." Snowpaw curled his tail around Minty's shoulders. "We'll look after you."

Bramblestar watched the apprentices lead Minty away. The

young cats were bubbling with curiosity.

"Are you really a kittypet?" Dewpaw asked, giving the black-and-white she-cat a fascinated stare. "What's it like, living with Twolegs?"

"Is it true you don't have to catch your own food?" Amberpaw mewed.

Purdy was standing beside the tunnel entrance. "You come wi' me," he meowed kindly to Minty. "You can make a nest beside mine. I was a kittypet once, y'know. I'll tell you all about it. . . ."

Bramblestar followed them into the tunnel to make sure that Minty wasn't too overwhelmed. Dewpaw and Snowpaw fetched more bedding and spread it out on the floor between their own nests and Purdy's.

"There!" Snowpaw mewed. "It's a bit wet, but it's not too bad when you get used to it."

Minty gasped when she saw the scanty heap of moss and bracken. "I can't sleep on *that*!" she exclaimed. "At home I have a *basket*! And a *blanket*!"

The three apprentices looked at one another. "We don't know what those are," Amberpaw meowed. "But look, I've got some feathers in my nest. You can have them if you like."

"Th-thank you." Minty gave her nest a dubious look as Amberpaw generously added the feathers.

Bramblestar was distracted from Minty's troubles as Squirrelflight and Leafpool walked into the tunnel and came up to him.

"There's a real problem with the bedding," Squirrelflight

began. "Everything's soaking wet, and cats are getting aches from sleeping on the cold stone floor in the tunnels."

"Well, we can't sleep outside," Bramblestar told her. "It might rain again."

Squirrelflight and Leafpool exchanged a glance.

"That's true," Leafpool meowed. "But we need to find some decent dry bedding or we're all going to catch whitecough."

As if to prove her words, a hacking cough sounded from where Briarlight was lying, deeper inside the tunnel. Bramblestar blinked, peering into the shadows. Jayfeather was crouched beside the dark-pawed she-cat, concern visible in every line of his body, while nearby Millie anxiously scuffled her claws on the rock floor.

Bramblestar felt heavy with worry as he headed outside. *Where do they expect me to get dry bedding? Out of my ears?*

Cloudtail was trudging up the slope, dangling a couple of mice from his jaws. Brightheart, Rosepetal, and Blossomfall followed him; Brightheart was carrying a squirrel, while Rosepetal and Blossomfall both had starlings.

"I think the prey is starting to come back," Cloudtail reported when he had dropped his catch on the fresh-kill pile. "Better than yesterday, anyway."

"Good," Bramblestar mewed, grateful for any scrap of good news. There was already prey on the pile; hunting patrols must have been out earlier, too. "Squirrelflight, can you take charge of doling it out? There should be enough for every cat to have something."

Squirrelflight nodded and set about efficiently dividing up

the catch, while Brightheart helped carry each share to their Clanmates.

Minty stared in horror as Brightheart dropped a starling in front of her.

"I'm not eating *that!*" she declared, screwing her nose.

"It's tasty," Amberpaw reassured her. "And when you've eaten it, you can add the feathers to your nest."

Minty just turned away with her nose in the air.

"Okay, I'll have it if you don't want it," mewed Dewpaw, who had already gulped down his portion of squirrel.

"You will not," Brightheart told him, gently shoving the apprentice away. "Queens and elders eat first, remember. Purdy, would you like it?"

The old tabby shook his head. "No, thanks, that mouse was plenty for me."

"Then I'll take it back to the fresh-kill pile for later," Brightheart meowed. "Minty, if you change your mind, ask me and I'll fetch it for you."

Minty didn't reply, but Dewpaw watched with a disappointed look as Brightheart picked up the starling and carried it away.

By the time the fresh-kill was eaten, the daylight was dying, and gray shadows invaded the tunnel. Bramblestar made a point of settling down near Minty; it had been his decision to bring her back to the Clan, so he felt responsible for her, at least until she was more settled.

The kittypet was crouching on the moss and bracken, her paws tucked under her. Bramblestar could hear her belly rumbling, but she looked too stunned to complain. After a few moments she heaved a gusty sigh and curled up with her tail over her nose.

But she didn't go to sleep. Wakeful himself, Bramblestar heard her tossing and turning, and once she let out a miserable whimper. At the sound, Millie rose from her nest beside Briarlight and padded past Bramblestar to sit down next to Minty.

"I know just how you feel," she murmured. "I was a kittypet once. It took me a long time to learn how to live in the wild."

In the half light, Bramblestar saw Minty raise her head and stare at Millie. "*You* were a kittypet? Did your housefolk leave you behind, or did you choose to live out here like this?"

"I chose to go with Graystripe when he came back to the Clan," Millie purred. "It's worth all the soft beds and all the food the Twolegs gave me, to be here with him."

"Don't you ever wish you could go back?"

"I wouldn't change a thing," Millie assured her. "Except that I wish my daughter Briarlight hadn't been injured. I'll never leave ThunderClan, but I'll never forget that there's another way to live, either."

I never knew Millie felt like that, Bramblestar thought, with a pang of guilt that Millie had never been one of his favorite cats, with her perpetual fussing over Briarlight. *I'll show her more respect in the future.*

At least the conversation with Millie seemed to have settled Minty; soon she curled up again and her steady breathing told Bramblestar she was asleep at last.

* * *

Bramblestar woke to see pale dawn light trickling into the tunnel. It looked as dull and gray as the day before, he thought. *We need proper sunlight to dry out the forest.*

While he was giving his pelt a quick grooming, he heard the sound of paw steps, and cats brushing through the undergrowth. Rosepetal, who was on guard at the entrance to the tunnel, stuck her head inside.

"Bramblestar, there are a couple of cats coming up from the direction of ShadowClan."

"Thanks, Rosepetal." Bramblestar looked around and saw that Lionblaze and Mousewhisker were stirring too. He beckoned them with a flick of his ears. "Let's go see what they want."

As Bramblestar stepped out of the tunnel he spotted two cats emerging from the sodden undergrowth: Rowanclaw, the ShadowClan deputy, and Littlecloud, their medicine cat. Bramblestar's paws tingled. Could he guess what this visit was about?

"Greetings," he meowed, padding forward.

"Greetings, Bramblestar," Littlecloud responded. With a glance at Rowanclaw he added, "We're on our way to the Moonpool. I don't know if it's escaped the flooding, but it's high up in the mountains, so we're going to take the risk that it's survived." He sighed. "If it hasn't, I fear for the Clans. . . ."

"I'm ShadowClan leader now," Rowanclaw explained, though no explanation was necessary. "Blackstar lost his ninth life in the storm."

"I'm sorry." Bramblestar regretted the death of any Clan

leader, though he was pleased that Rowanclaw would succeed Blackstar. His sister Tawnypelt's mate would make a strong and vigorous leader. "May he walk in peace with StarClan. And may your leadership go well," he added.

Rowanclaw nodded. "Thanks. How are things in Thunder-Clan?" he asked. "Did all your cats survive?"

"Yes," Bramblestar replied. "It was a struggle, but we're all okay." He stopped himself from saying more, especially not that the whole Clan was living in the tunnel.

Rowanclaw didn't offer any more information about ShadowClan, either. *I know how tough it is for them,* Bramblestar thought, remembering the journey through their waterlogged territory the day before.

"This is a hard day for all the Clans," Rowanclaw mewed. He seemed subdued, clearly grieving for Blackstar and worried about his own leadership in this crisis. "StarClan grant that we all survive."

Bramblestar murmured agreement. He watched the two ShadowClan cats trek farther up the hill in the direction of the Moonpool until they were out of sight. Then Bramblestar turned back to the tunnel to meet Jayfeather, who was just emerging. The medicine cat raised his head and gave a good sniff.

"Rowanclaw and Littlecloud were here?" he meowed.

"Yes. On their way to the Moonpool."

Jayfeather bowed his head for a heartbeat. "I'm not surprised Blackstar lost his last life," he mewed at last. "He was old, and he'd seen so much."

Bramblestar felt how odd it was to hear Jayfeather talking

like this. *It's like he's an old cat himself. But then, Jayfeather has seen more than most of us, in spite of being blind.*

By now the other cats were waking up and climbing stiffly into the open. The day was growing brighter, though the sun had not yet risen, and a cold breeze rattled the branches and spun raindrops into the air.

Squirrelflight appeared from the tunnel and spoke through a massive yawn. "What patrols do you want today?"

"We need to concentrate on hunting," Bramblestar told her. "Get Sandstorm and Cloudtail to lead patrols. And will you lead one too, along the WindClan border? I'll take one to ShadowClan."

Squirrelflight nodded. "What do you want done about the WindClan stream?"

Bramblestar hesitated, remembering the WindClan patrol's frenzied assertion of their rights over the water. "Nothing, for now," he decided. "I hope the problem will resolve itself once the floodwater goes down. Take cats with you who'll keep their heads if WindClan cats challenge you."

As Squirrelflight turned away to divide the cats into patrols, Briarlight emerged from the tunnel with Millie beside her. Bramblestar noticed that the young she-cat winced as she dragged herself along the ground.

"Is something wrong?" he called.

It was Millie who replied. "She's getting sores on her belly from the damp bedding. Bramblestar, you have to do something!"

"I'll be okay," Briarlight muttered. "Don't fuss!"

"Jayfeather?" Bramblestar glanced toward his medicine cat. "What do you think?"

Jayfeather padded up to Briarlight. "Why didn't you tell me you were getting sores?" he asked brusquely.

Briarlight looked at her paws. "I didn't want to bother you."

"StarClan help us!" Jayfeather puffed out a sigh. "What do you think a medicine cat is for?" To Bramblestar he added, "I'll examine her sores and find her some herbs, but Millie is right. Sleeping on stone and wet bedding won't do Briarlight any good at all."

Before Bramblestar could respond, a squeal sounded from the tunnel entrance. He glanced over his shoulder to see that Minty had appeared with Amberpaw.

"Oh, wow!" the kittypet exclaimed, her blue eyes round with shock. "That cat has no legs!"

Stupid furball, Bramblestar thought, as Briarlight shrank with embarrassment.

"Of course she's got legs," Amberpaw mewed, brisk and sensible. "The back ones don't work, that's all."

"And she's still alive?" Minty asked. "Don't you have to feed her and stuff?"

"Yes, we catch prey for her," Amberpaw replied. "What do you take us for? She's our Clanmate! Do you think we wouldn't help her?"

Minty gave Briarlight a fascinated glance. "You're not really wild at all, then," she murmured.

"Yes, we are," Amberpaw meowed with a decisive flick of her tail. "*Wild*'s not the same as *savage.*"

Bramblestar gave the apprentice a nod of approval. He still couldn't see any answer to the problem of the wet bedding, and hoped that something would occur to him on patrol. It would be a relief to get away from the makeshift camp for a while.

"Dovewing," he began, beckoning to the cat nearest him. "I want you to come with me to patrol the ShadowClan border."

"Sure," Dovewing mewed. "I need some exercise to take the stiffness out of my legs."

"Let's take the two older apprentices," Bramblestar suggested. "They've missed out on a lot of training lately. And their mentors, of course."

"I'll round them up." Dovewing padded into the tunnel with a whisk of her tail. Moments later she reappeared with Poppyfrost and Bumblestripe, Lilypaw and Seedpaw bouncing with anticipation behind their mentors.

"We're really going to patrol the ShadowClan border?" Seedpaw chirped.

Bramblestar nodded. "What's left of it. And there might be dangers we're not used to, so both of you need to be sensible and not go dashing off."

"We won't," Lilypaw promised.

Bramblestar led the patrol along the ridge toward Shadow-Clan, setting scent markers at the edge of the territory until they reached the border stream. Swollen by the heavy rain, it had burst its banks and become a brown, churning torrent as it rolled toward the lake. Pausing to taste the air, Bramblestar realized that he could only pick up faint traces of ShadowClan scent. "They haven't renewed their scent markers since yesterday," he mewed.

"We haven't renewed ours yet, either," Poppyfrost pointed out. "There's not much point in all this wet," she added with a shiver.

"No cat will try to cross this stream, that's for sure," Bumblestripe agreed.

"Still, I think we will go on leaving markers," Bramblestar decided. "The apprentices can practice setting them."

"Yes!" Lilypaw jumped into the air. "We'll feel like real warriors."

Gradually they worked their way downstream, finding new places to set the markers at the edge of the water. The boundary was farther into ThunderClan territory than it used to be, thanks to the flooded stream.

"I hope ShadowClan doesn't think we're giving them more territory when the floods go down," Bumblestripe murmured.

"If they do, they'll soon find out they're wrong," Bramblestar responded grimly.

A thin drizzle began to fall, soaking their pelts and striking a chill right through to their bones. Apart from the patter of droplets, the forest was silent. Bramblestar felt his neck fur begin to rise at the strangeness of pushing through the drenched undergrowth, under dripping trees, and finding no trace of prey or any other cats. Even the birds had stopped singing.

The apprentices, who had been scampering a few paw steps ahead, slithered to a halt.

"Wow, look at that!" Lilypaw exclaimed.

Bramblestar trotted forward to join the young cats. They had reached the edge of the flooded lake. The water stretched in front of them in an endless silver pool, with the tops of trees poking out of it.

"The water's risen above the old Thunderpath," Seedpaw meowed. "That's more fox-lengths from the lake than I can count!"

Lilypaw was blinking unhappily as she gazed out over the flood.

"What's the matter?" Seedpaw asked.

"I was thinking of all the drowned prey," Lilypaw mewed. "How are we going to find enough to eat?"

"That's easy!" Seedpaw replied. "We'll have to expand our territory over the other side of the ridge."

Bramblestar stared at the golden-brown cat in astonishment. Could this be the answer to the shortage of prey? It had never occurred to him to hunt anywhere but in the remains of their own territory.

"You know, Seedpaw could be right," Dovewing murmured.

"I don't know. . . ." Bramblestar felt that as leader he had to be more cautious. "It's a big paw step, to consider changing our boundaries."

"But we'd be unchallenged if we hunted beyond the ridge," Bumblestripe pointed out. "No other cats live there."

Poppyfrost's tail twitched. "There would be foxes and badgers. We had enough trouble with them when Thunder-Clan first made its territory here. Can we take on that kind of challenge when we're in this state?" she added, gesturing with her tail at their skinny bodies and sodden pelts.

"We could always start with hunting patrols," Bramblestar mewed, beginning to be intrigued by the prospect of more prey. "We don't need to mark out a whole territory."

While they were talking, the apprentices had been running along the water's edge, half-thrilled and half-fearful as they gazed out at the surging water.

"Look!" Lilypaw let out a squeak. "It's the Stick of Fallen Warriors!"

Bramblestar looked where she was pointing and spotted the stick that Jayfeather had marked with scratches as a memorial to the cats who had died in the Great Battle. It was half-floating, half-submerged in the floodwater, wedged among the branches of an oak tree.

"We have to get it!" Seedpaw exclaimed.

Both young cats were poised to plunge into the lake; Bramblestar reached them just in time to block their path.

"Stop!" he ordered. "It's far too dangerous to swim in the floodwater!"

"But the stick . . ." Seedpaw protested. "It's important!"

"And it will still be there when the water goes down," Poppyfrost meowed firmly. "Now come away from the edge."

She and Bumblestripe herded their apprentices away from the sucking edge of the floodwater, and turned back toward the camp.

"Hey!" Bumblestripe halted, looking back. "I can see a fish, swimming among the trees."

Bramblestar spotted it too, a swift, silver glimmer among

the drowned leaves. For a heartbeat he wondered if they should try to catch it. *No*, he decided. *We're all wet enough.*

"We'll try hunting beyond the ridge," he told the others as they plodded over the muddy ground. "That was a good idea, Seedpaw."

Seedpaw puffed out her chest. "Please let me come on the patrol!" she begged.

"No," Bumblestripe replied. "Only experienced warriors should go beyond the boundaries." Glancing at Bramblestar, who nodded in agreement, he added, "There could be other cats hunting there because of the flood, as well as badgers and foxes."

"But I'm a great hunter!" Seedpaw insisted. "I can pounce really well. Watch!"

She leaped into the air and landed with her front claws sunk deep into a clump of soggy moss. "I caught it!" she yowled. But when she tried to step back and withdraw her claws, the moss was so wet that it clung to her fur and she couldn't get it off. "This is yucky!" she complained as she shook her paws.

"Keep still," Lilypaw mewed, padding up to her sister and stripping off the moss with careful scrapes of her claws. "Honestly, Seedpaw, sometimes you're such a stupid furball."

Seedpaw blinked in embarrassment and her tail drooped.

"But you're right, that was a great pounce," Dovewing put in. "And Bumblestripe tells me you're an awesome hunter. Maybe you'd like to show me some of your skills?"

Seedpaw brightened up a little. "I know you're only try-ing to make me feel better," she mewed. "And hoping I won't think about hunting over the ridge anymore. But sure, I'll show you if you want."

"Thanks, that would be great," Dovewing responded, with a hint of amusement.

As the patrol moved off again, Bumblestripe padded along-side Dovewing. "That was kind," he murmured, brushing his muzzle against the she-cat's shoulder. "Thanks, Dovewing."

"I like working with the apprentices," Dovewing purred.

"I can't wait for us to have our own kits," Bumblestripe went on. "I know you'll be a great mother."

To Bramblestar's surprise, Dovewing stepped away from her mate. "There's plenty of time for that," she mewed. "We need to deal with the flood first."

Bumblestripe flattened his ears. "Right, okay," he mur-mured, but Bramblestar wondered if Dovewing had seen the hurt look in his eyes. Were things all right between them?

CHAPTER 13

The rain stopped, but the clouds didn't clear, so it was impossible to tell when it was sunhigh. But when the sky seemed brightest overhead, Bramblestar gathered the cats together to share the meager prey the hunters had brought back.

"I can't stand biting through soggy fur," Cloudtail complained, prodding the limp body of a mouse with his front paw. "What I wouldn't give to be tucking in to a nice juicy vole, back in the hollow in the sunshine!"

"Well, wet mouse is all you're going to get," his mate, Brightheart, told him. "You'll have to make the best of it."

Cloudtail grunted, and began to eat in small, fastidious bites.

Bramblestar noticed that Minty had emerged from the tunnel with Millie and the younger apprentices. She was staring in dismay at the sparrow Amberpaw put in front of her.

"I'm so hungry!" she moaned. "But eating that . . . it's yucky!"

Amberpaw rolled her eyes.

"Just try it," Millie coaxed the kittypet, her tone sympathetic. "You might find you like it." As Minty gave her a disbelieving glance, she continued, "I remember the first time I ate wild prey. It was a bit of a shock, after Twoleg food! But I wouldn't want to go back to eating that dry stuff now."

Minty gave the sparrow a wary sniff. "It's covered in feathers. I can't eat those."

"Bite down hard, like this." Amberpaw demonstrated with her own blackbird. "You can spit the feathers out after."

Minty shuddered, but sank her teeth into the sparrow as Amberpaw had demonstrated. Bramblestar saw her gulp down the mouthful with a stunned expression and a feather stuck to her nose.

At least she's eating, he thought.

"The hunting was poor today," he commented to Squirrelflight, who was sharing a vole with him. "Seedpaw suggested sending a patrol outside the territory."

Squirrelflight blinked in surprise, then nodded. "It might be worth a try."

"I'll go," Thornclaw meowed instantly, looking up from the scrawny rabbit he was sharing with Brackenfur, Cherryfall, and Blossomfall. "Anything to stop my belly rumbling."

"Count me in too," Brackenfur added.

"And me," Blossomfall mewed. "It sounds like a great idea."

"Thanks." Bramblestar felt proud of his Clanmates for volunteering so quickly to go into unknown and possibly dangerous territory. "I'll come with you."

"Bramblestar . . ." Squirrelflight gave him a nudge, and motioned with her ears for him to move out of earshot of the others. "You need to rest," she went on when she was sure that they couldn't be overheard. "You can't do every patrol. I'll go instead."

"But you've already hunted today," Bramblestar objected.

"And you did the ShadowClan border patrol." Squirrelflight's tail-tip was twitching, though she kept her voice low. "And yesterday you trekked all the way over to RiverClan and risked your life rescuing that kittypet."

"So?" Bramblestar began to feel frustrated. "I'm fine. It's not a problem."

"It'll be a problem for the rest of us if our Clan leader collapses from exhaustion."

Bramblestar heaved a long sigh. "Remind me why I chose you to be my deputy," he muttered through his teeth.

"Because I won't let you boss me around," Squirrelflight retorted, her green eyes flashing.

True, Bramblestar thought ruefully. "Okay," he mewed, giving in. "I'll just go as far as the border and make sure that things seem okay over there. Then I'll come back."

Squirrelflight didn't look satisfied, but she muttered something under her breath and didn't argue any more.

When Bramblestar had finished his share of the vole, and was waiting for the rest of his patrol to finish scraping the last shreds of flesh off the rabbit, Jayfeather came up from where he had been eating with Dustpelt and Leafpool. Bramblestar's paws tingled when he saw the troubled expression on the face of his medicine cat.

"Is Briarlight's whitecough worse?" he asked anxiously.

"No, thank StarClan," Jayfeather replied. "Though it's

worrying me that Amberpaw and Sandstorm have both started coughing. But that's not the real problem," he went on rapidly. "Look at this." He held up a forepaw and Bramblestar saw that blood was trickling from one of his pads.

"I'll get Leafpool," Bramblestar mewed immediately.

"No, it's nothing. Only a scratch." Jayfeather swiped his tongue over the injured pad. "The point is, I trod on a branch that hadn't been there a moment before."

"Is that so unusual?" Bramblestar asked.

"You know me." Jayfeather twitched his tail. "I don't trip over things just because I can't see them. When did I last hurt myself?"

Bramblestar couldn't remember. Jayfeather never needed his own healing herbs, unlike the other cats, who were always getting thorns in their paws or scratching themselves on bramble tendrils. An unpleasant suspicion occurred to Bramblestar, making the prey he had just eaten feel like a rock in his belly.

"Do you think this is a sign from StarClan?" he asked. "Some other danger we have to face?"

"I'm not sure," Jayfeather admitted, ruffling up his pelt. "The storm has changed everything in the forest. Maybe I just made a mistake."

Bramblestar's ears flicked up in surprise. *When does Jayfeather ever admit to being mistaken?*

"In any case," the medicine cat went on, "I think we should take careful note of everything. Tell the patrol to be extra cautious beyond the territory. They won't know where they're putting their paws, and this could be a warning of injury."

"Maybe we shouldn't hunt over there after all," Bramble-star mused.

"Oh, come on, Bramblestar," Thornclaw interrupted, pausing as he cleaned his whiskers. Bramblestar jumped, not realizing that the other warriors had overheard. "Jayfeather's right to warn us, but we'll be fine," Thornclaw continued. "We know we'll be on unfamiliar ground, so we'll tread carefully."

Reluctantly Bramblestar agreed, if only because he didn't want to worry his Clanmates with thoughts of omens. He took the lead as the patrol climbed up to the ridge. The morning's scent markers were still fresh and strong; a shiver crept right through his pelt from nose to tail as he stepped across them and stood in unfamiliar territory.

Though the border was less than a tail-length behind him, the forest ahead of him looked dark and threatening, full of sinister smells. Tasting the air, Bramblestar picked up traces of fox and badger. Fear swelled inside him, and for a moment he wanted to wail like a lost kit. He was tempted to change his mind and lead the patrol back to the safety of their own territory.

Then he looked at his Clanmates and saw that their fur was bristling with excitement, not fear.

"I can smell rabbits!" Thornclaw exclaimed in a hoarse whisper.

"And squirrels," Blossomfall added. "There should be plenty of them. This is where the prey would have fled when the water started to rise."

Bramblestar realized that he needed to have faith in his warriors' skills. They were strong and experienced, fully capable of dealing with any danger they were likely to meet. *Squirrelflight was right,* he thought. *I can't do everything.*

"What about those hazel bushes over there?" Brackenfur meowed, pointing with his tail. "I'll bet a moon of dawn patrols there's something lurking in there."

"And in that bramble thicket," Cherryfall mewed. "Mice and shrews love hiding in that kind of dense brush."

"Okay." Thornclaw took charge. "Spread out in a line, but let's not lose sight of one another. If you scent prey, signal with your tail. The wind's blowing toward us, so that should help."

Bramblestar watched his Clanmates bound into the trees. Almost at once Cherryfall waved her tail wildly. "Squirrel!" she called. "Over here!"

The rest of the patrol headed toward her, falling into the familiar hunting pattern of surrounding the tree where she had scented prey. Bramblestar's paws felt heavy as he turned away and began padding down to the tunnel. He would much rather have stayed and joined the hunt.

When he returned to the temporary camp, he found Millie outside with Briarlight, helping the injured cat with her exercises. Briarlight couldn't clear her chest; she seemed to be coughing every heartbeat, and nothing Millie did was helping. Minty was standing close by, her fur bristling while her horrified gaze was fixed on Briarlight.

The last thing Briarlight needs is to have a stranger staring at her, Bramblestar thought, his whiskers twitching with annoyance.

Glancing around, he spotted Daisy a couple of tail-lengths away, spreading out some of the bedding yet again in a futile attempt to dry it out. He beckoned her over with his tail.

"Is there something I can do?" Daisy asked as she padded up.

Bramblestar angled his ears toward Minty. "I'd like you to show her the forest," he meowed. "Don't scare her, but give her an idea of where the territory lies, where she should avoid, that kind of thing."

"Sure, Bramblestar," Daisy responded cheerfully. "We can look for extra bedding on the way. Minty might be happier if she has a job to do."

"Amberpaw and I will come, too," Spiderleg meowed, strolling up from where he had been helping his apprentice to practice her hunter's crouch.

Amberpaw coughed as she followed him, and Daisy turned to her with a look of concern. "Are you sure you're fit enough?"

"I'll be fine. It's only a tickle. I—" Amberpaw broke off as another fit of coughing seized her. "I don't want to be stuck in that horrible tunnel. Besides, I think Minty trusts me." She bounded over to the kittypet and gave her a friendly nudge. "Come on, we're going to show you the forest," she urged. "It'll be fun."

Minty blinked at her. "What if there are foxes or badgers?"

"There aren't," Amberpaw replied robustly. "We cleared them all out of our territory. They know better than to come back."

"Well . . . okay." Minty got up and followed Amberpaw back to the two warriors.

Bramblestar noticed that she managed to trip over a half-buried stone and a stray twig before she even reached them. *Good luck with taking her anywhere,* he thought. *Maybe that's what Jayfeather's omen meant.*

"Keep a close eye on her," he murmured to Daisy. "She may be mouse-brained, but I don't want her hurt."

"Don't worry," Daisy reassured him. "I'll treat her like a kit, the first day out of the nursery."

"I'll help, too." Sandstorm padded up from where she had been grooming her fur in the shelter of a bush. With an amused glance at Bramblestar, she added quietly, "Spiderleg was very quick to offer to go too. I wonder if he wants to get back together with Daisy." A cough ended her words.

Bramblestar doubted that the two cats would ever be mates again, and he was more worried about Sandstorm. "I don't think you should be trekking through the forest with that cough," he meowed. "It's important to stay dry and warm."

Sandstorm's look of amusement deepened. "And how do you suggest I do that?" she asked teasingly. "I've only got a choice of wet bedding or hard stone to sleep on."

Daisy's patrol turned to leave, but before they had gone a couple of paw steps, the sound of scuffling broke out in the undergrowth above the tunnel entrance.

Minty let out a scared squeal. "Foxes!"

Before any cat could react, Snowpaw and Dewpaw rolled into the open, their legs fastened around each other as they wrestled. Whitewing and Ivypool scrambled out of the bracken behind them.

"Careful!" Whitewing called. "Watch where you're going!"

"Keep away from the edge, or you'll fall," Whitewing added.

The two apprentices broke apart, shaking their pelts, then suddenly froze. "I'm slipping!" Snowpaw cried in a shrill caterwaul, his paws paddling in the soil above the tunnel as if it were water.

"Mudslide!" Ivypool screeched.

For a heartbeat Bramblestar's paws were rooted to the ground as he watched a chunk of earth above the tunnel entrance begin to give way, carrying the four cats with it. Then he pulled himself together. "Out of the way!" he yowled.

Before the words were out he flung himself across to where Briarlight was lying. With Millie's help he heaved her onto his back, crumbling earth falling all around them, then raced toward the trees. Cats shot away from the entrance, wailing in panic, as the soil roared down, fierce as another storm.

As the sound died away Bramblestar halted and turned around, letting Briarlight slide down from his back. A mound of earth covered the entrance to the tunnel. At first he couldn't see any of the four cats who had been caught in the slide, and his pelt prickled with the memory of the tunnel collapse that had buried Hollyleaf, so many moons ago.

Then Ivypool popped her head out of the heap, spitting earth and floundering through the loose soil as she dragged herself clear. Snowpaw reappeared a moment later, burrowing his way out. The soil at the top of the mound heaved and fell away to reveal Whitewing; she was helping Dewpaw, who seemed dazed, hardly moving at all.

Dustpelt, Cloudtail, and Brightheart dashed up to the heap

of earth and helped the four cats to struggle free. Bramble-star followed hard on their paws. To his relief, none of them seemed seriously hurt. Even Dewpaw, who looked a little unsteady when he stood on solid ground again, soon recovered and began shaking himself furiously to get the soil out of his pelt.

"Ugh! I'll never be clean again!" Ivypool spat. She had shaken off the loose soil, but her fur was still plastered with mud, and her claws were clogged with it.

"Let's thank StarClan it was no worse," Whitewing meowed.

Bramblestar looked at the pile of earth. At first he thought that it was blocking the tunnel, and that cats would have to burrow to release their Clanmates trapped inside. But then he realized that there was a narrow gap beside the mound of soil, just wide enough to let cats in and out of the tunnel.

"Are you all okay in there?" he called.

Purdy squeezed his way out and looked around with a disgusted expression. "What next?" he grunted. "Haven't we got enough trouble, without the forest throwin' earth at us?"

Bramblestar guessed that the rain must have loosened the ground above the tunnel, and the weight of four cats on top of it had been enough to bring it down. "No cat is to go up there again," he ordered. "Not until everything has had a chance to dry out."

"Don't worry, we won't," Whitewing muttered. "I thought I was on my way to StarClan when the ground started disappearing under my paws."

The rest of the Clan gathered around, surveying the mess with wide, wary eyes. Minty looked terrified; Daisy had curled her tail around the kittypet's shoulders, and was mewing something to her in a low voice. Briarlight was managing to drag herself back, with Millie at her side as always.

Dustpelt padded up to Bramblestar and gave the earth mound an experimental prod with one paw. "You know," he meowed, "maybe we shouldn't clear this away. When the wind's in the wrong direction it whistles straight down the tunnel and freezes our fur off, and this would make a good windbreak."

"But won't the wind scatter it?" Bramblestar asked.

"Not if we find something to shore it up with," Dustpelt told him.

Bramblestar nodded to the older warrior. "I'll put you in charge of it, then," he mewed. "See what you can do."

As Dustpelt studied the heap, Bramblestar glanced around again. The panic was over by now and the cats were chatting excitedly about what had happened. He could sense that they were dizzy with relief, that what had seemed to be a dreadful accident had turned out to be not too bad after all.

Bramblestar spotted Dewpaw scooping up a pawful of mud and throwing it at Snowpaw, who ducked to dodge it before scraping up some mud of his own.

"That's enough of that!" Ivypool scolded.

"We can't get any dirtier than we already are," Dewpaw pointed out with a cheeky glint in his eye.

Ivypool sighed. "Apprentices!"

Meanwhile Poppyfrost, Dovewing, and Bumblestripe were helping Leafpool and Jayfeather to check every cat who had been close to the mudslide for possible injuries. But even the cats who had fallen were unhurt.

If this is what Jayfeather's omen foretold, Bramblestar thought, *then we've had a lucky escape.*

"We want to take Whitewing, Ivypool, and the apprentices to the WindClan stream to get a wash," Dovewing reported, padding up to Bramblestar.

Bramblestar flicked his ears back uneasily. "Is that a good idea after all that trouble with WindClan?" he asked. "Can't they wash in the lake?"

"No, the lake water has that awful tang of salt," Whitewing meowed, picking her way over the muddy ground to join Dovewing. "We'd never get it out of our fur."

"Okay, then," Bramblestar decided. "But if you do meet a WindClan patrol, *don't* get into a fight about the water. We have enough problems without that."

"We won't," Dovewing promised. Waving her tail to beckon the apprentices, she led the way across the hill in the direction of the WindClan border.

"What do we need to do?" Squirrelflight asked, padding around the mudpile with a disgusted look on her face. "Don't tell me we have to shift all this."

"No, Dustpelt thinks we can shore it up and use it as a windbreak," Bramblestar replied. "There's still room to get in and out."

Dustpelt struggled up at that moment, dragging a branch.

"We need more of these," he panted. "And stones, as big as you can manage. If we pack them in at the bottom of the pile, they'll stop it from spreading."

"Right," Squirrelflight mewed. "I'll find some other cats to help." She bounded off.

As Bramblestar helped Dustpelt to shove the branch into position, he heard Lilypaw's voice coming from behind him.

"We're supposed to be having hunting practice. But I can't find Poppyfrost and Bumblestripe anywhere."

"Nor can I," Seedpaw added.

Bramblestar glanced over his shoulder. "They've gone to the WindClan stream," he told the apprentices. "They'll be back soon."

Lilypaw and Seedpaw looked disappointed.

"Can we help you instead?" Seedpaw asked. "What are you doing? What do you need?"

The two apprentices crowded up, sniffing curiously at the branch that Dustpelt was still pushing into place.

"We'll get more!" Lilypaw announced, but as she turned she skidded in the mud and Seedpaw tripped over her.

"For StarClan's sake!" Dustpelt snapped. "A cat can't move around here for nuisancy apprentices!"

"But we want to do something useful!" Seedpaw protested, scrambling to her paws.

"Then go and do it someplace else," Dustpelt muttered. "I'm sure you can think of something."

"Find a warrior to take you hunting," Bramblestar suggested, but the two apprentices were already scampering away.

I hope they don't get into trouble, he thought.

He was about to follow them when he was distracted by Leafpool, who came limping up to him, wincing at every paw step.

"What's the matter?" Bramblestar meowed. "Did you wrench your paw when the earth fell?"

Leafpool shook her head. "No, it's that wretched piece of wood again, the one that caught Jayfeather earlier," she complained. "I was sure we'd moved it out of the way, but it must have rolled back."

"You're not badly hurt?"

"No, just annoyed," Leafpool replied. "That stick is more trouble than the mudfall!"

A stick? Bramblestar thought suddenly. *A stick causing trouble? Where have I heard of a stick recently?* Then he remembered. *Jayfeather's Stick of the Fallen! The apprentices spotted it this morning, wedged in the branches of that oak tree. What if they've gone back to fetch it?*

He glanced around, but Lilypaw and Seedpaw were nowhere to be seen.

This is ridiculous! Bramblestar told himself. *You're not a medicine cat; you can't interpret omens.* But uneasiness was rising inside him like the lake water, his paws itching to be on the move. *Maybe I have bees in my brain, but I have to go check for myself.*

Telling Leafpool to carry the troublesome branch a long way away, he headed briskly after the apprentices. *They shouldn't be wandering about by themselves, even if they haven't gone to the lake. They're still very inexperienced.* He tried to remember exactly where they had seen the stick, then realized he would do better to follow the apprentices' scent trail. In spite of the soaking ground and undergrowth, he soon managed to pick it up. His apprehension increased as he realized it was leading straight for the edge of the floods.

As he drew closer to the lake, the unnatural silence of the forest was split by a terrified screech.

"Help!"

Lilypaw!

Bramblestar broke into a run, crashing through the brambles, oblivious of the thorns that tore at his fur. As he broke out of a thicket beside the edge of the flood, he spotted the half-submerged oak tree and Lilypaw thrashing desperately beside it. Peering closer, Bramblestar realized that she was caught up in the ivy that twined around the tree, and she was being pulled underneath the water.

Seedpaw was crouching on the bank, and as Bramblestar charged toward her, she straightened up and leaped into the water. "I'll help you, Lilypaw!"

"Seedpaw! No!" Bramblestar yowled.

But the young cat didn't hear him. Flailing her paws, she swam toward her sister. When she reached the oak tree, she dived underwater to reach Lilypaw, who had given up struggling and disappeared.

Bramblestar pushed as hard as he could, but he felt as if he was wading through mud. Reaching the nearest point of the shore to the submerged tree, he plunged into the water and swam out in a frenzy of fear. Both apprentices bobbed up for a moment, then vanished again. As Bramblestar reached the tree, Lilypaw reappeared alone. Bramblestar grabbed her scruff and supported her, thrashing his paws to keep them both afloat.

"Are you still trapped?" he gasped, speaking around the mouthful of fur.

Lilypaw shook her head. Bramblestar adjusted his grip on her scruff and started to swim back toward dry land, dragging the apprentice with him. She was too exhausted to swim, and by the time Bramblestar hauled her out of the flood, her eyes were closed.

"Lilypaw! Wake up!" he begged, shaking her.

Lilypaw twitched, then rolled over and coughed up several mouthfuls of water. "Where's Seedpaw?" she rasped. "She freed me. . . . She bit through the ivy. . . ."

Bramblestar looked over his shoulder. The water around the oak tree was ruffled but there was no sign of the other apprentice. "Stay there," he ordered. "I'll get Seedpaw."

Back at the oak tree, Bramblestar dived down, barely able to see in the murky water. Unseen tendrils grappled with his legs and head and twined around one paw; he had to wrench hard to pull it free. Then he bumped into a lump of sodden fur, clamped his jaws hard on it, and hauled it to the surface. Seedpaw was a dead weight, motionless and heavy as Bramblestar dragged her back to dry ground.

As he laid Seedpaw beside her sister, Bramblestar heard movement from among the trees. He looked up to see Brightheart and Cinderheart break out from the bushes.

"We heard the yowling," Cinderheart panted. "What happened?"

Brightheart said nothing, just pounced on Seedpaw and

began pressing her belly with rhythmic thrusts. Every so often she paused to put her ear to Seedpaw's chest, before opening the little cat's mouth with one paw to check it was clear. Then she started pounding at Seedpaw's belly again, her face grim. Lilypaw watched, her claws flexing in the sodden ground, while Bramblestar thanked StarClan for all the times Brightheart had helped Cinderpelt, Leafpool, and Jayfeather in their medicine-cat duties.

But this time Seedpaw didn't stir. Water trickled from her jaws, but her eyes didn't open. At last Brightheart sat back, her gaze clouding. "I'm sorry," she whispered. "She's gone."

"Oh, no, no!" Lilypaw flung herself down beside her sister. "It's all my fault! It was my idea to get the stick. I just wanted to be helpful!"

"It wasn't your fault," Cinderheart told her gently. "Come with me. We'll go find your father." She urged Lilypaw to her paws and began to lead her away. Lilypaw went with her reluctantly, looking over her shoulder at the limp body of her sister.

Horror coursed through Bramblestar as he gazed down at Seedpaw. *It's not Lilypaw's fault; it's mine. Why didn't I listen more carefully to Jayfeather and Leafpool? A stick that caused trouble? It should have been obvious!*

A sudden yowl pierced through the air and Brackenfur came hurtling through the trees. "What's going on?" he demanded.

Lilypaw broke away from Cinderheart and flung herself at the golden-brown warrior. "It's Seedpaw!" she sobbed.

Brackenfur wrapped his tail around his daughter's

shoulders. On trembling paws father and daughter approached Seedpaw's body and stood looking down at her.

"How can I bear this?" Brackenfur asked hoarsely. "To lose her mother, and now this . . ."

"She walks with Sorreltail in StarClan now," Bramblestar murmured, but he knew that his words were no comfort at all. "I'll carry her back to camp," he added, crouching down so that Brackenfur could load Seedpaw's body onto his back.

Bramblestar walked slowly back to the tunnel, the other cats in a silent group behind him. He felt as though the weight of the whole forest was crushing down on him in Seedpaw's fragile body.

Is this the role of a Clan leader? he wondered. *To watch my cats die one by one while I can do nothing to save them?*

CHAPTER 14

Another gray dawn found the grief-stricken Clan outside the tunnel, grouped around Seedpaw's body as they kept vigil for her. At length, as the light strengthened, Purdy rose stiffly to his paws. "It's time to bury her," he announced.

"I'll help you," Daisy meowed. "I know it's a duty of the elders, but you can't do it all by yourself, Purdy."

"I'll help too," Brackenfur added from where he sat at Seedpaw's head, with Lilypaw pressed close to his side.

The three cats picked up Seedpaw's body between them and gently carried her away into the trees. Sandstorm padded over to Lilypaw and sat beside her, giving her ears a comforting lick. Bramblestar saw that the little cat couldn't stop shivering.

Beckoning Leafpool, he asked, "Is Lilypaw ill?"

"I'm not sure," Leafpool replied, her eyes sorrowful as she gazed at the apprentice. "It may be the onset of whitecough, or it may just be grief. It's so hard when we can't get properly dry and warm."

"At least yesterday's patrol over the border brought back a decent haul of fresh-kill," Thornclaw put in. "I'll lead another patrol there today, if you like."

"Good idea," meowed Squirrelflight. "I'll go too."

"We have to find some dry bedding," Bramblestar declared. His pelt still prickled with concern for Lilypaw, but he was aware that it was his duty to pull the Clan out of its grief and get back to normal. And if he could find the bedding they needed, it would help Lilypaw, as well as Briarlight and the other cats with whitecough.

"Where are you going to look?" Spiderleg asked. "Even if it's not underwater, it's soaked through. There's no sun to dry anything out, and it looks like it's going to rain again soon."

"Spiderleg's right," Daisy mewed. "I've looked everywhere for moss, feathers, dry leaves, even inside hollow trees, and there's nothing."

Dovewing took a pace forward, her eyes shining. "What about those pelts in the Twoleg dens, Bramblestar?" she mewed. "Remember? They were dry, and really soft, too."

For a moment Bramblestar was struck silent by Dovewing's extraordinary suggestion. *Raid Twoleg dens for bedding?* Then he realized that she could be right. *This could be our only chance of getting dry bedding to help Briarlight—and stop the rest of the Clan from getting whitecough.* But a sense of dread stirred in him, as if he were looking down into dark water. *Can I really justify taking cats back into that dangerous, flooded place?*

"I'll go if you want, Bramblestar," Graystripe offered, stepping up to his shoulder.

His Clanmate's courage made up Bramblestar's mind. "No, you've done it once," he meowed. "This time I'll take

Poppyfrost, Lionblaze, and Cinderheart, if they're willing."

The three warriors nodded, looking somber.

"You've done it once, too, Bramblestar," Squirrelflight pointed out with an edge to her tone.

"And I'm going to do it again," he snapped.

Squirrelflight snorted. "Being Clan leader isn't just about being the bravest, you mouse-brained idiot."

Bramblestar dug his claws into the wet ground. "I'm going," he insisted stubbornly. "I can't ask my Clanmates to do something that I wouldn't do myself. Come on, the sooner we go, the sooner we'll be back."

Refusing to argue anymore, he set out with his patrol to cross ShadowClan territory. Clouds surged black and ominous above their heads, though so far that day there had been no more rain.

"I wonder where all the ShadowClan cats are," Lionblaze meowed as they headed through the deserted pinewoods. "I'd have expected to see a dawn patrol by now."

"There are no fresh scents, either," Poppyfrost added.

"Maybe they've stayed in their camp to welcome Rowanstar back from the Moonpool," Bramblestar suggested.

A stab of fellowship for the new ShadowClan leader pierced through Bramblestar as he remembered how awe-inspiring his own nine-lives ceremony had been. *I had to deal with the aftermath of the Great Battle, and Rowanstar will have to deal with the flood,* he thought. *Great StarClan, let the water go down soon, so we can all get back to normal!*

When they emerged from the trees near the small

Thunderpath, Lionblaze and the others stood aghast to see how far the floodwater stretched.

"Where's RiverClan?" Cinderheart asked, her voice shaking.

"Farther away from the lake," Bramblestar replied, reminding her how he and his patrol had located the RiverClan cats on their first expedition. "They're okay, for now at least."

Though he said nothing to the others, Bramblestar was alarmed to see that the water level was no lower. If anything, the flood was a bit deeper. *We'll have to be extra careful,* he told himself, pushing down the stirring of fear in his belly.

He led his three Clanmates alongside the Thunderpath and showed them how they could cross using the top of the drowned monster.

"I never thought monsters could be useful for *anything!*" Lionblaze muttered as he launched himself into the water.

On the other side, Bramblestar took the lead along the fences until he spotted the Twoleg den where they had found Minty. He was thankful to see that the entrance was still open. "This way," he meowed, readying himself for the awkward leap from the fence. "See that thing wedging the piece of wood ajar?" he added. "Graystripe says it's called a chair. We have to jump onto it, and then we can get inside."

"What should we do if we fall in?" Poppyfrost asked nervously.

"Swim," Bramblestar told her, pushing off with a massive effort and landing with all four paws safely on the flat, wooden surface of the chair.

He stepped aside to make room for Lionblaze to follow, and then Poppyfrost. The tortoiseshell she-cat misjudged the distance, and though her forepaws struck the Twoleg chair, her hind paws slid into the water. For a moment she thrashed helplessly, until Lionblaze grabbed her by the scruff and pulled her on.

"Thanks!" she gasped. "I never want to see any more water as long as I live!"

Once Cinderheart had made the jump safely, Bramblestar led the way to the upper level of the den. His pelt stood on end along his spine, even though there was no sign of Twolegs, and he saw that his companions were equally wary. All their coats were bristling as they gazed around at the unfamiliar Twoleg things, and they set their paws down as lightly as if they were stalking mice.

Cinderheart was the only one of them to show anything but alarm and the need to get out of there as soon as possible. Her eyes looked ready to pop out as she studied their surroundings. "Can't we explore a bit?" she begged. "I've never been inside a Twoleg den before."

"No, we can't," Lionblaze responded before Bramblestar had the chance to reply. "Let's just do what we've come to do."

The Twoleg pelts were still heaped on the floor on the upper level, where the first patrol had found them.

"These are great!" Poppyfrost purred, kneading one with her forepaws. "So soft and dry, and the whole Clan could sleep on just one of them."

Bramblestar sniffed warily at the pelts. "They smell like

sheep," he muttered. "But I can't imagine how sheep pelts would get inside a Twoleg den." *Actually, I don't want to imagine....*

Struggling with the heavy folds, the cats dragged the pelts down to the lower level, as far as the edge of the flood.

"How are we going to carry these across the water?" Cinderheart asked. "We don't want to get them wet."

Bramblestar thought for a moment. He pictured Minty in her tub and glanced around, looking for something the same size and shape. Finally he spotted a round black object, lying on its side near the edge of the water. It had a weird smell, but when he tested it with his teeth it felt strong and slightly chewy.

"It seems okay," he commented. "Let's see if it floats."

With Poppyfrost helping, he dragged the black tub to the edge of the water and pushed it in. It bobbed on the surface, and when Bramblestar stretched out his neck to peer inside, he couldn't see any leaks.

"It's fine," he announced. "Let's get the pelts inside. We should be able to push it across the water and keep them dry."

It was an awkward job to haul the tub out again and pack the pelts inside. By now the strain of working inside a Twoleg den was beginning to get to Bramblestar. His skin crawled with nervousness, though he wasn't sure exactly what he was afraid of. The rest of the patrol felt the same, he could tell, their ears laid back and their tails twitching. Every cat jumped at the slightest sound.

"We can only fit one pelt in here," Lionblaze meowed, kneading at the fluffy folds with his paws to pack it down harder.

"Then let's leave the others and go," Bramblestar responded. He was beginning to wonder if this mission had been a good idea. *I just want to get back to camp.*

Nudging the tub with their paws, the cats managed to make their way across the kitchen to the den's entrance. Lionblaze took the lead to jump onto the fence, with Poppyfrost and Cinderheart following.

I guess I get to swim again, Bramblestar thought with a sigh. Taking a deep breath, he plunged into the water and began swimming behind the tub, pushing it along with his nose. The current tugged at him, while unseen things below the surface swiped at his furiously paddling legs. He had to push away the hideous memory of Lilypaw trapped in the ivy around the oak tree, and Seedpaw's pathetic drowned body lying above the waterline.

Bramblestar saw that the ground rose steeply on the other side of the Thunderpath, just beyond the row of Twoleg dens, so he pushed the tub in that direction, toward the closest stretch of dry ground. His Clanmates kept pace with him along fences and across the roofs of drowned monsters.

I wish I'd never agreed to this, Bramblestar told himself as he struggled to keep his aching legs moving. *I hate swimming, and I can't see why RiverClan cats would ever want to get their paws wet.*

At last he made it to the sloping ground and staggered out of the water onto the slippery, muddy grass. While he stood there, panting, his Clanmates raced over and helped him to haul up the tub that held the pelt. It was awkward to move, and tipped to one side, spilling part of the pelt out onto the ground.

"Now it's all muddy," Poppyfrost murmured, looking

disappointed as she tried to brush off the sticky streaks.

"It's still more or less dry," Lionblaze pointed out, shoving the folds back into the tub as fast as he could. "It'll be fine."

"We did it!" Cinderheart exclaimed, her eyes glowing.

Glancing around, Bramblestar realized they still had a stretch of water to cross before they could reach the lakeside and follow the shore back to their camp. *At least we can keep our paws dry for a while on this bank,* he thought, bounding up to the highest point to get a good view of their surroundings.

On the other side of the shallow ridge, he saw a Twoleg den built into the slope. He was about to turn away again when he heard the thin wail of a cat. Looking more closely, he saw a dark brown she-cat pawing at something on the ground, close to the wall of the den. Her movements were frantic, matching the noise she was making. Bramblestar tried to hear what she was saying, but the wind in his ears meant he couldn't make out the words.

Oh, no! he thought. *Another kittypet that needs rescuing! Could this one be stuck in the mud?*

For a moment Bramblestar was tempted to turn away and pretend he hadn't seen. But he knew that the sight and sound of the distressed cat would haunt him if he refused to help. Bramblestar raced down the slope until he reached the Twoleg den, and approached the kittypet. "What's wrong? Can I help?" he called.

To his astonishment the kittypet swung around to face him with her lips drawn back in a snarl. "Stay out of this!" she meowed, giving him a shove in the chest to emphasize her words.

Bramblestar stared at her. The she-cat's amber gaze met his without flinching. *She's bold, for a kittypet!* he thought, admiring her courage in spite of her hostility.

The faint sound of yowling drew Bramblestar's attention to the den. At ground level there was a narrow opening covered by transparent Twoleg stuff. The yowls were coming from a gray tabby tom who had pressed his face against the transparent barrier and was caterwauling for help.

"There must be a way to get him out of there," Bramblestar mewed, pawing at the gap.

"What would you know about it, flea-pelt?" the kittypet hissed.

Bramblestar felt his shoulder fur begin to bristle and consciously forced it to lie flat again. *She's asking for a clawed ear!*

"I've seen stuff like this before," he replied, remembering the way that he and the others had got into the Twoleg den from the ledge while they were rescuing Minty. Experimentally he pressed his forepaws against the top of the transparent barrier, and let out a grunt of satisfaction as it swung inward, opening a narrow gap at the bottom.

But the space wasn't wide enough for the tabby tom to get out.

"Press harder," the she-cat ordered, adding her weight to Bramblestar's. "Frankie, you push from the bottom."

With all three cats heaving, the gap opened up and the tabby tom, Frankie, was able to squeeze out. His pelt was bristling and his eyes glared with a mixture of fury and terror. His pelt was soaked up to his belly fur, and when Bramblestar peered down into the den he could see floodwater sloshing about just below the opening.

"Thanks!" Frankie gasped. "I thought I was going to drown!"

The brown she-cat's gaze raked over Bramblestar, her hostility fading, though she still remained wary. "Yeah, thanks." Her tone was grudging. "My name's Jessy, and this is Frankie."

"I'm Bramblestar." He eyed Jessy, intrigued by her independence and spirit. "You're pretty brave, for a kittypet."

"Really?" Jessy's tail lashed. "Well, you keep a pretty civil tongue in your head, for a wild cat."

Bramblestar was looking for a retort when he heard paw steps approaching from behind and turned to see the rest of his patrol running down the slope.

Lionblaze halted a couple of tail-lengths away, his eyes wide with shock. "Great StarClan!" he exclaimed. "More kittypets!"

CHAPTER 15

❧

Bramblestar surveyed the kittypets more closely. Jessy looked in fairly good shape, but Frankie's fur was wet and clumped, his ribs were showing, and he was shivering.

"Jessy, have you seen Benny?" the tabby asked urgently. "I saw him get washed away when the water came. I couldn't reach him!"

Jessy shook her head. "No, I haven't. I'm sorry."

Frankie spun around to face Bramblestar and the rest of the patrol, his eyes wide and distraught. "Have you seen him?" he demanded. "He's my brother—he's tabby like me, but darker."

"No, sorry," Bramblestar replied. "Look," he added, reluctant to offer more help to kittypets, but aware that he couldn't just leave them, "why don't you come back to our camp? There's food there, and—"

"No!" Frankie exclaimed, backing away with his ears flattened. "I have to stay here, in case Benny comes back."

Bramblestar exchanged glances with his patrol. They were all looking uncomfortable and impatient. "We can't hang around here," he meowed to Jessy. "But we'd like to help. Can you persuade Frankie to come with us? He looks ill, and there are cats in our camp who can help him."

Jessy gave him a thoughtful nod and padded up to Frankie. "Are you flea-brained?" she snapped. "These cats just saved your life. The least you can do is come with them, so you can get better."

Bramblestar repressed a purr of amusement. *It hasn't taken Jessy long to start trusting us!*

Frankie's shoulders sagged. "Okay," he mewed in a small voice.

Jessy stayed close beside him as Bramblestar led the way back to where he had left the tub and the pelt. "What are you doing?" she exclaimed, giving the Twoleg stuff a sniff. "You *stole* this tub and blanket from the Twolegs? I have to say, wild cat, I like your style!"

"Whatever," Bramblestar muttered, feeling embarrassed.

Lionblaze and Cinderheart pushed the tub along in the shallow water while the rest of the patrol padded beside them, dry-pawed. Jessy stayed close to Frankie, quietly encouraging him when his paw steps faltered.

Eventually the cats reached the end of the bank and the stretch of water that extended from the lake. Bramblestar gazed at it in dismay. A strong current flowed into the lake, but water was surging from the other direction too, and where the two currents met the floodwater tossed about in choppy waves.

"It's too dangerous to swim across here," Cinderheart warned.

"Why don't we see if we can get closer to the lake?" Poppyfrost suggested. "The water's quieter there, where we crossed before."

Bramblestar nodded. "Good idea."

But as they began hauling the tub along the edge of the turbulent water, Cinderheart stopped with her ears pricked. "Wait—listen! What's that?"

Every cat halted. Bramblestar heard a faint buzzing noise. "It sounds like a monster," he murmured. "But there haven't been any monsters around here since the water rose."

"Only the drowned ones," Lionblaze agreed.

A few more moments passed, and Bramblestar was about to give the order to move on, when Cinderheart exclaimed, "There it is!"

Following where her tail was pointing, Bramblestar spotted a water monster with two Twolegs standing on its back as it swam back and forth across the flooded Thunderpath. They seemed to be looking into each of the Twoleg dens.

"That settles it," he hissed. "We can't go that way. We can't let them see us."

Wearily they retraced their steps to where the two currents met. "We'll have to cross here," Bramblestar announced.

His Clanmates exchanged glances; Bramblestar could see them bracing themselves for the ordeal ahead. Jessy's tail-tip was twitching apprehensively, but she didn't protest.

Frankie, however, had flattened himself close to the ground, trembling, his eyes glazed with terror. "I can't. . . ." he moaned. "I saw Benny get swept away. I know I'll drown!"

"I'll help you," Jessy began, but the tabby tom only moaned more loudly and began backing away from the water's edge.

Jessy turned to Bramblestar, letting out a soft hiss of

frustration through her teeth. "We can't leave him here," she mewed. "What if we put him into the tub with the blanket?"

Bramblestar thought the idea sounded crazy, but there was no alternative. They couldn't hang around much longer on this side of the water, in case the Twolegs saw them. "We'll give it a try," he agreed.

Jessy went up to Frankie and nudged him. "Come on, Frankie. We're going to give you a ride." She explained her suggestion to the terrified tom. "You'll die if you stay here," she finished dramatically.

Dumb with fear, Frankie allowed Jessy to shove him over to the tub. He climbed in on top of the pelt, digging his claws hard into the folds. Bramblestar and Lionblaze pushed the tub onto the turbulent water and waded in after it. The force of the current nearly knocked Bramblestar off his paws, and he drew in his breath in a gasp of terror. *There's no turning back now.*

The other cats followed as they began to swim. All Bramblestar could see was the tub, the swirling water, and Lionblaze's drenched golden head beside him.

Then Cinderheart appeared a tail-length away. "Steer over this way," she panted. "It's not far now."

As Bramblestar tried to turn, a wave slapped against the side of the tub. It lurched over, and Frankie let out a terrified screech as water slopped inside it. Lionblaze managed to give the tub a shove, righting it and sending it on its new course. At the same moment Poppyfrost's head appeared among the waves, bobbing up and down as she swam right into the path of the tub.

"Poppyfrost, look out!" Bramblestar yowled.

The tortoiseshell she-cat, focused on struggling through the waves, hadn't seen that the tub had changed course. She turned at Bramblestar's yowl and her eyes widened in terror as she saw the tub bearing down on her. She thrashed her legs faster, and Bramblestar tried to thrust the tub aside, but it was too late. The side of it knocked into Poppyfrost, driving her under the surface of the water.

Bramblestar took a gulp of air and dived down, dark thoughts of Seedpaw's death flickering through his mind. Would he even find his Clanmate in this swollen river? He wanted to let out a screech of joy when he bumped into Poppyfrost's body. He grabbed her and hauled her back to the surface.

Poppyfrost was still conscious, writhing and coughing up water. "Thanks, Bramblestar," she gasped after a few moments. "I'm okay. I can swim."

Bramblestar was reluctant to let her go, but just then he caught sight of Cinderheart paddling up to them.

"I'll swim beside her," the gray she-cat mewed. "I'll make sure she's okay."

Bramblestar swam back to the tub, which was riding lower in the water. Frankie was peering over the edge, letting out terrified whimpers. Bramblestar joined Lionblaze in pushing, and spotted Jessy still swimming strongly a fox-length away.

"We're nearly there!" the brown kittypet called.

At last Bramblestar felt the tub scrape against solid ground, and realized that he could lower his paws and stand. He and Lionblaze dragged the tub to the very edge of the water so that

Frankie could crawl out. The tabby tom looked stunned, as if he didn't know where he was or what was happening anymore.

Looking down into the tub, Bramblestar saw that the pelt was soaked through with the water that had splashed in during the crossing. *I've risked all our lives for a wet pelt and two homeless kittypets,* he thought with mingled disgust and guilt.

He took the lead as the patrol headed back through ShadowClan territory, still pushing the tub containing the pelt along at the edge of the floodwater. They figured it was easy to keep the pelt where it was, to keep it from getting even muddier.

Suddenly Poppyfrost, who was bringing up the rear, called out, "I can smell ShadowClan!"

Bramblestar stopped and tasted the air. The scent was strong and fresh, and getting stronger, telling him that several ShadowClan cats were approaching. Swiftly he shoved the tub into the shelter of a bramble thicket.

"Climb trees!" he ordered in a low voice.

Cinderheart and Poppyfrost obeyed instantly, streaking up the trunk of the nearest pine tree and peering down from its branches.

Lionblaze hesitated. "You think they'll be hostile?" he asked.

"We're on their territory, with *kittypets*," Bramblestar retorted. "What do you think?"

"Good point," Lionblaze muttered.

Bramblestar turned to Jessy. "Can you climb?"

"Yes, I'll be fine, but Frankie won't."

The gray tabby tom had slumped into a sodden bundle of misery at the foot of a tree. Jessy bounded over and nudged him. "Frankie, wake up! You have to climb!"

"Leave me alone!"

Bramblestar tasted the air again and realized that the ShadowClan patrol would reach them in a few heartbeats. He knew that if he left Frankie where he was, the ShadowClan cats would try to drive him off, and probably injure him badly if he couldn't run away fast enough.

"Jessy, climb the tree," he ordered. "Lionblaze and I will help Frankie."

To his relief the she-cat didn't argue. She clawed her way up the trunk, clumsily but fast, and joined Cinderheart and Poppyfrost in the branches.

Bramblestar turned to Lionblaze. "You push and I'll pull," he meowed.

Grabbing Frankie by the scruff, Bramblestar dug his claws into the trunk of the pine tree. It felt like hauling a piece of dead prey, although Frankie was heavier than even the biggest squirrel. Lionblaze boosted him from below, and gradually they began to climb.

Bramblestar's belly churned because they were taking so long to reach the denser branches, where they would be hidden. Frankie wasn't even trying to help himself; he seemed paralyzed by fear. As they forced themselves higher, Bramblestar could hear racing paw steps and the sounds of cats brushing through undergrowth.

They must have seen us!

Panting, he dragged Frankie onto the closest branch.

Lionblaze joined them a moment later, and the dark pine needles enfolded them. Peering down, Bramblestar saw the ShadowClan patrol burst out of the bushes. Crowfrost was in the lead, with Pinenose, Ferretclaw, and his apprentice, Spikepaw.

For a heartbeat Bramblestar expected them to surround the tree and yowl out a challenge. Instead they just dashed on, passing right under the tree without picking up the Thunder-Clan or kittypet scent. Their fur was bristling and their eyes were wide with tension, darting here and there as they ran.

"What's wrong with them?" Lionblaze whispered, staring after the ShadowClan patrol. "They're not hunting, or checking scent markers."

"Who knows?" Bramblestar meowed tiredly. "At least they didn't spot us. Now, help me get Frankie down off this branch."

By the time the cats reached the ThunderClan border they were all wet and exhausted.

"This is where we live," Bramblestar told Jessy and Frankie.

"Here? Really?" Jessy sounded incredulous as she gazed around.

Bramblestar could understand the kittypet's disbelief. *The territory looks so different since the storm.* Everywhere had the harsh tang of the sun-drown-water, and even the trees that were clear of the flood looked sick. Bramblestar wished he could show his home to Jessy on a sunny day in greenleaf, with leaves rustling above and the warm scent of prey in every thicket.

They had abandoned the tub at the edge of the lake because

it was too awkward to push through the undergrowth. Poppy-frost and Lionblaze dragged the pelt between them as the patrol headed for the tunnel. By now it was wet, filthy, and stinking, and kept tearing when it caught on concealed roots or sharp stones.

As they approached the makeshift camp, Bramblestar spotted several cats outside the tunnel and saw their looks of shock as they realized that he was bringing more kittypets to join them.

Jayfeather, who had been supervising Briarlight's exercises, came to meet the returning patrol. "What's this?" he demanded, giving Jessy and Frankie a disdainful sniff. "Are you turning ThunderClan into a home for lost kittypets?"

Bramblestar glared at his medicine cat; even though he knew he was adding to the Clan's problems, he thought Jayfeather could have sounded more welcoming. "They needed our help," he retorted. "Frankie especially. Do you have anything to calm him down?"

Jayfeather heaved a deep sigh. "Like I don't have enough to do. Okay, I'll take a look." He trotted back to the tunnel entrance and vanished. Soon he reappeared with a bundle of thyme leaves in his jaws. "Here," he mewed to Frankie, dropping the leaves in front of him. "Eat these. They're good for shock. When you're feeling better, I'll give you poppy seed so you can sleep."

Frankie sniffed the leaves and took a step back, curling his lip. "I don't eat green stuff," he mewed.

Jayfeather shrugged. "Okay, so suffer. Your choice."

"You should eat them," Cinderheart urged him. "They really will make you feel better."

Frankie still hesitated until Jessy gave him a hard nudge. "Eat, flea-brain."

Still reluctant, Frankie licked up the leaves and swallowed them, then kept passing his tongue over his jaws as if he was trying to get rid of the taste.

Bramblestar realized that Squirrelflight had padded up beside him and was surveying the kittypets with a disapproving gaze. "Honestly, Bramblestar," she meowed, "what were you thinking? Two more kittypets! How are we going to feed all these extra mouths? It's not like they can hunt for themselves."

"Would you rather I left them behind to die?" Bramblestar asked.

Squirrelflight rolled her eyes. "No, I suppose not. But it's not making life any easier. Did you at least bring back something useful?"

"There's this Twoleg pelt," Bramblestar meowed, pointing with his tail at the sodden object Lionblaze and Poppyfrost had dragged up.

"That?" Squirrelflight wrinkled her nose. "You went all that way and put your Clanmates in danger for that? It's disgusting!"

"No, it might not be so bad," Daisy mewed, looking up from where she and Leafpool were sniffing the pelt. "We can stretch it over a bush to dry it."

Squirrelflight just let out a snort.

Even though Bramblestar had to agree with her, he was hurt by his deputy's dismissiveness. Before he could reply, Jessy pushed her way forward.

"Who do you think you are?" she snarled at Squirrelflight. "You should be grateful to Bramblestar. He risked his life to get that!"

Squirrelflight seemed too taken aback to match the kittypet's aggressiveness. "I know how brave Bramblestar is," she responded, then added, "I'm going to sort out patrols. Bramblestar, you need to rest and eat."

Jessy watched Squirrelflight as she stalked off. "Wow, is she always like that?"

"Yeah, pretty much," Bramblestar replied.

Jessy went over to join Frankie, who was still shivering. Minty poked her head out of the tunnel, then picked her way carefully over the muddy ground to touch noses with the other two kittypets. It seemed as if they already knew one another, but it was hardly a joy-filled reunion.

"Thanks for getting the pelt." Graystripe had padded up while Bramblestar was watching the kittypets. "It looks like the floods are more dangerous than we realized," he commented with a nod at the three.

Bramblestar murmured in agreement. All three kittypets were huddled together, small and hunched against the wind. Even Jessy looked out of place and miserable. *What are we going to do with them?* Bramblestar wondered.

CHAPTER 16

❧

Bramblestar woke from a restless sleep, feeling the cold of the tunnel floor striking through his pelt all the way to his bones. Staggering to his paws, he picked his way among his sleeping Clanmates until he could slip past the mudfall and into the open. He padded forward a couple of tail-lengths and stood watching as the sky paled toward dawn and the last warriors of StarClan winked out.

A light rain was falling, swept across the forest by a chilly breeze, but the cloud cover seemed thinner, as if the storm might be over at last. Looking downward through the trees, Bramblestar could just make out the silver shimmer of the lake. Behind him in the shadowy tunnel he could hear rasping coughs coming from Amberpaw. Another cat stirred and muttered something grumpily.

"Here, Amberpaw." Bramblestar's ears twitched at Leafpool's whispered words. "Have a drink from this wet moss. It should help your throat."

A loud snore drowned any response from Amberpaw. *Purdy,* Bramblestar thought, pleased that the old cat was getting some rest. But his relief died away a moment later as he heard a whimper from deeper in the tunnel.

"Seedpaw . . . I want Seedpaw."

"I'm here, Lilypaw." That was Dewpaw, his voice comforting. "Lie closer to me. Seedpaw's in StarClan now."

Bramblestar's heart felt as heavy as a rock. *Too many cats have been lost. . . . There are too many scratches on the Stick of the Fallen.* And now the stick itself had caused the death of a young apprentice. Urgent questions swept through Bramblestar's mind like leaves driven by the wind. *Will the waters ever recede? Will the Clans be forced to look for yet another home? What would Firestar have done?*

He was still vainly searching for answers in his thoughts when he heard soft paw steps behind him. Glancing over his shoulder, he saw Jessy emerge from the tunnel, shivering as the rain spattered against her pelt. *I bet Firestar wouldn't have filled the Clan with kittypet mouths to feed,* he thought ruefully.

Jessy's jaws gaped in a yawn; her tail was drooping, and she was clearly tired. Her gaze darted from side to side as she left the safety of the tunnel. But her paw steps were firm as she walked over to stand beside Bramblestar.

"You don't live in this tunnel all the time, do you?" she asked curiously.

"No, our real camp is much better than this," Bramblestar replied. "Do you want to see it? I could show you some of the territory if you like." *We'll be back before patrols have to go out,* he told himself, feeling slightly guilty at the thought of going off alone. *And we could both do with a brisk run to warm up.*

"Okay," Jessy agreed. "Lead the way, wild cat."

As they headed down the slope toward the stone hollow, Bramblestar realized that Jessy was stumbling over roots and bramble tendrils. She winced and let out a startled yelp as water showered over her from the low branch of a hazel bush.

"Are you okay?" he called. "We can go back if you want."

"I'm fine," Jessy insisted, giving her pelt a shake.

Bramblestar was half-amused and half-impressed by her determination. *She's not like any kittypet I've ever met before.*

Reaching the top of the cliff, Bramblestar pushed through the brambles, leaving a tunnel for Jessy to follow, until they could look down into the flooded hollow. "You see that ledge with the hole in the rock?" he meowed, pointing with his tail to where the Highledge was just visible above the water. "That's the Clan leader's den . . . my den, now. Just below it, but a bit closer to us, used to be the warriors' den. The apprentices' den and the nursery were over the other side. The elders'—"

"Wow!" Jessy interrupted, her eyes wide. "You're really well organized!"

"We have to look after ourselves," Bramblestar meowed. "We can't rely on Twolegs out here."

Annoyance flashed briefly in Jessy's eyes. "Just because we're kittypets doesn't mean we're weak and lazy," she retorted.

"I never said it did." To avoid an argument Bramblestar retreated from the cliff edge and beckoned with his tail. "Do you want to see some more of our territory?"

He led the way along the top of the floodwater toward the WindClan border. Jessy padded at his shoulder. She seemed to have forgotten her irritation, instead gazing around her with interest, though she still tended to jump at the creaking of a branch or the sucking sound of water as it lapped against the slope.

Soon Bramblestar heard the rushing of the stream that marked the border, and his nose twitched at a strong scent of WindClan. Emerging from the trees, he spotted four cats heading downstream on the ThunderClan side: the Wind-Clan deputy, Harespring, with his apprentice, Slightpaw, along with Crowfeather and Heathertail.

Bramblestar stiffened with rage. The WindClan warriors were blatantly trespassing. *They're so determined to keep the fresh water to themselves!* He knew he couldn't confront the Wind-Clan cats when he was out here alone except for a kittypet. "Let's go this way," he suggested, thankful that Jessy didn't seem to have noticed the patrol, and steered her away toward the top of the ridge.

Jessy followed, keeping on determinedly even though she started puffing as they headed up the steep hillside. When they reached the ridge, the brown she-cat's eyes stretched wide with amazement at the view over the flooded lake and the remains of the forest.

"It's amazing up here! I feel like a bird! I didn't realize how far the water stretches," she added more seriously. "Look, that's my housefolk's den over there. The floods are all around it."

Bramblestar wasn't sure which of the Twoleg dens she was pointing at. They all looked the same to him, poking up out of the waste of water.

"I used to like hunting in the backyard," Jessy went on, "and in Frankie and Benny's yard. Theirs was the best—full of thick bushes!"

By now Bramblestar was feeling colder than ever, and anxious to get back to the camp after spotting the WindClan patrol on the wrong side of the stream. "Yes, but you didn't really hunt, did you?" he mewed. "It's not like you needed to catch your own food. I bet you never caught a thing."

"Catching your own food doesn't make you better than me," Jessy snapped. "Stop being so smug. No cat can help where they're born!"

Bramblestar was taken aback by the strength of feeling in her tone and her blazing eyes. "Okay, you have a point," he admitted. "You know," he went on, hoping to make it up to her, "our last leader, Firestar, was a kittypet. He came into the forest when he was six moons old, and he was the best cat in the forest. Every cat in ThunderClan misses him." His voice shook on the last few words.

Jessy's anger faded. "Really? I wish I'd had a chance to meet him."

"I wish you had, too," Bramblestar responded, sadness washing over him as he realized how impossible that was. *I'd give every bit of prey in the forest to have Firestar back.*

When he and Jessy returned to the tunnel, Bramblestar found the cats milling about outside while Squirrelflight sorted out the first patrols of the day.

"Where have you been?" she demanded, swinging around to confront Bramblestar. Her green eyes sparked with annoyance.

"I took Jessy for a walk, to show her some of the territory," Bramblestar explained.

Squirrelflight curled her lip. "If Jessy wants to see the territory, she can join a patrol!"

Irritation sparked beneath Bramblestar's fur. *Am I Clan leader or aren't I?* "I can walk where I like, and with any cat I like," he retorted.

Squirrelflight said no more, but her shoulder fur was bristling, and Bramblestar felt as if the air between them had become as cold as ice. "Dovewing, Lionblaze," she meowed, ignoring Bramblestar, "take a patrol each and check the ShadowClan border. Start at opposite ends and meet in the middle—and make sure the scent marks are good and strong," she finished.

Lionblaze dipped his head. "Which cats should we take?"

"Let's see . . ." Squirrelflight glanced around. "Blossomfall, Dustpelt, and Birchfall can go with you. Dovewing, take Spiderleg, Brightheart, and Cherryfall."

Unseen by his deputy, Bramblestar gave a nod of approval. She was right to double the patrols on the ShadowClan border. *We can't trust those cats to stay inside their own markers, and we know how badly their territory has been affected!*

"I'll help by going on patrol if you like," Frankie offered, padding up to stand beside Squirrelflight.

Bramblestar twitched his whiskers in surprise. The gray tabby tom was looking brighter and more determined this morning, very different from the shrinking, moaning creature who had come to the camp the night before. *Good job, Jayfeather! Your herbs have really helped him.*

Glancing at the gathering patrols, Bramblestar realized that all the warriors looked distinctly unimpressed at the idea of Frankie taking part. "No, thanks, Frankie," he meowed. "It's a bit soon for that. Get some rest today, and we'll find you something to do soon."

"Patrolling with a kittypet?" Blossomfall muttered. "I'd sooner eat fox dung!"

"Yeah," Spiderleg agreed. "He'd *really* scare ShadowClan."

Bramblestar glared at them, hoping that Frankie hadn't heard. "The sick cats shouldn't go out," he mewed to Squirrelflight as the ShadowClan patrols moved off. "Sandstorm and Amberpaw need to rest and stay dry."

Squirrelflight nodded, her previous annoyance seemingly forgotten. "Mousewhisker has started coughing," she reported. "And Berrynose is looking pretty sorry himself. I think they should stay in camp, too." She flicked her tail toward the tunnel entrance, where Berrynose was crouched miserably, his cream-colored fur ungroomed. Poppyfrost sat beside him, giving his ears a comforting lick.

"Okay, fine," Bramblestar meowed, trying to push down a swell of anxiety. *How many more of us will get sick before this is over?*

"I'm going to lead a patrol along the WindClan border," Squirrelflight went on. "Poppyfrost, Cloudtail, and Thornclaw, you can come with me."

Poppyfrost quickly said good-bye to Berrynose. She and the other cats gathered around Squirrelflight and set out. They had gone several fox-lengths down the slope before Bramblestar remembered what he had seen that morning.

"Hey, Squirrelflight, hold on a moment!" he called.

Squirrelflight turned and padded back up the slope toward him. "What?"

"When I was out with Jessy I spotted a WindClan patrol on our side of the stream," Bramblestar told her. "You should keep a lookout for—"

"What, you only think to tell us that now?" Squirrelflight's tail lashed and her green eyes narrowed in fury. "There are trespassers on our territory and it slipped your mind?"

Bramblestar forced his neck fur to lie flat, knowing that his deputy had some reason for her anger. *I should have come straight back here and sent out a patrol.*

"Those crow-food eaters! How dare they?" Thornclaw exclaimed, following Squirrelflight back up the slope.

"Let's chase them off!" Ivypool hissed, coming to join her Clanmates with Bumblestripe just behind.

"They're probably back in their own camp by now," Squirrelflight snapped with another flick of her tail.

"You know," Bumblestripe began thoughtfully, "they must have had trouble crossing the stream. Now that it's flooded, it's too wide to jump across for the whole length of the border, and the current is far too strong for them to swim. They must be crossing farther up. If we could find the place, there might be a way to guard or block it."

"That's a great idea," Bramblestar mewed. "I'll lead a patrol upstream right away and check it out. You can come with me to investigate, Bumblestripe, and you too, Ivypool."

"I'll get Snowpaw," Ivypool mewed, racing back to the tunnel mouth and calling for her apprentice.

"Can I come too?" Jessy asked, bright-eyed. When Bramblestar hesitated, unsure about taking a kittypet on what could be a dangerous patrol, she added, "I'd like to help, and I know I can't hunt." Blinking, she shot him a look of exaggerated innocence, and Bramblestar knew she was reminding him of their earlier conversation.

"Okay," he agreed. "But do exactly what I tell you."

Squirrelflight looked annoyed at the addition of the kitty-pet; then Bramblestar reflected that perhaps she was just worried about the invasion. "I'll take my patrol to the bottom of the stream and we'll work our way up," she meowed. "If we meet the trespassers, we'll chase them off."

"Oh, yes," Thornclaw added, baring his teeth in a snarl.

"If you find the crossing place," Squirrelflight went on to Bramblestar, "you should hide there and let the WindClan cats go back to their own territory. Then do what you can to block it."

"Right," Bramblestar responded, feeling amused. *Just who's Clan leader here?* He waited until Squirrelflight had left at the head of her patrol, and Ivypool had returned with Snowpaw, who was bouncing excitedly at the thought of tackling Wind-Clan.

"Stay close to your mentor," Bramblestar warned him. He wasn't sure it was wise to add an apprentice to the group. *Still, Snowpaw can look after himself better than Jessy.* He was about to set out when he heard his name being called, and spotted Jayfeather emerging from the tunnel. Bramblestar waited for his medicine cat to cross the wet grass to his side.

"Bramblestar, be careful," Jayfeather mewed breathlessly.

"Have you had another dream?" Bramblestar demanded. "Another omen?"

Jayfeather shook his head, looking troubled. "I just don't want to risk any more lives."

Bramblestar guessed that Jayfeather was feeling distressed

by the way that he had failed to interpret the warnings about the Stick of the Fallen. "Don't worry," he reassured the medicine cat. "We'll be careful. I don't want to lose any more cats, either."

Bramblestar and his patrol trekked up to the ridge, then trudged along the top toward the swollen stream. Once out of the shelter of the trees, the wind blustered around them, flattening their pelts to their sides, and rain flicked in their faces. Though he kept halting to look and listen for WindClan cats, Bramblestar couldn't pick up any trace of them, not even a whiff of their scent. But from here there was no clear view down to the lake. *That patrol could be anywhere.*

When they reached the stream, Bramblestar detected WindClan scent along the bank; it was fairly fresh, as if it might have been left by the patrol he had seen earlier. "They came this way," he meowed. "So they must have crossed farther up. Let's go."

Before they had traveled many more fox-lengths, they crossed their own border scent markers. Bramblestar's paws tingled as he led his patrol out of Clan territory.

"This is the way to the Moonpool," Snowpaw informed Jessy, pattering along beside her. "I wish I could go there. It sounds so cool!"

"What's the Moonpool?" Jessy asked.

"All the medicine cats go there," Snowpaw told her. He seemed delighted to be teaching a cat who knew even less about the forest than he did. "That's where they meet with StarClan."

Jessy opened her jaws to ask another question, but Snow-paw forestalled her. "StarClan are the spirits of our dead ancestors," he informed her. "They tell medicine cats omens and stuff."

Jessy blinked and shot Bramblestar a glance full of confusion. "StarClan? Dead cats?"

"Shh." Bramblestar raised his tail to silence them. "There might be WindClan cats about."

The patrol's pace slowed as the ground became rockier. The stream was still fast flowing and overfull, but narrower here as it cut through a deeper channel. Bramblestar began to think it might be possible to leap over it. *Though I wouldn't want to try it,* he thought with a shiver as he watched the roiling water.

Ivypool had bounded ahead of the rest of the patrol. Suddenly she turned back, gesturing with her tail. "Come and see this!" she called.

Bramblestar picked up the pace until he reached Ivypool's side and saw a fallen tree wedged across the stream. *The flood must have washed it down from the mountains,* he realized. The current had thrown debris against the tree on both sides of the stream, and water was breaking over the top, but Bramblestar had no doubt that this was the crossing place. The whole area reeked of WindClan scent.

"Those impudent rabbit-chasers!" Ivypool exclaimed. "Now what are we going to do?"

CHAPTER 17

❧

"We have to dislodge the tree," Bramblestar mused, examining it carefully. He couldn't imagine how they were going to manage that; the trunk was firmly wedged among the rocks on both sides of the stream.

"I'll take a closer look," Jessy meowed, leaping onto the trunk and running confidently along it.

Bramblestar admired how light-pawed and nimble she was, realizing she must have had practice walking along the fence-tops by the Twoleg dens. His Clanmates looked a bit startled, though they said nothing.

"Dovewing told me how she and the others dislodged the beaver dam," Ivypool told Bramblestar as they waited for Jessy to return. "It sounds as if it must have been similar to this. But they waded into the stream and attacked the dam from the bottom. The water here is too deep and fast flowing for us to do that."

Bramblestar nodded. "We can't risk—"

"Bramblestar!" Bumblestripe broke in. "I can smell Wind-Clan cats. They're coming this way."

Turning away from the tree trunk, Bramblestar parted his

jaws to taste the air. Bumblestripe was right. He drew in fresh WindClan scent, growing stronger with every heartbeat. And it was on their side of the stream. "Hide!" he ordered. "Jessy, get back here!"

While the brown kittypet ran back along the tree trunk, Ivypool and Snowpaw dived into the shelter of the rocks. Bumblestripe flattened himself underneath a low-growing thorn bush, and Bramblestar shoved Jessy in beside him. She peered out at him, wide-eyed with excitement at the sudden crisis.

"They'll see my white fur!" Snowpaw gasped from behind a rock.

"No, they won't." Bramblestar threw himself down on top of the apprentice, who wriggled underneath him and stuck his head out, gasping for breath.

Cautiously Bramblestar craned his neck to see around the rock. The WindClan patrol he had seen earlier was heading up the stream, panting and scrambling over the stones. Squirrelflight and her patrol were bounding after them, screeching. Harespring skidded to a stop beside the tree trunk and turned to face the pursuing ThunderClan patrol while the other three WindClan cats ran across the log. All of them looked disheveled, as if the ThunderClan cats had given them a few swipes, but no cat was seriously hurt. Once his Clanmates were across safely, Harespring sprang after them, with a final hiss at Squirrelflight and her warriors.

Bramblestar waited until the WindClan patrol had vanished downstream, heading back toward their own territory, then emerged from hiding. The rest of his patrol followed to meet Squirrelflight and her cats beside the stream. To his relief, all of Squirrelflight's patrol seemed unhurt, except for Thornclaw, who was dabbing at a scratch on his muzzle. Actually, they looked better than they had for days, energized by the skirmish that had driven off the rival Clan.

"They won't come back in a hurry," Squirrelflight mewed, twitching her whiskers in satisfaction.

"Let's hope not," Bramblestar responded. "But to make sure of it, we have to move this tree."

To his surprise, Ivypool and Jessy already had their heads together, thinking of ways to shift the temporary bridge.

"We can't break the tree trunk, or chew through it," Ivypool muttered.

Jessy nodded. "Suppose we dislodge all this rubbish that's piled up against it," she suggested. "Then the extra force of the current might wash the log away."

"That might work. . . ." Ivypool sounded doubtful. "But where would we stand to do it? Besides, that would mean at least one cat being stuck over the other side."

"Then we have to dislodge just one end," Bramblestar meowed, padding over to join the discussion. "That way, the whole thing might fall into the stream."

"Okay, let's give it a try," Cloudtail mewed impatiently.

All the cats clustered together and tried to push the end of the log. But there wasn't enough room on the bank for all of them to reach and add their strength. The log didn't move.

Jessy leaped down onto the collection of twigs and debris

washed up by the stream, to try pushing from there, but it rocked alarmingly under her paws. Panic rushed through Bramblestar as he saw her stagger, about to lose her balance and fall into the torrent. Leaning over precariously, he grabbed her by the scruff and hauled her back to the bank.

"Thanks!" Jessy gasped.

"I won't lose another cat to the floods," Bramblestar meowed grimly.

Jessy looked up at him. "But you've already seen me swim," she reminded him, "and I managed just fine."

"Actually, that was a good idea," Squirrelflight told Jessy, turning away from the tree trunk. "If we could strengthen that twiggy stuff so we could stand on it, then we could give the log a bigger shove than we can from the bank."

"Then let's look for something to do that," Bramblestar mewed. As the group of cats scattered in different directions, he added to Jessy, "Stay close to me, just in case."

"In case of what?" Jessy asked with a gleam in her eyes.

"Anything," Bramblestar muttered.

The bleak moorland didn't seem to offer much that would be useful. A few rocks jutted out here and there from the rough grass, but they were far too big to move into the stream. Bramblestar was beginning to think that they would have to trek back into the forest to fetch bracken when he heard Cloudtail's voice calling him.

"Bramblestar! We found something!"

Bramblestar bounded back to the stream to find Cloudtail and Poppyfrost waiting for him. "What is it?" he asked, glancing around; he couldn't see anything.

"There's a huge bush upstream," Poppyfrost reported as the other cats came racing to join them. "It must have been uprooted and washed up on the bank."

"If we could drag it down here, it could be enough for all of us to stand on," Cloudtail added.

"Let's take a look," Bramblestar meowed. He led the way upstream until they came to a hawthorn bush with dense, prickly branches, caught between two rocks at the edge of the stream.

"Oh, great!" Thornclaw sighed. "I'm *really* looking forward to putting my paws on that!"

Working together, the ThunderClan cats managed to haul the bush out of the water and began dragging it down the slope toward the log. Before they had gone many paw steps, Jessy leaped back with a yelp.

"What's the matter?" Bramblestar puffed.

"A branch poked me in the eye," Jessy explained, blinking rapidly. "But I'm fine. Let's just get on with it."

As the slope grew steeper, the bush began to slither down under its own weight. Bumblestripe had to dart quickly out of the way to avoid being crushed by it.

"Stop it!" Cloudtail yowled. "If it slides past the tree, we'll never drag it up again!"

Bramblestar leaped at the bush from the side, letting all his weight fall onto the outermost branches and wincing as the prickles drove into his pads. Ivypool thrust herself in next to him, trying to help, while Squirrelflight and Thornclaw did the same at the other side. Their efforts slowed the bush down, but it still didn't stop. Poppyfrost, Bumblestripe, and Jessy vainly tugged at it from the back, and even Snowpaw dug in his small claws. Bramblestar looked up to see that the tree trunk was very close.

We'll slip past it for sure. Fox dung!

With heartbeats to spare, Cloudtail raced around to the front of the bush and stood bracing himself on the bank beside the fallen tree. The full weight of the bush settled over him as it finally slid to a halt. Bramblestar heard a massive *oof!* from the middle of the branches. A moment later Cloudtail crawled out, his long white fur snagging on the twigs.

"Good job," Bramblestar mewed, padding up to him. "Are you okay?"

Cloudtail let out a disgusted snort. "I've got every thorn in the bush stuck in my pelt," he hissed. "But apart from that I'm fine."

With Thornclaw and Squirrelflight helping, Bramblestar managed to push the hawthorn bush into the stream above the log so that the current shoved it firmly against the tree trunk.

"It worked!" Poppyfrost exclaimed.

"Let's hope so," Bramblestar muttered. "There's still a long way to go."

Balancing carefully, Squirrelflight ventured out onto the bush. The branches sagged under her weight, but she stayed on her paws. "I think it'll be okay," she reported. "But we'd better have the lightest cats out here, and the rest should stay on the bank."

Poppyfrost leaped forward, but she was a bit too eager. The

bush shifted under her weight and she almost slid backward into the stream until she dug in her claws and hauled herself into position beside Squirrelflight.

"Not you," Bramblestar meowed to Snowpaw as the apprentice got ready to follow the two she-cats. *I'm not going to risk losing another apprentice.* The young cat looked disappointed, so Bramblestar added, "I need a cat to keep watch. Let us know if you see any warriors coming up from WindClan."

Snowpaw brightened up immediately. "Right, Bramblestar!" He puffed out his chest and stood on the bank just downstream of the tree trunk, his ears pricked and his gaze fixed on the WindClan side of the torrent.

Meanwhile Bumblestripe, Ivypool, and Jessy scrambled out onto the hawthorn bush, the branches dipping dangerously under the weight of so many cats. Ivypool's hind paws slipped and water slopped over her hindquarters. She let out a hiss of annoyance as Bumblestripe steadied her.

"I can't even shake my pelt when I'm perched out here!" she grumbled.

Bramblestar, Thornclaw, and Cloudtail remained on the bank. "Okay, is every cat ready?" Bramblestar called.

"Just get on with it, before this bush gives way," Squirrelflight grunted.

Bramblestar braced himself. "When I say *push* . . . push!"

Digging in with his hind paws to hold himself steady, Bramblestar heaved at the end of the tree trunk. Cloudtail and Thornclaw strained beside him. At first he thought nothing was happening, but then he felt the log shift slightly under his paws.

"It's moving!" he gasped.

The cats on the bush threw all their weight against the tree. It shifted again, then with a grating sound slipped free of the rocks that held it and crashed into the stream with a massive splash that soaked the cats' pelts.

"Back to the bank!" Bramblestar yowled.

With the tree trunk gone, the hawthorn bush was already tossing on the current. The cats who were balancing there pushed off in massive leaps for the bank. Jessy landed neatly, then whirled around to help Squirrelflight, who had been farthest away. The ThunderClan deputy was scrambling frantically among the branches as the bush started to roll over in the clutch of the rushing stream.

"I can manage!" she panted, clawing her way through the dense thorns.

Bramblestar leaned out and fastened his teeth in her scruff to haul her the last tail-length onto the bank. Squirrelflight's paws had scarcely touched solid ground when the current finally swept the bush away and rolled it over and over downstream. Bramblestar looked around to make sure that all his Clanmates were safe. Every cat was spattered with mud, their pelts soaked through and torn by the prickly bush, and yet the light of triumph shone in their eyes.

"We did it!" Ivypool yowled. "WindClan can't get across here anymore."

"They might find another place higher upstream," Bramblestar pointed out, "but ThunderClan should be safe for a while. Great job, all of you."

Squirrelflight nodded. "Let's get back to camp."

Bramblestar felt worn out and battered as he led the way down the hill, back onto ThunderClan territory. But success had set his paws buzzing with new energy, and for the first time since the storm had broken he began to feel hopeful that they might get through this.

"You two can set scent markers along the bank of the stream," he told Ivypool and Poppyfrost. "We'll make it clear to WindClan that we're taking back our territory."

"I'll help too!" Snowpaw chirped.

Bramblestar watched with satisfaction as his Clanmates left enough ThunderClan scent to swamp the remaining traces of WindClan. *Let's hope they've learned their lesson. After all, it's not like they can't drink from the stream on their own side.*

"You know," Cloudtail meowed as he padded along beside Bramblestar, "it feels weird to be completely cut off from WindClan like this. Back in the old forest, Firestar and Tallstar were such good friends. It's a pity that's all changed, now that Onestar is leader."

"I know." Bramblestar sighed. "Especially since Onestar got on well with Firestar when he was Onewhisker."

"I appreciate that we're separate Clans," Cloudtail went on, "but these days the WindClan cats look at us as if they want to rip our fur off. It bothered Firestar, too."

"Tell me more about Firestar," Jessy begged, bounding up to join them. "You all seem to respect him so much."

"There was never a cat like Firestar," Cloudtail told her. "I'm proud to be his kin."

Jessy's eyes stretched wide. "You're his kin? Does that

mean you were a kittypet too?"

Cloudtail nodded, looking faintly embarrassed, and from somewhere behind him Bramblestar heard a snort of amusement from Thornclaw.

Cloudtail ignored it. "My mother was Firestar's sister, a kittypet called Princess," he explained to Jessy. "She never wanted to leave her Twolegs, but she was proud of Firestar for making his home in the forest, so she gave one of her kits to him to bring up."

"And that was you?" Jessy prompted. "Wasn't it awfully hard, leaving your mother and learning to live in the forest when you were only a kit?"

"It was tough," Cloudtail admitted. "There was a lot to learn, and I missed my Twolegs and their den."

And their food, Bramblestar thought, remembering the stories he had heard.

"So why didn't you go back?" Jessy went on.

Ouch! Bramblestar knew that Cloudtail would find that hard to answer. When Cloudtail was an apprentice, he had kept sneaking into a Twoleg nest to eat kittypet food, until the Twolegs shut him inside to stop him from straying. The whole Clan knew how Firestar and some of his Clanmates had risked their lives to rescue him. *But Cloudtail became a loyal warrior,* Bramblestar reminded himself. *He earned his place in ThunderClan.*

"I got used to it," Cloudtail replied. "I wouldn't live anywhere else now."

"Are there a lot of kittypets in the Clans?" Jessy went on.

Cloudtail's tail-tip twitched as if he was getting irritated by the flow of questions, but he answered readily enough. *Maybe he's relieved not to be talking about himself anymore,* Bramblestar thought.

"No, the Clans don't usually welcome kittypets," the white warrior meowed. "Firestar was different, because he'd been a kittypet himself."

"That's right," Thornclaw added, bounding forward to catch up to them. "And they're *very* unpopular in the other Clans. Whatever you do, don't cross the border into any other Clan's territory. They'd chase you off as soon as look at you. And you might end up leaving some of your fur behind."

Jessy halted, staring in shock at the golden-brown tom. "Really? But I'm not their enemy!"

"The warrior code says that we have to challenge all trespassing cats," Poppyfrost told her as she turned from setting a scent marker.

Jessy looked puzzled. "What's the warrior code?"

"It's the rules we live by," Bramblestar mewed. "Without it, we'd be no better than rogues."

"So you broke the code to give me shelter—and Frankie and Minty too?" Jessy sounded even more astonished.

Bramblestar shifted his paws uncomfortably. "The code doesn't allow me to watch cats die for no reason," he responded after a moment's pause. "I have to keep you safe until you can go back home."

Jessy nodded and padded on thoughtfully, her stream of questions silenced.

Squirrelflight moved closer to Bramblestar and spoke softly into his ear. "I'm not sure that the code can be stretched to include kittypets," she murmured. "You know that Firestar would always put his Clanmates first."

Bramblestar shrugged. "I know. There are really good reasons why I shouldn't have brought those three into the Clan. But I didn't feel I had any choice. I think Firestar would have done the same," he finished.

"Maybe you're right," Squirrelflight meowed.

Back at the temporary camp, Bramblestar discovered that Brackenfur and Cinderheart had each led a hunting patrol into the woods beyond the border, and brought back a good catch. The Clan had begun to eat well since they extended their territory.

Bramblestar could sense relief spreading throughout the Clan as he reported on the successful expedition to the Wind-Clan border and the destruction of the tree-bridge. There was a mood of celebration as he and his Clanmates settled down to tuck in to the fresh-kill. Even Frankie and Minty looked more relaxed, Bramblestar noticed, as they settled down to share a blackbird with Millie and Graystripe. The positive mood survived when every cat had finished eating.

"Let's see if we can't get the nests sorted out," Bramblestar suggested. "We should be able to organize the sleeping places so every cat gets better rest."

There was a murmur of agreement from the cats around him. Cinderheart led the three youngest apprentices into the undergrowth to look for anything that could be used for extra bedding. Daisy supervised while Molewhisker and Rosepetal clawed and chewed at the Twoleg pelt to divide it into smaller pieces. Dustpelt and Brackenfur dragged a branch into the tunnel and began using the end to mark out the limits of dens on the floor.

"This will help a lot," Bramblestar mewed as he padded into the tunnel to watch. "Better put Purdy and the sick cats farthest from the entrance to keep them out of the wind."

"Good idea," Brackenfur responded. With Dustpelt's help he maneuvered the branch to trace a half circle next to the tunnel wall. "Leafpool and Jayfeather should sleep down here, too," he added. "Then they'll be close to the cats who need their help."

Dustpelt angled his ears toward a niche in the tunnel wall where the earth and stone had crumbled away. "That could be useful," he meowed. "The medicine cats can store their herbs in those cracks."

"Look!" An excited squeal came from the entrance to the tunnel.

Bramblestar turned to see Dewpaw and Snowpaw dragging a huge bundle of bracken inside. It was Snowpaw who had called out.

"We found this really dense patch of fern," Dewpaw added. "There's lots of dry bracken inside. Cinderheart and Amberpaw are bringing some more."

"That's great news," Bramblestar purred.

The bracken wasn't entirely dry, and even with the second

bundle there wasn't enough to make a dry nest for every cat, but it was a big improvement on what they'd had until now.

"Bring one bundle down here for the sick cats," Bramblestar directed, "and then divide the rest among all the nests."

"Where do you want to put your . . . uh . . . visitors?" Dustpelt asked Bramblestar, while the apprentices scrambled around them making nests from the bracken.

"The kittypets? They'd better go with the apprentices," Bramblestar replied after a moment's thought. "After all, they'll be learning how we do things, too."

"We won't have to do yucky stuff, will we?" Minty had poked her head inside the tunnel to watch what was going on. Her pink nose was creased in disgust. "I mean, I saw Amberpaw searching Purdy's pelt for fleas. *I* haven't got fleas," she insisted, giving her shoulder a lick.

"I could find you a few," Dustpelt muttered.

"Every cat has to pull their weight," Bramblestar told her, with a flick of his tail at Dustpelt.

Minty blinked at him, wide-eyed and unhappy.

"I don't mind helping out where I can," Frankie meowed, looking over Minty's shoulder.

"Thanks, Frankie." Bramblestar flicked his tail at him. "And as for you, Minty, don't worry. You'll soon get used to living in a Clan."

Minty's only response was a long sigh.

Bramblestar watched as the remaining dens were marked out and the bedding organized. The pieces of the Twoleg pelt had almost dried out on the bush where Daisy had spread them, and the nests suddenly began to look comfortable.

Squirrelflight padded up to his side and the two watched their Clanmates working for a few heartbeats. "You know," she mewed, "I'm starting to believe that we will get through this."

Bramblestar nodded. "I'm sure we will. It takes more than a storm to destroy ThunderClan."

CHAPTER 18

❧

Bramblestar padded through his territory, weaving a path among the trees. The line of floodwater glinted silver a couple of tail-lengths away. Above his head the full moon shone down, so bright that the night was almost as clear as day. Walking to the water's edge, Bramblestar looked out across the lake. At first the surface rippled with a pure, pale light. Then a scarlet stain began to spread, stretching its tendrils toward the shore. Bramblestar's belly cramped with horror as he caught the tang of blood and saw thick red coils floating to the surface and swirling through the depths.

No! A cat must be injured. . . . I have to get them out of the water before they drown!

Bramblestar jumped into the lake. Silver droplets splashed around him, but before he could dive below the surface, he felt the teeth of another cat sink into his scruff. He let out a yowl and flailed his paws, but he couldn't break the grip. The unseen cat dragged him back to the shore before it let go.

Bramblestar whirled around and froze, his mouth falling open as he recognized the tom with the flame-colored pelt who stood in front of him.

"Firestar!" he gasped. "There's a cat in trouble," he blurted out. "Look, it's bleeding into the water! I have to find it!"

Firestar's green eyes glowed in the moonlight. "It's okay," he reassured Bramblestar. "Your Clanmates are safe. There are no cats in the lake."

Bramblestar took a long breath. "Then am I . . . am I dreaming? Oh, Firestar, it's so great to see you!"

Firestar dipped his head. "It's good to be back in my old territory."

"I've tried to look after your Clan," Bramblestar meowed, struggling with a mixture of joy and guilt that made his voice shake. "But I—I lost Seedpaw. I'm so sorry! If only I'd kept a closer watch on the apprentices."

"Seedpaw is safe in StarClan," Firestar told him. "And you need to learn that you cannot guard every one of your Clanmates all the time. As their leader, they'll look to you to make the big decisions, and to keep them safe from outside enemies, but they have to make their own choices as well. I promise you, you're doing a good job."

Bramblestar began to feel soothed by his former leader's confidence in him. "But what about the visitors? The kitty-pets?" he asked. "Would you have brought them into the Clan? And would you—?" The words began to spill out of him; he wanted to ask about every single thing he had done since Firestar died.

Firestar raised a paw to silence him. "You know the answers already," he mewed gently. "They are in your heart." As Bramblestar blinked at him, he went on, "This is not my

Clan anymore. You are ThunderClan's leader now. Trust the cats who gave you your nine lives. They all knew you would do well—including me," he added with a glint in his eyes.

"Thank you, Firestar." Bramblestar bowed his head. When he raised it again, he was startled to realize that the ginger cat was beginning to fade, and Bramblestar could see the stones on the shore through his starlit pelt.

"I have come to tell you something very important," Firestar meowed. "When water meets blood, blood will rise."

Bramblestar stared at him. "What does that mean?"

"Look at the floodwater," Firestar urged. "See how the blood cannot be drowned?"

Bramblestar turned his head to gaze at the lake again. The strange upswelling of blood still shone scarlet among the waves.

Firestar spoke from behind him. "I can't tell you any more than this. Just remember . . ."

His voice died away. When Bramblestar turned back, he was gone, and the forest was dark and silent. The moonlight too was blotted out, and Bramblestar was alone in the dark.

Somewhere nearby, a cat sneezed. Bramblestar knew that he was back in the tunnel, surrounded by the warm scents of his sleeping Clanmates. The strangeness of his dream still wreathed around him, and Firestar's mysterious words echoed in his head.

When water meets blood, blood will rise. . . .

What kind of prophecy was that? *It can't mean that no cats will drown, because Seedpaw has already died. So what does it mean?*

After a long time wrestling with different meanings, and discarding them all, Bramblestar gave up and curled deeper into his nest. He slipped back into sleep to the sound of Gray-stripe's muffled snores.

The voices and movement of cats around him woke Bramblestar. He lifted his head to see pale light spilling into the tunnel as his Clanmates headed out to start the new day. Yawning, he scrambled to his paws and followed them. For once it wasn't raining, though the sky was still gray and there was a damp, chilly breeze.

Squirrelflight was already outside, choosing cats for the dawn patrols. "Greetings, sleepyhead," she mewed, dipping her head to Bramblestar.

With a jolt Bramblestar remembered his dream. "I have to talk to you," he told her. "Leafpool and Jayfeather, too. This is important."

His deputy gave him a worried look but didn't ask any questions, just called Lionblaze and asked him to take over sorting out the patrols. Meanwhile Bramblestar headed back into the tunnel to find the two medicine cats.

When all four cats were gathered it took a while to find a spot where they could talk without the rest of the Clan over-hearing them. Not for the first time, Bramblestar missed the privacy of his old den on the Highledge. Finally they found a hollowed-out spot among the roots of a nearby oak tree.

"Firestar came to me in a dream last night," Bramblestar told his Clanmates once they were settled around him. "He told me, 'When water meets blood, blood will rise.' But I have no idea what that means."

Leafpool's gaze lit up. "Firestar is watching over us!" she exclaimed.

Jayfeather looked less impressed. "He might have been a bit clearer," he grumbled.

"And told us what we need to do," Squirrelflight agreed, looking frustrated.

"Jayfeather," Leafpool began, "you know as well as any cat that omens and prophecies are often difficult to understand at first."

Just like the troublesome stick, Bramblestar thought, guessing that the tabby she-cat had deliberately not mentioned it. *If only we'd understood that a bit sooner.*

"Often prophecies are only clear after they've come true," Leafpool continued.

"Then what's the point of having them?" Bramblestar asked, exchanging a glance with Squirrelflight.

"Keep the prophecy in mind as you listen to your instincts," Leafpool advised him. "Then the meaning should appear."

Bramblestar still wasn't sure that he understood, but he realized this was the best advice he was going to get. "Tell me right away if StarClan speaks to either of you," he ordered the two medicine cats. "And if you have any more ideas about this prophecy."

"Of course," Jayfeather responded. "Come on, Leafpool. We have herbs to sort."

As the medicine cats padded away, Squirrelflight turned to

Bramblestar. "Thanks for sharing the prophecy with me," she meowed. "I promise to keep watch for what it might mean."

Her support warmed Bramblestar as he led the way back to the other cats, but before he could tell Squirrelflight this, Jessy emerged from the tunnel and came bouncing up to him. The other two kittypets followed more slowly.

"Hi, Bramblestar," Jessy chirped. "I had a great time yesterday. What are we doing today?"

Bramblestar was slightly taken aback by the brown she-cat's enthusiasm. "If you really want to help the Clan," he meowed, "you need to learn how to hunt. Frankie and Minty, too."

Frankie, who came up in time to hear what Bramblestar said, looked interested, but Minty blinked doubtfully and took a step back.

"Minty, you have to learn," Frankie told her, touching her shoulder with his tail-tip. "You can't stay here and expect these cats to feed you."

"But as soon as the water goes away, we'll be able to go home," Minty objected. "My housefolk will be so worried about me. Perhaps we're too far away from them up here," she fretted. "Maybe we should move closer to our homes, so when our housefolk come back they can find us quickly."

Millie, who was standing nearby with Graystripe, turned to the kittypet with a compassionate look in her eyes. "I don't think the floods will go away for another quarter moon," she mewed gently. "You're safe here, safer than you would be in any other Clan's territory, and you'll be able to see when the water starts to go down. Then you can go home—but not before, not when it isn't safe."

Minty's eyes clouded with sadness. "We might be stuck here for ages," she wailed. "My poor housefolk!"

"I know it's not ideal," Frankie comforted her. "I want to go back and look for Benny. But we have to keep away from more risks. Surely that's what our housefolk want most of all: for us to survive?"

Minty sighed, but she didn't argue any more.

Bramblestar felt a pang of sympathy for the kittypets. It had been a shock for them to lose their homes, and even Minty was trying to be brave and sensible. "I'll take you hunting myself," he meowed. "Dovewing, will you come too?"

Dovewing, who had been waiting to join a patrol, spun around at the sound of her leader's voice. "Me? But Ivypool is much better at hunting than me." She sighed. "In fact, every cat is better than me now. . . ."

Bramblestar knew that she was still regretting the loss of her special powers, which had helped her to pinpoint prey more accurately than any cat in the Clan. "And that's what makes you the best cat to train these kittypets," he told her briskly. "You know what it's like to learn from the very beginning, when you're feeling blind and deaf and lost in the trees."

"Oh!" Dovewing was obviously surprised by this idea. "Okay, I'd be glad to help," she agreed.

By this time the early patrols were ready to set out. Lionblaze was taking his cats to the WindClan border, to check the crossing place and to make sure there were no new WindClan scents. Squirrelflight was leading cats along the ShadowClan border, while Brightheart and Birchfall were both heading up hunting patrols in the woods beyond the territory.

"We're all being asked to travel much farther than we're used to," Squirrelflight murmured as the patrols set out.

Bramblestar nodded, his gaze traveling across his thin, weary Clanmates. "We have no choice," he reminded his deputy, feeling bad for them but knowing that they would all do what they had to, to protect the Clan and survive.

He took Dovewing and the kittypets into the trees in the direction of the ShadowClan border, treading in Squirrelflight's paw steps but letting her patrol draw ahead. Once they were well away from the tunnel among dense undergrowth, he halted.

"First you have to learn the hunter's crouch," he began. "That's essential for every ThunderClan cat—or any cat who happens to be living in ThunderClan for a time," he added as Minty opened her jaws to object. "Dovewing, show them how."

Dovewing crouched down with her paws drawn up under her and her hind legs braced for a pounce.

"See how she's ready to leap?" Bramblestar meowed. "She's putting all her strength into her hind legs—like this." He pressed himself to the ground, copying Dovewing's crouch. "Dovewing, show them the pounce."

Dovewing sprang forward, her forepaws extended and her claws ready to grip her quarry.

"Great," Bramblestar commented. "See how her forepaws flashed out? Her prey wouldn't have a chance."

"Now you try," Dovewing suggested.

Bramblestar stayed in the crouching position so that the kittypets could copy him. All three looked nervous, but they wriggled into position and tucked in their paws neatly.

"Very good," Dovewing mewed, pacing around them and checking their position. "Frankie, pull your hind paws a bit farther in. That's right."

"Excellent." Bramblestar rose and arched his back in a stretch, loosening up after the crouch. "Now let's try pouncing." He peeled a bunch of moss off a nearby tree root and padded forward until he emerged in a small clearing. "Suppose this moss is a mouse," he continued, dropping the bundle in the middle. "I want you to stalk it, crouch, and then pounce."

"Is this what you do with your apprentices?" Jessy asked.

"Yes," Bramblestar replied.

Jessy let out a snort that was half-amused, though her tail-tip flicked frustratedly. "But we're not apprentices!" she pointed out. "We've all hunted before, whatever you think of our skills. Why don't you let us show you what we can do?"

"I don't think—" Bramblestar began, his neck fur beginning to rise defensively.

"That's a great idea," Dovewing interrupted. "That way, we'll see what we need to teach you."

Bramblestar nodded, appreciating the sense in what his Clanmate said. "Okay. Frankie, you go first. Can you scent any prey?"

The tabby tom cast him a nervous glance, then stood with his ears pricked and his jaws parted to taste the air.

Bramblestar was slightly surprised that he knew what to do.

After a moment Frankie turned to him. "I think there's a squirrel under there," he mewed, angling his ears toward a holly bush at the edge of the clearing.

"I think so, too," Bramblestar replied; he had picked up the scent several heartbeats before Frankie. "See if you can catch it."

Forgetting all about stalking, Frankie tore across the clearing with a yowl, startling the squirrel, which shot out from beneath the holly bush and raced around a bramble thicket with its tail streaming out behind it. Frankie hurtled after it, crashing through the brambles, only to halt in frustration as the squirrel swarmed up the trunk of a nearby beech tree and vanished among the branches.

His head and tail drooping, Frankie trudged back to the other cats. "I'm sorry, I messed up," he muttered. He looked thoroughly depressed, and he had lost several tufts of fur in his mad dash through the brambles.

"It wasn't so bad," Dovewing meowed bracingly. "Okay, you didn't catch it, but you picked up its scent quickly, and you kept after it, even with brambles in the way. You just need to work on being quieter."

Frankie perked up. "I'll remember that," he promised.

Dovewing gave him a nod and turned to Minty. "You try now."

Minty looked even more nervous than Frankie, but she stood still with her ears pricked just as he had done, though she forgot to taste the air for scent. She kept jumping at the sound of creaking branches or rustling leaves, as if she thought a fox or a badger might be sneaking up on her. At last she glanced at Bramblestar and whispered, "I think I've found something."

Bramblestar was confused. He couldn't scent any nearby prey at all. *Don't tell me that kittypet is better at this than me!* "Okay, go ahead," he mewed.

Minty started to stalk forward, setting her paws down lightly. *At least she's learned something from what Frankie did,* Bramblestar thought, still wondering what she thought she was going to catch.

Then Minty dropped into an untidy hunter's crouch, and jumped forward with her forepaws stretching out. "Got it!" she yowled as she landed, sinking her claws into something brown, almost hidden by an arching fern. "Oh . . ." she added a moment later, looking disconcerted.

Bramblestar padded over to look. He hid an amused purr when he saw that Minty's prey was actually an old log half-buried in the grass.

"I thought it was a rat," she murmured, scrabbling her paws in embarrassment.

"We don't get many rats in this part of the forest," Bramblestar told her. "But don't worry, Minty. That was pretty good. If it had been a rat, you'd have stood a good chance of catching it."

Minty looked unconvinced.

"My turn now," Jessy announced.

Instead of standing still, she began slipping quietly through the undergrowth, her paws hardly touching the ground, while she stared up into the trees. Bramblestar and the others followed her at a distance. Eventually Jessy froze, her gaze fixed on a low branch where a thrush was perched.

Hunting in trees? Bramblestar thought. *Not a chance!*

To his surprise, Jessy leaped up the tree trunk, quick as a fox. The thrush spotted her, and with a loud alarm call fluttered away into the next tree. Without hesitating, Jessy ran out along the branch and jumped after the thrush, pinning it to the next branch with one paw. The thrush struggled and nearly got free; Jessy almost overbalanced as she lowered her head and managed to bite it in the throat. She hopped down neatly with the thrush in her jaws and dropped it at Bramblestar's paws.

Bramblestar thought he had never seen a cat look so smug. *And I told her I bet she'd never caught anything!*

"Wow, that was great!" Dovewing exclaimed.

"Oh, Jessy's a brilliant hunter," Frankie told them. "And she loves to climb. Hey, Jessy, did you tell them about the time your housefolk thought you were stuck on the roof?"

Jessy tossed her head. "I can't believe they thought I couldn't get down!"

"Yes," Frankie purred, "but you could have shown them before they climbed onto the roof themselves."

Jessy swished her tail and looked innocent.

"I shouldn't have dismissed your skills," Bramblestar admitted to her. "That's a rare skill, being able to jump between trees. Firestar wanted ThunderClan cats to learn, but it doesn't come easily to us."

"I've never felt comfortable being off the ground," Dove-wing agreed. "I don't have wings, in spite of my name."

"Maybe I should give you some lessons," Jessy suggested. There was a teasing glint in her eye.

"Maybe you should," Bramblestar mewed, meeting her gaze. "Meanwhile let's head for the ShadowClan border and see what else we can find. Jessy, if you scratch some earth over that thrush, we'll pick it up on the way back."

As the five cats headed off, Bramblestar felt more relaxed than he had for days. It was good to be part of a patrol, without the weight of his duties as Clan leader. And he was impressed by how well Jessy was fitting in.

Every cat was keeping a lookout for prey; Dovewing was the first to spot a shrew scrabbling in the grass at the foot of a mossy bank. "Frankie," she murmured, angling her ears toward the tiny creature. "See that? Try catching it. And remember . . . quiet!"

Looking determined, the gray tabby tom crept toward the shrew. He remembered to set his paws down carefully, but he had forgotten about his tail, which swept over a clump of long grass. The shrew darted away as the shadow of the grass fell across it. Frankie hurled himself at it in an enormous leap, but his claws hit the ground just short of his prey. The shrew veered away in a panic, right into the claws of Dovewing, who killed it with one quick blow.

"I missed it!" Frankie wailed.

"But you drove it straight into my paws," Dovewing pointed

out. "We make a great team!"

A pleased purr rose in Frankie's throat.

"What about you, Minty?" Bramblestar asked. "Can you spot anything? Or hear anything?"

Minty gazed around confusedly. "It's all so strange," she confessed.

Bramblestar twitched his tail in rising frustration. *Can't she even tell the difference between a branch creaking and a mouse scuffling?*

He opened his jaws, ready for a harsh comment, when Dovewing stepped between him and Minty, motioning him away with a jerk of her head. "Come on, Minty," she mewed. "Let's listen together. Can you hear that loud creaking noise? The one that's repeated every couple of heartbeats?"

Minty listened for a moment, then nodded.

"What do you think that is?" Dovewing asked.

"Er . . . a branch moving in the wind?"

"Very good," Dovewing praised her. "Now . . . that rustling sound, just behind you. No—don't turn your head and look!"

"Ferns." This time Minty sounded more confident.

Bramblestar realized that Dovewing was drawing on her own experience of being able to hear everything. Her patience with Minty was clearly comforting the kittypet, making her feel less out of place.

Frankie was busy practicing his stalking and crouching, so Bramblestar padded on slowly with Jessy by his side. "Where did you learn to climb?" he asked the brown she-cat.

"My mother taught me," Jessy replied. "I've always dreamed of living among trees!"

"Well, now you are," Bramblestar purred. "And it's even better than this when the lake isn't flooded." Halting to point through the woods with his tail, he added, "There are lots of different trees down there, closer to the shore. Well, there used to be. I don't know if they'll survive being underwater."

"You're really worried that the water won't go down, aren't you?" Jessy guessed.

"Yes, I am," Bramblestar meowed. "Not just for Thunder-Clan, but for all the Clans."

Together the two cats wandered on in companionable silence. But while they were still some way from the Shadow-Clan border, Bramblestar heard a faint hiss coming from the trees ahead. Pausing to taste the air, he stiffened, feeling every hair on his pelt begin to rise.

ShadowClan scent!

Bramblestar suspected that a ShadowClan patrol had crossed the border. He motioned Jessy to get back with a wave of his tail, wishing that he weren't stuck out here alone with only a kittypet.

Then a tortoiseshell head peered out from behind a bush, and Bramblestar let out a puff of relief.

"Tawnypelt!" he cried. "What are you doing here?"

CHAPTER 19

As Tawnypelt emerged from behind the bush, Bramblestar was aware of Jessy stiffening, her claws sliding out and her neck fur bristling as if she was ready for a fight.

Of course, Bramblestar thought, *she's heard all about how hostile ShadowClan is, and she saw the WindClan intruders for herself.*

"It's okay, Jessy," he meowed. "This is Tawnypelt, my sister. Wait here while I speak to her." He padded forward the few paw steps that brought him close to his sister. Tawnypelt was looking very thin, her tortoiseshell fur ruffled and her eyes wide. "Is Rowanstar okay?" Bramblestar asked.

"He's as well as the rest of us," Tawnypelt replied. "But . . . oh, Bramblestar, ShadowClan is in big trouble. We've lost our camp and nearly all our hunting grounds. Our territory is so low-lying that the water has covered nearly all of it."

"You're right, that's bad," Bramblestar mewed. "Thunder-Clan is struggling, too. We've started hunting beyond the top border; has Rowanstar thought of doing that?"

"Yes, but our patrols ran into some trouble. . . ." Tawnypelt lowered her head, looking uncomfortable, and scrabbled her paws in the grass.

"What kind of trouble?" Bramblestar prompted her.

Tawnypelt took a deep breath. "There are kittypets who seem to think that part of the forest belongs to them," she told her brother. "They attacked our patrols."

"Kittypets?" Bramblestar blinked in surprise. "Not the ones who live in the Twoleg nest in your territory? I thought we'd taught them a lesson."

Tawnypelt shook her head. "No, they went off with their Twolegs when the water started to rise. These are different cats."

"And they managed to chase off ShadowClan warriors?" Bramblestar found that hard to believe.

"There were a lot of them!" Tawnypelt protested. "And we . . . we're so hungry all the time, we're not as strong as we were."

Bramblestar could understand that. Compassion for his sister clawed at him; he could see she was torn between pride and the desperate need for help. "What do you want me to do?" he meowed. "Do you want me to give you some of our fresh-kill? That could be difficult. . . ."

Before Tawnypelt could reply, Jessy bounded up to his side. "Hi!" she mewed to Tawnypelt.

Bramblestar wished that the kittypet had stayed where he left her. "This is Jessy," he told his sister. "She's staying with us for a while."

"I live with my housefolk over there," Jessy added with a wave of her tail across the lake. "But they left when the floods came."

"You're a *kittypet?*" Tawnypelt's eyes stretched wide as she gazed over Bramblestar's shoulder. "And there are *more* of you?"

Glancing back, Bramblestar saw that Frankie and Minty had appeared from the trees with Dovewing.

"Are you completely mouse-brained?" Tawnypelt yelped. "Giving food and shelter to kittypets at a time like this?"

"They would have died if I'd left them in the flood!" Bramblestar growled, aware of Jessy bristling by his side.

"That's hardly your problem," Tawnypelt retorted. "Well, I guess I can't expect you to help us if you're too busy feeding kittypets."

Bramblestar forced himself not to get angry. *She's not usually this short tempered. It's only because she and her Clan are in trouble.* "Firestar showed me that compassion is a sign of strength," he responded calmly.

"Firestar would have put Clan cats first!" Tawnypelt snapped. She turned and stalked away, then paused to look back over her shoulder. "Forget I said anything, Bramblestar," she hissed. "Rowanstar will figure out a way to save us."

"Wow!" Minty exclaimed, watching Tawnypelt vanish into the bushes. "She's really fiery! I can see why you don't get along with ShadowClan."

"That's Bramblestar's sister, Tawnypelt," Dovewing informed her. "She's okay."

Bramblestar was torn between anger and worry for his sister. *Things must be really bad in ShadowClan if she's coming here to ask for help.* He knew how proud Tawnypelt was of her adopted Clan. *I'm sure Rowanstar knows nothing about this.*

"Is everything okay with Tawnypelt?" Dovewing asked him.

Bramblestar hesitated, not sure how much he wanted to give away. "Not really," he replied at last. "But she's no worse than the rest of us, struggling to survive the flood."

Bramblestar led his patrol back to the camp, pausing to pick up Jessy's thrush on the way. When they reached the tunnel, Frankie headed straight for Millie, who was helping Briarlight with her exercises near the entrance.

"Look what Dovewing and I caught," he meowed, laying the shrew proudly at Millie's paws.

"Very good!" Millie's eyes glowed as she gazed at the kittypet. "You see, it just takes a little while for you to settle in here."

"And Jessy caught a thrush all by herself," Minty added as some of the other cats gathered around to look. "She climbed up the tree and leaped through the branches just like a real forest cat!" Minty sounded as pleased as if she had caught the thrush herself.

"Good job," Squirrelflight mewed, giving the thrush a sniff. "We'll take you out with the apprentices next time."

"They're all doing well," Dovewing put in. Half joking, she added, "Maybe we should give them some fighting lessons next."

Jessy and Frankie exchanged a glance. "I'm up for it," Jessy declared. Frankie looked less certain, but nodded a heartbeat later.

Minty took a step back. "I'll stick with hunting, if that's okay."

Bramblestar went to look for Sandstorm, and found her

inside the tunnel, fluffing up the bedding to help it dry out. He remembered she'd been ill; though she wasn't coughing now, he didn't like the sound of her rasping breath.

"Did you want something, Bramblestar?" she asked, turning toward him.

Bramblestar paced the tunnel restlessly as he told her about his meeting with Tawnypelt. "What do you think Firestar would have done?" he asked her.

Sandstorm had listened quietly, sitting with her tail wrapped around her paws. "I think you're asking the wrong question," she mewed. Her green gaze was fixed on him. "You should be asking yourself what *you* should do."

"I don't know," Bramblestar confessed. "That's why I'm asking for your opinion."

Sandstorm flicked her tail-tip back and forth for a couple of heartbeats, thinking. "You haven't welcomed Rowanstar formally as ShadowClan's leader yet," she pointed out at last. "And there'll be no more Gatherings until the water goes down. Why not visit him? If his Clan is obviously in trouble, it wouldn't be too difficult to ask if he wants help. Then he can make the decision whether to accept or not."

Bramblestar sagged with relief. "You're right," he meowed. "Why didn't I think of that? What kind of leader am I if I have to ask you what to do all the time?"

"You don't ask me all the time," Sandstorm mewed briskly. "You're doing fine. I'm glad Tawnypelt felt that she could come and ask you for help," she added. "Sometimes Clan boundaries cause more damage than they're worth."

* * *

The two hunting parties returned at sunhigh. *Not that we can see the sun,* Bramblestar thought. *Sometimes I think we'll never feel its warmth again.* When every cat had finished eating, Squirrelflight began to organize the afternoon patrols.

"I don't mind going out again," Jessy offered. "Hunting this morning was fun."

"I'll go too," Frankie mewed.

Bramblestar was glad that the two kittypets were adapting so well, but he could see that they were both tired after the morning's unaccustomed exercise. "No, you've already done your bit," he meowed. He had been watching the two medicine cats patiently trekking back and forth with mouthfuls of herbs, and now he suggested, "Why don't you help Jayfeather and Leafpool sort out their supplies?"

"That would be great." Leafpool padded over to them. "We're managing to build up a store again, but we lost everything so we had to start over."

Bramblestar spotted Dovewing talking to Brightheart, who had also been helping the medicine cats. "Do you think you could take Minty with you to look for herbs? It would help her get used to the forest."

"Sure," Brightheart responded.

Bramblestar gave Dovewing a grateful nod, impressed by her kindness and her good sense in guessing what would help Minty to feel better about her new surroundings.

Cherryfall and Mousewhisker puffed past him, dragging branches, with Brackenfur and Dustpelt to supervise.

"Careful as you go past the mudfall," Dustpelt warned. "We spent a lot of time getting it secure, and I don't want you to dislodge it."

"We're *being* careful," Cherryfall panted.

"It'll be fine," Brackenfur reassured Dustpelt. "Think how much more comfortable the nests will be when we install these windbreaks."

Bramblestar watched them as they disappeared into the tunnel. He couldn't help noticing how old Dustpelt and Brackenfur were looking, the fur around their muzzles fading to gray and their movements growing stiffer. *I'm glad they have the younger cats to help them.*

"No, Purdy, you don't need to go on patrol." Squirrelflight's voice interrupted Bramblestar's thoughts. "I need you to help look after the sick cats—Briarlight especially."

Bramblestar purred. *I'd be lost without Squirrelflight to keep every cat in line! She has a knack for making them all feel useful and important, even Purdy.*

When the sturdy tabby had gone bumbling off into the tunnel, Squirrelflight noticed that Bramblestar was looking at her, and padded across to him. "Do you have any special tasks for today?"

"I'm thinking of going over to ShadowClan to have a word with Rowanstar," Bramblestar meowed. "Just to see how he's coping."

Squirrelflight blinked in surprise. "I don't think Rowanstar will appreciate another Clan muscling in," she told him.

"Blackstar was generous to me when I first became Clan

leader," Bramblestar responded. "I'd like to return the favor." He didn't tell Squirrelflight about his encounter with Tawny-pelt.

Squirrelflight still didn't look impressed, but she didn't argue any more. "Then I'll stay here and keep an eye on the camp," she mewed.

Bramblestar glanced around to see which cats were free to come with him, and beckoned Leafpool with a wave of his tail. "I'm going to visit ShadowClan," he informed her. "Now that Jayfeather has some help, I'd like you to come with me."

"Sure, Bramblestar."

"Spiderleg, Cinderheart!" Bramblestar called.

The long-legged black warrior came bounding over, while Cinderheart, who had been talking to Lionblaze under a nearby elder bush, followed more slowly, with Lionblaze still at her side.

"Can I come too?" Lionblaze asked when he heard where his Clan leader and the others were going.

Bramblestar shook his head. "I'm not expecting trouble," he meowed, "so I don't want to take too many warriors with me. Besides, Lionblaze, you have a habit of bringing trouble to ShadowClan all by yourself."

"Okay," Lionblaze agreed without protest. He touched noses with Cinderheart. "Take care," he mewed softly. "You don't know what you're going to find over there."

Cinderheart gave his ear a lick. "Don't worry. I'll be fine."

Watching their farewell, Leafpool leaned close to Bramble-star. "I wouldn't be surprised if we have some new kits in the

Clan soon," she murmured.

Kits! Bramblestar thought happily. Then he let out a sigh. *I hope they aren't born outside the hollow, in this cold, damp tunnel.*

As Bramblestar's patrol was getting ready to leave, Jessy looked up from where she was sorting herbs with Jayfeather and came racing over to them. "Good luck, Bramblestar," she meowed. "You're being a good brother to do this."

Squirrelflight looked puzzled. "What does she mean, 'a good brother'?" she asked, her tail-tip twitching.

Bramblestar began to regret that he hadn't told Squirrelflight about his meeting with Tawnypelt. *But it's too late now.* "Oh . . . uh . . . I guess Jessy knows my sister is in ShadowClan, and that I'm worried about her."

Squirrelflight didn't look convinced by his reply, her green gaze flicking from Bramblestar to Jessy and back again. "Well, isn't Jessy learning quickly," she commented after a moment.

Realizing anything he said would just make things worse, Bramblestar led his patrol out of the camp and through the trees to the ShadowClan border. When they reached it and saw the extent of the flooding in their rivals' territory, Spiderleg and Leafpool halted, gazing in shock at the waste of water.

"I had no idea the lake had stretched so far!" Leafpool exclaimed.

"It's pretty bad." Cinderheart, who had seen this on her previous patrol, was calmer. "Life must be so hard for Shadow-Clan now."

"Life's hard for all of us," Spiderleg mewed unsympathetically.

Bramblestar had no idea how to find ShadowClan's temporary camp, so he led his patrol along the border, staying on the ThunderClan side, his ears pricked for the sound of cats and his jaws parted to pick up their scent. Eventually a whiff of ShadowClan scent reached him and he heard the swish of long grass as cats brushed through it.

"Hey, ShadowClan!" he called out, stopping. "Over here!"

He waited, his Clanmates bunched around him, until Crowfrost appeared around a bramble thicket with Tigerheart and Scorchfur a pace or two behind. All three cats looked desperately thin, their ribs showing beneath their pelts.

"What do you want?" Crowfrost growled as he stopped in front of Bramblestar. "You have no business being here."

"We haven't crossed your border," Bramblestar pointed out mildly. "But we'd like to visit Rowanstar. I want to welcome him as your new leader."

"I think they just want to find out where we've made our new camp," Scorchfur put in, glaring over Crowfrost's shoulder.

"Well, we don't have to take them there," Crowfrost responded. "If that's really what you want," he added to Bramblestar, "then we'll bring Rowanstar to you here."

Bramblestar would have been prepared to settle for that, but Spiderleg broke in. "Look, we're all suffering from the floods," he snapped. "The last thing we want is to attack your camp. Just take us there!"

"That's enough!" Bramblestar warned him, raising his tail.

Before he could say anything to the ShadowClan cats,

Crowfrost's shoulders sagged. "Okay, then, come on," he meowed, sounding too weary to argue anymore.

The ThunderClan patrol crossed out of their own territory and followed the ShadowClan cats, heading toward the top border. The ground began to rise steeply and a cold wind whipped their fur the wrong way and rattled the tops of the spindly trees. Crowfrost came to a halt in front of a dense bramble thicket. There was a strong reek of ShadowClan, and Bramblestar could hear sounds of movement and muted mews coming from deep within the brambles. *It looks like they camped as high up as they could because they were afraid the water wouldn't stop rising.*

"Wait here," Crowfrost ordered. "I'll bring Rowanstar out to you." Pressing himself to the ground, he wriggled his way inside. Scorchfur and Tigerheart remained outside on guard. *Ready to spring if we put a paw wrong,* Bramblestar thought.

Eventually there was movement among the brambles and Rowanstar appeared, followed by Crowfrost and two or three other ShadowClan cats.

"Greetings, Bramblestar," the ShadowClan leader mewed. "Crowfrost, thank you for bringing them to see me. Crowfrost is my new deputy," he added to the ThunderClan cats, who murmured congratulations.

"And of course we congratulate you on receiving your nine lives, Rowanstar," Bramblestar meowed. "We know you will be a strong leader for ShadowClan. I see that you've managed to find a good place to camp while the water is high."

Rowanstar gave a brief nod. "Yes, we've had to move, just as you have, no doubt. But the water will soon go down, and meanwhile we're surviving."

For all his brave words, Bramblestar could see the panic in the Clan leader's eyes. His tucked-up flanks suggested that he had been giving all the fresh-kill to his Clanmates. But Bramblestar knew there was no point in challenging him directly about the trouble he was in. *There's no way he would ever admit it.*

Leafpool stepped forward, dipping her head to Rowanstar. "May I speak to Littlecloud?"

"Yes, of course," Rowanstar replied, respect for the medicine cat showing in his eyes. "Dawnpelt, please go get him."

The cream-furred she-cat, her belly swollen with kits, turned and pushed her way back into the brambles. *That's Tawnypelt's daughter,* Bramblestar thought. *My kin . . . and her kits will come soon. I must do something to help this Clan.*

Littlecloud emerged from the thicket a moment later. Bramblestar was shocked to see how old and frail he looked; his eyes seemed to be fixed on some point in the distance, and his haunches quivered as he lowered himself to the ground.

Bramblestar's shock was reflected in Leafpool's eyes as she padded up to Littlecloud and touched noses with him. "How are you, Littlecloud?" she asked.

"Fine," the old tabby rasped. "The apprentices are finding herbs to replenish my stores, and all the cats are healthy."

"Would you like me to take a look at your supplies?" Leafpool offered. "I might have some spare herbs that you're missing."

A pleased glimmer appeared in Littlecloud's eyes. "Thank you, Leafpool. That would be very helpful."

Rowanstar's neck fur bristled slightly, but he didn't protest as his medicine cat led the way into the thicket and Leafpool followed.

The medicine cats had hardly disappeared when Pinenose and Pouncetail padded up from the direction of the lake, dragging dry bracken fronds behind them. Bramblestar exchanged a surprised glance with Cinderheart that warriors were fetching bedding; then he recalled that ShadowClan had so few apprentices that some of the everyday tasks would have to be carried out by warriors.

"Great, you found some!" Scorchfur exclaimed, looking pleased, as the two cats approached.

"We'll take this straight to the nursery," Pinenose mumbled around her mouthful of bracken. "Snowbird and your kits will sleep warm tonight."

"Let me help you carry it in," Cinderheart suggested, stepping forward.

"I'll come, too," Spiderleg added.

The warriors who were struggling with the bracken looked willing to accept help, but Rowanstar lashed his tail. "Shadow-Clan can manage without ThunderClan's interference," he snapped.

"No cat doubts that," Bramblestar mewed, keeping his voice calm. "But equally it's not a sign of weakness to accept help sometimes."

Rowanstar's nostrils flared, while Pinenose and Pouncetail quickly started dragging the bracken into the camp before a full-blown argument developed. The ThunderClan warriors stayed where they were.

With a twitch of his ears Bramblestar beckoned Rowan-star a little way from the bramble thicket, so that they could talk privately. "Look," he began, deciding to get straight to the point, "I know about the kittypets who have been stopping you from hunting beyond the border. If you want, I could send some warriors to help you defeat them, just like we did when you first moved into the territory."

Rowanstar lashed his tail and his shoulder fur bristled up into spikes. "Who told you?" he demanded.

As if his words had summoned her, Tawnypelt appeared from the bushes, carrying a scrawny blackbird in her jaws. The rest of her hunting patrol followed with a few more puny scraps of prey. She halted at the sight of Bramblestar standing beside Rowanstar.

Understanding flashed into Rowanstar's eyes. "Tawny-pelt!" he snarled. "Over here—now!"

Tawnypelt gave her blackbird to another member of her patrol and padded over.

"It was you, wasn't it?" Rowanstar challenged her. "You told a cat from another Clan that ShadowClan needed help."

Tawnypelt gave Bramblestar a glare as if to ask him why he had come blundering in. "Yes, it was me. Of course I'll ask my brother for help if I need it."

"And you call that being loyal to ShadowClan?" Rowanstar demanded.

"You've never had reason to doubt my loyalty." Tawnypelt's voice was scathing. Then she softened, taking a step toward Rowanstar. "Please let ThunderClan help us," she begged.

Rowanstar lifted his head proudly. "Never. This is my

Clan, and we will stand alone."

Bramblestar felt a sudden rush of sympathy. *I should never have expected that Rowanstar would fall at our paws and beg for help.* "Cinderheart, Spiderleg, we're leaving," he meowed. "Will some cat please get Leafpool?"

Scorchfur slid into the thicket, and emerged a moment later with Leafpool and Littlecloud. She padded over to Bramblestar, and he saw with a sharp stab of concern that her eyes were full of trouble.

"Bramblestar, I want to stay here," she mewed. "Please let me."

Bramblestar blinked. "Why?"

"Dawnpelt is very close to kitting," Leafpool explained in a rapid undertone. "And Littlecloud's herb store is pitiful. I could be a real help to him, and Jayfeather can manage without me for a few days."

Rowanstar was staring at her with horror in his eyes. "Are you mouse-brained?" he began. "Do you imagine—"

Leafpool cut him off. "Rowanstar, do you want a healthy litter of kits, or don't you?" While the ShadowClan leader was spluttering for an answer, she went on, "You know that Clan rivalries mean nothing to medicine cats. Will you deny me the chance to do the role that StarClan chose for me?"

Her logic silenced Rowanstar, while Bramblestar regarded his medicine cat with admiration.

"I could do with some help," Littlecloud admitted. "Just for a few days."

Rowanstar turned to the old medicine cat with compassion

in his gaze. "Very well," he meowed.

"Please, Bramblestar," Leafpool begged. "I'll be back soon."
Bramblestar hesitated, then dipped his head. "Whatever you want."

Beckoning Spiderleg and Cinderheart with a flourish of his tail, he said good-bye to Rowanstar and led the way toward ThunderClan territory. He was still reeling from Leafpool's unexpected decision.

"Do you think Leafpool will stay with ShadowClan forever?" Cinderheart mewed. "After all, Littlecloud hasn't had an apprentice since Flametail died."

A cold shiver passed through Bramblestar to hear his own fears voiced out loud. "Of course she'll come back!" he snapped. "She's a ThunderClan cat."

But even though he silenced Cinderheart, he couldn't silence his own misgivings.

Am I losing control of my Clan? I feel as though my cats are slipping through my paws like water.

CHAPTER 20

The first cat Bramblestar spotted when he reached the makeshift ThunderClan camp was Jayfeather, padding up from the opposite direction with Brightheart. Both cats were carrying bunches of herbs in their jaws. Jayfeather halted in front of the tunnel entrance, turned toward Bramblestar's patrol as though he could see them. Then he dropped his herbs and bounded over to them.

"Where's Leafpool?" he demanded.

"She stayed behind to help Littlecloud," Bramblestar explained. *This isn't going to go well.*

Jayfeather's neck fur stood on end. "And you let her? What about ThunderClan? Don't you think I've got enough on my paws, looking after the cats with whitecough?"

"You have Brightheart to help you," Bramblestar pointed out.

"It's not the same," Jayfeather hissed.

Brightheart, who had followed him over, blinked at him, completely unoffended. "I'll do whatever I can," she mewed.

Jayfeather gave a disgusted snort and stalked off. Brightheart shot an apologetic glance at Bramblestar and hurried after him.

Across the clearing, Squirrelflight was organizing Mouse-whisker, Dovewing, and Thornclaw into a hunting patrol. On the way out she halted beside Bramblestar.

"How did the meeting go with Rowanstar?"

Bramblestar described his offer to help ShadowClan cope with the fierce kittypets, and how Rowanstar had refused.

Squirrelflight shrugged, though there was compassion in her green eyes. "That's Rowanstar's decision to make," she commented.

As Squirrelflight headed off with her patrol, Bramblestar noticed Jessy standing close by, listening to his account of the visit. He was about to beckon her over when Rosepetal, who was spreading the bits of Twoleg pelt on a holly bush, called out to her.

"Hey, Jessy, come and help me freshen up these pelts!"

Jessy bounded across to her immediately. Bramblestar was pleased and a little surprised to see how well she was settling in.

"You'd almost think she was a Clan cat," he remarked to Graystripe, who was padding past him with a starling in his jaws.

Graystripe nodded, dropping his prey to reply. "We should have learned by now not to be surprised by kittypets," he mewed with a wry twist to his mouth.

"Hey, Bramblestar!" Cherryfall popped her head out of the tunnel. "Look what we've done with the new dens!"

Bramblestar headed toward her, leaving Graystripe to carry his prey to the fresh-kill pile. Inside the tunnels, he saw that each section had been marked out by low walls of interwoven branches that would give even more protection from drafts. Within each wall were several nests of moss and bracken; stretching out a paw, he felt that they were hardly damp at all.

"How do you like it?" Cherryfall prompted.

"It's great," Bramblestar replied. *It looks almost comfortable.*

"It'll be even better once Rosepetal gets the Twoleg pelts back in," Cherryfall mewed. "Dustpelt and Brackenfur worked out the breaks, and Mousewhisker and I helped build them."

"Good job, all of you," Bramblestar purred. "I think we'll all sleep better from now on."

He padded farther down the tunnel, spotting Purdy curled up asleep in the den he shared with the apprentices, and lastly reaching the section where Jayfeather and Leafpool had their den, next to the sick cats. Jayfeather and Brightheart were arranging their newly gathered herbs in cracks in the rock.

Berrynose and Molewhisker were both sleeping; their breathing sounded almost back to normal. Amberpaw looked much better too, helping Briarlight with her exercises by tossing a ball of moss for her to catch. Bramblestar noticed uneasily that the injured cat couldn't manage more than a couple of throws without having to stop to catch her breath.

Sandstorm was curled up in her nest, but she raised her head and greeted Bramblestar as he approached. "How did the visit to ShadowClan go?" she asked.

"Not good," Bramblestar admitted. "Rowanstar wouldn't let us help him with the kittypets."

"But he was quick enough to accept *our* medicine cat," Jayfeather put in with a snarl.

"Leafpool will be back soon," Bramblestar told him, hoping that was true. A cough from Sandstorm drew his attention back to her, and he thought how ill she looked, her green eyes bright with fever. "How are you feeling?"

"Oh, fine," Sandstorm replied. "This fern dust gets in my throat, though. I'm going outside for some fresh air." Rising to her paws, she shook some scraps of bracken out of her pelt and padded off.

"How is she really?" Bramblestar asked Jayfeather, unable to stifle his anxiety about the ginger she-cat.

"She doesn't have greencough," Jayfeather answered, "so she should be okay. But living in a cold, damp tunnel doesn't help."

I wish we could go back to the hollow, Bramblestar thought. Aloud he mewed, "I think I'll go check the water levels, and see if they're starting to go down."

"I'll come with you." Jayfeather pushed a few stems of tansy into a crack and turned to Brightheart. "Stay and finish up here. I won't be long."

Outside in the clearing, Bramblestar spotted Lionblaze and Daisy on their way back into the clearing with a load of moss. "We're going to check the water levels," Bramblestar called. "Do you want to come with us?"

Lionblaze paused, his bundle of moss tucked under his chin.

Daisy gave him a nudge. "Go on," she urged him. "I'll sort out the bedding."

"Thanks!" Lionblaze dropped the moss and bounded over

to join Bramblestar and Jayfeather.

Heading into the trees, Bramblestar caught a whiff of ThunderClan scent, and came upon Squirrelflight's hunting patrol, already heading back to camp. Squirrelflight was carrying a thrush, while Dovewing and Thornclaw both had mice.

"You've done well!" Bramblestar purred.

Squirrelflight nodded. "I think the prey is starting to come back," she mumbled around her mouthful of feathers.

"Why don't you come with us to check the water levels?" Bramblestar suggested.

"Sure." Squirrelflight dropped her catch at Mousewhisker's paws. "You can take that in. And Thornclaw, you can lead the patrol out again. It seems like the prey's running well, so we ought to make the most of it."

As the rest of the patrol headed for the camp, Bramblestar led the way down the slope with Squirrelflight at his side, and Lionblaze and Jayfeather just behind. He suddenly felt at ease, comfortable and happy to be with these cats he knew so well. The others seemed to feel the same, their tension and anxiety relaxing as they trotted through the trees.

Scuffling broke out behind them with a mock growl from Lionblaze. "Die, ShadowClan trespasser!"

"Get off, you great lump!" Jayfeather protested, though there was laughter in his voice.

Squirrelflight whipped around. "Honestly! How old are you both?"

The two brothers broke apart. "Sorry," Lionblaze muttered,

though his eyes glimmered with mischief. "I don't know what came over me."

"I'll get you later," Jayfeather promised as they set out again.

It's almost like they are kits again . . . our kits, Bramblestar thought. A pang of sorrow pierced him as he pictured Hollyleaf. *She should be with us. I hope she found peace in StarClan.*

Reaching the top of the hollow, the four cats peered over, scanning the floodwater that covered their dens.

"It's just as deep as it was before," Bramblestar meowed, discouraged.

"I'm not so sure." Lionblaze pointed with his tail to a tangle of soggy roots that stuck out of the cliff above where the nursery had been. "See those? They look as if they might have been uncovered recently."

Bramblestar nodded slowly, trying to remember whether the roots had been visible the last time he looked.

"When we went down into the tunnels," Lionblaze meowed, "you scratched on the floor to mark the water level. Maybe we could do the same here." He frowned. "Though I don't see how we could make scratch marks on the side of the cliffs."

"Maybe we don't need to," Squirrelflight put in. "We could go to the edge of the flood among the trees, and mark the water level there with sticks instead."

"Great idea!" Bramblestar agreed.

Following the top of the hollow, the cats reached the water's edge and paused for a moment, gazing out across the lake and the drowned forest. Bramblestar felt his paws sinking into mud.

"Mouse dung!" Jayfeather cursed. He had taken an extra pace forward, and now the mud was creeping up his legs, hampering him as he tried to backtrack.

Lionblaze leaned over and grabbed his brother by the scruff, hauling him back. "Use your nose, mouse-brain!" he hissed.

Jayfeather shrugged him off, and raised each paw in turn to shake off sticky clots of mud. Lionblaze jumped back to avoid the shower.

"The scents are all different," Jayfeather mewed after a moment. "And the air feels weird on my fur."

For a few heartbeats longer Bramblestar stood still, contemplating his flooded territory and realizing how much had changed—perhaps forever. *I wonder if we'll ever hunt in that part of the forest again.*

Then Squirrelflight gave him a shove. "Wake up!" she meowed. "Let's look for some sticks."

She and Bramblestar and Lionblaze scattered up the slope, searching for long, thin sticks that would be easy to drive into the mud as markers. They brought them back to Jayfeather, who chewed one end into a point.

"This tastes disgusting," he muttered, spitting out bark.

"I wish we could mark the level in the hollow like this," Squirrelflight meowed as she drove the first stick into the marshy ground.

"So do I," Bramblestar agreed. "We'll just have to take note of where the water reaches up to on the cliffs."

They continued to set markers along the water's edge

between the hollow and an ash tree that stood with its roots washed by floodwater.

The training clearing is under there, Bramblestar thought sadly. Then he spotted Jayfeather creeping up on Lionblaze, who was busy pushing a stick into the mud with his back turned. Bramblestar opened his jaws to warn Lionblaze, then closed them again, watching to see what would happen.

Jayfeather sneaked up until he was a tail-length away from his brother. Then he slammed his paws down into the water, throwing up an enormous splash that showered Lionblaze from ears to tail. Leaping backward, Jayfeather avoided the worst of it.

Lionblaze spun around with a hiss of fury. "Stupid furball!"

"I said I'd get you." Jayfeather licked one paw complacently and drew it over his ear.

"You wait!" Lionblaze bared his teeth and leaped for his brother, who dashed away into the trees.

Bramblestar listened to them crashing about, and suppressed a *mrrow* of amusement.

"It's good to see them having fun for once," Squirrelflight observed, padding up to him. She gave another push to Lionblaze's stick. "There. We're all done." She broke off, and Bramblestar realized that she was staring over his shoulder. Turning, he saw that Jessy was watching them from a few tail-lengths away.

"What does she want?" Squirrelflight meowed.

Bramblestar felt slightly uneasy. "I don't know. I'll go and ask her." He padded up to the kittypet, wondering whether some disaster had overtaken their temporary camp. "Is everything okay?"

Jessy blinked at him, her eyes gleaming. "I'm sorry if I'm interrupting," she mewed. "Everything's fine. This can wait until later if you're busy."

"No, now's a good time," Bramblestar told her. Glancing back at Squirrelflight, he called, "Round up those two daft furballs and go back to camp." Then he led Jessy along the top of the flood, heading toward the ShadowClan border. "What can I do for you?" he asked.

Instead of replying, Jessy stopped and looked out over the drowned forest. "I wonder what it was like here before the floods came," she murmured.

"It was beautiful," Bramblestar replied at once. "There was long grass, and patches of fern and bramble where the prey could hide. In greenleaf the sun would shine through the branches and make patterns on the ground. The air would be full of scents—fresh green growth, and the warm scents of prey. And then in leaf-bare, in the frost and snow, the cold would make your pelt tingle, and you'd feel so alive!"

"You love living here, don't you?"

"Yes, I do," Bramblestar meowed, walking on. "I can remember our old home, and I still walk there in my dreams, but—but I have always believed that StarClan has led us to the right place here."

"Are you quite sure about that?" Jessy pressed, picking up the note of doubt in his voice.

"I have to have faith that the floods will go down,"

Bramblestar told her. "But come on, Jessy," he added. "You didn't come looking for me just to chat about the forest."

Jessy narrowed her eyes. "No, I wanted to talk about the kittypets who are giving ShadowClan all that trouble. I think I know who they are."

"You do?" Bramblestar felt suddenly excited. "Who?"

"There's a gang of kittypets and a few strays who like to claim that part of the forest for themselves," Jessy replied. "They hunt there—not that they ever catch anything," she added with a sly sideways glance at Bramblestar.

Will she ever forget that I said that to her? "Go on," he mewed.

"I don't know these kittypets well," Jessy continued. "I think one's called Ziggy, and another one is Riga. But I know where they live and where they like to roam."

Bramblestar felt the fur along his spine start to rise. "Are you suggesting we attack them *without* ShadowClan's approval?"

Jessy shrugged. "It's a possibility."

For a moment Bramblestar was filled with admiration for Jessy's courage, and for how she was willing to help wild cats who were completely unknown to her.

"I can see how much your sister means to you," Jessy added. Taken aback by her perceptiveness, Bramblestar couldn't think of anything to say before she went on. "Do lots of cats have kin in other Clans?"

"Great StarClan, no!" Bramblestar exclaimed. "Cats are supposed to stay in the Clan where they were born. Clan loyalty is very important to us. A cat who changed Clans would be thought of as a traitor, and it would be hard for their new

Clan to trust them. Tawnypelt only went to live in Shadow-Clan because our father became their leader."

"Wow!" Jessy's eyes stretched wide. "Why didn't you go with her?"

Bramblestar hesitated. *I can't tell her about Tigerstar! We'd be here all day!* "It's . . . complicated," he meowed at last. "ThunderClan has always been my home. I miss Tawnypelt, but I've never regretted my decision."

He and Jessy padded on in silence for a few moments, until Bramblestar began to pick up the scent of ShadowClan border markers. "We should turn back here," he mewed.

"Okay." Jessy bounced on her paws. "But we're going to attack these kittypets, right? I can show you where to find them. They often go out at night, and that would be a really good time to sneak up on them." She jumped up and swiped one paw at a head of cow parsley, scattering the tiny white flowers on the grass. "We'll soon teach them to stay away from Clan cats!"

"Hang on," Bramblestar warned. "I haven't said we're doing it yet. I have to speak with my Clanmates first."

For a moment Jessy looked wounded. "But—"

She broke off at the sound of cats brushing through the undergrowth. Bramblestar stiffened, then relaxed as he picked up ThunderClan scent. A patrol came into view with Cloudtail in the lead, followed by Birchfall and Whitewing, with her apprentice, Dewpaw.

"Bramblestar!" Cloudtail ran up to his leader with his ears flattened. "Those mangy crow-food eaters from ShadowClan have been trespassing again!"

Bramblestar saw that all the cats in the patrol were bristling with anger, their eyes glittering.

"We picked up their scent several tail-lengths inside our border," Birchfall confirmed.

"Those kittypets you heard about must be attacking them on their other border," Whitewing meowed, "so they're trying to hunt on our territory."

"We can't let them get away with it!" Cloudtail growled.

"No, we can't," Bramblestar agreed. Turning to Jessy, he meowed, "It looks like we need your plan."

The evening was clear and calm, with a few gaps in the clouds that let through stray gleams of red sunlight. Long shadows stretched across the clearing outside the tunnel, and a fresh breeze stirred the branches.

This is the best weather we've had since the floods came, Bramblestar thought hopefully. *Maybe things are changing.*

Jumping to the top of the mudfall, he gave a yowl. "Let all cats who are old enough to catch their own prey come here outside the tunnel for a Clan meeting!"

Surprised mews burst from the cats nearest the tunnel, who were trying to warm their fur in the last of the sunlight. The apprentices broke off their fighting practice at the far side of the clearing and pattered eagerly across to the bottom of the mudfall, followed by their mentors. Daisy, Cherryfall, and Blossomfall popped out of the tunnel. Purdy appeared a moment later, his pelt stuck all over with moss, and plopped himself down beside the apprentices. Jessy bounded over to Frankie and Minty, who were sharing a blackbird under an arching clump of fern, and chivvied them over to join the rest. Jayfeather came to sit at the mouth of the tunnel, with the sick cats clustered around him.

"Cats of ThunderClan," Bramblestar began when all the cats were assembled, "and our guests." He dipped his head to the three kittypets. "You all know that kittypets have been harassing ShadowClan in the woods beyond their top border. Tomorrow I'm going to lead a patrol to get rid of them."

"What?" Dustpelt sprang to his paws. "Have you got bees in your brain?"

"You offered ShadowClan our help and they turned you down," Graystripe pointed out. "Rowanstar won't thank you for interfering."

Several other cats echoed their protests. Bramblestar looked down on their bristling fur and twitching tails. *It's just as well I haven't told them this was Jessy's idea.*

"If the kittypets are allowed to keep attacking Shadow-Clan," he went on, forcing himself to stay calm, "then ShadowClan will start to hunt in our territory, or in the woods beyond our border. It's in our own interest to deal with the kittypets." He was relieved to see that several of his cats were looking interested, but he knew that he hadn't won them over yet.

"Why can't ShadowClan deal with their own problems?" Mousewhisker protested. "These are *kittypets*, for StarClan's sake! How dangerous can they be?"

"Well, we've met fierce kittypets in our time," Sandstorm pointed out from her place just inside the tunnel. "And ShadowClan is weakened by the floods."

"So are we," Rosepetal retorted. "Why should we risk injury to help ShadowClan? What have they ever done for us?"

"Yes, we didn't survive the Great Battle to fight on behalf of ShadowClan," Brackenfur agreed.

Bramblestar glanced down and caught Jessy's eye. She looked shocked by the strength of the objections to the plan. He noticed that Squirrelflight was watching Jessy, too; then she fixed her green gaze straight on him. She hadn't spoken yet.

One by one the warriors turned to look at their deputy, waiting for her to give her opinion. Squirrelflight kept her eyes fixed on Bramblestar for a long moment, then rose to her paws. Bramblestar found himself holding his breath as he waited for her to speak.

"I think we should take action," she meowed. "We can't let a bunch of kittypets force ShadowClan onto our territory. If ShadowClan isn't strong enough to deal with them, then we'll have to!"

Bramblestar saw a ripple of enthusiasm pass through the Clan in response to his deputy's rousing words. Loud caterwauls rose into the air from almost all the cats, Mousewhisker and Rosepetal among them.

"That makes sense," Graystripe declared.

"Yes! Let's drive them off!" Thornclaw yowled.

Blossomfall worked her claws into the ground. "The forest

is for warriors, not for kittypets!"

Bramblestar noticed that Frankie and Minty were looking a bit unnerved by the protests against kittypets. Millie leaned over to them and Bramblestar heard her whisper, "Don't worry, they don't mean you. They get like this sometimes."

"Then that's settled," Bramblestar announced. "Warriors who are prepared to fight, join me now." He slithered down from the mudfall, with mud sticking to his fur and clogging his claws. At the foot of the pile he met Cloudtail, Thornclaw, Cinderheart, Lionblaze, Blossomfall, Ivypool, and her apprentice, Snowpaw, all pressing forward to volunteer.

"I can't let apprentices come," Bramblestar meowed with a glance at Snowpaw.

Snowpaw took a pace back, looking hurt.

"Why not?" Ivypool asked Bramblestar. "They have to fight sooner or later, and a battle against kittypets won't be as dangerous as fighting another Clan."

Bramblestar tipped his head on one side. "Good point. Okay, Snowpaw, you can come."

Snowpaw let out a squeal of delight and leaped straight into the air, while his sister, Amberpaw, slid out of the tunnel and ran forward. "Me too!" she begged.

Jayfeather snaked his tail around her neck and hauled her back. "Don't even think about it. You're far too sick." He ignored Amberpaw's protests and herded her back into the tunnel.

"What about you, Dewpaw?" Bramblestar prompted, seeing the third of the litter hovering close by. His eyes were wide and his gray-and-white fur looked ruffled.

"I'm going to stay and help guard the camp," Whitewing announced before her apprentice could reply. "Dewpaw can come with you if he likes," she added, glancing at the little cat beside her.

Dewpaw shook his head. "It's okay, I'll stay and help you, Whitewing. You might need me."

Bramblestar noticed that Lilypaw had crept closer to the front of the crowd of warriors, and he shook his head firmly at her mentor, Poppyfrost. *Lilypaw is still too vulnerable to fight, so soon after Seedpaw's death.* Poppyfrost nodded agreement and bent her head to speak gently to Lilypaw.

Squirrelflight thrust her way through the crowd of warriors around Bramblestar. "When do we leave?"

"You don't," Bramblestar told her. "I need you to stay and take charge here."

Squirrelflight's green eyes widened in surprise. "You mean you're going yourself? This is just a minor skirmish. It doesn't need the Clan leader!"

"It was my suggestion," Bramblestar reminded her. "I have to take part and share the risks with my Clanmates."

Squirrelflight nodded reluctantly. "All right, I'll stay."

Bramblestar glanced around until he spotted Jessy sitting with Frankie and Minty. "Jessy," he called to her, "will you come with us, please? We need you to show us where to go."

Jessy nodded and rose to her paws to make her way over to Bramblestar.

"A kittypet fighting kittypets?" Squirrelflight hissed into Bramblestar's ear.

"Actually, this was Jessy's idea," Bramblestar whispered

back. "She knows these kittypets."

Squirrelflight's eyes narrowed to green slits. "Why does she want to help ShadowClan?" she asked suspiciously. "Are we settling an old score for her against her enemies?"

Bramblestar realized that was a fair question. "No, I trust her," he replied. "And I respect her for having the courage to suggest it."

Squirrelflight let out a snort. "Just be careful, and remember that we don't really know her at all."

Frankie had followed Jessy over to the Clan leader, and now he spoke up. "I'll come too, Bramblestar, if you like."

Bramblestar looked at him, and at Minty, who was peering around his shoulder, her eyes wide with horror at the thought of going into battle. "No," he meowed. "Thanks for offering, but you stay here and go on with your training. You too, Minty." His gaze swept around his assembled warriors. "The rest of us leave at dawn!"

CHAPTER 21
❧

Thin, gray light covered the forest. Long before the sun would crest the ridge, Bramblestar led his cats out of camp and brushed through the dew-soaked undergrowth, straight up the slope to the top border. His paws tingled with anticipation as he and his Clanmates passed their own scent markers and entered the unknown forest.

Crossing the ridge, Bramblestar let Jessy take the lead along the downward slope, well outside ShadowClan territory. None of them had ever set paw in this part of the forest before. They padded warily among huge oak trees, their gnarled roots stretched out as if to trip careless paws. Everything was silent in the dawn chill.

Gradually the oaks thinned out, to be replaced by dark, slender pines. The ground was thick with fallen needles that gave way slightly under every paw step. Blossomfall sprang a tail-length from the ground at the loud alarm call of some hidden bird, then licked her chest fur in embarrassment and tried to look unconcerned.

"Don't worry," Bramblestar told her. "We're all getting nervous. This is new for all of us."

"I don't like the way we can be seen at such a distance," Cloudtail meowed, waving his tail at the ranks of pine trees, the ground between them clear of undergrowth. "I'll stick out like a mushroom."

"So will I," Snowpaw added worriedly.

"You could try rolling in mud and pine needles," Thornclaw suggested. "Then these kittypets might think that you're a couple of bushes."

"That's not a bad idea," Cloudtail responded. He spotted a muddy hollow underneath a tree and led Snowpaw over there. Bramblestar and the others watched as the two cats rolled over in the mud until their fur stood out in sticky spikes.

"That's so weird!" Jessy exclaimed, intrigued and with a glint of amusement in her eyes. "The lengths you warriors will go to in order to stalk an enemy!"

Thornclaw gave her a defensive look. "We're not kittypets, you know!"

As the cats set out again, Bramblestar began picking up traces of ShadowClan scent, but they were all stale, and though at one point the scent was mixed with a tang of squirrel blood, he didn't think that ShadowClan had been this way for some days.

Before they had gone much farther, Cloudtail came to walk alongside Bramblestar, who tried not to let his nose twitch at the reek of mud coming from the warrior's white pelt. "I'm a bit worried about Jessy," Cloudtail whispered. "Should we really be taking a kittypet into battle?"

"I know she hasn't had much training," Bramblestar

mewed. "We'll just have to make sure she doesn't get cornered one-on-one."

Cloudtail grunted. "We might all be too busy watching out for our own tails."

"I'm looking forward to this!" Bramblestar heard Lionblaze speaking just behind him, excitement in his voice. "It's been moons since we've had to use our battle moves."

"Which is a *good* thing," Cinderheart replied.

"I know," Lionblaze told her. "It's not like I want to go through the Great Battle again; don't think that. But how dangerous will it be, teaching a few kittypets to keep away from Clan cats?"

Bramblestar glanced back over his shoulder. "Kittypets who have already defeated ShadowClan," he pointed out.

Lionblaze's eyes gleamed. "Oh, ShadowClan!"

"Remember that you don't have your—your *power* anymore," Cinderheart warned him. "You can get injured, just like any other cat."

"I'll be careful," Lionblaze told her, flexing his claws. "Don't worry."

Cinderheart looked doubtful, as if she didn't quite believe him, but she said no more.

"Hey, Bramblestar!" Ivypool's voice came from a few foxlengths away. "Come and look at this!"

Ivypool and her apprentice had been ranging away on one side; now they were standing in front of a drift of white on the ground. Padding closer, Bramblestar picked up the scent of ShadowClan, and realized that the white stuff was a scatter of pigeon feathers.

"ShadowClan must have killed here," Ivypool meowed.

Bramblestar nodded; the scent was fresh, too, much more recent than the other traces he had picked up.

"ShadowClan seems to be doing well enough on their own," Thornclaw declared, bounding up and giving the feathers a sniff. "Do they really need our help with these kittypets?"

"One dead pigeon doesn't mean a full fresh-kill pile," Bramblestar meowed. "And remember that our borders will be threatened if ShadowClan goes hungry."

But as the patrol set out again, Bramblestar admitted to himself that he was starting to have his own doubts about their mission. *I can't let Tawnypelt's Clan suffer,* he insisted. *And we need to protect our own territory.* But his paws prickled at the thought of being caught here by a ShadowClan patrol.

A little farther on, Bramblestar realized that the pine trees had begun to thin out. He stiffened as he caught a faint trace of a Twoleg and a dog, then relaxed as he realized that they were long gone.

Jessy trotted up to his side. "Do you see that tree stump?" she mewed, waving her tail at the remains of a lightning-blasted tree. "I'm pretty sure I recognize it. We must be getting close." She went on more cautiously, sniffing here and there, while the rest of the patrol bunched together as they followed.

"There's kittypet scent here," Jessy announced, raising her head. "And I'm pretty sure they're the ones who have been harassing ShadowClan."

"How sure are you?" Blossomfall pressed. "We can't attack innocent kittypets."

"No kittypets are innocent!" Snowpaw declared. "They're all fat and lazy."

Jessy cleared her throat meaningfully.

Snowpaw glanced sideways at her, his ears flattened. "Sorry," he muttered.

"We won't fight any needless battles," Bramblestar assured his Clanmates. "Ivypool, you go off in that direction"—he waved his tail—"and Cinderheart, you go that way. Look for more traces of the kittypets, and any sign of ShadowClan patrols."

I really don't want to be caught here, he thought as the two she-cats headed off in opposite directions. *These are ShadowClan hunting grounds now.*

Bramblestar waited until Cinderheart and Ivypool returned, reporting no further traces of the kittypets.

"We'll have to go closer to their dens," Jessy meowed. "This way." She led them on until the trees thinned out even more, and dense undergrowth filled the gaps between the trunks. Wriggling his way through thick bushes that snagged his fur and soaked him to the skin, Bramblestar emerged into an open space with a line of Twoleg fences at the far side. Twoleg dens, built of reddish stone, reared up beyond the fences.

The rest of the patrol emerged, bristling at the unfamiliar surroundings and the strong scent of Twolegs, though Cloudtail padded over to Bramblestar and murmured, "This reminds me of the old forest, where the trees met the Twolegplace."

"You're right," Bramblestar agreed. "The same plants, the same kind of smells . . ."

"My mother, Princess, came from a den like these," Cloudtail added. "So did Firestar."

Bramblestar nodded, feeling a pang of unexpected regret that he would never see the old forest again. But a heartbeat later he was distracted by Jessy calling to him.

"I know where I am now! I recognize that big tree with the white flowers. Come on!"

She began running ahead, more confident with every stride, while the rest of the patrol raced after her.

"Look, there's the den with the broken fence!" Jessy meowed. "And the place where I played with some little Twolegs. It's not far now."

"I think she's just showing off," Thornclaw grumbled as he bounded along at Bramblestar's side.

"We'd be lost without her," Lionblaze pointed out. "Literally."

Finally Jessy stopped and the patrol gathered around her. "The kittypet who lives behind this fence is called Victor, I think," she began. "He comes into the woods with Ziggy and Riga. If any cats are going to cause trouble, it'll be those three."

"Thanks, Jessy." Bramblestar turned to his Clanmates. "Stay here," he ordered. "Jessy and I will scout ahead."

He noticed that the warriors didn't look too happy, but none of them protested as he jumped up to the top of the fence. Jessy followed him and together they looked down onto the neat square of grass behind the Twoleg den, surrounded by bushes and brightly colored Twoleg flowers.

"No sign of Victor," Jessy commented. "He might have gone to visit the others."

"Then let's go look," Bramblestar meowed.

With Jessy in the lead they ran along the top of the fence, checking the enclosed spaces, each with its square of grass. Bramblestar could scent several different cats, but they didn't see any.

Suddenly a stronger aroma wafted over Bramblestar. "Who are you, and what do you want?" a voice growled from behind him.

Bramblestar turned, balancing awkwardly on the narrow fence-top. A muscular black-and-white tom stood in front of him, his teeth bared in the beginnings of a snarl.

"Who wants to know?" Bramblestar asked. "Are you Victor?"

"No, I'm a friend of his," the black-and-white tom replied. "My name's Webster." He peered around Bramblestar and spoke to Jessy. "I've seen you around, whatever your name is. What are you doing with these wild cats?"

"I'm Jessy, and this is Bramblestar," Jessy replied. "We've come to tell you to leave the wild cats alone."

In spite of the defiance in her voice, her statement sounded feeble. *Why should they do what we say, unless we back it up with our claws?* Bramblestar thought.

"Oh, sure." Webster was scornful. "We'll do exactly what you tell us—not!"

Bramblestar felt exposed on the fence-top, his legs wobbling as he unsheathed his claws. Webster flicked his tail-tip contemptuously and took a threatening stride forward so that he was almost nose-to-nose with Bramblestar. Though Bramblestar was aware that behind him Jessy was bristling, ready for a fight, he knew that he couldn't take on cats like this, so far above the forest floor.

Is Webster really going to pounce while we're on top of the fence? Bramblestar wondered. *Sure, kittypets have good balance, but not that good!*

"Get ready to jump down," he muttered to Jessy. "Take the fight to the ground."

"Oh, yes," a new voice purred from behind him, beyond Jessy. "What a good idea."

Bramblestar glanced over his shoulder to see three kittypets crowding up to Jessy on top of the fence. All three of them had bristling fur and bright, bold eyes.

"That's Victor," Jessy murmured, pointing with her tail at the pale brown tabby who was in the lead. "The ginger she-cat behind him is Scarlet, and the silver tabby is O'Hara. Ziggy and Riga will be somewhere close by; you can be sure of that."

O'Hara waved his tail at Bramblestar. "*So* pleased to meet you," he purred.

As if his words were a signal, all four kittypets charged at Bramblestar and Jessy.

"Jump!" Bramblestar yowled.

Together he and Jessy sprang down from the fence on the forest side. Screeching furiously, the kittypets launched themselves after them. Bramblestar was knocked off his paws as

O'Hara landed on top of him. He rolled over and sprang up again, raking his claws along the silver tabby's side.

Jessy was bravely tussling with Webster, but for all her courage she was much lighter than Webster and she was getting the worst of it. Webster was obviously an experienced fighter, gripping Jessy in his claws so she couldn't maneuver to strike. O'Hara had backed off, and Bramblestar was about to leap to help Jessy when two bodies slammed into him from behind. He let out a yowl as he felt claws digging into his shoulders. Twisting around, he found himself facing Victor and Scarlet, their eyes gleaming and their shoulder fur bristling as they tried to thrust him to the ground.

Remembering his battle training, Bramblestar let himself go limp, sinking to the ground with the two kittypets on top of him.

"Coward!" Scarlet jeered. "I thought you wild cats could fight."

Not wasting breath on a reply, Bramblestar exploded upward, balancing on his hind paws while he struck out at his enemies with both forepaws. His claws scored down Victor's muzzle; the kittypet let out a yelp of pain and scrambled back out of range. But although Bramblestar's second blow caught Scarlet across her ear, she barely paused, shaking her head to clear it, then leaped at Bramblestar again. Victor recovered himself and joined her, bearing Bramblestar to the ground. As his paws gave way he caught a glimpse of a slender black cat dashing up to join the fray, with a ginger-and-white kittypet hard on his paws.

Oh, no! That must be Ziggy and Riga! Jessy and I are crow-food! "ThunderClan, attack!" he screeched.

Bramblestar struggled under the weight of Scarlet and Victor. He was beginning to think his Clanmates hadn't heard him when he heard yowls of defiance, so loud that they swamped the screeches of the battle, and the sound of cats crashing through the undergrowth.

Thank StarClan! My warriors are here!

A heartbeat later the weight of the kittypets vanished and Bramblestar caught a glimpse of Cinderheart chasing Victor into the bushes. Ivypool darted in to slash at Scarlet from one side, while Snowpaw copied her on the other side, leaving Scarlet not knowing where to defend herself.

You've taught your apprentice well, Ivypool, Bramblestar thought.

Cloudtail had torn Webster away from Jessy and was driving him back with repeated blows to his ears. Jessy staggered to her paws, battered and bleeding, but still looking around for the next attack. Bramblestar headed toward her, but was blocked by the ginger-and-white kittypet, who hurtled toward him with growls of anger and aimed a blow at him with claws extended. Bramblestar ducked under the blow and thrust himself at the kittypet's chest, driving him to the ground, then leaped on top of him, battering at his belly with all four paws. The kittypet wriggled free and fled.

Bramblestar rose and looked around him, his head reeling from the force of the battle. *I never thought kittypets could fight like this!* He saw O'Hara trip Lionblaze, then crouch on top of him, raking his claws across Lionblaze's shoulders, until

Cinderheart grabbed him and chased him off. Lionblaze rose to his paws, glaring after Cinderheart with fury in his eyes. Bramblestar could feel his rage that Cinderheart thought he had to be rescued, even though blood was dripping from her wounds too.

Gradually the ThunderClan cats began to drive the kittypets back toward the Twoleg fences, their warrior skills overcoming their adversaries' uncontrolled attack. Bramblestar spotted Jessy copying his move of ducking under a blow from the black kittypet and shoving her to the ground. The black kittypet rolled away from Jessy's claws and fled.

Jessy learns fast! Bramblestar thought admiringly. "Great move!" he called to her.

Victor lunged out of a nearby bush and hurled himself at Blossomfall, who staggered under the weight of his body. Bramblestar sprang after them and hauled Victor off, sinking his teeth into the kittypet's tail. Victor let out a shriek of pain and whirled to face him, but he was off-balance, and Bramblestar easily crushed him to the ground.

Standing over Victor, pinning him down with both hind paws, Bramblestar raised his claws to slash through Victor's throat. "Do you give in?" he growled.

Victor bared his teeth in a snarl. "Kill me if you want, flea-pelt!"

Bramblestar stepped back, letting the defeated kittypet scramble to his paws. "Do you give in?" he repeated.

Victor gave him a puzzled look, as if he wasn't sure why he was still alive. The rest of the kittypets, apart from the black cat who had fled, gathered around, their expressions still threatening.

"Warriors do not kill if there is no need," Bramblestar told them. "But you must let the wild cats hunt here in the forest."

"Why should we?" Scarlet sneered.

"Because if you don't, we'll come back with more warriors, and show less mercy," Blossomfall growled.

The kittypets still hesitated, until Lionblaze stepped forward. His golden pelt was soaked in blood, and his eyes glared menace. He didn't need to speak; all the kittypets edged away from him.

"All right," Victor agreed at last, dull anger in his voice. "We'll leave the squirrel munchers alone."

"Good." Bramblestar was about to call his patrol together to leave, when a new voice spoke behind him.

"What in the name of StarClan do you think you're doing?"

CHAPTER 22
❧

Bramblestar whirled around. Rowanstar stood a fox-length away, flanked by Pinenose, Ferretclaw, and his apprentice, Spikepaw. The fur of all four cats was bristling with rage, so that they looked twice their normal size. Their furious gazes were fixed on the ThunderClan cats.

"How dare you come here?" Rowanstar hissed.

Bramblestar was aware of the kittypets slinking away. He took a pace forward, trying to find the right words to defend himself and his patrol. *Fox dung! I'd hoped we could get away without ShadowClan knowing we were here.*

"What makes you think you have to fight our battles for us?" Rowanstar snarled. "This is our hunting territory now. What gives you the right even to set paw here?" He dug his claws hard into the ground as if what he really wanted was to rake them across Bramblestar's face. "You came to offer us help, and we refused. Why couldn't you take no for an answer?"

"I thought—" Bramblestar began.

"Thought!" Rowanstar spat. "That was Firestar's problem, too. He always thought he knew what was best for every Clan."

Stung, Bramblestar forced himself to stay calm. He didn't want other cats to think he viewed himself as superior to the other leaders, interfering when it wasn't needed. "I found out Jessy had inside information," he meowed, angling his ears toward the brown she-cat. "She knew where these troublesome kittypets lived."

Rowanstar stared at Jessy. "Because she's a kittypet herself, right? So ThunderClan is taking in kittypets now?" he sneered. "*What* a surprise!" He lashed his tail. "Stay out of our business, Bramblestar, and concentrate on your own Clan."

At a word of command from Rowanstar, the ShadowClan cats encircled the ThunderClan patrol and began to drive them back toward their own territory, keeping them tightly bunched together. Bramblestar felt as though they were being escorted back to the border like trespassers. *Whatever Rowanstar says, we saved their miserable pelts,* he thought furiously, but he remained silent, recognizing that nothing he could say would help matters.

They crossed ShadowClan territory and reached the ThunderClan border near the grassy clearing.

"Now get out and stay out," Rowanstar growled. With a nod of his head he gathered his patrol and headed back into his own territory.

"The ungrateful, mange-ridden furballs!" Snowpaw's words exploded from him as soon as the ShadowClan cats had vanished into the undergrowth. "We were helping them! They should be thanking us!"

"Hmm . . ." Ivypool flicked her ears. "Maybe we should

have waited to be asked before we helped."

"Maybe we shouldn't have helped at all," Thornclaw mewed.

"I can't believe they were so angry," Jessy murmured, her eyes still wide with shock. "I'm sorry, Bramblestar. I didn't mean to get you into trouble."

"It's not your fault," Bramblestar told her. "I made the decision, and if it keeps ShadowClan patrols out of our territory, it was the right one."

I wish I was really convinced of that, he thought to himself. Gazing at his battered warriors, he wondered if he had gone into battle for the right reasons, or if he had allowed himself to be swayed by Jessy's bold ideas.

It was after sunhigh by the time Bramblestar led his cats back into their camp. Most of the cats were stretched out in the clearing, trying to warm themselves in a few pale gleams of sunlight that pierced the ragged cloud. Squirrelflight, who was talking to Brackenfur near the tunnel entrance, sprang to her paws as soon as she spotted the returning patrol.

"Great StarClan!" she exclaimed, bounding over to them. "What happened?"

"The kittypets happened," Bramblestar responded briefly.

"But . . . you're so badly hurt!" Squirrelflight's green gaze was filled with horror as she turned and raced back to the tunnel. "Jayfeather!" she yowled. "Come here! You're needed!"

Immediately the medicine cat popped out of the tunnel. His jaws parted to taste the air; Bramblestar realized he would recognize the reek of blood at once.

"I knew this was a mistake," Jayfeather mewed as he approached the patrol and began to sniff at their wounds. "Especially when Leafpool is still in the ShadowClan camp. I need her here!"

Oh, StarClan! Bramblestar thought. *I hope Rowanstar isn't taking out his anger on my medicine cat!*

Frankie and Minty bounded across the clearing to Jessy, looking shocked when they saw the blood welling from the scratches on her shoulders.

"Did you really fight?" Minty asked, her eyes stretched wide.

"Did you chase off the kittypets?" meowed Frankie.

Bramblestar listened while Jessy described the battle, apparently relishing the danger and pleased that they had defeated Victor and his friends. Frankie and Minty listened breathlessly.

"Wow!" Frankie looked more impressed than scared. "I wish I'd been with you."

Minty shuddered. "I don't."

"It was great!" Jessy's eyes glowed with the memory. "I know we got hurt, but it was worth it to teach those arrogant kittypets a lesson!"

Bramblestar realized that while the kittypets were talking, Brackenfur had padded up to his side. "Are you sure you weren't settling kittypet scores?" he murmured.

For a heartbeat, Bramblestar wasn't sure. *No,* he told himself firmly. *Jessy was only trying to help.*

Before he could reply to Brackenfur, a groan from Lionblaze distracted him. The golden-furred warrior staggered and flopped over on his side. "The pain . . ." he gasped.

"I told you so!" Cinderheart shrieked as she ran to his side. "When will you learn that you're not invulnerable anymore?"

She nudged Lionblaze to his paws while Jayfeather helped to support him on the other side. Together the two cats half carried, half dragged him into the tunnel to have his wounds treated. The rest of the patrol followed.

"Mouse-brain!" Jayfeather muttered angrily as he went. "You're *all* mouse-brained. And all over a bunch of kittypets!"

Discouraged, Bramblestar watched them go. He could sense the depression among the Clan, the sense that although they had won the battle, it was a hollow victory. Only the kittypets seemed to be happy.

"Come on," he meowed to Jessy, touching her shoulder with his tail. "You need to go to Jayfeather and have your wounds treated." As she turned away from her friends and followed him to the tunnel, he added, "Thank you for your courage, Jessy. I know the battle was harder for you than for any of us."

Jessy halted, gazing into his eyes. "I just copied what you did," she mewed. "I had the best teacher."

For a moment Bramblestar didn't know what to say to her. But before the silence could stretch out, Squirrelflight came padding up. Jessy dipped her head to Bramblestar and headed inside to see Jayfeather.

Bramblestar braced himself for a scolding from his deputy,

ready to defend himself. But to his surprise, Squirrelflight's gaze was sympathetic.

"You had to do something," she meowed. "We can't have ShadowClan hunting in our territory, and this was a way to stop them."

"That's what I wanted to do," Bramblestar responded.

"The trouble is," Squirrelflight went on, "it could be seen as interfering, insulting to ShadowClan, and a stupid risk to our own warriors."

Bramblestar sighed. "You're right," he admitted.

Squirrelflight leaned toward him and gave his ears a brisk lick. "It's behind us," she told him. "We need to focus on our own Clanmates now."

As she finished speaking, Sandstorm padded up with a mouse dangling from her jaws. "Come on, Bramblestar, you need to eat."

Bramblestar realized that his belly was growling with hunger. The warm scent of the mouse made his jaws water, but he hesitated for a moment, looking around until he had checked that all his patrol had headed into the tunnel to have Jayfeather deal with their injuries. Then he crouched down and bit into the mouse.

"Thanks, Sandstorm," he mumbled around his mouthful.

While he was eating, Graystripe appeared, giving him a friendly nod. "I know you're worried about whether you did the right thing," he began. "But you shouldn't. Firestar would have done exactly the same."

Bramblestar winced. "That's what Rowanstar said."

Graystripe was quiet for a moment, while Bramblestar gulped down the rest of the mouse. When he spoke again, he seemed to be aware of exactly what Bramblestar was thinking. "You know, Firestar wouldn't have seen it as interfering. He truly believed that if another Clan needed our help, it was our duty to give it."

"But it's not," Bramblestar pointed out, swiping his tongue around his whiskers. "Not according to the warrior code. My loyalty should be to my own Clanmates, no other cats."

Graystripe snorted. "There's such a thing as basic decency," he pointed out.

"What would you have done?" Bramblestar asked.

"Followed Firestar," Graystripe replied without hesitation.

While Bramblestar was thinking that over, Purdy ambled out of the tunnel and settled down beside him. "Y'know, this reminds me of when I was a young cat, livin' with my Upwalker," he began.

Bramblestar suppressed a sigh. *Purdy, this isn't the time for one of your long-winded stories.* But there was no stopping Purdy, who embarked on a complicated tale of how he had helped a cat in the den next door deal with his Upwalker's new dog, and how the cat had then crept into Purdy's den and stolen his food.

"Well, I said to myself, *I'm not puttin' up with that*, so I . . ."

Bramblestar stopped listening as a clump of fern at the edge of the clearing shivered and Leafpool emerged. Her fur was ruffled and she had an agitated air.

Bramblestar bounded across the clearing to her side. "Leafpool! Are you okay?"

"Rowanstar asked me to leave!" Leafpool's eyes were sparkling with indignation. "He said he'd had enough of ThunderClan interference. Bramblestar, what have you done?"

Ivypool and Cinderheart appeared from the tunnel at that moment, their wounds treated with cobwebs and poultices of marigold. They helped Bramblestar explain to Leafpool what had happened in the battle with the kittypets.

"How could you be so mouse-brained?" Leafpool sighed, shaking her head. "The medicine-cat code extends to helping other Clans, but not the warrior code. You should stop trying to imagine what Firestar would have done, and be true to yourself."

"And Lionblaze is badly hurt," Cinderheart added.

"What?" Leafpool paused for a heartbeat, her eyes stretched wide with shock. Then without another word she raced to the tunnel and vanished inside.

Be true to myself? Bramblestar thought, looking after her glumly. His responsibilities weighed as heavy on his shoulders as if he were trying to carry the whole forest.

I wish I knew how.

CHAPTER 23

❧

Bramblestar sat in the shelter of a hazel bush, watching Minty creep up on a mouse. Frankie and Jessy, the other members of the patrol, were watching from farther around the edge of the clearing.

I can't believe this! Bramblestar thought wryly. *A hunting patrol of kittypets!*

But in the quarter moon since the expedition into Shadow-Clan's hunting grounds, all three of them were improving their tracking skills—even Minty, who had the twin advantages of being small and light-pawed. The mouse, nibbling something among the roots of a beech tree, had no idea that she was stalking it. She had even remembered to check the wind direction.

Suddenly Minty leaped forward and trapped the mouse under an outstretched paw. "Got it!" she exclaimed.

The mouse let out a squeal of terror.

"Oh, poor thing!" Minty sprang back, raising her paw, and the mouse scuttled off.

Frankie shook his head with an exaggerated sigh, then took off after the mouse and killed it with a quick blow to the head.

"Neat catch!" Bramblestar praised him as he padded back with the body dangling from his jaws.

Minty's head was hanging as she rejoined the patrol. "I'm sorry," she mewed. "It freaks me out when they squeal."

"It doesn't freak you out anymore when you eat them, though," Jessy pointed out.

"I know. I'll try to do better next time," Minty promised.

"Your stalking was very good," Bramblestar told her. "Why don't you see if you can scent some more prey?"

Obediently Minty began sniffing around, and soon picked up another scent trail, following it across the clearing with her nose to the ground.

"Well done!" Bramblestar called to her.

"This is odd," Minty muttered. "I don't know this scent, but it must be prey, right?"

Bramblestar and the others watched as she vanished among some brambles at the other side of the clearing, then froze with only her hindquarters and her tail sticking out. Feeling his pelt begin to prickle with apprehension, Bramblestar opened his jaws to taste the air. In the same heartbeat, Minty began to back slowly out of the thicket.

"Er . . . this isn't prey at all," she mewed.

The reek of fox hit Bramblestar in the throat as a snarl sounded from the midst of the brambles. Minty turned and fled across the clearing, her belly fur brushing the grass and her tail streaming out. A young fox exploded out of the thicket behind her.

"Stay back!" Bramblestar snapped at the kittypets.

Bounding forward, Bramblestar met the fox at the center of

the clearing and reared up on his hind legs to rake the claws of both forepaws across the fox's muzzle. The fox let out a bark of mingled pain and surprise, and lunged at Bramblestar, its jaws gaping. Bramblestar ducked aside and managed to land a blow on the fox's flank before he darted back out of range.

The fox whirled to follow him, but it was already looking confused. *It didn't expect its prey to fight back,* Bramblestar thought with satisfaction as he dashed in again and clawed its ears with a swift slash of his paw. Letting out a high-pitched screech of terror, the fox backed off, then spun around and fled out of the clearing, vanishing among a thick clump of ferns. At the same moment another ThunderClan hunting patrol raced into the clearing, with Mousewhisker in the lead.

"We heard the fight!" Mousewhisker gasped. "Are you okay?"

"Fine," Bramblestar panted. "Take your patrol and follow it," he added, "all the way to its den."

"Right." Mousewhisker waved his tail to the rest of his patrol, and vanished into the ferns on the trail of the fox.

It's a good thing they turned up, Bramblestar thought. *We can't hope to clear all the forest of foxes, but we need to know where they are, especially now that we're hunting across the border.*

The three kittypets crowded around Bramblestar, their eyes wide with shock.

"That was amazing!" Frankie exclaimed.

"I never thought a cat could take on a fox like that," Jessy added, her eyes glowing. "It was the bravest thing I've ever seen!"

"It wasn't hard," Bramblestar mewed, wanting to scuffle

his paws in the earth like an embarrassed apprentice. "It was a young fox, and easy to confuse. Besides, it's quite common for us to have to chase off a fox or a badger."

"A badger!" Minty squeaked. "Purdy told me about those. They're huge!" She glanced around her fearfully as if she expected a massive black-and-white animal to erupt out of the bushes at any moment.

"Believe me, they're really rare," Bramblestar reassured. "We chased the badgers out of the forest a long time ago. But I can show you a few techniques to keep in mind, if you like."

Minty took a pace back, looking as if she might never leave the tunnels again. But Jessy and Frankie both pricked their ears with interest.

"Yes, show us," Frankie mewed. "You never know; we might meet something nasty."

"Mostly you use the fighting techniques you're already learning," Bramblestar explained. "But you need to practice dashing in to strike and then away again, like I did just now. That works even better with badgers, because they're slower than foxes. Another move you can try is to spring onto the badger's back. You can claw it to your heart's content up there, and it can't get at you."

"On its *back*?" Minty breathed, horrified.

"Show me the spring," Jessy urged.

"Okay." Bramblestar took a pace forward that brought him to her side. "First, get into the hunter's crouch." As Jessy pressed herself to the ground, he added, "Now, remember that your hind legs—"

He broke off as he spotted movement in the corner of his eye, and looked around to see Squirrelflight emerge into the clearing. She bounded over to him with an anxious look in her green eyes.

"I heard about the fox," she told him. "Is everything okay?" Glancing down at Jessy, she went on, "Uh . . . what are you doing?"

"Discussing ways to fight off a badger," Bramblestar meowed.

"Oh . . . are you?" There was an odd note of strain in Squirrelflight's voice. "We met a badger once in the old forest; do you remember? Me and you and Thornclaw, when I was your apprentice."

She raised her head, and her eyes locked with Bramblestar's. His memories came flooding back. *She looked at me like that back then, too,* he recalled. *Just for a heartbeat, as we ran from that badger.*

Squirrelflight gave her pelt a shake. "I'll go check for any more traces of that fox," she mewed.

"Be careful," Bramblestar warned her.

"I can look after myself," Squirrelflight responded. "You trained me well." There was warmth in her voice, but the brilliance of her gaze faded as she looked down at Jessy. She swung around abruptly and loped out of the clearing.

Bramblestar glanced down at Jessy, patiently waiting. *Great StarClan!* he thought. *Is Squirrelflight jealous because I'm training Jessy now? That's ridiculous!*

Jessy wriggled out of the crouch and turned half away,

giving her chest fur a few vigorous licks. Bramblestar thought she looked embarrassed.

"We should head back to the tunnels," he decided. "Frankie, don't forget your mouse."

"I've decided that if I meet any foxes or badgers I'm going to run away very fast," Minty announced as they trekked back toward the camp. "Or climb a tree. They can't climb trees, can they?" she added anxiously to Bramblestar.

"No, they can't," he reassured her.

"Then that's what I'll do," Minty decided.

On the way back, a light rain began to fall, quickly becoming heavier. Bramblestar lashed his tail with frustration. After a few dry days, he had hoped that the bad weather was over.

When they arrived at the tunnel entrance, he found Lilypaw, Snowpaw, Dewpaw, and Amberpaw dashing up with bunches of leaves in their jaws to cover up the fresh-kill pile, which had only been moved into the open the day before. Poppyfrost, Lilypaw's mentor, was supervising them.

"Hurry up," she urged them. "Or we'll all be eating soggy mice!"

"Amberpaw!" Spiderleg called from the tunnel mouth. "Get in here right away! Your cough will get worse if you stay out in the rain."

"My cough's fine," Amberpaw grumbled, though she obeyed her mentor and trotted into the tunnel.

The remaining apprentices quickly covered the fresh-kill pile, pausing for a moment so that Frankie could deposit his mouse. Graystripe and Millie appeared, dragging a squirrel between them, then headed for shelter, pausing to shake rain off their pelts before they slipped past the mudfall. Poppy-frost and the apprentices raced after them.

Bramblestar thought how much easier it was to cope with rain in the stone hollow, where all the den roofs were re-inforced with brambles and ivy to keep the nests dry. *We could settle in to talk or take a nap, and wait for the sun to come out again. Here, it's uncomfortable whatever we do.*

The kittypets headed for the tunnel, and Bramblestar was about to follow when he spotted Leafpool brushing through the sodden undergrowth with a bundle of herbs gripped in her mouth. Bramblestar nodded to her as she padded up, rain dripping from her whiskers. "That looks like a good haul," he commented.

"I went nearly to the top border to find them," Leafpool told him, setting her bundle down. "They're daisy leaves, to help ease the aches and pains in the older cats. Purdy, of course, and Graystripe, Sandstorm, and Dustpelt. Not that they'll admit they're old," she added with a half-amused, half-impatient snort.

"Don't look at me," Bramblestar protested. "It's not up to me to tell them when to become elders."

"I know." Leafpool sighed. "But living in this tunnel isn't helping, I can tell you."

She picked up her herbs again and slid past the mudfall. Bramblestar followed her to see that most of the Clan was already there. The tunnel was unpleasantly crowded, the air thick with the scent of wet fur.

From farther down the passage, Bramblestar could hear Daisy's voice raised in annoyance. "What were you apprentices thinking of?" she scolded. "How many times have you been told not to go farther down the tunnel than the last nests? Does every cat have to watch you every moment of the day? And as for you, Cherryfall and Molewhisker, you should be ashamed of yourselves for encouraging them."

"Sorry," Cherryfall muttered.

"But it's boring down here," Molewhisker retorted. "I've been stuck in this tunnel for moons!"

"Boring?" Daisy was unimpressed. "I'll show you boring. If you need something to do, you can play hunt the tick on Purdy."

"What, all of them?" Purdy grunted. "I'll be prodded to death!"

The thick air and the voices of his Clanmates seemed to press in on Bramblestar. For a moment he felt that he couldn't breathe. *I have to get out of here.* "I'm going to check the water levels," he announced to no cat in particular.

"I'll come with you," Lionblaze offered, rising from his nest and pushing between Birchfall and Cloudtail to reach his leader.

Bramblestar noticed that the golden-furred warrior was still limping badly from the wounds he had suffered in the battle with the kittypets. "No, you need to rest," he ordered.

"I've rested until I'm sick of it!" Lionblaze snapped.

"Bramblestar's right," Cinderheart mewed, stroking Lionblaze's side with her tail. "You need to be more patient."

Lionblaze glared at his mate. "I've *been* patient!"

"I'll come with you, Bramblestar," Cloudtail offered, heaving himself to his paws.

"Thanks. Let's go," Bramblestar meowed, turning away from Lionblaze. *He'll have to accept that things are different for him now.*

Outside the rain was as heavy as ever, but after the crowded tunnel Bramblestar didn't mind the cold water seeping through his pelt. He took deep breaths of the damp air as he and Cloudtail headed through the dripping trees.

"The Great Battle seems so long ago," Cloudtail meowed after they had trotted in silence for a while. "And at the same time, it feels as if it was less than a moon away." He sighed deeply. "I miss Firestar."

Is he telling me I'm no good as leader? Bramblestar wondered for a moment, guilt clawing at him. Then he remembered that Cloudtail was Firestar's kin.

"I miss him too," he murmured.

"Oh, you're doing a great job!" Cloudtail assured him, suddenly cheerful. "Just trust your instincts, and trust Firestar to have made the right choice!"

The older warrior's praise warmed Bramblestar, and he felt more optimistic as they came into sight of the floodwater. But he was puzzled as he padded along the water's edge looking for the marker sticks.

"Have they all fallen over?" he muttered. "I'm sure I put one just here!"

"Hey, Bramblestar!" Cloudtail called.

Turning, Bramblestar saw that the white warrior was standing a couple of fox-lengths up the slope, a marker stick poking out of the ground beside him. Another stick stood a few tail-lengths away, and another: a whole line of them stretching along the slope well above the edge of the flood.

Relief surged through Bramblestar, making him dizzy. "The water's going down!"

"Brilliant!" Cloudtail's blue eyes gleamed. "We will get our home back; you can be sure of that."

CHAPTER 24

✿

"What?" *Mousewhisker was the first cat* to leap to his paws when Bramblestar and Cloudtail returned to the tunnel to announce that the water was going down. "I've got to see this!"

He charged out of the tunnel, almost knocking Bramblestar and Cloudtail off their paws. Rosepetal, Thornclaw, Birchfall, and several other cats streamed after him and disappeared into the trees.

Lionblaze rose and tried to limp after them, but Jayfeather blocked him before he could leave the tunnel. "Stay here, fleabrain!" he hissed.

Lionblaze raised a paw as if he was going to swipe his brother across his ears, but he stopped himself at the last moment and went back to his nest with an angry twitch of his tail. Cinderheart gave his ears a lick as he flopped down into the moss, but Lionblaze didn't respond to her. The gray she-cat's blue eyes were filled with worry and frustration.

"Speak to Cinderheart." Sandstorm appeared at Bramblestar's side and spoke quietly. "Tell her that all warriors get hurt, and it's tough learning how to heal."

Bramblestar sighed. *I'm no good at talking to cats about their feelings.* But he recognized the wisdom in Sandstorm's words, and he called Cinderheart over to him with a wave of his tail.

"I know you're having a tough time. . . ." he began awkwardly.

"I'm so afraid!" The words burst out of Cinderheart. "Lionblaze just won't accept that he's not invincible anymore. He'll end up getting himself killed!"

"No, he won't." Bramblestar tried his best to reassure her. "He's not stupid. He'll adjust in time." He tried to understand how Lionblaze must be feeling, after living so long without fearing injury. "He'll have to find a different kind of courage, that's all," he went on. "One that takes account of his limitations. He can't fight alone now; he must stay with his Clanmates. That might feel like failure to him, even though it's not."

Cinderheart nodded. "I know I shouldn't nag him about being reckless," she mewed. "I need to try to understand what it must feel like, to be in danger of getting hurt when it's never happened before. You're right: He must feel like he is letting us all down because he can't fight like he used to. Thanks, Bramblestar." Looking much happier, she went back to Lionblaze and curled up beside him in silent sympathy.

"There was good sense in what you told her," Sandstorm murmured, appearing at Bramblestar's side once more.

Bramblestar hadn't realized that the ginger she-cat was listening. "You gave me good advice," he responded.

Sandstorm dipped her head. "You're welcome."

Glancing around the camp, Bramblestar realized that

Millie was looking anxious, and for once it didn't seem to be about Briarlight. Her gaze was flickering up and down the tunnel, and when the cats began to return from checking the water level, she got up and went to join them at the entrance.

"Has any cat seen Frankie?" she asked.

Birchfall shook his head. "He didn't come with us."

"Isn't he with the kittypets?" Poppyfrost meowed.

But Jessy and Minty were curled up in their own nests, drowsily sharing tongues, and there was no sign of Frankie. Millie wove her way through the other cats toward them, and Bramblestar, sensing a problem, padded over as well.

"Have you seen Frankie?" Millie called to them.

"No," Jessy replied. "Not since we got back from our patrol."

"Any cat seen Frankie?" Bramblestar yowled, raising his voice so all his Clanmates could hear him.

There was no response except for shaken heads and murmurs of confusion.

Minty sprang to her paws, all her fur fluffed up and her tail brushed out. "Oh, no!" she wailed. "He's been eaten by a fox!"

"No, I'm sure—" Bramblestar began, although he had a horrible suspicion that something equally bad might have happened to the kittypet, and he could sense that tension was rising among the rest of the Clan. Then he broke off as he spotted movement at the tunnel entrance and Frankie staggered in, soaked through and exhausted.

"Frankie!" Minty screeched. "You're not dead!"

"Where have you been?" Millie demanded, stumbling over other cats as she hurried toward him.

Frankie glanced around, bewildered to see all his Clanmates' gazes fixed on him. "What's all the fuss about?" he panted. "I just went hunting on my own. I'm sorry, I didn't catch anything."

"I thought you'd been eaten!" Minty mewed with a shudder.

"I'm fine."

Frankie headed toward the other kittypets, but Bramblestar intercepted him before he reached them. "Listen," he mewed, "don't go off on your own like that. It's not safe."

"I can look after myself!" Frankie snapped.

And hedgehogs fly, Bramblestar thought. But Frankie seemed tense and upset, so all he said was, "Go get some food and rest."

After he had watched Frankie head back out to the fresh-kill pile, Bramblestar realized that Squirrelflight had appeared at his side. "You know," she mewed gently, "you mustn't let the kittypets take up so much of your attention. They are just visitors, after all. And now that the floods are going down, they'll be able to return to their Twoleg dens soon."

Bramblestar glanced across at the kittypets. Frankie was gulping down a thrush, while Jessy was teaching Minty how to pounce directly from a crouch. He felt a pang of loss run through him from ears to tail-tip at the idea of saying goodbye. "I've kind of gotten used to having them around," he admitted.

"We have enough mouths to feed," Squirrelflight pointed out.

"They're learning to hunt!" Bramblestar protested.

Squirrelflight's gaze rested on him for a long moment. "You don't know that they want to stay here. Let them decide where they want to be," she meowed at last.

When Bramblestar woke the next morning, he could hardly believe what he was seeing. Faint rays of sunlight were angling in through the tunnel entrance, and the air felt soft, laden with green scents. His pads tingling with optimism, he headed outside, enjoying the hint of newleaf warmth on his fur.

Squirrelflight was already in the open, arranging the patrols, with several of their Clanmates around her. "Cloudtail has gone to check the ShadowClan border," she reported to Bramblestar.

"Then I'll take a patrol over to WindClan," Bramblestar decided. "I want to find out what they're up to now that the water has started to go down."

"I'll come." Berrynose thrust his way through the other cats. "Jayfeather says I'm fit for warrior duties again."

"Great," Bramblestar meowed. Glancing around, he spotted Whitewing with Dewpaw. "I'll take you two as well. And you, Thornclaw, and . . . yes, Brightheart." *I'd better have a good number of cats, just in case WindClan causes any trouble.*

But when Bramblestar and his patrol reached the WindClan border, there was no trace of WindClan scent on ThunderClan territory. Padding up to the edge of the stream, Bramblestar saw that the current was wider and deeper than before, but had retreated within its banks again. *We really are getting back to normal.*

Bramblestar led his cats as far as the top border without meeting any WindClan cats, but on their way back they spotted Crowfeather with his apprentice, Featherpaw, as well as Furzepelt and Gorsetail making their way upstream on the opposite side. Bramblestar halted and waited for them.

"Greetings, Crowfeather," Bramblestar mewed as the WindClan patrol reached them. "How's the prey running in WindClan?"

"No better for you asking," Crowfeather retorted. "And before you start accusing us, no, we haven't crossed over to your side of the stream."

"I know that," Bramblestar told him, not mentioning the log they had unjammed. *WindClan isn't saying a word about it, either.*

"And we're not *going* to cross." Furzepelt's gray-and-white fur was bristling. "So keep your filthy ThunderClan paws off our side."

"You and your kittypet friends," Crowfeather added.

"Oh, yes." Gorsetail's voice was full of scorn. "We've seen the latest additions to your hunting patrols. Very effective— *not!*"

"But ThunderClan never seems to mind who they let into their Clan," Furzepelt meowed. "Maybe you're missing Firestar so much that you're looking for a kittypet replacement."

A growl of anger woke deep in Berrynose's chest. Thornclaw and Brightheart were both bristling, while Dewpaw raced to the very edge of the stream and glared furiously at the WindClan patrol.

Bramblestar raised his tail in warning. "Careful," he murmured. "We don't want trouble with them, and it's none of their business who we let into the Clan."

"You mean we have to let them say what they like?" Thornclaw demanded.

"I mean we need to pick our battles." Bramblestar made himself sound calm, although inwardly he was ruffled to learn how much WindClan knew about the kittypets. He'd deliberately kept them out of border patrols for that very reason. "There's no WindClan scent all along this side of the stream, so our border is safe."

"They'd better not think of invading." Berrynose sounded troubled rather than aggressive. "Those kittypets could be a weak link."

"It won't come to that," Bramblestar told him. "At least, Whitewing, it won't if you can sort out your apprentice."

Dewpaw was still standing on the bank, flexing his claws and hissing at the WindClan patrol. "Come over here and insult Firestar's memory!" he yowled.

Whitewing padded over and patted Dewpaw with her tail. "That's enough. It's time to go back to camp."

"But they—" Dewpaw began to protest.

"I said, *enough*. Do you want them to see me dragging you away by the scruff?"

Dewpaw shot one last glare at the WindClan cats and retreated, his fur still bristling. "They'd better not come over here," he muttered.

Bramblestar made a polite farewell to Crowfeather and his cats, guessing that would irritate them far more than hurling abuse. Then he led his patrol away, conscious of unfriendly stares following them until undergrowth cut off the view.

As soon as Bramblestar and his patrol returned to camp, Brackenfur came bounding up. "Now we've lost Frankie *and* Minty!" he complained. "They were supposed to be with me on the late-morning hunting patrol."

"Never mind." Bramblestar tried to sound soothing, though his pads prickled with apprehension at the news. Glancing around to see which cats were available, he added, "Take Cherryfall instead, and Poppyfrost and Lilypaw."

"Can I come too?" Jessy asked, turning from where she was hanging one of the Twoleg pelts on a nearby bush. "Daisy asked me to hang these pelts out in the sun, but this is the last one."

"Sure." Brackenfur invited her over with a friendly wave of his tail. "You can show me these hunting skills Bramblestar keeps telling me about."

As soon as the patrol had left, Bramblestar sniffed around the clearing and finally picked up faint traces of Frankie and Minty leading out of the clearing side by side. *They've been gone some time,* he thought, judging by the faintness of the scent.

The trail led Bramblestar toward the ridge, up to the outcrop of rocks where once there had been another tunnel entrance. *The one that collapsed behind Hollyleaf, all those moons ago.* Bramblestar shivered at the memory, still missing the cat he had once believed to be his daughter. As the rocks loomed into full view, he spotted a small black-and-white she-cat basking in a patch of sunlight, fast asleep. He bounded up and stood over her. "Minty!"

Minty's eyes flew open and she jumped to her paws. "Oh!" she squeaked. "It's you!"

"What are you doing here?" Bramblestar meowed.

Minty gave her chest fur a few embarrassed licks. "Frankie suggested coming out here to lie in the sun," she explained. "He said we'd be back in plenty of time for the patrol." She blinked in confusion. "Did I oversleep? Where's Frankie? Did you wake him already?"

"Frankie's not here." Bramblestar's tail-tip began to twitch. *StarClan preserve me from clawing this silly cat's ears off!* He felt disappointed that the kittypets had been so irresponsible, when he had thought they were beginning to fit into the life of the Clan. "I don't have time to round up missing kittypets," he snapped. "Come on, back to the tunnel!"

Minty's eyes widened. "Aren't you going to look for Frankie?"

"No." Bramblestar was too fed up with the kittypets to waste one more heartbeat on them. "He'll come back when he's hungry, no doubt."

Back in the camp, Spiderleg, Ivypool, and Whitewing were teaching their apprentices a new fighting move where they rolled over on their backs and battered their opponents with their hind paws.

"Can I join in?" Minty asked, trotting over to them.

Spiderleg turned to her with a cold stare. "No. This isn't for cats who go wandering off and miss their patrols."

Minty turned away, her head and tail drooping. Bramblestar thought that Spiderleg had been a bit harsh; it was encouraging to see Minty actually wanting to learn to fight. He was pleased a moment later when Brightheart padded up to the crestfallen kittypet and rested her tail on Minty's shoulder.

"I'm going into the forest to look for herbs," she meowed. "Do you want to come with me?"

Minty brightened up. "Sure!"

Bramblestar watched them go, then decided that he'd had enough of worrying about pesky kittypets for one day. *I'll see if I can catch up with the hunting patrol.*

The trail led up to the ridge and across the top border into the woods beyond. Bramblestar relished the experience of being alone, listening to the scurrying of small creatures in the undergrowth and the twittering of birds overhead. The air was full of the scent of fresh growth after the long leaf-bare.

As Bramblestar inhaled the signs of returning life, he detected a faint bitter scent among the newleaf richness. *Badger?* he wondered, his neck fur beginning to fluff up. Bramblestar tried to tell himself that he had been spooked by Minty's fussing, but he knew that he had to check. Following the traces deeper into the undergrowth, he realized that his first instinct had been right. At least two badgers had passed that way. He found flattened bracken and holes filled with badger droppings that confirmed his first suspicions.

His pelt bristling, Bramblestar backed away, taking careful note of the spot so that he could warn the patrols to keep watch. As soon as he retraced his steps to the hunting patrol's scent trail, he heard sounds up ahead as if some cat was brushing swiftly through undergrowth. A mouse appeared out of the shelter of a clump of ferns and scuttled across the open ground. A heartbeat later the ferns waved wildly as Lilypaw burst out of them and hurled herself at the mouse.

Bramblestar waited for her to make the kill, then stepped forward as Lilypaw straightened up with her catch in her mouth. "Good job!" he meowed. "Your hunting skills are coming along well."

Lilypaw jumped at the sound of his voice and turned toward him. Her eyes glowed with pleasure. "Thanks, Bramblestar," she mumbled around the mouse.

She may be small, but she's brave and she works hard, Bramblestar thought as he followed Lilypaw to join the rest of the hunting party. A pang of sorrow stabbed through him, sharp as a thorn, when he remembered how much she had lost. *I must remember to take Brackenfur aside and tell him how well his daughter is doing.*

That night in his nest, Bramblestar couldn't sleep. There was a hard knot in his belly; he blamed the tough blackbird he had eaten earlier. However often he changed his position, he felt as if a sharp piece of twig was poking into him.

"For StarClan's sake," Squirrelflight hissed, coming to sit beside him, "stop fidgeting about. You're keeping every cat awake! Except for Frankie," she added. "He came back late, so exhausted he just flopped into his nest."

"Sorry," Bramblestar muttered. "I'm worried about Frankie," he went on.

He was slightly surprised when Squirrelflight agreed. "So

am I. Why don't we follow him the next time he wanders off by himself?"

Bramblestar's whiskers quivered. "Do you think he's plotting with another Clan?"

Squirrelflight let out a snort of disbelief. "No. He's a kittypet. But he's our responsibility at the moment, so we need to find out where he's going." She poked her paw into his nest and yanked out a single long thorn. "There, you should stop wriggling now. Sleep well."

CHAPTER 25
❧

"Seeing that the water's going down," Bramblestar meowed, "we need to think about repairing the dens in the hollow."

A couple of days had passed without any more rain. Now a pale sun was shining and the clouds were thinning out, drifting across the sky like white mist. Bramblestar felt his energy rise at the thought of returning to their home.

Dustpelt and Brackenfur were discussing the practicalities with him just outside the entrance to the tunnel, along with Cherryfall and Molewhisker. The life of the Clan went on busily around them. The apprentices were dragging bedding outside to let it dry off in the sun, with Daisy supervising them.

"Stop it, Amberpaw!" Bramblestar heard her scold the young she-cat. "You won't make that moss fit to sleep on by throwing it at Dewpaw."

Farther across the clearing, Millie was helping Briarlight with her exercises. The warmer weather was helping her, Bramblestar noticed; she wasn't coughing nearly as much. *In fact, most of the sick cats are getting better.*

Dustpelt twitched his whiskers thoughtfully before replying to Bramblestar. "It'll be a long job," he murmured. "Before we can repair anything, we'll have to get rid of all the mess."

"But we'll be *home*; that's the most important thing," Brackenfur added.

"I suggest we split up the tasks," Dustpelt went on. Bramblestar saw that his eyes were brighter as he considered the problem. He looked more like the cat he had been before he lost Ferncloud. "Some cats to clear up, some to fetch brambles and moss from the forest, some to start the actual rebuilding . . ."

"And still keep up with hunting and border patrols," Bramblestar pointed out.

"Yeah, we need to keep an eye on ShadowClan," Cherryfall put in, working her claws eagerly in the ground.

"Let's hope that ShadowClan has enough to do repairing their own camp, to have time to come bothering us," Bramblestar responded. "And that goes for the other Clans, too."

"Then we should start by organizing work patrols," Brackenfur suggested. "As soon as the water level sinks low enough to let us back in."

"That would be a task for Squirrelflight," Bramblestar mewed. He glanced around for his deputy, who had been sorting out hunting patrols at the far side of the clearing. Now the patrols were leaving, and Squirrelflight was already heading toward him.

"Bramblestar," she began as soon as she was within earshot, "remember what we were talking about the other night? Well, Frankie is at it again. I was about to put him in a patrol when I saw him sneaking off."

Bramblestar rose to his paws with a frustrated lash of his

tail. "I hoped he'd given that up. He was in a hunting patrol with me yesterday, and he made a couple of really good catches. Which way did he go?" he asked Squirrelflight.

His deputy angled her ears in the direction of the ridge. "Up there."

"Sorry," Bramblestar meowed to Dustpelt and the others. "I have to deal with this. Discuss the hollow among yourselves, and let me know what you decide when I get back."

Padding across the clearing, Bramblestar easily picked out Frankie's trail from the mingled scents of the other cats. To his surprise, it led straight up to the ridge, then across the border and into the woods above ShadowClan territory. Before long, he spotted Frankie, trotting along swiftly and purposefully.

Bramblestar quickened his pace to catch up. He was almost close enough to call out: *Hey, what do you think you're doing?* Then he saw Frankie freeze and hurl himself into the shelter of a clump of bracken. Quickly Bramblestar leaped up into the nearest tree, hiding himself among the tiny, unfurling leaves, and peered downward. A heartbeat later he spotted a Shadow-Clan patrol padding past, focused and alert as if they were looking for prey. Rowanstar himself was in the lead.

Thank StarClan they didn't spot us! Bramblestar thought as the patrol vanished and their scent died away.

Frankie emerged from the bracken and set off again, swift as a fox, into the dark pine forest in the direction of the Twolegplace. *Is he going to visit Victor and those other kittypets?* Bramblestar wondered, deciding not to call out to Frankie until he knew what was going on.

But Frankie veered away from the Twolegplace and headed toward the border between ShadowClan and RiverClan. Suddenly Bramblestar realized that he was going back to his own nest. *Does he want to leave us?* Bramblestar felt a stab of disappointment that Frankie would just go without even saying good-bye. *But if this is where he disappeared to before, he has already been and come back twice. What is he playing at?*

Bramblestar tracked Frankie in silence as his paw steps turned toward the lake. The stream leading down into it was much shallower now, not the turbulent current they had risked their lives to swim such a short time before. Frankie waded across it without hesitating, even though in the middle of the stream the water came up to his head and shoulders. Bramblestar waited for him to get a little farther ahead before following.

Even though the water had gone down, Bramblestar could see the evidence of the terrible flood everywhere he looked. Vast swathes of mud covered the ground, clinging to his paws as he picked his way through it. The ground was littered with broken Twoleg things and branches swept along in the surge. Sometimes there was no way around it, so that Bramblestar and Frankie had to clamber over the heaps of flotsam, getting even wetter and muddier. As they drew closer to the Twoleg dens, Bramblestar saw that some of the Twolegs had returned. They waded in and out of the flooded dens, pushing water out with long branches that were bushy at the end, and yowling at one another in angry voices. Bramblestar's fur began to bristle as he drew closer to them, but soon he realized that they were too busy to notice a couple of cats.

By now Bramblestar was close enough to Frankie to have called to him easily, but he kept silent, in the grip of curiosity, and ducked out of sight whenever Frankie paused to look around. *I want to know exactly what this kittypet is up to.* Soon Frankie reached the flooded Thunderpath that led away from the lake. The water came up no farther than his belly fur now, and he waded along, venturing into each Twoleg den but staying out of sight of the Twolegs.

What is he doing? Is he trying to steal food because hunting prey is too hard? Or looking for his Twolegs?

When Frankie emerged from the next Twoleg den, he paused, looking around with his head raised. "Benny! Benny!" he called.

Bramblestar stared at the kittypet in dismay. *He's looking for his brother! Why didn't I think of that?* He kept close as the gray tabby cat went on, searching under bushes, in abandoned Twoleg dens and monsters, underneath the bigger chunks of debris that littered the ground. His frantic, uncoordinated movements and his wide-stretched eyes gave away his growing despair.

At last Frankie jumped up onto a fence. "Benny, where are you?" he yowled.

Bramblestar couldn't let him suffer on his own anymore. "Frankie!" he meowed, jumping up onto the fence beside him.

Frankie whirled to face him, so startled that he almost lost his balance. "I—I'm sorry. . . ." he stammered when he had regained his footing.

Bramblestar silenced him with a wave of his tail. "You have nothing to be sorry for. We should have known you'd come looking for Benny. We all know how it feels to lose kin. It's part of Clan life."

Frankie lowered his head. "Then it's a part of Clan life I can't accept."

"I didn't say we accepted it, either," Bramblestar mewed. "Come on, I'll help you look."

He leaped down from the fence and headed farther along the flooded Thunderpath, trying to remember which of the Twoleg nests Frankie had been trapped in when Jessy found him. "Show me your den," he told Frankie. "Maybe we can work out which way Benny would have gone. That is where you saw him last, right?"

Frankie nodded, beckoning with his tail. "This way."

He waded across the Thunderpath and up the slope on the far side. At the top, Bramblestar spotted the den set into the bank where he had first seen Jessy trying to get through the window to release Frankie. Following the kitty-pet, he bounded down the slope until they reached the fence that surrounded the den.

"Benny and I were here when the flood came," Frankie explained, jumping over the fence and landing on a stretch of soggy grass. "The water came up from the lake like a huge wave. It knocked us off our paws and washed us that way." He angled his ears toward the opposite fence. "I hit the fence and dug my claws in. I thought I was going to drown." He shuddered and his eyes clouded.

"What happened next?" Bramblestar prompted him.

"I spotted that the basement window was open. I managed to get inside. I thought Benny was right behind me . . . but he must have been swept away." His voice shook on the last few words.

Bramblestar touched Frankie's shoulder with his nose, then padded across the garden to inspect the fence at the opposite side. Water had washed away all traces of scent, but after a few moments he found a narrow gap at the bottom with a tuft of black-and-white fur caught on a splinter.

"Hey, Frankie!" he called. "Benny is black and white, right? Could this be his?"

Frankie ran over and stared at the scrap of fur. "Yes, that's Benny's," he meowed.

"Looks like he went this way, then."

Bramblestar squeezed through the gap, with Frankie close behind. On the other side a broad swathe of destruction—broken fencing, stinking mud, scattered branches and other debris, and even a small monster tipped over onto its side—revealed the path of the huge wave. Ignoring their wet paws and drenched fur, the two cats followed the trail, checking each possible hiding place to see if Benny was there.

"Why are you helping me?" Frankie asked after a few moments.

"Because right now you are my Clanmate," Bramblestar replied, drawing his tail-tip along Frankie's flank. "I would do the same for any of my cats."

The trail led to a narrow opening in the ground. At first Bramblestar thought it was another entrance to the tunnels, but then he realized it was something made by Twolegs. A neat square hole had been built into a raised bank of earth, supported by stones like the ones used to build Twoleg dens.

"That's a drain," Frankie meowed. "There's usually a cover on it, but it must have been washed away."

Bramblestar felt his fur start to prickle as he pictured what might have happened to a struggling cat, his fur heavy with floodwater, swept off his paws by a wall of water. *I don't like this one bit, but some cat has to check it out.* Then he took a deep breath and crawled into the drain.

The air was damp and full of a thick, rotting stench. This was nothing like the tunnels, which seemed light and spacious compared with this dank hole. Bramblestar's pelt brushed against the slimy walls on either side. His own body was blocking the light, and ahead of him was only choking darkness. *Oh, StarClan, please don't let me get stuck!*

Bramblestar's heart was pounding hard, and it took a massive effort for him to keep putting one paw in front of another. He was wondering how long he ought to go on when he bumped into something soft and furry. A tiny slice of light from a gap overhead revealed a heap of black-and-white fur, cold and solid and a long way from life. Every muscle in Bramblestar's body stiffened as he realized that he had found Benny.

Gagging at the smell, Bramblestar nosed about until he located one of the dead cat's legs and fastened his teeth in it. Then he tried to crawl backward, but Benny's body was stuck against something, and wouldn't move. Bramblestar reached out one forepaw and felt around for whatever was blocking Benny. His paw touched something hard and chilled, lodged slantwise in the drain and wedging Benny's body underneath it.

Bramblestar gave it a shove. *Maybe it's the drain cover that Frankie said was missing.*

At first nothing Bramblestar could do would shift the obstacle. His legs started to ache as he heaved at it, stretched to his limit to reach past Benny's unmoving body. He was on the verge of giving up when it gave way with an echoing clang against the side of the drain and slipped to one side.

Bramblestar tried moving Benny again and this time the cat's body slid easily toward him. Carefully he backed away, dragging Benny with him, until he felt a welcome draft of fresh air on his haunches, and emerged into the daylight. Frankie was waiting beside the drain entrance and helped him to pull Benny the last couple of tail-lengths out into the light.

Bramblestar coughed to clear the stench of the drain from his throat. "Is that your brother?" he meowed hoarsely, though he was in no doubt about the answer.

Frankie crouched beside the body, his head bowed. The dead tom looked small and pathetic out here, his black-and-white pelt plastered to his sides, covered in mud and slime.

"Oh, Benny . . ." Frankie touched his nose to his brother's cold side. His voice began as a whisper, then rose to a grief-stricken wail. "What am I going to do? I can't leave him here!"

"We'll bury him," Bramblestar told him. "We'll give him a warrior's farewell."

Together he and Frankie managed to hoist Benny onto their backs and carry him up the slope to the top of the hill, where the ground was drier. They laid Benny on the grass while they scratched a hole. The sun was setting, bathing the hill with scarlet light, as they settled him inside it and covered him with earth. Bramblestar stood beside the small, dark mound of soil and spoke the words that a medicine cat would say over the body of a fallen warrior.

"May StarClan light your path, Benny." His voice rang out over the heap of stones and earth. "May you find good hunting, swift running, and shelter when you sleep."

Frankie looked up to where the warriors of StarClan were beginning to appear, crossing the sky in a glittering pathway of stars. "Do all cats go to StarClan?" he asked. "Even Benny?"

Bramblestar wasn't sure if a kittypet would be welcomed into StarClan. He guessed that even Jayfeather or Leafpool would have trouble answering that question. But he knew that he had to give Frankie some comfort. "Well . . . there are a lot of stars," he mewed. "More than there have ever been warriors, I'm sure."

Frankie peered more closely at the shimmering swathe of light. "I wonder which one is Benny?" His voice quivered. "Benny, I'll look up at you every night. If you look down on me, then we'll still be together."

Bramblestar leaned closer to Frankie, lending him his warmth and feeling him tremble from more than cold.

After a moment Frankie spoke, his gaze still fixed on the stars. "Don't you need to get back to the Clan?"

Yes, Bramblestar thought, *but that's not important right now.* "There's plenty of time," he murmured. "I'll stay with you for as long as you need."

CHAPTER 26

❧

The last of the sun had gone and shadows were gathering fast before Frankie stirred, lowering his gaze from the stars. "What will happen to me now?" he mewed sadly. "My housefolk have left, and my home is still full of water. Everything has gone."

"But the water is going down." Bramblestar tried to sound encouraging. "Your Twolegs will come back."

"But what will I do right now?" Frankie wailed.

"Come back to ThunderClan." The answer was so obvious to Bramblestar that he found it hard to understand why Frankie was asking the question. "We'll look after you until you can go home."

Frankie let out a sigh. "Thank you."

Bramblestar led the way back to ThunderClan territory, retracing their previous route. Night had fallen by the time they reached the woods above ShadowClan, and Bramblestar felt his pelt rise at the eerie silence. The scents of ShadowClan warriors wreathed around him from every side, as if they had been hunting regularly beyond their border since Thunder-Clan had dealt with Victor and the other kittypets.

"If we spot a ShadowClan patrol, climb a tree, quick as you

can," he murmured to Frankie. "I know we're not actually trespassing, but I don't want them to catch us."

When they reached the forest above ThunderClan, Bramblestar relaxed briefly, only to stiffen again as he picked up a trace of the bitter scent of badger. "Let's get a move on," he meowed, not telling Frankie anything about his fears. "I can't wait to get back to my nest."

A quarter moon was shining down on the clearing when Bramblestar and Frankie returned to the makeshift camp. Squirrelflight was stalking up and down in front of the tunnel entrance, her tail-tip flicking and her whiskers quivering.

"Bramblestar!" she exclaimed as the two cats limped out of the undergrowth. "Where have you been?"

At the sound of her voice, Minty, Jessy, and Millie erupted out of the tunnel.

"Are you two mouse-brained?" Millie demanded as she shot across the clearing. "Do you know how worried we've been? Do you *care*?"

"Great StarClan, look at you!" Squirrelflight gasped.

Bramblestar realized how they must appear: thorn-scratched and exhausted, their fur soaked and muddy, stinking of death. "It's been a long day," he muttered.

Millie's anger died as she reached Frankie and Bramblestar and saw them more clearly. "What happened?" she hissed. "Are you hurt?"

"Did you fight a badger?" Minty asked, bounding up and giving Frankie's filthy pelt a shocked sniff.

"Benny's dead," Frankie responded wearily.

Minty's eyes stretched wide. "Oh, no! How?"

While Bramblestar gave a brief account of their search and the discovery of Benny's body inside the drain, more of his Clanmates emerged from the tunnel. Murmurs of sympathy arose from them as they listened.

"We buried him on a little hill overlooking the lake," Bramblestar finished.

"I'm sure StarClan was with him at the end," Leafpool mewed, padding up to Frankie and giving his ear a comforting lick.

"I hope so." Frankie's voice was bleak. "Because I wasn't."

"You did all you could," Millie told him. "At least now you know what happened."

"Yes," Jessy added. "You don't have to worry anymore, and you can grieve for him properly."

Frankie nodded, gazing around at the group of cats who surrounded him with looks of sadness, but he said nothing.

"You should have told us where you were going," Cherryfall meowed. "We could have come with you. I'd have helped you find him."

"Come on." Leafpool gave Frankie a gentle shove. "Into the tunnel, and I'll take a look at you. You can have some thyme leaves for the shock."

"I'll bring you some fresh-kill," Minty offered as the medicine cat led Frankie away.

Once Frankie had gone, Jessy padded over to Bramblestar. "Thank you," she mewed. "You didn't have to do that."

Bramblestar dipped his head toward her. "My cats never

have to suffer alone," he told her.

Jessy's ears flicked up. "Is that true?" she pressed. "That we are your cats?"

"For now," Bramblestar replied, feeling a purr rise in his throat.

Jessy touched her nose to his. "Good."

Bramblestar opened his eyes to see dawn light seeping into the tunnel. For a moment he felt as if he couldn't move a muscle. Weariness from the long trek the day before, and the struggle to free Benny's body from the drain, weighed down his limbs. He staggered to his paws and stumbled out of his nest, still half-asleep.

"Hey, that's my tail!" Jessy's voice meowed.

Bramblestar turned to see that the brown she-cat had dragged her nest next to to his, and was looking up at him with amusement in her golden eyes. "Sorry," he mumbled.

"It's okay. How do you feel? You had a tough time yesterday."

"I'll be fine." Bramblestar shook each leg in turn, his muscles protesting, then arched his back in a long stretch. "I need to get moving, that's all."

Jessy followed him as he headed along the tunnel and into the cool dawn. The sky was a pale, milky blue with small puffs of white cloud. *No rain today,* Bramblestar thought gratefully.

In the clearing most of his cats were milling around Squirrelflight, who was organizing patrols. "Cloudtail," she was mewing, "you can go and check the border with WindClan.

Take—" She broke off as she spotted Bramblestar and Jessy emerge from the tunnel, held Bramblestar's gaze for a heart-beat, and then turned back to Cloudtail. "Take Mousewhisker, Berrynose, and Birchfall with you," she finished.

As Cloudtail gathered his patrol together, Bramblestar padded up to his deputy. "I want to lead a patrol out beyond the top border," he announced.

"I'll come!" Jessy offered.

Bramblestar was acutely conscious of his Clanmates exchanging glances. "Sure," he replied.

"Spiderleg and Amberpaw as well?" Squirrelflight suggested.

"Of course," Bramblestar agreed, wanting to be off as soon as possible. "Let's go."

With Bramblestar in the lead, the four cats headed straight up the ridge and across the border into the woods beyond. The sun rose in front of them, sending shafts of golden warmth between the trees. The last of Bramblestar's weariness faded away, and he felt ready for anything.

"Are we looking for signs of ShadowClan trespassing?" Spiderleg asked as they crossed their own scent marks.

"No," Bramblestar replied. "Badgers."

"Badgers?" Amberpaw echoed, her voice rising to a squeak. "Wow!" She slid out her claws and let her shoulder fur bristle up. "Are we going to fight them?"

Spiderleg gave his apprentice a friendly nudge. "You'd be better off running away," he mewed. "You'd hardly make a mouthful for one of those huge beasts."

"I'll *never* run away!" Amberpaw exclaimed.

"Don't tease her," Jessy protested to Spiderleg. Turning to Amberpaw, she added, "Don't worry. Bramblestar taught me some moves for when a badger attacks. I'll show you if you like."

"That's okay," Spiderleg told her. "Amberpaw is *my* apprentice." His tone was frosty, and Bramblestar could understand why.

A kittypet trying to take over his apprentice's training! But Jessy learns so fast, she'd make a good mentor one day.

"We're not going to fight," Bramblestar meowed. "I've spotted a few traces, smelled a few scents, and I just want to make sure there isn't a badger set anywhere we're hunting right now."

Amberpaw was wide-eyed as the patrol padded onward. She paused beside every tree or clump of bracken to have a good sniff. "I've scented one!" she squealed, backing away from a tangle of gnarled oak roots.

Bramblestar padded up to check. "No, that's fox," he told the bristling apprentice. "And it's several days old. But well done for spotting it."

Eyes shining, Amberpaw went on sniffing, expecting at any moment to detect an entire den of badgers. But it was Spiderleg who found the first traces, a heap of droppings in the shelter of a bramble thicket.

"They're pretty stale," he commented, backing away and passing his tongue over his lips in disgust.

Bramblestar studied the scent for himself. "Three days old,

at a guess," he meowed. "And I think the badger went that way." He angled his ears in the direction of the Twoleg nests where Victor and his friends lived.

"The kittypets are welcome to them," Spiderleg grunted.

"That's amazing!" Jessy exclaimed. "Bramblestar, can you really tell how old those droppings are, and which way the badger was heading?"

"It's all part of warrior training," Bramblestar told her. "I think we should follow the scent for a while," he went on. "Just to be sure that there isn't a set nearby."

With Bramblestar in the lead, the patrol tracked the badger until they drew close to the ShadowClan border. There was no sign of a set. "We may as well turn back," Bramblestar decided. "I don't want Rowanstar to accuse us of trespassing again. We—"

He broke off at a harsh squawk and a squeal of terror from Amberpaw. Spinning around, he saw that a rook had flown down and was attacking the small apprentice, stabbing her with its beak. Amberpaw bared her teeth and lashed out with one paw, but the rook was too big and fierce for her, pressing into the attack in a flurry of feathers.

Spiderleg flashed past Bramblestar and flung himself on top of Amberpaw, hiding her from the rook. The bird battered at him with its wings and tried to fasten its claws into his back. Bramblestar let out a defiant yowl and hurled himself at the rook, his claws slashing at it. The rook squawked again and beat its wings to avoid his blows. Before it could gain height, Jessy leaped into the air and grabbed it. She fell back to the ground and rolled over, the rook flapping furiously in an attempt to escape. Its harsh cry was cut off as it went limp. Panting, Jessy rose to her paws and stood over her prey.

"That was outstanding!" Bramblestar meowed. "Great job, Jessy!"

Jessy's eyes shone with pride.

"We're on a border patrol," Spiderleg muttered as he scrambled off Amberpaw and smoothed down his ruffled fur. "Not a hunting patrol."

"All fresh-kill is welcome," Bramblestar retorted. "Amberpaw, are you okay?"

The apprentice tottered a little as she regained her paws, and checked herself for injuries. "I'm fine, thanks, Bramblestar."

"If that rook attacked us," Bramblestar mewed thoughtfully, "there must be a new nest somewhere close by." He peered up into the trees and spotted an untidy cluster of twigs lodged in the fork of a branch in a nearby ash tree. "Up there," he murmured.

Stealthily he began to climb the trunk, trying to stay out of sight of the nest until he could look down on it from above. A moment later he realized that Jessy was following him, leaving her catch at the bottom of the tree.

Soon Bramblestar reached a branch from where he could see into the nest. A mother rook was sitting there; at the sight of Bramblestar she half rose, revealing a small clutch of pale blue, brown-speckled eggs. As she settled again, her berry-bright eyes still fixed on him, Bramblestar slid out his claws, intent on more fresh-kill.

"No, leave her!" Jessy protested. "She's about to be a mother. You'd be killing her chicks as well!" Then she paused and gave her chest fur a few embarrassed licks. "Okay, I'm talking like a kittypet," she admitted.

"No, we'll leave her," Bramblestar meowed. As they turned to climb down the tree, he added mischievously, "We'll come back when the chicks have hatched."

Jessy swiped at him, her claws sheathed, before leaping to the ground.

Spiderleg, waiting at the bottom of the tree, looked unimpressed. "Are we going home, or what?" he grumbled.

When the patrol arrived back at the tunnel, Frankie and Minty hurried forward to admire Jessy's rook. Bramblestar looked around for Squirrelflight, to report to her about the badger traces, but before he spotted her Bumblestripe sprang up from where he was sitting beside the mudpile and raced over to him.

"I've been waiting for you," the young warrior meowed. "I need to talk to you about Dovewing."

Anxiety sprang up inside Bramblestar. "Is something wrong?"

Bumblestripe shifted his paws uncomfortably. "Follow me," he mewed.

At Bramblestar's nod, he led the way along the tunnel and past the nests, into the shadows beyond.

"You haven't been going down here, have you?" Bramblestar asked, astonishment and fear making his heart thud. "You know the tunnels are dangerous!"

"I know," Bumblestripe assured him. "But Dovewing's safe.

You just need to see this."

Unpleasant memories of the drain and Benny's body filled Bramblestar's mind as he followed Bumblestripe into the narrow, dripping darkness. For all his efforts to concentrate, he kept bumping into the walls. His pads grew numb from the cold, damp floor and every hair on his pelt longed to turn and head back to the light.

Then Bramblestar heard a faint meowing coming from somewhere ahead. "What's that?" he asked sharply, halting.

"Shh!" Bumblestripe whispered. "Listen!"

"Hello! Hello!" The sound came echoing up the tunnel.

Now Bramblestar recognized the voice. "It's Dovewing! Is she lost?" he gasped.

"No," Bumblestripe replied. "Come on."

Bramblestar followed him, creeping forward until they came to a place where three tunnels met. A thin shaft of light pierced the darkness from a crack in the roof. Peering over Bumblestripe's shoulder, Bramblestar could see Dovewing standing with her back toward them. Clearly she had no idea they were there.

"Hello! Hello!" she called again. Then she waited in silence, her ears pricked, as her voice echoed away down the tunnels.

"What's she doing?" Bramblestar whispered.

Bumblestripe glanced back at him, his eyes filled with pain. "She's testing how long she can hear the echoes," he told Bramblestar. "She—she wants to be able to hear again."

CHAPTER 27

"Hello!" Dovewing called again. "Hello!"

"But she's not deaf," Bramblestar murmured in dismay. *I thought she had accepted that her powers had gone.*

"She thinks she is," Bumblestripe responded. "Compared with how she was . . . before."

Bramblestar thought of Lionblaze, furious that he had to wait for his wounds to heal. *Was it worth these cats having their special powers,* he wondered, *when they suffer such agony losing them?* Only Jayfeather seemed untroubled, but he was still able to be a medicine cat, just like before. *And I've never known what goes through Jayfeather's mind.*

Bramblestar padded forward. Dovewing jumped at the sound of his paw steps, and spun around to face him. After one glance into his eyes she hung her head and shuffled her front paws on the stone.

"Bumblestripe told me what you're trying to do," Bramblestar began.

"It's none of his business!" Dovewing's tone was indignant.

"Of course it is," Bramblestar meowed. "He's your mate, and he cares for you."

Dovewing let out a long, frustrated sigh. "It's awful, not being able to hear anymore," she told Bramblestar. "I feel as if I've let my Clanmates down."

"Of course you haven't!" Bramblestar assured her. "It's not your fault."

Dovewing's eyes were pools of sadness in the dim light. "In spite of the powers the three of us had, the Clans were still devastated by the Great Battle," she mewed.

"But without you, we would have suffered much more." Bramblestar wasn't sure what he could say to comfort Dovewing, and he paused for a moment, hoping that StarClan would give him the right words. But no words came.

Maybe StarClan can't see me under all this rock, he thought. *I'll have to figure this out on my own.*

"StarClan gave you those powers for a good reason," he went on at last. "You knew where the Dark Forest warriors were attacking. Lionblaze fought like a whole Clan of warriors without shedding a drop of blood, and Jayfeather united StarClan."

Dovewing shook her head. "So why have we lost our powers, if we needed them so badly?"

"Perhaps because StarClan knows you don't need them now," Bramblestar suggested. "We will still face challenges, like the flood, but we can survive them using our Clanborn knowledge. You and Lionblaze can still hunt and fight as well as any cat. Jayfeather still heals us."

"Maybe you're right. . . ."

Bumblestripe stepped forward out of the shadows.

"Dovewing, you're not angry with me, are you, that I told Bramblestar?"

"No." But Dovewing brushed past him quickly and headed toward the camp without looking back.

When Bramblestar emerged from the tunnel he spotted Jessy at the other side of the clearing, spreading moss out in the sun with Brightheart and Whitewing. As soon as she saw Bramblestar she rose and bounded over to him.

"Is everything okay?" she asked. "Those tunnels look pretty scary!"

"Oh, they're not that bad," Bramblestar replied. "We've fought battles in them before."

"Really?" Jessy sounded impressed.

Bramblestar was about to embark on the story of the trouble with Sol and WindClan when he saw Squirrelflight returning at the head of a hunting patrol. She was carrying a blackbird; Graystripe and Brackenfur both had mice, while Rosepetal was dragging along a squirrel.

"I'll tell you about it later," Bramblestar mewed to Jessy. "I need to have a word with Squirrelflight now." He padded over to the fresh-kill pile, where Squirrelflight and the others were depositing their catch, and beckoned her aside with a flick of his tail.

"Is there a problem?" his deputy mewed.

"I've just heard Dovewing calling in the tunnels," Bramblestar explained. "She was trying to get her old hearing back. And Cinderheart is afraid that Lionblaze will take too many risks in battle because he can't accept that he can be hurt now."

Squirrelflight riffled her whiskers thoughtfully, her concern clear in her green eyes. "It's tough on them," she meowed after a moment, "but I'm sure they'll find a new balance in the end. After all, they see every day how their Clanmates have to live, and they both care deeply about the Clan."

Bramblestar blinked gratefully. "Thanks, you're probably right. Look, I'm going to give the kittypets a battle-training session," he went on. "Do you want to join us?"

Squirrelflight gazed at him, her eyes narrowed with faint amusement. "Oh, no, I think I'll leave that to you," she mewed. "I don't want to get in the way."

Bramblestar's pelt suddenly felt hot and uncomfortable. "Okay," he mumbled.

To his relief, the sound of cats brushing through the undergrowth distracted him and his deputy. He turned to see Millie emerging into the open at the head of her patrol, followed by Thornclaw, Ivypool, and Snowpaw. All four cats were bristling with agitation. Bramblestar padded across the clearing to meet them, with Squirrelflight at his shoulder. Brightheart and Whitewing looked up from their task with the bedding, and the rest of Squirrelflight's hunting patrol gathered around to listen.

"Bramblestar!" Millie burst out. "We found fresh badger scent!"

Bramblestar's ears pricked and he felt an unpleasant hollowness in his belly. "Where?"

"Across our top border," Millie replied. "Just at the edge of ShadowClan's forest. There were at least two of them."

"I'd better go take a look," Bramblestar meowed. Glancing around, he beckoned to the two most senior warriors. "Brackenfur, Graystripe, you can come with me."

Jessy pushed herself to the front of the group. "And me!"

"No," Bramblestar responded. "Remember that you and Frankie and Minty are due for a battle-training session. Brightheart," he added, turning to the ginger-and-white she-cat, "will you take that over for me, please?"

Brightheart dipped her head. "Sure."

Jessy looked disappointed. "I'll learn a new move, so you'd better watch out when you come back!"

As she turned away, Bramblestar touched her shoulder with his tail-tip. "We'll take a walk together later on," he mewed. "Maybe up to the ridge at sunset?"

Jessy's eyes sparkled. "I'd like that!"

Bramblestar headed out of the clearing, with Brackenfur and Graystripe flanking him.

"You know," Graystripe murmured as they headed for the ridge, "not all kittypets are bad news. After all, Millie was a kittypet. She settled down well in the Clan, and we've been very happy together."

"Yes, of course . . ." Bramblestar wondered where Graystripe was going with this subject. *Besides, it seems harsh to be discussing mates when Brackenfur is still grieving for Sorreltail.* "I'm worried about these badgers," he meowed. "I wonder if they're the same ones who attacked us before in the hollow."

"I thought we taught that lot a lesson," Graystripe growled.

The patrol crossed their own top border and headed for

the woods beyond ShadowClan territory. As they drew closer, Bramblestar began to pick up the strongest badger scent he had smelled yet, mingled with the scent of terrified cats. He exchanged a glance with Brackenfur and Graystripe. "Something's seriously wrong here," he muttered.

The scent grew stronger. Determined to find out more, Bramblestar risked venturing into the trees above Shadow-Clan's border, his Clanmates treading warily behind him. Thrusting through a dense patch of ferns, he halted on the edge of a clearing and stared in horror at the scene of destruction.

Grass and bracken were trampled down over a wide area. The reek of blood hit Bramblestar in the throat, and he spotted streaks and splotches of it on the grass. Tufts of fur lay scattered, most of it from cats.

"Oh, StarClan!" he whispered. "Did any cats die here?"

Brackenfur gave him a hard prod in the side. "Shadow-Clan's coming!" he hissed.

Bramblestar hadn't heard the approaching patrol. Rapidly he backed into the ferns and crouched down with Graystripe and Brackenfur beside him, hoping that the stench of battle in the clearing would hide their ThunderClan scent. Peering through the arching fern fronds, Bramblestar watched the ShadowClan patrol cross the clearing, heading deeper into the woods. Rowanstar was in the lead, with Tigerheart, Ferretclaw, and Tawnypelt. All of them looked battered and scarred.

That must be from fighting with the badgers, Bramblestar thought.

As the patrol disappeared into the undergrowth, Tawny-pelt, who was bringing up the rear, suddenly halted. She looked around, her jaws parted to taste the air. Then she ran across the clearing toward the ferns. Bramblestar rose to his paws and stepped out into the open to meet her.

"We're not trying to cause trouble," he meowed before she could speak. "We never meant for you to know we'd been here."

"You're my brother," Tawnypelt responded. "I'd recognize your scent anywhere."

Bramblestar winced when he saw fresh cuts across his sister's muzzle and a clump of fur missing from her shoulder. "We were tracking the badgers," he explained. "Have they moved into your territory?"

"Not our usual territory," Tawnypelt mewed. "But there are some old sandy sets in these woods. It looks like several badgers have moved in since the flood. The water must have driven them out of their original homes."

"Well, the floods are going down now," Bramblestar mewed, trying to sound hopeful. "Maybe they'll go back where they came from."

"And maybe hedgehogs will fly," Tawnypelt growled. "Bramblestar, my Clan is suffering so much. . . . The kittypets have stopped bothering us since you fought them, but now the badgers are making it impossible for us to hunt here. And most of our old territory is still underwater." She lowered her head, and her voice was full of shame as she continued. "I was too harsh with you before," she confessed. "Rowanstar and

I—and all of ShadowClan—should have been more grateful for your help with the kittypets."

"That doesn't matter," Bramblestar murmured, touching his nose to her ear. "I know we should never have interfered. It won't happen again."

Tawnypelt raised her head again, her green gaze locking with her brother's. "Do you really mean that? Because I don't think we can fight these badgers alone. We're too weak, too hungry."

Bramblestar gazed at her. "Are you asking for Thunder-Clan's help?"

Tawnypelt took a deep breath. "Yes," she meowed. "I am."

CHAPTER 28

Bramblestar's mind was whirling as he went back to Brackenfur and Graystripe. He said nothing to his warriors, and they accepted his silence and didn't question him.

Rowanstar made it clear that he didn't want any more interference from ThunderClan, Bramblestar thought as he led the way back to camp. *I respect that. But it's clear that ShadowClan is in great trouble. Can I stand aside and let them fall?* That night, as he curled up in his nest, Bramblestar raised his head and prayed silently to StarClan. *Send me a dream,* he begged. *Speak to me and tell me what I should do.*

As sleep surged over him, Bramblestar found himself walking beside the lake—a lake shrunk back into its old boundaries. Pale sunlight glinted on the water, turning it to silver, the surface ruffled by a gentle breeze. Bramblestar looked around, expecting to see Firestar. Instead the wispy shape of an enormous cat began to appear on the other side of the lake, taller than the trees, broader than a Twoleg den, the tips of her ears reaching up to the clouds. As the figure grew more solid, Bramblestar saw that it was a dark gray she-cat with a broad, flat face and amber eyes. Not Firestar, but Yellowfang!

The former medicine cat stood at the edge of the lake, and at her paws the silver water turned red with blood: swirls of blood that rose to the surface of the water until the whole lake was scarlet.

Bramblestar's eyes stretched wide. "Is that how much blood is going to be spilled?" he whispered.

"Blood does not have to mean death," Yellowfang meowed, her voice echoing from the hills. "It can bring more strength than you can imagine."

"What do you mean?" Bramblestar protested. "I don't understand!"

But Yellowfang didn't reply. Her form began to fade again, and at the same moment the scarlet water rose and flooded over Bramblestar, sweeping him off his feet. He struggled, flailing his paws, but the water choked him in its salty grip and he sank into a swirling darkness.

Bramblestar jolted awake, trembling. Faint moonlight spilled into the tunnel. He felt a paw on his shoulder, gently calming him, and looked up to see that Jessy had left her nest and was bending over him.

"Was it a bad dream?" she murmured.

"More than that," Bramblestar muttered, staggering to his paws. "I need to speak with the medicine cats."

"You can talk to me if you want," Jessy offered.

"No, this is medicine-cat stuff." Seeing Jessy's hurt expression, Bramblestar added, "I'll tell you later."

He picked his way through the sleeping cats, heading farther down the tunnel to where the medicine cats slept.

Jayfeather roused at the sound of his approach, though Leaf-pool remained curled up, sunk deeply in sleep.

"What do you want?" Jayfeather asked as Bramblestar reached his side.

"I need to talk to you and Leafpool."

Jayfeather whisked out his tail to block Bramblestar as he reached out a paw to shake Leafpool's shoulder. "Let her sleep," he warned. "She was up earlier to give Sandstorm some tansy for her cough. We can wake her later if we need her."

Bramblestar nodded. "Let's talk outside."

In the open, he took a long breath of the clear, cool air. The night was calm and quiet, with not even a faint breeze to stir the branches. The moon was floating above the trees, begin-ning to swell toward full.

"Leafpool and I have missed a medicine-cat meeting at the Moonpool," Jayfeather remarked. "But I doubt many of the others were there. RiverClan is still cut off, and we don't know what the floods are like in the mountains."

"I hope we can get to the next Gathering," Bramblestar mewed. "We've already missed one. Have you had any omens about the water going down?"

Jayfeather shook his head. "Not a whisper. Only the signs of the waterline dropping below the sticks on the slope."

Bramblestar sighed. "I suppose we can only wait. But meanwhile," he continued, trying to feel more optimistic, "the kittypets are settling in well. Especially Jessy. Did you hear how much fresh-kill she brought in from her last patrol?"

Jayfeather gave him a sidelong glance, his narrowed blue

eyes so sharp that it was hard to remember he was blind. "You're spending a lot of time with Jessy. . . ." he murmured. "You shouldn't let any cats think you care more for the kitty-pets than your Clanmates."

For a moment Bramblestar was outraged. *I raised this cat! I licked him warm when he was a kit, and comforted him when he got a thorn in his pad. And now he's making comments about my private life!* Then he remembered that Jayfeather wasn't a kit anymore. He was ThunderClan's medicine cat, with every right to poke his nose into his Clan leader's business.

"All the kittypets need my time if they're to fit into the Clan," he responded, aware that he wasn't being entirely truthful.

Jayfeather hesitated for a moment, and Bramblestar braced himself for a stinging retort. But then the medicine cat shrugged, as if he too wasn't comfortable talking about Jessy. "Did you bring me out here to enjoy the night air?" he meowed.

"No," Bramblestar replied. "I had a dream. . . ." Struggling to find the right words, he told Jayfeather about Yellowfang's appearance beside the lake, and the blood that had risen when her paws touched the water. He repeated the mysterious words she had spoken. "She said, 'Blood does not have to mean death. It can bring more strength than you can imagine.' Jayfeather, what do you think she meant? Is there going to be another terrible battle? Was Yellowfang trying to warn me?"

Jayfeather twitched his whiskers. "It doesn't sound like a warning of doom," he admitted. "It's more like . . . something strong. It's obviously connected with that other dream you had, about Firestar," he continued. "'When water meets blood, blood will rise.'"

"And what does *that* mean?" Bramblestar asked tartly. "Why can't StarClan tell us something clearly, instead of talking in riddles?"

"StarClan tells us as much as they want us to know," Jayfeather retorted. "And sometimes even they don't hold all the answers. You can't expect them to know everything. Sometimes they are just cats, like us. Trust your own instincts, Bramblestar. That's why StarClan made you leader, because they had faith in you."

Bramblestar returned to his nest, and this time his sleep was untroubled by dreams. When he woke, sunlight was pouring in through the tunnel mouth, and most of the nests around him were empty. He sprang to his paws, alarmed that he had overslept.

"Take it easy, Bramblestar."

At the sound of Jessy's voice Bramblestar turned to see the brown she-cat sitting in her nest with her tail wrapped neatly around her paws.

"I told the others not to disturb you," she mewed. "I know you were awake during the night."

"That's kind of you," Bramblestar responded, half-appreciative and half-annoyed, "but a Clan leader can expect to have broken nights."

"But you're not just a Clan leader," Jessy pointed out, rising to her paws and padding over to Bramblestar. "You're a cat, too. You need to look after yourself as well as everyone else."

Bramblestar touched his nose to her ear. "Maybe you're right."

He padded out into the clearing with Jessy following him, to discover that the first patrols had already gone out. Squirrelflight was heading down the slope with Bumblestripe, Berrynose, and Rosepetal behind her.

"Squirrelflight!" Bramblestar called, pleased that he had caught her. "I need a word with you."

His deputy halted and turned to Bumblestripe. "You lead the patrol," she ordered. "Check the water levels, then try hunting over toward WindClan. We haven't been there for a day or two." She watched the patrol leave before bounding over to Bramblestar. She looked faintly surprised when she saw Jessy with him, but gave the she-cat a polite nod. "How can I help?"

Bramblestar glanced around, spotting Graystripe beside the fresh-kill pile and beckoning him over with a wave of his tail. "Are any of the other senior warriors still here? I need to speak with all of them."

"Cloudtail and Thornclaw are on a border patrol," Squirrelflight replied. "Brackenfur and Dustpelt went to look for more branches for the dens, but they only just left. I'll see if I can catch them." She shot off into the undergrowth.

While he waited for her to return, Bramblestar went back into the tunnel, where he found Sandstorm talking to Purdy. For once she was telling *him* a story. "So Firestar—he was Firepaw then—was hunting in the old forest and he came upon this skinny old gray she-cat . . ."

"Sandstorm, I need you outside for a moment," Bramblestar meowed.

"Sure." Sandstorm rose to her paws. "I'll finish the story later, Purdy."

The elder looked up at her, blinking. "See that you do," he purred. "You spin a good yarn."

Sandstorm stifled a *mrrow* of amusement. "Praise indeed!"

Bramblestar padded farther down the tunnel, where he found Jayfeather hauling himself out of his nest, his jaws parted in a massive yawn. Leafpool was still asleep.

"Jayfeather, I've called a meeting," Bramblestar meowed. "Come and join us outside."

When he emerged into the clearing again, followed by the medicine cat, he saw Squirrelflight returning with Dustpelt and Brackenfur. They all gathered together at the foot of the mudpile.

Jessy was standing nearby, her eyes bright with interest, but she didn't join the others, as if she wasn't sure if she was invited.

"Jessy," Bramblestar mewed, "could you find Frankie and Minty and help them practice their hunting moves?"

"Sure," Jessy replied, heading off cheerfully with her tail in the air.

"So what's all this about?" Squirrelflight asked when the kittypet had gone.

"I think I can guess," Brackenfur growled.

Graystripe nodded. "The badgers, right?"

Bramblestar told them about his patrol the day before, and how they had found badger scent and the evidence of a battle just inside ShadowClan's extended hunting grounds. He added what he hadn't even told Graystripe and Brackenfur yet: his conversation with Tawnypelt and her plea for help.

"Are you completely mouse-brained?" Dustpelt growled when he had finished. "You know how much trouble we got into with Rowanstar when we fought off those kittypets."

"Yes, let ShadowClan fight their own battles now," Brackenfur agreed.

Bramblestar had expected to get this response, but at the same time he couldn't bear to picture his sister and her Clan struggling against the badgers alone. "What do you think, Graystripe?"

"I know how you feel, Bramblestar," Graystripe began, "but none of us want to fight again. Look how badly injured Lionblaze was. You could easily lose warriors if we take on the badgers. Is that what you want?"

"But the badgers are very close to *our* territory," Squirrelflight reminded the others. "If we don't deal with them now, we could be storing up trouble for later."

"True." Dustpelt raised one hind paw and scratched his ear. "But we can meet that trouble when it happens."

A cough shook Sandstorm's body before she spoke. "Remember the time the badgers attacked us in the stone hollow?" she rasped. "What if we fight them and they follow us back here? We're barely surviving as it is."

"So what you're all saying," Bramblestar mewed, "is that we should deal with the badgers if they interfere with our hunting, but not before?"

Murmurs of agreement came from all the cats, though he thought Squirrelflight remained doubtful. He knew he couldn't argue anymore. "Okay," he decided, "I see your point. But I want to lead a patrol up there now, to see if there are any new developments. We'll have to keep a close watch on ShadowClan territory from now on. The first sign that those badgers are crossing into our adopted territory, we have to be ready for them."

No cat objected to that. Bramblestar led them all out, except for Sandstorm, who went back to finish her story for Purdy. For once the graceful she-cat didn't ask to go with the warriors, but seemed happy to go back to the tunnel.

By now the forest beyond the border was becoming familiar to the ThunderClan cats. Bramblestar was aware of the moment when they reached the invisible boundary with ShadowClan. There were no scent markers, but fresh scents of the rival Clan drifted to his nose from close by.

"This is weird," Brackenfur muttered. "Do you think these borders could ever become permanent?"

"You mean, extend our territory out here and still keep it safe?" Dustpelt sounded doubtful. "Could we even do that?"

"Let's hope we don't have to," Bramblestar meowed, dismayed at the thought of trying to keep such a long border efficiently patrolled.

As the patrol padded along the edge of ShadowClan

territory Bramblestar began to pick up new scents of blood and fear, along with the strong reek of badger. His pelt prickled. "There must have been another fight since yesterday."

"That's not our problem," Dustpelt reminded him sharply.

"Especially if Rowanstar hasn't asked for our help," Graystripe added. "We could find ourselves fighting ShadowClan as well as the badgers."

With no evidence that the badgers had come any closer to ThunderClan hunting territory, Bramblestar knew there was nothing to do but turn around and head back to camp. His anxiety for ShadowClan and Tawnypelt was growing with every sign of conflict, yet he didn't know what he could say to his Clanmates to change their minds.

Desperate for a quiet place to think, when he reached the camp he climbed the slope until he could sit alone above the tunnel entrance. Warmed by the sun on his shoulders, he looked down at his Clanmates.

Lionblaze had just entered the clearing at the head of a hunting patrol. They were loaded down with prey: two squirrels, a blackbird, and more mice than Bramblestar could count. Lionblaze had recovered from his wounds, and his golden tabby pelt gleamed in the sunlight. When he had dropped his catch on the fresh-kill pile he padded up to Cinderheart, touched noses with her, and gave her ears a loving lick. The two cats withdrew to a sunny spot and stretched out together to share tongues.

Jayfeather was out in the weak sunshine too, taking Briarlight through her exercises. Bramblestar was pleased to see that she had regained some of her strength; she was fast and nimble on her front paws. She was practicing pulling herself up on the low-hanging branch of an elder bush, then letting herself roll onto her back with a yowl of triumph.

"What? What's all the yowlin' about?" Just below Bramblestar, Purdy rushed out of the tunnel. "Is it badgers? Just let me at 'em!"

"It's okay, Purdy," Millie reassured him. "It's only Briarlight." She turned to Graystripe, her eyes glowing with pride. "Just look what she can do!"

Briarlight repeated her exercise, while her mother and father stood close together to watch, their pelts brushing. Bramblestar felt his heart warmed, his troubles fading for a moment.

Movement behind Bramblestar distracted him and he turned, expecting to see Jessy. But the newcomer was Squirrelflight.

"You're going to take us into battle against those badgers, aren't you?" she mewed, coming to sit beside him.

Bramblestar nodded; until that moment he hadn't realized that he had made the decision.

"Why would you risk your own Clan to help Tawnypelt and ShadowClan?" Squirrelflight asked.

Bramblestar thought of the scene he had just watched in the clearing. He knew that it might be destroyed if he went ahead with his plan. But it didn't change a thing in his mind.

"Because I'd do anything to help my sister," he meowed, meeting his deputy's green gaze. "As would you."

As he spoke, Bramblestar finally understood why Squirrel-flight had lied to him about the kits. He had already forgiven her, because he knew that she had been trying to do the best for every cat, but only now did he appreciate the impulse that had made her build so much upon something that wasn't true. "That's why you did what you did, isn't it? You took Leaf-pool's kits because you loved her."

Squirrelflight nodded, her eyes so full of feeling that he guessed she couldn't find words to answer.

"I have nothing but respect for your courage," he told her. Looking down into the clearing again, he saw Lionblaze sprawled contentedly beside his mate, and Jayfeather happily bossing Briarlight around. "We raised three fine cats," he mewed, remembering Hollyleaf's brave death when she sacrificed herself to save Ivypool.

He and Squirrelflight sat in silence, gazing down at their kits and their other Clanmates, cheerful in the sunlight below. Bramblestar felt Squirrelflight's fur touch his, and he felt closer to her than he had for seasons, as if the glow of sunshine was enfolding them.

"I'll support you, Bramblestar," Squirrelflight murmured. "If you want to take ThunderClan into battle on Shadow-Clan's behalf, I will be with you."

CHAPTER 29

Bramblestar scrambled to the top of the mudpile. "Let all cats who are old enough to catch their own prey join here outside the tunnel for a Clan meeting!" he yowled.

The cats who were already outside looked up at him curiously, then clustered closer together at the foot of the mudpile. Leafpool emerged from the tunnel with Sandstorm and Purdy. Daisy and the apprentices trotted out of the undergrowth carrying balls of moss, which they dropped near the tunnel entrance before sitting down to listen. Jessy sprang down from the branch of a tree, where she had been practicing climbing techniques with Frankie and Minty.

Bramblestar looked down at his Clan and took a deep breath. *They aren't going to like what I have to tell them.*

"Cats of ThunderClan," he began. "I've thought hard about this, and I've come to a decision. It's possible that Shadow-Clan will drive out the badgers by themselves, but if that doesn't happen within the next quarter moon, then we will help them."

"What?" Thornclaw sprang to his paws. "Have you got bees in your brain?"

"After what Rowanstar said to you?" Dustpelt challenged.

Daisy was looking up at Bramblestar with outrage in her eyes. "Must mothers watch their kits die again?"

More angry yowls rose up from the rest of the Clan. Bramblestar felt as if he were standing in the blast from a storm, and he dug his claws deep into the mud as if he was afraid of being swept away. For a moment he was tempted to start justifying himself. *No,* he thought, *the word of the Clan leader has to be obeyed. It is part of the warrior code.*

But Bramblestar was still worried that he was wrong. This was the first decision he had made as Clan leader that was unpopular with all his Clan—except for Squirrelflight, standing silently supportive above the tunnel entrance, and Jessy, who was watching him with bright eyes and ears pricked. *I respect each one of these warriors,* he thought unhappily. *I don't like it when they challenge me.*

"We will begin training at once, so we can be ready," he finished curtly, and jumped down from the mudpile.

His paws had scarcely touched the ground when Daisy pushed her way through the crowd of cats. "I chose to stay with ThunderClan because I trusted that my kits and I would be kept safe," she told him, her normally gentle voice deepened to a growl. "I thought I could trust you, too, Bramblestar. Why do we need to face danger again so soon?"

Before Bramblestar could reply, Jessy skirted the nearest group of cats to stand at his side. "You're a Clan cat through and through," she told Daisy with a respectful nod of her head. "You've had courage to survive in the past, and you'll survive again."

Daisy twitched her ears, as if she wasn't sure if she should be offended by a kittypet telling her how to behave. "But that doesn't mean we have to go looking for trouble," she protested.

"Sooner or later, trouble will come to you," Jessy meowed. "I've learned that much about living in a Clan! Bramblestar's right to deal with the badgers now, before they try to take over ThunderClan territory."

Daisy was silent for a moment. At last she raised her eyes to gaze directly at Bramblestar. "You're our Clan leader," she mewed. "I trust you. But that doesn't mean I have to like it."

"Thank you, Daisy." Bramblestar dipped his head. "No warrior should enjoy going into battle. But sometimes we have no other option. Thanks, Jessy," he added when Daisy had walked away. "You said exactly the right thing." He let out a long sigh. "I wish I felt as certain about this as my Clanmates think I am," he confessed. "Would Firestar have done this? Probably not," he answered his own question. "He had no kin in ShadowClan. Oh, for StarClan's sake, why does this have to be so difficult?"

"Well, you can't change your mind now," Jessy pointed out.

Murmuring agreement, Bramblestar turned toward the rest of his Clanmates. They were clustered around Squirrelflight, who was organizing them into groups to train for the battle.

"I don't see why we're doing this," Mousewhisker grumbled. "The badgers are ShadowClan's problem."

"And I'm *your* problem," Squirrelflight flashed back at him. "So just get on with it."

She continued quietly dividing up the groups. Bramblestar

noticed that she was choosing cats who had taken part in the battle against the badgers in the hollow, so many seasons ago, to lead the training. Graystripe, Brackenfur, and Cloudtail gathered younger warriors around them, and Squirrelflight led another group herself, including all three kittypets.

"Remember that some of us have fought badgers before," she reminded them when the groups were ready. "We know what works and what doesn't. The badgers are a lot bigger and stronger than you, so you should focus on what you do better than them: moving swiftly, darting in to strike, and getting out of range before they can retaliate. Work in pairs, with one of you distracting the badger while the other gets a blow in. And don't forget that you can jump onto their backs. It's far harder for them to throw you off than it would be for another cat."

Bramblestar joined Brackenfur's group, with Ivypool, Snowpaw, Poppyfrost, and Lilypaw. Brackenfur took a pace back, prepared to give up the leadership to Bramblestar, but Bramblestar shook his head and gestured with his tail to tell Brackenfur to go on.

Brackenfur led his group up toward the ridge until they found a clearing. "Right," he meowed. "We'll start with the move Squirrelflight mentioned, leaping onto the badger's back. It's a good tactic, because up there the badger can't get at you. Snowpaw, do you want to start? I'll be the badger."

While Snowpaw faced up to Brackenfur, Bramblestar spotted a gap between the trees and padded over to gaze across into ShadowClan's territory. *I wonder what's happening over there?*

What are the badgers doing? Is Rowanstar able to deal with them after all?

Turning back into the clearing, he saw that Snowpaw and Lilypaw were having trouble learning the move. They should have been able to use their speed to spring up and balance on the badger's shoulder, to claw its fur, or even topple it off its paws. But they couldn't stay on Brackenfur's back for more than a couple of heartbeats before they fell off. Their waving legs and exposed bellies made them vulnerable before they could scramble upright again. Even though Lilypaw was older and more experienced, she was so small that she had the same difficulties as Snowpaw.

"I'd have eaten you both by now," Brackenfur meowed frustratedly.

Bramblestar was about to offer his help when Ivypool stepped forward. "Listen," she hissed. "The badgers are going to tear you apart if you don't shape up. When you leap, dig your claws in *hard*. Bite down on their neck, and if you can get close enough, rip their eyelids and claw out their eyes."

Ivypool's voice was low but powerful, and for a moment Bramblestar was shocked by her ruthless advice. Then he remembered the many moons that Ivypool had spent being trained in the Dark Forest. She had learned more savagery there than most warriors could imagine. *Thornclaw, Blossomfall, and Birchfall must know how to fight like this, too,* he thought. *At least their experiences will be useful here.*

When the apprentices tried the move again, Bramblestar could see the effects of Ivypool's advice. They kept their balance, their claws digging into Brackenfur's back. Lilypaw bent over Brackenfur's shoulder until her ears almost brushed the grass and hooked his paws out from under him. As he fell onto his side, Snowpaw flexed his claws, aiming for Brackenfur's eyes.

"Hey!" Brackenfur yowled. "Don't do that for real!"

Snowpaw leaped back, giving Brackenfur the chance to haul himself back onto his paws. "Sorry," he mewed. "I got carried away."

"No harm done," Brackenfur responded.

Ivypool gave an approving nod. "Much better. That was *fierce.*"

When his patrol returned to the camp, Bramblestar noticed that the atmosphere had improved. All the cats were discussing the battle practice, the younger warriors especially pleased with what they had learned. Even though Bramblestar figured they were still not thrilled about going into battle on behalf of another Clan, there was a new sense of purpose and pride in their skills.

"I think they'll be okay," Squirrelflight remarked, padding up to him where he sat at the foot of the mudpile.

"How did you get on with the kittypets?" Bramblestar asked.

"Frankie and Jessy did well," Squirrelflight replied. "But Minty has no confidence at all."

Bramblestar nodded. "She's not bred to fight. And they're kittypets: Can we even ask them to take part in this battle at all?"

"Jessy and Frankie are keen to join in," Squirrelflight told him. "I can't stop them."

Daisy poked her head out of the tunnel; clearly she had overheard what they were discussing. "Minty could stay behind with me and the other cats who don't fight," she meowed. "You can't risk the lives of your entire Clan. This isn't the battle against the Dark Forest all over again."

Bramblestar nodded. "Who else do you think should stay behind?"

"Enough warriors to defend the camp," Daisy meowed. "Maybe Brackenfur and Spiderleg, for a start." She gave her whiskers a twitch. "I'd ask Graystripe and Dustpelt, too, but it's no use expecting those gray muzzles to listen to me!"

While she was speaking, Leafpool emerged from the bushes with a mouthful of chervil and padded up to Bramblestar. She set down her bundle of herbs and waited patiently for a chance to speak.

"Do you need something?" Bramblestar mewed.

"It's about Cinderheart." Leafpool looked troubled. "I think she should stay here in camp, too."

Baffled, Bramblestar exchanged a glance with Squirrelflight. Was there a problem with Cinderheart that he didn't know about? Squirrelflight shrugged. "Why do you think that?" Bramblestar prompted.

Leafpool hesitated. "I just don't think you can expect Cinderheart to face badgers."

"Okay." Bramblestar was still puzzled. "If she wants to stay behind, that's fine by me."

"No, I want you to tell her—" Leafpool began, then broke off.

Bramblestar had a feeling that his medicine cat knew something she wasn't telling him. "I can't force Cinderheart not to fight," he meowed. "She is a warrior, after all."

Leafpool sighed, shaking her head, then picked up her bunch of chervil and headed into the tunnel. A cold trickle of apprehension crept down Bramblestar's spine, and after a heartbeat's hesitation he followed her.

"Are you okay?" he asked. "Have you had a bad omen about this battle?"

Leafpool stopped and faced him, her blue eyes clouded with distress. In a rush Bramblestar remembered the last battle against the badgers, in the hollow. Leafpool had returned to find the whole camp in torment and her mentor, Cinderpelt, dying in the nursery, torn apart by a badger as she protected Sorreltail while she gave birth. *Mouse-brain!* he scolded himself. *No wonder the thought of fighting badgers frightens her.*

"It won't be like the last time," he promised. "These badgers won't come anywhere near where we live. I will keep our Clanmates safe."

"Thank you, Bramblestar." Leafpool's response was quiet, and Bramblestar sensed that for some reason she still wasn't reassured.

When he headed out of the tunnel again, the sun was setting, the long shadows of the trees already covering the clearing. Above the topmost branches, scarlet light was fading from a sky barred with cloud, and a single warrior of StarClan shone overhead. Bramblestar spotted Jessy choosing prey from the fresh-kill pile, and padded over to join her. As he drew closer he noticed that one of her ears was scratched and she had lost a tuft of fur from near her tail.

"You look a bit battered from the training," he commented as he joined her. "You know, you don't have to fight."

Jessy looked up from her blackbird and narrowed her eyes. "If I choose to fight, will you stop me?"

"Of course not," Bramblestar replied. He felt a warm glow of admiration for her courage, her readiness to fight on behalf of cats she had known for barely a moon, and he leaned closer to her until his shoulder rested on her flank. Jessy jerked backward, wincing and drawing in a sharp, hissing breath.

"Sorry," she mewed. "I've got a massive bruise there."

"I hope your opponent has one, too," Bramblestar responded.

Jessy's eyes glinted with amusement. "Let's just say that Birchfall will take kittypets more seriously from now on!"

The sun had cleared the tops of the trees by the time Bramblestar ventured into ShadowClan territory at the head of a border patrol. Two sunrises had passed since his decision to go into battle, and there had been no more news from ShadowClan. Previous patrols had found more fresh scent, more traces of blood, but no sign of cats or badgers.

Something has to happen soon, Bramblestar thought.

The forest was silent as he brushed through the long grass, with Dovewing, Cherryfall, and Molewhisker behind him. His ears were pricked and his jaws parted to taste the air. At every paw step his gaze darted around to make sure that nothing unexpected was creeping up on them. Dovewing looked strained and anxious, and Bramblestar guessed that she was still trying to hear as far as she had before the Great Battle. *I'd love to know what's going on in ShadowClan,* Bramblestar thought. *But I'm not going to tell her that!*

He halted as he breathed in a familiar scent. *Tawnypelt!* "You go on ahead," he told the others. "Dovewing, take the lead."

When the rest of his patrol had vanished into the undergrowth, Bramblestar followed his sister's scent trail until he spotted her pushing her way out from a clump of ferns, with a mouse hanging limply in her jaws.

"Tawnypelt!" he meowed in a low voice.

His sister stiffened, then whipped around to face him, so startled that she dropped the mouse. "Bramblestar! Get out—there's a patrol in the trees over there."

Bramblestar beckoned with his tail. "Come here, then."

Tawnypelt snatched up her prey and sped toward him; together they slid under the low-growing branches of a holly bush.

"ThunderClan will help ShadowClan attack the badgers," Bramblestar told his sister, his voice rapid and urgent. "But we need to know what's happening. Has Rowanstar planned a strike?"

Tawnypelt's green eyes widened in astonishment. "You'll do that with your whole Clan?"

Bramblestar gave her a terse nod. "Don't try to talk me out of it. I know you need help—and we don't want badgers settling in these woods either."

Tawnypelt rested her tail-tip on his flank. "I asked for your help. I'm not going to turn it down now."

"Tell me what's going on," Bramblestar prompted.

"Rowanstar plans to attack tomorrow night," his sister meowed, "before the moon gets any brighter."

"Okay. We'll be there."

"Tawnypelt!" A cat yowled in the distance.

"I've got to go," Tawnypelt muttered. "Thanks, Bramblestar." She wriggled out on her belly from under the bush and disappeared.

Bramblestar tracked down the rest of his patrol and returned to camp, where he found Squirrelflight and his other Clanmates returning from battle practice.

"I saw Tawnypelt," he told his deputy. "She says that Rowanstar is planning to attack the badgers tomorrow night."

"This is it, then." Squirrelflight flexed her claws. "Well, we're as ready as we'll ever be."

In the clearing outside the tunnel, all the talk was of the forthcoming battle as Bramblestar's Clanmates discussed different moves, arguing about which ones worked best. Suddenly feeling in need of some space, he headed down the slope toward the lake.

"Hey, Bramblestar!" Lionblaze called after him. "Can I come with you?"

"Sure." Bramblestar waited while the golden tabby tom bounded across the clearing. "I'm just going to check the water levels."

Companiably the two cats trotted through the trees side by side.

"I've got something to tell you," Lionblaze confessed as they skirted the top of the cliffs that surrounded the hollow. "Cinderheart is expecting my kits."

Bramblestar halted. "That's *wonderful*! I can't say I'm surprised."

Lionblaze scrabbled in the leaf-mold with his front claws, ducking his head in embarrassment. "Uh . . . well . . . Cinderheart's such a great cat."

"And she'll make a great mother," Bramblestar meowed. "Lionblaze, this is the best news I've heard in moons. Kits are the future of the Clan."

"I need to ask you something," Lionblaze went on as they continued toward the lake. "I don't want Cinderheart fighting the badgers. Will you tell her not to come?"

"I'm not sure any cat can tell Cinderheart what to do," Bramblestar replied. "But I'll do my best."

Of course—Leafpool must know about this, and that's why she was so worried about Cinderheart fighting! Bramblestar realized. But he was still puzzled. *Why couldn't she just say so?*

Lionblaze's eyes were shining and his paw steps were light as he brushed through the undergrowth. Bramblestar felt his heart warmed by the happiness of the cat he still thought of as his son, and yet concern about the battle hung over him like a stormcloud in an otherwise clear sky.

I must keep Lionblaze safe as well. These kits deserve to grow up with both their parents.

Lionblaze picked up the pace, so that he was the first to burst out of the trees on the shore above the lake. "Look!" he yowled.

Bramblestar hurried to catch up with him, and found him standing next to one of the sticks they had positioned to check the change in water level. Now it stood high and dry several fox-lengths away from the edge of the flood.

"See how far the water has gone down!" Lionblaze exclaimed. "It won't be long before we can go home. Our kits will be born in the nursery!"

Bramblestar nodded. "Let's reposition the sticks, and then we'll go look at the hollow."

When they had retrieved the sticks and driven them into the ground at the water's edge, the two cats climbed the slope again until they reached the cliff top. This time they padded right up to the edge and peered over. The water had dropped down far enough to reveal dark shapes rising up, thorny and misshapen by the weight of the flood.

"Look, those branches must be the top of the warriors' den." Lionblaze pointed with his tail. "And over there's the nursery— I can just see the roof with the interwoven brambles."

Bramblestar crouched beside him, scanning the cliffs where the marks of the flood still remained, and the debris thrown among the tumbled rocks that led up to the Highledge. "It's going to take a lot of work to rebuild," he murmured, thinking of how the surging water must have torn all of the nests away, and how much mud and litter would have been swept in on the flood. "But we'll do it, however long it takes," he added.

Returning to camp, Bramblestar looked for Cinderheart and found her in the tunnel with Leafpool and Sandstorm. She lay on one side; Bramblestar guessed that Leafpool had been examining her.

"Lionblaze told me about the kits," Bramblestar announced. "Congratulations, Cinderheart."

"Thank you," Cinderheart purred. "I've hoped for this for so long."

"So with the kits in mind," Bramblestar went on, "I thought you might not want to fight the badgers."

Cinderheart raised her head, a glint of annoyance in her blue eyes. "I'm expecting kits," she snapped. "I'm not sick! I can fight just as well as any cat."

Bramblestar knew she was right, and wasn't quite sure how to argue with her. He could order her to stay in camp, but he didn't want to offend her.

While he was still searching for the right words, Sandstorm stretched out a paw and laid it gently on Cinderheart's flank. "Remember you're not making decisions for yourself alone now," she mewed, her voice still hoarse from her attack of whitecough. "You have to think of the kits inside you. Is it fair to put them at risk before they've even been born?'

Cinderheart opened her jaws to reply, then hesitated.

"There'll still be a lot to do in the camp, preparing for the wounded and keeping the fresh-kill pile stocked," Sandstorm went on.

"I could certainly use the help," Leafpool added.

The annoyance faded from Cinderheart's gaze. Finally she nodded. "Okay, I'll stay," she meowed. "Sandstorm, what was it like when you were carrying Leafpool and Squirrelflight? What should I do to make sure my kits are born healthy?"

Aware that he couldn't add anything to this conversation,

Bramblestar crept quietly away. None of the she-cats saw him go. Outside the tunnel he spotted Squirrelflight giving herself a quick groom in a patch of sunlight. "Hi," he meowed, bounding over to her. "Lionblaze just told me some good news: He and Cinderheart are having kits."

Squirrelflight froze in the middle of drawing her paw over her ear. "Wow!" she exclaimed, her eyes widening. "Our kit having kits! That's awesome." A deep purr rumbled up from her chest.

Bramblestar gulped. *I hadn't looked at it quite like that before.* "Great StarClan, that makes me feel old!" he mewed.

Squirrelflight flicked her tail at him. "Don't be mousebrained."

Bramblestar gazed at her, stifling a small *mrrow* of amusement. Then he remembered the badgers, and his amusement faded.

"At sunrise tomorrow, don't organize any more battle-training patrols," he told Squirrelflight. "Just the usual hunting and border patrols. They'll need to save their strength for the end of the day."

Looking suddenly somber, Squirrelflight nodded. "Your warriors are ready, Bramblestar. And may StarClan be with us all."

CHAPTER 30

Dusk was gathering under the trees as the last glance of sunlight faded from the sky. The air was warm and filled with the fresh scents of newleaf. The whole forest seemed full of hope and recovery, and yet Bramblestar knew, as he leaped onto the top of the mudpile, that he was about to lead his Clanmates into another deadly battle. Looking down on them, seeing the gleaming eyes of every cat turned toward him, Bramblestar's courage wavered and for a moment he didn't know what to say. Then he met Squirrelflight's calm, trusting gaze, and he felt stronger again.

"Cats of ThunderClan," he announced. "I know what I'm asking of you, and I want you to know that I trust every one of you to fight with courage tonight. Remember that we've taken on badgers before and won. We defeated the Dark Forest cats, and they were far more dangerous than a few badgers! StarClan fought alongside us then, and they may be not with us in the same way now, but they'll be watching over us, just as they always have. ThunderClan warriors, to victory!"

"Bramblestar! Bramblestar!" his Clanmates yowled.

Bramblestar realized with a stab of relief that after their

earlier hostility they were all with him now, ready to risk their lives to save ShadowClan and to rid the forest of the threat from badgers.

Jessy and Frankie looked as enthusiastic as the Clan cats, joining in to call his name. Jessy's eyes were sparkling with excitement. Bramblestar nodded to her, inviting her to walk beside him as he sprang down from the mudpile and prepared to lead his cats out of the camp.

Leafpool, Jayfeather, Purdy, and Sandstorm were clustered together just outside the tunnel. Minty and Daisy were with them, while Graystripe, Thornclaw, and Cherryfall, who had agreed to stay behind and defend the camp, took up positions around the edge of the clearing and stood there watchfully.

As the rest of the Clan began to move off, Cinderheart bounded up to Lionblaze and touched noses with him. Lionblaze gave her a tender lick around the ears, and briefly twined his tail with hers.

"Please be careful," Cinderheart begged. "Think of our kits and stay away from danger."

"I can't promise that, but I promise I'll come back to you," Lionblaze murmured.

Bramblestar led his warriors out of the clearing, hearing the voices of the cats who remained echoing through the trees behind him.

"Good-bye! Good luck!"

"Give the badgers a few good scratches from me!"

"We'll keep the camp safe!"

At last the voices died away, and the ThunderClan cats

padded in silence through the darkening forest. The moon appeared above the tops of the trees, shedding a silver light over the open spaces, while the shadows of the undergrowth seemed even darker. The warriors crossed the top border into the wild woods, and along the line of the ridge to the invisible border with ShadowClan's extended territory.

Here Bramblestar paused. He could feel that his cats were tense and anxious as the moment of the battle drew closer. Turning to face them, he spoke to them again, his voice lower so that they had to gather around tightly to listen.

"Remember that this is ShadowClan's battle first," he meowed. "Our help is unexpected."

"More like unwanted," Dustpelt muttered, glaring into the darkness.

Bramblestar ignored the interruption. "Whatever happens," he went on, "however ShadowClan reacts, we do not get into fights with them. We're here to drive out badgers. Nothing else."

Murmurs of agreement rose from the assembled cats. They waited, quivering with anticipation, a few tail-lengths inside ShadowClan territory. Bramblestar's ears were pricked for the first sounds of battle, but he was still aware of Dovewing by his side. She was shaking from ears to tail-tip, and working her claws frantically into the loose earth.

"Are you okay?" Bramblestar whispered, pressing himself against her for a heartbeat.

Dovewing gazed up at him, her blue eyes wide and scared. "I don't know how I can fight without being able to see or hear," she confessed.

"Like any other cat," Bramblestar told her. "Dovewing, you're an *amazing* fighter. I know you can do this. You won't let ThunderClan down."

To his relief, his words seemed to calm Dovewing. Her trembling died away and her chest heaved as she took deep breaths.

Dovewing had distracted Bramblestar briefly, and an outbreak of distant screeches, ripping through the dusky air, took him by surprise. A heartbeat later he recovered himself. "The battle has begun!" he hissed. "With me—now!"

Waving his tail for his warriors to follow him, Bramblestar leaped forward through the trees, charging around bushes and pushing his way through sodden, rotten-smelling undergrowth. His Clanmates raced behind him, silent except for thudding paws and the splash of wet ground.

The sounds of battle grew louder as they bounded on; the shrieks and yowls of fighting cats mingled with deeper growls and snarls from the badgers. The scent of blood and badgers was so thick that Bramblestar almost thought he could see it in the air like fog. He and his Clanmates pushed through a stretch of thickly growing hazel saplings and burst into a clearing. Bramblestar realized they were close to the Twoleg dens where they had met the hostile kittypets.

At first Bramblestar could see nothing but badgers: their broad shoulders and blunt claws; their pointed black heads with a white stripe down the nose swinging from side to side as they searched for their prey; their enormous teeth gleaming in the moonlight. Then he noticed the smaller, swifter bodies of ShadowClan cats weaving in and out among the badgers, darting forward to slash with outstretched claws, and just as quickly falling back out of range.

But there are so few of them! Bramblestar thought in horror.

With less than a heartbeat's hesitation the ThunderClan warriors leaped forward, letting out furious screeches of challenge. Bramblestar heard yowls of amazement coming from the ShadowClan cats as they realized they were not alone. Rowanstar whirled around from the badger he was facing and glared at Bramblestar.

"We didn't ask for your help!" he spat.

At the same moment the badger lurched forward and swatted Rowanstar across the head with a powerful forepaw. Rowanstar staggered and fell.

Bramblestar sprang forward to stand over his body and bared his teeth at the badger. "Get back or I'll slit your throat!" he snarled.

He knew the badger wouldn't understand his threat, and bunched his muscles to spring, hoping to avoid those terrifying teeth. But before he could move, Owlclaw darted in and slashed his claws down the badger's side. The badger, distracted, swung around and lumbered off after Owlclaw.

Bramblestar helped Rowanstar to his paws. "You may not have asked for our help," he panted, "but you've got it."

Rowanstar didn't reply. For a heartbeat he stood dazedly shaking his head, then flung himself back into the battle.

Bramblestar paused to let his gaze sweep around the clearing. In the shifting moonlight and shadow he couldn't be sure, but he thought he could count eight badgers. *Two of them look young,* he thought, spotting two smaller black-and-white shapes. *They might not give us too much trouble. No, who am I kidding?* he added to himself, noticing two old, ferocious boars that roared and trampled through the undergrowth, fighting as if they belonged to the legendary LionClan. *They're* all *trouble!*

Bramblestar let out a fearsome screech and hurled himself forward. The badger closest to him had picked up a gray-and-black cat by his scruff and was shaking him like a piece of prey. Bramblestar recognized Ferretclaw from ShadowClan. His paws flailed furiously, but he couldn't reach the badger to strike a blow.

Bramblestar launched himself upward and dug his claws into the huge beast's shoulder. The badger jerked its head and flung Ferretclaw away; Bramblestar lost sight of the warrior as he plummeted into a clump of ferns. Scrambling up to avoid the creature's snapping jaws, Bramblestar balanced on the badger's neck and raked his claws over and over again through its thick fur. He felt fierce satisfaction as blood welled up from the marks of his claws. With a bellow of pain the badger reared up on its hind paws. Bramblestar lost his grip and slid to the ground, landing with a thump that briefly drove all the breath from his body. He staggered back to his paws to see his enemy lumbering off.

By now the clearing was full of battling cats and badgers. ThunderClan and ShadowClan fought side by side. Their nimble shapes wove between the clumsy forms of the badgers, using speed and skill to avoid the badgers' slashing claws and teeth.

Bramblestar spotted a badger looming over Poppyfrost, who stood bravely in front of it, hissing defiance. He raced across the open ground to help her. But before he reached her he tripped and rolled over, hitting the ground hard, with rocks driving their sharp points into his side. Springing up, he found himself at the foot of a bank, the steep slope hidden by a thick growth of fern.

This is what we get for fighting outside our territory, he thought, shaking his pelt. *We don't know where the hollows are, or the brambles, or the fallen trees that could trap us in a corner.* The battle inside the ThunderClan camp had been hideous, but at least they had known their own terrain well.

Poppyfrost had disappeared in the moments it took Bramblestar to recover. Now he spotted Dovewing dashing up to a badger and raking its side with her claws before leaping back out of range. All her fears seemed to have vanished in the heat of the battle. As she prepared to dart in for a second blow, she seemed to notice a ShadowClan warrior writhing on the ground with the foot of another badger planted on his back. Dovewing whirled and raced toward the huge beast, sinking her claws and teeth into its leg. The badger shifted to attack her, raising its paw enough for the ShadowClan cat to crawl away, and Dovewing ducked away from the badger's snapping jaws with one last well-aimed blow at its muzzle.

She may have lost her powers to see and hear afar, Bramblestar thought, *but she's managing pretty well without them.*

A few tail-lengths away Lionblaze was fighting with one of the old badgers, snarling defiance as he leaped up over and over again to slash his claws across its eyes and ears. The badger lurched from side to side, swiping with its huge paws, but it couldn't land a blow on the whirling, dodging, golden-furred warrior.

"He's being too reckless!" Squirrelflight gasped, appearing at Bramblestar's side. "Doesn't he know that he can be hurt now?"

"Oh, he knows," Bramblestar replied, pride in the young warrior warming him through. "But he's going to be a father. He's fighting to protect Cinderheart and their unborn kits. That gives him all the courage he needs." He hesitated, then added, "Once I felt the same."

Squirrelflight's green gaze rested on him for a heartbeat that seemed to last for seasons. "You are still their father," she meowed. Then she darted away, back into the chaos of the battle.

Bramblestar glanced around, checking to see if any of his cats needed help. He glimpsed Cloudtail and Dustpelt, flinging themselves into the thick of the fighting together. Blossomfall, Rosepetal, and Berrynose had surrounded a badger, confusing it with matching attacks until the creature stood helplessly roaring in pain. Lionblaze was fighting side by side with Pinenose, while Mousewhisker and Stoatfur attacked a badger from each side, nimbly leaping out of the range of its massive paws.

Bramblestar noticed that the two kittypets had taken on one of the younger badgers. Jessy stood in front of it, teasing it by jumping in to tap its nose lightly with her paws, her blows hardly grazing its skin, while Frankie attacked from behind, digging his claws into its hindquarters and biting down hard on its tail. The badger roared in fury and frustration, turning around and around in its efforts to get at Frankie, while the she-cat in front of him kept distracting him.

That's a new move, Bramblestar thought, amused in the midst of danger. *I'll have to remember it.*

In the next heartbeat the badger broke away, with Frankie pursuing it into the darkness under the trees. Bramblestar lost sight of Jessy too, as he dodged around a tree stump to help Scorchfur, who was battering vainly with his hind paws at a badger that held him in its claws. Bramblestar launched himself at the badger with an earsplitting screech, scoring his claws down its shoulder. The badger dropped Scorchfur, and for a few moments the dark gray tom and Bramblestar fought together, attacking the badger from one side and then the other. It was already injured, blood pouring from a wound in its side, and too slow for its blows to land on the swifter cats. Soon it turned and staggered away, thrusting a path through a dense thicket of brambles.

Scorchfur and Bramblestar faced each other for a heart-beat, breathing hard. Then Scorchfur gave a tiny nod. "You fight well, ThunderClan cat."

"You're not so bad yourself," Bramblestar responded.

Turning back to the battle, he spotted Jessy again, this time perched on the back of a badger with Ivypool and Snowpaw. She and Snowpaw were clawing vigorously at the badger's back, while Ivypool balanced on its neck and raked her claws across its eyes.

Bramblestar shuddered. *A Dark Forest move . . .*

A badger charged in front of Bramblestar, cutting him off from Jessy and the others. Poppyfrost and Lilypaw raced after it alongside Pinenose from ShadowClan. As the badger slowed down, looking for a gap in the undergrowth at the edge of the clearing, Lilypaw outpaced the other she-cats and with a wild screech sprang up to fasten her claws and teeth in the badger's tail. She swung there, all her fur bushed out, until the badger found its escape route and blundered away. Then she dropped lightly to her paws and bounded back to her mentor.

Bramblestar raced up to meet her. "Lilypaw, that was brilliant!" he meowed. "Great job!"

Lilypaw's eyes shone with reflected moonlight. "I'm fighting for Seedpaw too!" she gasped.

Once again Bramblestar paused to check on the state of the battle. The crowd of struggling animals seemed to have thinned out. *I saw two badgers leave. . . . Maybe we're going to win this fight!*

Then Bramblestar spotted another pair of badgers at the far side of the clearing. They were crouching over the body of a cat who snarled and lashed out at them, but couldn't attack both of them at once. The cat was half-hidden by the badgers' bodies, but a ray of moonlight showed Bramblestar a familiar patch of tortoiseshell fur.

Tawnypelt!

One of the badgers had raised a paw, braced to bring it slamming down on the ShadowClan she-cat. Bramblestar began racing toward them, but he already knew he would be too late.

It's too far. I'll never get to them in time. Tawnypelt's going to die. . . .

CHAPTER 31

❧

Then Bramblestar saw Squirrelflight. The dark ginger she-cat bunched her muscles and soared upward in a massive leap, clearing the back of a badger that stood in her way. Her paws barely touched the ground before she sprang up again, reached a low-growing beech branch, then leaped to the fork between an ash branch and the tree's trunk. From there she hurled herself down with a terrifying shriek on top of the badger looming over Tawnypelt.

The badger's blow fell, but it barely grazed Tawnypelt, who rolled clear. The badger reared up, throwing Squirrelflight off. Bramblestar winced at the hard thump as his deputy's body hit the ground, but the next moment she was on her paws again. As Bramblestar finally raced up to them she met his gaze and nodded before throwing herself into the battle.

Tawnypelt sprang to her paws and faced the second badger. Side by side, she and Bramblestar forced it back, ducking beneath its gaping jaws to slash at its throat. Tawnypelt's shoulder was oozing blood, but the wound didn't seem to slow her down.

"Get off our territory!" she snarled at the vast creature. "Or

I'll line my nest with your fur!"

The badger lumbered away, with Tawnypelt following, harrying it with nips at its hind paws. Bramblestar, confident that his sister was okay, spun around and flung himself at a badger that held Crowfrost, the ShadowClan deputy, down with one huge paw, while its teeth bit hard into his shoulder. Bramblestar leaped up and dug his claws into the badger's neck. It let out an enraged bellow and let itself fall sideways, crushing Bramblestar underneath its massive body.

Letting out a howl of pain, Bramblestar struggled to free himself, but the badger had him pinned to the ground, its stinking flank pressing on his face and filling his mouth with fur. He couldn't get a paw free to defend himself. As he fought to breathe, Bramblestar felt as if he was sinking into a glittering darkness.

StarClan, help me!

Suddenly the weight lifted off Bramblestar. Gasping for breath, he scrabbled to his paws, confused for a moment by the roaring and screeching all around him, the crashes from the undergrowth and the reek of blood. As his vision cleared he saw that Bumblestripe had taken on the badger, bravely crouching low to lash out at the creature's belly. From the corner of his eye Bramblestar spotted Crowfrost stretched out on the ground, his twitching tail-tip all that showed he was alive. As he watched, Spiderleg darted out of a nearby bush, fastened his teeth in Crowfrost's scruff, and dragged him away.

Bramblestar staggered toward the badger to help Bumblestripe, but at the same moment the badger turned tail and headed out of the clearing, leaving a trail of blood spattering the ground.

"Thanks," Bramblestar panted with a nod to Bumblestripe. "Where's Dovewing?"

Bumblestripe angled his ears across the clearing. "There," he mewed grimly.

Looking where he pointed, Bramblestar saw Dovewing attacking a young badger side by side with Tigerheart. First one, then the other would dart forward, slash at the badger's muzzle, and leap back, confusing the badger because it didn't know which cat to attack first.

Leap and slash . . . leap and slash . . . At first Bramblestar was impressed by the unspoken closeness between the two young cats, the natural rhythm they shared as they drove the badger back into a bramble thicket. But after a moment the sight began to trouble him. *Where did they learn to fight together like that? Any cat would think those two had known each other for moons, and trained together.*

But Bramblestar had no time to think about that. The sounds of battle were beginning to die away. Some of the badgers had already fled, and the others were yielding, ready to be chased off. Bramblestar allowed himself a sigh of relief.

It's almost over!

A heartbeat later he realized he had allowed himself to relax too soon. The biggest, most ferocious badger hadn't given up. Bramblestar gaped with amazement at its speed as it lumbered across the clearing away from the main throng of battle. He realized that its target was two small ShadowClan cats—apprentices by the look of them—who were crouching together in the shelter of a clump of ferns, licking each other's wounds. They looked up with horror in their eyes as the badger bore down on them.

Bramblestar launched himself forward, but he was too late to stop the creature. He raced after it, then spotted Jessy hurling herself at the badger from the opposite side.

She waved her tail when she saw Bramblestar. "With me!" she screeched.

Jessy shot straight in front of the badger, distracting it from snapping at the two young cats, who plunged deeper into the undergrowth with squeals of terror. Jumping up and down in front of the badger, backing away so that she was always just out of reach, Jessy lured it toward the edge of the trees.

"Come back!" Bramblestar yowled.

"No," Jessy responded. "I know what I'm doing!"

Terrified for her, Bramblestar streaked across to her side and kept pace with her as they pelted ahead of the badger. Tree roots tripped them and bramble tendrils reached out to snag their fur. Exhausted from the battle, Bramblestar knew he was too slow. He imagined he could already feel the badger's hot, stinking breath on his fur and braced himself for the sting of snapping teeth.

Suddenly the leaf-strewn ground vanished, and the two cats lurched to a halt at the edge of the stream on the far side of ShadowClan territory. The water had gone down, but it was still far too wide to jump across. And there was no hope of swimming across the swift-flowing current, which snatched debris and branches downriver in front of them.

"Great StarClan, we're trapped!" Bramblestar gasped. "We'll have to fight our way out."

Jessy ignored him; she was frantically scanning the water. "It's here somewhere," she muttered.

"What?" Bramblestar panted, aware of the badger crashing through the undergrowth, getting nearer with every heartbeat.

Jessy began running downstream, her gaze flicking back and forth. Suddenly she halted and turned to Bramblestar, balancing right on the edge of the surging black water. "Follow me," she meowed.

"We can't swim across that!" Bramblestar protested.

Jessy fixed her amber gaze on him. "Trust me."

Bramblestar hesitated, then touched his nose to hers. He nodded. "Lead on."

The badger broke out of the undergrowth and covered the open ground between them with massive strides. Bramblestar flexed his claws as it loomed over him and Jessy and he looked up into its tiny, malignant eyes.

Jessy gave one more glance around, took a deep breath, and jumped into the stream. Bramblestar flinched, waiting for her to be swept underwater, then realized that she was still standing, fighting the current, but with water only reaching up to her belly.

For a moment Bramblestar stood still, gaping in astonishment.

"Quick!" Jessy screeched.

Knowing that he was trusting her with his life, Bramblestar leaped into the water beside Jessy. His paws struck something hard just beneath the surface, but before he could get his balance he started to slip. Jessy grabbed his scruff in her teeth and hauled him back before he could fall into the stream.

"There's a tree trunk crossing the stream just here," she panted. "It's underwater now, but I remembered where it was."

I can't believe this! Bramblestar thought, stunned. Every hair on his pelt rose in alarm as he stood on top of the turbulent current. There was no way of seeing the tree beneath the surface, but it was definitely there, solid and steady against the flow of water. Bramblestar sank his claws into the perilously narrow trunk and braced himself. With Jessy beside him he stood firm as the badger let out a roar and lunged toward them.

But the badger didn't know where the tree trunk was. There was a huge splash, soaking both cats, as it plunged into the stream and vanished beneath the surface. Moments later it reappeared as the current washed it down toward the lake, sputtering and bellowing as it thrashed its paws.

Jessy's eyes gleamed as she watched it out of sight. Then both cats jumped back to the bank and shook water from their pelts. Bramblestar wanted to let out a yowl of pure joy and admiration for Jessy's courage and quick thinking.

Instead he gave her a nod. "Not bad—for a kittypet," he meowed.

Jessy let out a small *mrrow* of amusement. "Not bad—for a wild cat," she retorted.

Together Bramblestar and Jessy raced back to the clearing, to find that the rest of the badgers had gone. Warriors from ShadowClan and ThunderClan stood side by side, their chests heaving, blood trickling from their wounds, as they assessed the damage.

"How's Crowfrost?" Bramblestar demanded. He couldn't see the ShadowClan deputy, and knew how badly hurt he had been.

"He'll be okay," Pouncetail replied. "Pinenose and Stoatfur are helping him back to see Littlecloud."

Looking around at the rest of the cats, Bramblestar saw that none of them was unmarked. Spiderleg was one of the worst injured, with almost all his fur missing from one side, while Scorchfur had both ears slashed, and Ivypool was standing on three legs with one paw raised and bleeding. But all the wounds looked as if they would heal in time.

We won! Bramblestar thought, exhilaration flooding through him. *We defeated the badgers and survived!*

Then he felt a light touch on his shoulder. He turned to see Brightheart, her single eye full of sorrow. "It's Dustpelt," she whispered.

With a lurch of horror in his belly, Bramblestar followed Brightheart across the clearing. Dustpelt was lying on his side in the midst of the trampled debris from the battle. Blood was trickling from his mouth and his brown tabby body was lacerated with countless claw marks. His eyes were closed and his breath came in short, shallow puffs.

Bramblestar crouched beside him. "Hold on, Dustpelt," he begged. "We'll get help."

The tabby tom's eyes flickered open. "It's okay," he rasped. "It's my time."

"No!" cried Bramblestar. He leaned forward so that his forehead rested against Dustpelt's. "Not yet. Not here. You have served your Clan so well and for so long. Now it is our turn to serve you. The elders' den is waiting for you, Dustpelt."

The tip of Dustpelt's tail twitched. "That is not where I want to be," he murmured. "Thank you, Bramblestar, for everything. May StarClan light your path, always."

The ShadowClan cats stood back and allowed Dustpelt's Clanmates to gather around him as his breathing grew feebler and his eyes closed again. As Dustpelt sighed out his last breath, a pale gray shape appeared beside him, a cat with a pale gray pelt that glimmered in the moonlight, and the frosty glitter of stars around her paws. Her blue eyes shone with love as she gazed at the fallen warrior.

"Ferncloud!" Bramblestar breathed.

Other, fainter shapes appeared behind her: Bramblestar recognized Foxleap, who had died from his wounds after the Great Battle; Icecloud, who had succumbed to the recent bout of greencough; and others with them, all the lost kits of Dustpelt and Ferncloud, warriors of StarClan who had come to honor their father. Bramblestar stared in amazement as the spirit of Dustpelt rose from his mutilated body and padded up to Ferncloud, bending his head to touch noses with her. The two cats twined their tails together and for a moment the clearing shone even more brightly with silver light. Then the starry shapes began to fade, until all that was left was a few wisps of shimmering mist, and then nothing.

A long sigh escaped Bramblestar. His grief at Dustpelt's death was tinged with a strange feeling of joy. *He found it so hard to go on without Ferncloud, and now they're together again.*

Bramblestar realized that Tawnypelt was standing at his side. "I'm so sorry," she whispered, dipping her head toward Dustpelt. "He was a noble warrior. All of the Clans will grieve for him."

Bramblestar nodded. "May he be at peace now." He suddenly felt exhausted, bitterly aware of every scratch and bite on his pelt. He wondered if his legs had enough strength to carry him back to his own territory.

Tawnypelt traced his flank with the tip of her tail. "I can never thank you enough for what you did tonight," she purred. "This was more than ThunderClan protecting its own hunting grounds, wasn't it? You came because you are my brother, and I needed you."

Bramblestar gazed into her warm green eyes. "Always," he murmured. An image flashed into his mind of the lake filling with scarlet water that swirled to the surface until it swallowed the reflected starlight. Firestar's strange prophecy echoed in his ears: *When water meets blood, blood will rise.* His vision of Yellowfang had shown him the same thing. And finally Bramblestar understood.

Tawnypelt shares my blood. We are the son and daughter of Tigerstar and Goldenflower. When the flood threatened us both, our kinship gave us strength to survive. That's what the prophecy meant!

Bramblestar didn't try to explain all this to Tawnypelt. He

knew this wasn't the place or the time. But he raised his head to look at the stars glittering above him, and sent up a silent prayer of thanks to StarClan.

"Tawnypelt, it's time to go back to camp." Rowanstar's voice broke into Bramblestar's thoughts.

Tawnypelt dipped her head, then touched noses briefly with Bramblestar before turning away to join her Clanmates, who were limping out of the clearing.

Rowanstar faced Bramblestar. His orange pelt was ruffled and smeared with blood, and one eye was swollen closed. But he held his head high, and stood with his shoulders squared. "Thank you for your help," he meowed. Then hostility flashed into his eyes. "But we didn't ask for it!"

Bramblestar said nothing. He wasn't going to get Tawnypelt into trouble by telling her mate about the plea for help. He wondered when Rowanstar would realize that ThunderClan had enabled them to win this battle. He waited for one of the ShadowClan warriors to pitch in and point out that without ThunderClan, the badgers would have destroyed them all. But no cat spoke, and Rowanstar still glared at Bramblestar as if he was on the verge of continuing the battle.

"Don't be like Firestar," the ShadowClan leader growled, drawing his lips back in the beginnings of a snarl. "Stop interfering, Bramblestar. This is your last warning!"

CHAPTER 32

Sunlight, golden and thick as honey, bathed the forest. Outside the tunnel most of the cats of ThunderClan were basking in the sun's rays, licking their wounds and telling one another stories of the battle against the badgers. Two sunrises had passed since their expedition to help ShadowClan, but the excitement of their victory still bubbled up among them like springs of pure water.

"You should have seen Lionblaze fighting!" Amberpaw mewed. "He was like three cats, all on his own."

"And Jessy was brilliant," Frankie added. "She wasn't scared at all!"

Bramblestar couldn't share in their cheerful talk. A dark mood had settled over him as he wondered if he had been right to take his warriors to fight ShadowClan's battle. Rowanstar's furious parting shot had forced Bramblestar to question the risks he had taken for an ungrateful rival.

If I hadn't insisted on helping ShadowClan, Dustpelt would still be alive. Bramblestar was missing the sharp-tongued, cranky warrior more than he would have thought possible. Now he watched Dustpelt's son Spiderleg returning from the place where his father had been buried on the slope above the tunnel. Spider-leg's head drooped sadly and his tail trailed on the ground. *So much pain . . . Hasn't enough ThunderClan blood been spilled?*

In addition to grief for Dustpelt, Bramblestar wasn't looking forward to hearing what WindClan and RiverClan would have to say about the way ThunderClan had interfered again. He had no doubt that Rowanstar would claim it had been unnecessary and overconfident, and a threat to the independence of all the Clans.

Yes, the badgers have been driven off, but at what cost to my warriors?

A joyful yowl from the direction of the lake distracted Bramblestar from his gloomy thoughts. A moment later Jessy and Millie rushed out of the trees.

"The water has gone!" Millie announced. "We can get into the hollow!"

Several cats sprang up and crowded around the two she-cats. Their excited voices echoed around the clearing.

"Is it really dry?"

"We can go home!"

"No more sleeping in that horrible, dark tunnel!"

Brackenfur rose more slowly. "Calm down," he meowed, thrusting himself into the enthusiastic throng. "It'll take a lot of work to rebuild the old dens. I'll come down now and take a look at the damage."

"We'll come with you!" Snowpaw bounced up and down. "We'll all help!"

With the apprentices scampering ahead, all the cats ran into the trees and headed down the slope. Bramblestar fell in behind them, and found that Jessy had waited for him at the edge of the trees.

"Isn't this great?" she cried, bouncing up to him. "At last I can see your home!" Then she paused, tipping her head on one side. "Are you worried about how much damage has been done?" she asked more gently. "You don't seem as excited as the others."

Bramblestar shook his head. "No, I know we can repair our dens. Don't worry, I'm fine."

Together they followed the rest of the cats down to the hollow. The lower slopes, where the water had just retreated, were still wet and slippery. Bramblestar watched Amberpaw lose her footing and roll down, tail and paws waving, until she managed to stop herself by grabbing a tuft of long grass. She sprang up again, slicked with mud but not at all bothered by the fall, and pelted on after her littermates.

Bramblestar padded into the hollow and looked around. The thorn barrier at the entrance had been almost completely swept away; that would need restoring before they could feel safe. He was relieved to see that he could identify all the dens, though some of the branches and all of the moss and leaves that plugged holes in the roofs and walls had vanished. The nursery roof was sagging and washed-up branches blocked the entrance to the medicine cats' den.

Walking farther into the camp, Bramblestar had to pick his way among debris and a few surviving puddles. Scraps of bark, twigs, and leaves littered the ground, and there were even a few dead fish.

"Look, a fresh-kill pile already!" Berrynose joked as he padded past.

Poppyfrost wrinkled her nose and winced. "Not all that fresh," she muttered.

Brackenfur was moving from den to den, followed by Cherryfall and Mousewhisker as he inspected the damage. "We'll need a *lot* of brambles to patch that up," he warned, waving his tail at the roof of the warriors' den, which had a jagged hole in the middle. "Dustpelt, do you think—" he mewed, then broke off, flinching. "Sorry, I forgot," he mumbled. "I'm not sure I can do this without him."

Whitewing rested her tail across Brackenfur's shoulders. "You worked with Dustpelt for many seasons," she meowed encouragingly. "You know just what he would have done. And we'll all help rebuild our home. You're not alone."

Bramblestar watched the golden-brown tabby brace himself and examine the warriors' den more closely. "We'll need to find the longest bramble tendrils we can, to weave between the branches," he told Cherryfall and Molewhisker. "Ivy is good, too. And then plenty of moss to plug the gaps. But first we have to clear out all the mud and mess."

"How do we do that?" Mousewhisker asked, ducking under the branches of the fallen tree to peer at the clots of sludge that covered the floor of the den.

"Hmm . . ." Brackenfur narrowed his eyes. "There are plenty of dead leaves and ferns lying around. They should help to sop up the worst of the mud."

"Brackenfur!" Daisy's voice called from across the camp.

Bramblestar turned to see that the cream-furred cat had emerged from the nursery with a disgusted expression on her face. Cinderheart followed her a few paces behind.

"Brackenfur, the nursery is a disgrace!" Daisy announced. "Cinderheart's not having her kits in there."

"It's not that bad—" Cinderheart began to protest.

"It's worse than the tunnel!" Daisy hissed. Turning to Brackenfur, she added, "You have to do something right now, so it's ready for when the kits arrive."

"Okay, okay," Brackenfur soothed her. "I've only got four paws, you know. But I'll make sure the nursery's ready; don't worry. I'll come over with you now, and see what needs to be done."

Satisfied, Daisy turned to head back to the nursery, and was nearly knocked off her paws by all four apprentices, who were giving Frankie, Jessy, and Minty a tour of the camp.

"This is where we sleep," Dewpaw announced, waving his tail at the wreck of the apprentices' den. "You can go in if you like."

Minty peered over the waterlogged ferns that edged the den and drew back with a twitch of her whiskers. "Er . . . very nice," she murmured. "But I won't go in just yet, if you don't mind."

"Oh, I know it looks awful now," Amberpaw responded cheerfully. "But when it's dried out, and the floor covered with moss and bracken, it's so cozy and comfortable!"

"Except when you stick your tail in my ear," Snowpaw muttered, giving her a prod.

Lilypaw slipped between the two younger apprentices. "That's enough," she mewed. "Come on, we have to show the kittypets the medicine den."

"Yes!" Amberpaw yowled. "Come on, it's this way!"

The apprentices streamed across the clearing, paws slipping in the thick mud that covered the floor. "Oh, yuck, I've got it all over my pelt!" Snowpaw squealed.

The kittypets followed, their expressions torn between amusement and confusion.

"That's where the fresh-kill pile used to be!" Amberpaw explained, pointing with her tail.

"No, it's not, mouse-brain!" Dewpaw swatted her over the head with one paw. "It was over there!"

The sight of them lightened Bramblestar's mood. He watched them wriggling through a tangle of branches into the medicine cats' den. Dewpaw got stuck, his hind legs waving in the air until Snowpaw gave him a push. Frankie and Jessy used their greater strength to shift some of the branches aside and improve the entrance.

Bramblestar realized that Squirrelflight had padded up silently and was standing at his side. "We'll be home soon, won't we?" she asked.

Bramblestar turned to her and nodded, seeing his own joy and relief reflected in her face. "I'm sure we will," he responded, then added, "I wanted to talk to you about the badgers. It worries me that—"

He broke off as Brackenfur came bounding up, looking energized and purposeful. "Bramblestar," he meowed, "can I start organizing building patrols right away?"

"Of course," Bramblestar agreed. Glancing at Squirrel-flight, he added, "I'll tell you another time."

That night Bramblestar headed to his nest before the last traces of daylight had faded from the sky. Most of his Clan-mates were still gathered outside. Though they were tired, their fur muddy and full of twigs, they were still bubbling with excitement about rebuilding the camp in the hollow.

As he closed his eyes, Bramblestar could hear their cheerful voices drifting down into the tunnel.

"Berrynose, I'll never forget seeing you with that bramble stuck in your fur!" Poppyfrost purred. "You looked like a hedgehog!"

"It patched a good section of the nursery roof," Berrynose retorted good-humoredly.

"I thought Snowpaw had turned into a brown cat," his mentor, Ivypool, meowed. "It looked like he was trying to clear all the mud out of the camp with his pelt."

"And Molewhisker," Rosepetal teased, "remember that you have to get *off* the branch before Brackenfur puts it in place. You nearly ended up as part of the warriors' den."

Bramblestar drifted into sleep, lulled by the chatter. He found himself standing in the hollow on firm, dry ground, not the thick layer of mud that covered it now. Moonlight washed over his fur as he gazed around at the restored camp. The dens were as good as new, strong and safe and well constructed, and a thick barrier of thorns stretched across the entrance. But there was no sign of any of his Clanmates.

From the corner of his eye Bramblestar spotted a flash of flame, and turned to see Firestar pushing his way into the camp. He bounded across to his former leader and dipped his head.

"Firestar!" he meowed. "It's so good to see you."

"It's good to be here," Firestar responded. "Thank you for returning our Clan to its home."

"It hasn't happened yet," Bramblestar reminded him.

"No, but it will." Firestar's green eyes glowed. "You have done well."

"Really?" Bramblestar found that hard to believe. "Even by fighting ShadowClan's battle for them?"

"You did what you thought was right," Firestar told him.

No, Bramblestar thought. *I did what I thought you would think was right.*

"Those badgers could have caused trouble for Thunder-Clan," Firestar went on.

"I don't know that for sure," Bramblestar meowed. "Rowan-star is angry with me."

Firestar let out a long sigh. "So few cats understand how important it is for us to share dangers between all the Clans."

Bramblestar was puzzled. How could that be reconciled with keeping each Clan safe and independent, the way the Clans had lived for season upon season? "But each Clan leader is responsible for their own Clan, right?" he checked. "It's not up to us to make decisions for other Clans."

Firestar fixed him with an intense green gaze. He sat down

in the middle of the clearing and gestured with his tail for Bramblestar to sit beside him. "There's something you need to know," he began. "When I had been leader of ThunderClan for just a few moons, Bluestar came to me and told me about a terrible mistake that the four Clans had made a long time ago: that they allowed a fifth Clan to leave the forest."

Bramblestar stared at him in astonishment. "A fifth Clan? But there isn't a fifth Clan!"

"Once there was," Firestar continued. "They were called SkyClan, and their territory in the old forest lay next to ThunderClan's. Their skill was hunting aboveground in the trees, snatching birds from the air. They were strong and well respected. But the Twolegs began to build more dens, and they destroyed SkyClan's territory to make room for them."

Every hair on Bramblestar's pelt prickled. "Just like the Twolegs did to us," he breathed, "when the old forest was cut down and we had to make the Great Journey to find a new home by the lake."

Firestar nodded. "Exactly like that. SkyClan's leader, Cloudstar, asked the other Clan leaders to change the borders of their territories so that they would still have somewhere to live. The other leaders refused. SkyClan had no choice but to leave the forest and travel until they found somewhere else they could settle."

"What happened to them then?" Bramblestar felt like a kit begging the elders for a story.

"They made their home in a gorge where the forest river rises. But there were dangers that they never expected, and

SkyClan almost died out, until cats began to settle in the gorge again, and StarClan sent me and Sandstorm to help them form a new SkyClan."

"So that's where you went!" Bramblestar exclaimed. "That time you disappeared for moons and left Graystripe to lead the Clan."

Firestar dipped his head. "That's right. And it wasn't easy, let me tell you."

Bramblestar's head spun. How had the Clans kept this massive secret for so long? "What about SkyClan now? Did they survive?"

"I don't know," Firestar admitted. "They have their own warrior ancestors, and I can't see them from my StarClan, though Cloudstar once visited me here. But I have faith in Leafstar, the cat who became their leader, and her deputy, Sharpclaw, and their medicine cat, Echosong. And if they follow the warrior code, it will protect them." He paused for a moment, memories flickering in his eyes like minnows in a stream. "The four leaders who drove SkyClan out realized that they had been wrong," he meowed. "They came to Leafstar and each gave her one of her nine lives. It was more than an apology: It was an acknowledgment that one Clan cannot survive alone, that we owe the others a debt that is greater than we know. And that proved to me what I've known all along: that the safety of each Clan depends on all the others."

Bramblestar began to understand why Firestar had told him this story, but he didn't dare to interrupt.

"Fighting the badgers was your chance to do the right

thing," Firestar told him, "to save ShadowClan from being driven out of their territory altogether. The Clans traveled a long way to find this home. We can't lose it now. It's not up to any one Clan to protect the others; all of us have to fight together to survive."

"Like in the Great Battle," Bramblestar meowed.

"Exactly!"

"Tell me more about SkyClan," Bramblestar went on, his pelt pricking with curiosity about these cats he had never heard of before. "Did they—?"

He broke off as the sun began to rise above the treetops, spilling warm light into the hollow. Firestar's flame-colored form was already beginning to fade.

"There is one other cat who knows what happened with SkyClan," he mewed; the words seemed to come from an immense distance as the last glimmer of his green eyes vanished. "If you have any more questions, ask her."

Bramblestar woke to find his cats stirring around him, heading out of the tunnel in their eagerness to begin the new day. Firestar's last words echoed in his ears.

I know which cat he meant.

Following his Clanmates out of the tunnel, he padded over to Squirrelflight, who was starting to organize the first patrols. "Don't put me in a patrol just yet," he meowed. "There's something I have to do first."

Squirrelflight nodded. "No problem."

A paw poked Bramblestar in the side, and he turned to see

Jessy. "Hey," she protested. "I thought we were going hunting this morning."

Bramblestar dipped his head. "I know. But this is important. We'll go later, okay?"

Jessy gave him a light flick with her tail, and bounded off to join Frankie, Cloudtail, and Millie. Bramblestar watched her go, then went to look for Sandstorm. He found her sitting in a patch of sunlight near the mudpile. Jayfeather had just dropped a spray of leaves at her paws.

"But I'm perfectly capable of joining a patrol," Sandstorm was objecting. "I'm hardly coughing at all."

"You're capable when I say you are," Jayfeather retorted. "Now eat the tansy and get some rest."

Sandstorm sighed, rolling her eyes, but she licked up the leaves without any more argument. Bramblestar padded up as Jayfeather disappeared into the tunnel again.

"Firestar visited me in a dream last night," he announced as he sat down beside the pale ginger she-cat.

Joy glowed in Sandstorm's green eyes. "That's wonderful!" she exclaimed. "I dream about Firestar all the time, but it's not the same as a real visit."

"I know he's watching over you," Bramblestar assured her. "He sent me to talk to you."

"Oh?" Sandstorm's whiskers twitched. "What about?"

"In my dream, he told me about SkyClan. I wanted to know more, and he said that you were the cat I should ask."

"SkyClan . . . oh, yes." Sandstorm reached out with her forepaws to give herself a good stretch. "That was an amazing time! So scary . . . but it was fun, too, and what we did was important."

"Tell me about it," Bramblestar urged her.

Sandstorm described how the former SkyClan leader, Cloudstar, had visited Firestar in a dream and given him the task of traveling upriver to discover the remains of his Clan. "When we came to the gorge where the river rises, it seemed empty at first. But we learned that an old cat came to sit on the rocks at every full moon to watch the stars and speak to the spirits of his ancestors. His name was Sky."

"And he was the last surviving cat of SkyClan?" Bramblestar asked, fascinated.

Sandstorm shook her head. "No, but his mother's mother was born into the Clan. She passed down the warrior code to her daughter, who passed it down to Sky."

"And he kept the memories alive . . ." Bramblestar murmured. "What happened next?"

"Firestar thought that all he needed to do was find Sky-Clan, but the old cat Sky didn't agree. He wanted to see SkyClan restored. . . . So that's what we did, though it wasn't as easy as that makes it sound."

"Where did you find enough cats?"

"There were rogues living in the forest around the gorge. We had to rescue one she-cat and her kits from a Twoleg who was starving them. We scared him out of his fur! And there were two young kittypets who became our first apprentices: Cherrypaw and Sparrowpaw. They were a pawful, and no mistake! They took Firestar into the Twolegplace nearby to see if any other kittypets wanted to join."

"And did they?" Bramblestar asked, surprised.

"Oh, yes." Sandstorm's eyes glimmered with amusement. "Echosong, who became the medicine cat . . . She was a kittypet."

Bramblestar blinked in surprise.

"In the end," Sandstorm went on, "we discovered what had destroyed the original SkyClan. There was a huge Twoleg den that was full of rats. The rats started attacking the new Clan in the gorge, so we had to go and fight them." For a heartbeat her gaze became shadowed. "Firestar lost a life there."

Bramblestar pressed himself against her side. "It was hard for both of you. SkyClan owes you a lot."

Sandstorm dipped her head in agreement. "Yes, but they repaid us, in a way. Skywatcher—that was the warrior name Firestar gave to Sky—died while we were there, but before he died, he made a prophecy." Her voice dropped to a whisper. " 'There will be three, kin of your kin, who will hold the power of the stars in their paws.' "

Bramblestar felt his heart skip a beat. "The Prophecy of the Three came from SkyClan!" he murmured. "Everything is connected."

The two cats shared a few heartbeats of silence, until Bramblestar meowed, "Why didn't Firestar tell all the Clans about SkyClan when you came home?"

"I asked him that once," Sandstorm replied. "He said that the burden of guilt didn't need to be carried on. StarClan had done its best to make amends by sending Firestar and me to build a new SkyClan." Gently she added, "There is a time for guilt and shame to stop."

Bramblestar sighed. "I hope I can stop feeling guilty about the badger attack," he confided to Sandstorm. "I lost Dustpelt and I angered Rowanstar." Unfamiliar emotion surged through him, and more words spilled out of him. "I was just trying to do what Firestar would have done. He would have rescued the kittypets and helped ShadowClan not once, but twice."

Sandstorm's ears flicked up in surprise, and she fixed a compelling green gaze on Bramblestar. "That's not what you're supposed to do!" she exclaimed. "StarClan knew you would be a good leader in your own right. That's why they led your paws along this path. Firestar didn't appoint you to be his echo, but to be yourself. He trusted you to protect ThunderClan, to make decisions for them based on your own judgment and instincts." Tucking her paws underneath her, she went on, "Tell me honestly, if there was no ThunderClan, no Firestar, no expectations, would you still have helped the kittypets? Interfered with ShadowClan?"

Bramblestar thought about how he had made those decisions. He had felt compassion for the kittypets, unable to abandon them to drown or starve in the flood. His bond with Tawnypelt had led him to save her Clan.

He took a deep breath. "Yes, I would."

Sandstorm's eyes narrowed in approval. "You are the leader of ThunderClan now, Bramblestar," she mewed. "Not Firestar. Be the leader that you want to be. No cat expects anything else."

CHAPTER 33
❧

Repairs to the hollow progressed rapidly in the sunny days that followed. The Clan still lived in the tunnel, but their hunting
and border patrols had to be fitted around the task of rebuilding.

Just before sunhigh, Bramblestar headed for the hollow to
see how the work was going. He was tired after an early hunting
patrol, but he shared with all his Clanmates the sense of jubi-
lation that their home was being restored. As he approached
the camp, he spotted Squirrelflight in the entrance helping
Rosepetal and Bumblestripe, who were dragging brambles
and tendrils of ivy to form a new barrier. She broke off when
she spotted Bramblestar and padded up to him.

"It's going well," she mewed, looking exhausted but determined. "Come in and see."

Bramblestar followed her into the camp. The hollow was
swarming with cats, and for a moment he couldn't make any
sense of all the activity. Then he noticed Brackenfur moving
from den to den, pausing to direct the building work with a
great deal of calm meowing and waving of his tail. He looked
confident, as if at last he was comfortable alone in the role he

had once shared with Dustpelt.

Briarlight was sitting with Jayfeather and Leafpool at the mouth of their den, helping the medicine cats to sort herbs. Bramblestar realized with satisfaction that one of his Clanmates must have carried her down from the tunnel.

Jessy bounded over to Bramblestar, her eyes sparkling with triumph. "You have to see the nursery!" she announced.

Lionblaze was scrambling around on the nursery roof, patching the holes with tough stems of ivy. "Cinderheart!" he called, twisting around precariously to beckon his mate with one paw. "It's nearly finished. Our kits will be warm and safe in here!"

Cinderheart hurried over and stood looking up with a warm glow in her blue eyes. "It's perfect!" she purred.

Inside Bramblestar discovered Daisy with the other two kittypets, spreading huge bundles of moss over the nursery floor.

"Minty, make sure there aren't any thorns in there," Daisy mewed. "We don't want Cinderheart's kits to get scratched."

"I'll be careful, Daisy," Minty responded, drawing her claws through the moss and setting aside a huge thorn.

Lionblaze dropped to the ground and stuck his head inside the entrance, with Cinderheart peering over his shoulder. "It's great in here," he meowed. "I can't wait for our kits to be born. I'll visit as often as I can."

Daisy gave him a sharp flick with her tail. "You'll visit if I say you can," she told him. "Cinderheart and her kits will need a lot of rest. We all have to put mothers and their kits first."

Lionblaze nodded. "Of course, Daisy."

Jessy followed Bramblestar out as he left the nursery. "Daisy has enough help," she remarked. "Is there anything else I can do?"

Bramblestar glanced around and spotted the apprentices, who were hauling a tangle of bramble tendrils up to the warriors' den. "They could do with some extra paws," he mewed.

"I'm on it!" Jessy responded, bounding across the camp toward the young cats.

Bramblestar watched her go, then went over to Squirrelflight, who was struggling with a hazel branch outside the elders' den. "Let me help you with that," he offered.

Together they began wrestling the branch into position. Squirrelflight kept darting swift glances at Bramblestar. "I've noticed how well you're getting on with Jessy," she murmured after a few moments.

Bramblestar's pelt grew hot with embarrassment at the thought of discussing Jessy with Squirrelflight. "She's a nice cat," he responded; then, trying to sound lighthearted, he added, "for a kittypet."

"She doesn't seem like a kittypet now," Squirrelflight mewed. After a pause, she added, "Do you think she'll stay?" She didn't look at Bramblestar. "I mean, if you want her to, that's fine with me. Not that it's up to me, of course . . ." Her voice trailed off; she sounded as awkward as Bramblestar felt.

Bramblestar blinked. Until now he hadn't thought about what it would be like if Jessy stayed in the Clan forever, as a warrior and his mate. *Is that what I want?*

He looked at Squirrelflight, who had gone back to struggling with the branch. Behind him, he could hear Lionblaze talking to Cinderheart. "How many kits do you think we'll have?"

Then Jayfeather's voice, raised in annoyance, drifted across the camp. "How many times do I have to tell you apprentices? Watch where you're putting your paws when you come into my den. That's a whole bunch of yarrow crushed!"

My sons are so grown up, so confident and talented. How could I have regretted raising them for a single moment? Grief surged up inside Bramblestar. "I miss Hollyleaf," he blurted out.

Squirrelflight let the branch drop. "So do I."

She looked so heartbroken, her eyes wide and full of sorrow as if the pain had never left, that Bramblestar choked on the words he would have liked to stay. Instead he rested his head against Squirrelflight's, hoping that the touch would bring her comfort.

Neither of them said anything more about Jessy.

As the sun reached its height, Cloudtail appeared at the entrance to the hollow with Blossomfall, Dovewing, and Berrynose. All four cats were loaded with prey.

"Hey, Bramblestar!" Cloudtail dropped his catch in the middle of the clearing and waved his tail at his Clan leader. "We brought our fresh-kill so we can eat here!"

"Good idea," Bramblestar agreed.

Cheerful yowls rose from his Clanmates as they converged hungrily on the pile. Bramblestar chose a thrush and settled down to eat. As the noise died down while the cats gulped down their fresh-kill, he heard Blossomfall and Rosepetal talking together beside him.

"What's this I hear, that Bumblestripe and Dovewing aren't mates anymore?" Rosepetal asked.

Surprised, Bramblestar flicked a glance around the clearing and saw that the two warriors were eating on opposite sides of the group, about as far away from each other as they could get. Both of them looked downcast, and kept their gaze firmly fixed on their prey.

"That's right," Blossomfall replied to Rosepetal. "But I never did think Dovewing was right for my brother. She's always been a bit . . . different, hasn't she?"

Rosepetal murmured agreement. "I'm sure Bumblestripe will find another mate soon," she mewed. "He's so nice."

Blossomfall gave her a friendly prod. "I'll put in a good word for you, if you like!"

Bramblestar was distracted from the conversation as Jessy came to sit beside him and tucked into her mouse. He studied her warily, still not sure about what their future might be. Squirrelflight's comments had confronted him with something he had been aware of for a while. He was finishing his thrush when his deputy approached, picking her way through the crowd of feeding cats.

"Hey, Squirrelflight wants you," Jessy meowed, springing to her paws as she gulped down the last of her mouse. "I'll talk to you later." Resting her tail on Bramblestar's shoulder for a moment, she headed for the nursery.

Bramblestar noticed that Squirrelflight's gaze followed

her, but he said nothing. "Did you want something?" he asked.

"Yes," Squirrelflight mewed. "I thought we could celebrate the return to the hollow with a warrior ceremony. Lilypaw fought well against the badgers, don't you think? I know she hasn't had a formal assessment, but she's more than proved her skills."

"She sure has," Bramblestar agreed. "Let's do it." Glancing around, he saw that most of the Clan had finished eating. He rose to his paws. "Since we're all here," he began, "I'm going to hold a Clan meeting. I've got something important to do. Lilypaw, come here."

The apprentice's eyes widened with shock and she almost tripped over her own paws as she joined Bramblestar. The rest of the Clan moved into a ragged circle with Bramblestar at its center.

"Am I in trouble?" Lilypaw whispered.

Bramblestar shook his head. "Quite the opposite." Raising his voice, he began, "I, Bramblestar, leader of ThunderClan, call upon my warrior ancestors to look down upon this apprentice. She has trained hard to understand the ways of your noble code, and I commend her to you as a warrior in her turn."

Lilypaw looked astonished as Bramblestar spoke the words of the ceremony. Every hair on her pelt fluffed out, and she was trembling. A stir of excitement ran through her Clanmates as they realized what was happening.

"Lilypaw," Bramblestar went on, "do you promise to uphold the warrior code and to protect and defend this Clan, even at the cost of your life?"

Lilypaw's jaw's opened and for a moment Bramblestar thought nothing would come out. But her voice was clear and confident as she replied, "I do."

"Then by the power of StarClan, I give you your warrior name. Lilypaw, from this moment you will be known as Lilyheart. I give you this name in recognition of your courage, and because Seedpaw and Sorreltail will live forever in your heart. ThunderClan honors your bravery and dedication, and we welcome you as a full member of ThunderClan." He rested his muzzle on her head, and Lilyheart licked his shoulder in response.

"Lilyheart! Lilyheart!" the rest of ThunderClan called out in welcome.

Under cover of the jubilant cries, Lilyheart whispered to Bramblestar, "Thank you for my name. It's beautiful."

Poppyfrost bounded forward to congratulate her former apprentice, while Brackenfur padded up to Bramblestar's side. "Thank you, Bramblestar," he meowed, his eyes shining with pride as he gazed at his daughter. "You don't know what this means to me."

"She deserves it," Bramblestar meowed. "You both deserve it."

Before the circle of cats could disperse, Graystripe and Sandstorm stepped forward together to stand beside Bramblestar. Each of them dipped their head to him with great dignity.

"Bramblestar, we want to ask if we may enter the elders' den when the Clan returns to the hollow," Sandstorm mewed.

"We feel it's time to let the younger cats take over," Graystripe added. "Though we'll still be watching them!"

Even though he had been expecting this for a while, Bramblestar felt a pang of sorrow. Firestar and Dustpelt were dead; Graystripe and Sandstorm were the last remaining cats of their generation. "Of course you may join Purdy," he agreed. "If you're sure, we can hold your ceremony now."

Realizing that something more was about to happen, the Clan fell silent again, Lilyheart, Brackenfur, and Poppyfrost withdrawing to stand in the circle with their Clanmates.

"Cats of ThunderClan," Graystripe began, sounding slightly awkward but determined to have his say, "I'm so glad that I came back to find ThunderClan. I could never have made the journey without Millie, and I was so blessed by StarClan to have a second chance to raise kits." His glance traveled around the clearing, resting on each of his friends in turn. "I'll never forget Silverstream or Stonefur," he went on, "and I can scarcely believe that my daughter Mistystar is now leader of RiverClan. But I have no quarrel with StarClan for the path they chose for me, and I'm proud of all my kits. Blossomfall for her courage and skill in battle; Bumblestripe for his loyalty and compassion; and Briarlight for her bravery, her humbling spirit, and her hopefulness. I shall be watching all of you from the elders' den; you can be sure of that."

"I won't be long behind you, Graystripe," Millie purred, giving her mate a loving look.

Graystripe blinked at her. "I will wait for you, my dear."

Bramblestar waited for a moment, recalling the two cats' long relationship and the kits they had given to Thunder-Clan. Then he stepped forward and glanced from Graystripe to Sandstorm. "Are you ready?"

"Almost," Sandstorm mewed. "I just want to say that I will continue to serve my Clan and the warrior code, even from the elders' den." Her green gaze, full of love and loyalty, swept around the circle of her Clanmates. "I wish Firestar were here at my side," she went on, her voice shaking, "but I know he's watching over me, and over all of us." With great dignity she dipped her head to Bramblestar. "Go ahead."

"Sandstorm, Graystripe," Bramblestar began, "is it your wish to give up the role of warrior and go to join the elders?"

There was regret but no uncertainty in Sandstorm's voice. "It is."

"It is," Graystripe echoed.

"Your Clan honors you and all the service you have given us," Bramblestar went on. "I call upon StarClan to give you many seasons of rest." He laid his tail across Sandstorm's shoulders, and the ginger she-cat bowed her head, then stepped back. When Bramblestar had repeated the gesture for Graystripe, the two cats padded over to stand beside Purdy.

"I'm lookin' forward to company in the elders' den," the old tom meowed. "We'll have plenty o' stories to tell each other."

For a moment Bramblestar thought that he could see Firestar and Dustpelt weaving around the two new-made elders, the four cats united again. But before he could be certain, the image faded.

CHAPTER 34

"*Uh . . . Bramblestar?" Frankie walked into the* circle of cats. "Can I ask you something?"

Bramblestar dipped his head. "Of course."

"I want . . . that is, I'd like to join ThunderClan, and stay in the forest forever. If you'll have me," Frankie finished humbly.

Murmurs of surprise rose from the cats who surrounded them, but Bramblestar was pleased to see that none of them looked hostile at the idea of accepting a kittypet into the Clan. The gray tabby had more than proved his loyalty in the battle with the badgers, and his willingness to hunt and patrol.

"We'd be honored to have you," he responded.

Frankie's eyes shone with pride. "Thank you, Bramblestar!"

"Frankie," Bramblestar went on, "from this moment you will be known as Stormpaw, in recognition of the storm that brought you here, and as a memorial to your brother Benny. Squirrelflight, you will be mentor to Stormpaw. I'm sure that you will teach him everything he needs to know."

Squirrelflight's green gaze met Bramblestar's for a moment; then she dipped her head and beckoned to Stormpaw with her tail. "Touch noses with me," she murmured as he approached her.

"Stormpaw! Stormpaw!" the cats in the hollow yowled.

As the clamor died away, Minty stepped forward. "Er . . . I don't want to stay here! No offense—you've all been really kind—but please can I go home now? I want to see if my housefolk have come back."

"Of course," Bramblestar meowed with a purr. "We'll take you home. Thank you for everything you've done." He glanced at Jessy, but she said nothing, and did not meet his gaze. Bramblestar's pelt prickled. *There's a question waiting to be asked and answered, but neither of us is ready to say it out loud.*

Pushing that to the back of his mind, Bramblestar turned to Minty. "We'll take you home now, if you want."

Minty hesitated. "Please, may I stay one more night? I want to finish the nursery, and Purdy said he would tell me a story about a blind chicken, and I promised to help Leafpool sort some herbs, and . . . oh!" Her voice rose into a wail. "I will miss you all so much!" she blurted out.

Millie, who was standing nearby, rested her tail-tip on Minty's shoulder. "We'll always be here, if you ever want to visit," she meowed.

"Yes, you'll always be welcome." The rest of the Clan gathered around Minty, letting out friendly purrs.

"You have to come see my kits!" Cinderheart purred.

Brightheart nuzzled Minty's ears. "I'll be glad of help gathering herbs, if you feel like a walk in the forest some time."

Bramblestar watched, blinking in surprise. *I never thought Minty would end up being so popular. These kittypets have done more than adjust to our life in the Clan; they have become true Clanmates.*

* * *

The trees were outlined against a pale dawn sky as Bramblestar emerged from the tunnel and gathered a patrol to take Minty home. He chose Millie, who had always been especially kind to the little kittypet, and Dovewing, who had been part of the patrol that had rescued her from her flooded Twoleg nest.

"Stormpaw, do you want to come?" he asked.

Stormpaw shook his head. "No, thanks, Bramblestar. I don't want my old housefolk to see me. It's better if they think that Benny and I found a new home together," he finished sadly.

Cherryfall padded up to him and rested her ginger tail on his shoulder. "It's okay to be sad. If you ever want to talk about your brother, I'm always here."

Stormpaw bent his head toward hers, and Bramblestar caught Squirrelflight's eye across the backs of the two young cats. His deputy looked amused and pleased. Perhaps there was more behind Stormpaw's decision to stay than respect for the life of a warrior?

Bramblestar took the lead as his patrol headed down the slope. The water level was still much higher than the original shoreline, but they could make out the familiar shape of the lake. The border stream had shrunk back between its banks, so that they easily found a place where it was narrow enough for even Minty to leap across.

"I hope we don't get into trouble with ShadowClan," Minty mewed nervously as her paws struck the ground on the ShadowClan side.

"So do I," Millie agreed, landing next to her. "Rowan-star could still be angry that we joined in the battle with the badgers."

"There won't be any trouble," Bramblestar stated firmly. "We're within three fox-lengths of the water, so we're not trespassing."

Sure enough, before they were halfway across the terri-tory, a ShadowClan patrol came into view, picking their way through pine trees farther up the slope. Tigerheart was in the lead, with Stoatfur and Pinenose just behind him. When Tigerheart spotted Bramblestar and the others he veered toward them, loping briskly down until he met the Thunder-Clan patrol at the water's edge. "What are you doing here?" he demanded.

The other two ShadowClan warriors gave the Thunder-Clan cats a cold stare, without even a dip of the head as greeting. Bramblestar could still see their scars from the bat-tle against the badgers.

"We're taking Minty home," Bramblestar explained.

"Minty? Oh, yes, the kittypet." Tigerheart's glance raked across the patrol, coming to rest for a heartbeat on Dovewing. The gray she-cat was staring out across the lake as if it was more interesting than anything she had ever seen before.

There's something going on there, Bramblestar thought. *I wish I knew what it was. I know they went on the journey together to find the beavers, but that was seasons and seasons ago.*

"Well, I suppose you can pass," Tigerheart meowed, giv-ing Bramblestar a condescending nod. "But don't even think about putting a paw inside our territory."

"We won't," Bramblestar responded, doing his best to hide his irritation.

"See you stick to that." Tigerheart stood aside with a wave of his tail, leaving the path clear around the water's edge. "Because ShadowClan will be watching."

Bramblestar set off again. As he padded along the shoreline at the head of his patrol he could still feel the gaze of the ShadowClan cats boring into his back. By now the sun was rising above the trees, its pale rays turning the lake water to glittering silver. Around the Thunderpath and the half bridge, the flood was only belly-deep. Bramblestar was reminded of the hidden tree trunk that had saved him and Jessy from the old badger. *I hope I never have to do that again!*

He and his cats splashed through the water and headed up alongside the Twoleg dens. As they drew closer to her home, Minty picked up her pace and took the lead.

"The Twoleg dens are still empty and damaged with mud, just like the hollow," Millie remarked to Bramblestar. "But I expect the Twolegs will repair them, just like we're doing."

The doors of some of the dens stood open, with a few Twolegs hauling their stuff outside to dry in the sun. Bramblestar, Millie, and Dovewing instinctively ducked behind a hedge as a pair of them emerged close by, but Minty let out a joyful little trill and raced forward.

"I'm back! It's me!" she yowled. "I survived!"

The Twolegs stared at her, their jaws gaping, and let out sharp cries of surprise at the sight of the little black-and-white cat charging toward them. Minty took a flying leap into the forepaws of the nearest Twoleg, who held her close and pressed its face into her fur. For a moment it looked almost like a mother cat curling around the body of her kit.

They're really glad to see her, Bramblestar thought. *Just listen to them purring! I never thought Twolegs could feel that way.*

Minty looked up into her Twoleg's face. "I lived with wild cats!" she squealed. "I caught mice! And Purdy told me lots of stories, and I helped fix the nursery, and thrush tastes really good when you get past the feathers, and . . ."

Bramblestar exchanged an amused glance with Dovewing. "I don't suppose they have any idea what she's meowing about," he murmured. "Still, she's happy, and that's all that matters."

Beside him, Millie looked thoughtful as she watched the reunion.

"Are you thinking about your own Twolegs?" Dovewing asked her. "You must miss them very much."

Millie nodded. "I did, but not so much now," she mewed. "Sometimes I dream of them. I wonder if they dream of me." Then she turned away, giving her pelt a shake. "Come on, Minty is home now. Let's go back to ours."

There was no sign of ShadowClan cats as they padded back across the territory on their way home. By the time they reached the camp, the sun was beginning to dip down behind the tops of the trees. All the cats in the patrol were tired and wet through as far as their belly fur, their legs and paws caked with mud.

Squirrelflight and Stormpaw were sitting together outside the tunnel. "The warrior code says that the Clan must be fed first," Squirrelflight was explaining. "The elders and the nursing queens eat before any other cat. We take care of those who can't hunt for themselves."

Stormpaw nodded. "That makes sense."

Watching Squirrelflight teaching her apprentice, Bramblestar felt something warm well up inside him. *She's the best deputy a leader could hope for—and more than that* . . .

He was distracted as the other cats in the clearing noticed their return and pressed around them.

"Is everything okay?"

"Did Minty find her Twolegs?"

"Was there any trouble with ShadowClan?"

Mousewhisker pushed his way to the front of the crowd, a bundle of dry bracken in his jaws. "Here," he meowed. "Clean yourselves up with this. Honestly, I think if I see any more mud, I'll turn into a heap of earth!"

While Bramblestar was scraping the worst of the mud onto the bracken fronds, he realized that Jessy had slipped through the other cats to his side.

"Would you like to go for a walk while it's still light?" she offered.

Bramblestar nodded, though his belly began to churn with apprehension as they left the camp side by side. He knew that he couldn't put off questions about their future any longer.

They headed for the ridge, trotting silently over the soft, new grass. Shadows were gathering under the trees, and a light breeze swept down from the heights, stirring the cats' fur. When they reached the summit, they found a flat-topped rock where they could sit side by side, their pelts barely touching, and watch the sun go down in a blazing scarlet sky.

"I remember going this way to fight Victor and his friends," Jessy meowed. "We certainly taught them a lesson! And the battle against the badgers—that was so scary! But worth every moment of danger, because we helped ShadowClan and protected our own hunting grounds." She paused and looked at him, her amber eyes reflecting the orange sky. "Bramblestar, I'll never regret a moment of the time I spent with your Clan."

Bramblestar swallowed. "That sounds as if you're leaving."

Jessy rose to her paws. Her gaze was full of sadness. "I think you know I have to. If I stay, you—you might not follow where your heart truly lies."

For a moment Bramblestar was silent. Did she really know him so well, this brave, bold, sparkling kittypet? He had never meant to hurt her, not for a single heartbeat. "I'm sorry. I really am." He stood beside her, twining his tail with hers. Jessy leaned into him and they rested their heads together.

"I could have loved you," Bramblestar meowed.

"I know," Jessy murmured. "But you already love Squirrelflight. As you should. She is the mother of your kits."

Bramblestar opened his jaws to interrupt, but Jessy silenced him with a flick of her tail. "I know they weren't born to you," she went on. "But you are their father, just as Squirrelflight is their mother. That is not a bond that's easily broken. Not even washed away in a storm!"

"Will you go home to your housefolk?"

"I don't know," Jessy admitted. "They might not come back. Our den was very badly damaged. But I'll go that way first, and then see where my paws lead me." She raised her head, her eyes suddenly brighter. "Living with ThunderClan has given me a taste for adventure, and the life of a kittypet might be too tame for me!"

"You would have made a great warrior," Bramblestar told her.

"Oh, I know I would," Jessy assured him with a gleam in her eyes.

"I'll never forget you," Bramblestar mewed.

"Nor I you."

Bramblestar pressed himself closer against Jessy's side, breathing in her scent for the last time. *I wish things could have been different,* he thought. *It's hard to believe I'll never see her again.*

Looking over Jessy's head, he saw the lake turned scarlet by the setting sun. He remembered his vision of Yellowfang, the blood rising to meet her paws, and realized that blood ran deeper than anything else.

Jessy is right. Whatever I have felt for her, whatever might have been, Squirrelflight and I share a bond that cannot be broken.

CHAPTER 35

Bramblestar woke to find his Clanmates already heading outside. Two sunrises had passed since Jessy and Minty left, and the tunnel seemed oddly empty without them. He sat up, gave one ear a thorough scratch, and followed the others into the clearing outside the tunnel.

The rest of the cats were crowding around Squirrelflight as she sorted out the early patrols. "Cloudtail," she meowed, "I want you to lead the WindClan border patrol. Take Lilyheart with you, and . . . yes, Ivypool and Snowpaw. And can you take Stormpaw, too? It's time he learned what happens on a border patrol, and I have other things to do this morning."

Cloudtail dipped his head. "No problem."

Ivypool beckoned Stormpaw over with a twitch of her ears. "You can set the scent marks."

Stormpaw looked alarmed. "I don't know how to do that!"

"Don't worry." Lilyheart brushed her tail over his shoulder. "We'll show you what to do."

"We'll all help." Snowpaw looked delighted to be on patrol with an apprentice who knew less than he did. "It's easy!"

Bramblestar noticed Graystripe and Sandstorm standing

to one side, looking a little sad as the patrols formed up and moved off. He could guess how hard it must be for them to adjust to their new life as elders. But Sandstorm was already looking plumper now that she had the chance to rest, and Bramblestar hadn't heard her coughing for the last day or two. Now she and Graystripe settled themselves in a patch of sunlight where Purdy was already dozing, and began sharing tongues.

When the last of the patrols had left, Squirrelflight padded over to Bramblestar. She hadn't mentioned Jessy at all, except to say that she would be missed, on the morning after the brown she-cat had left.

"It's the night of the full moon," Squirrelflight meowed, sitting beside Bramblestar and wrapping her tail around her paws. "Every cat is excited at the thought of going to the Gathering. Do you think the water is low enough?"

Bramblestar nodded. "The lake is almost back to its normal level. The island will be muddy, but it should be dry enough for us to meet."

"Good!" Squirrelflight purred. "Who should we take with us?"

Bramblestar blinked. "Sandstorm and Graystripe will have to come. And Lilyheart and Stormpaw. I'll be mentioning them in my report. And either Jayfeather or Leafpool: We can let Jayfeather decide which."

"Jayfeather will decide, whether we *let* him or not," Squirrelflight commented, with a glint of amusement in her green eyes.

"True. What about Cherryfall and Molewhisker?" Bramblestar suggested. "They've worked so hard on rebuilding the camp; they deserve to come."

"Good idea," Squirrelflight agreed. "Brackenfur too, then."

"Right. And there should be a few more. . . . Give me some time to think about it. Oh, and could you tell Stormpaw what happens at a Gathering? He'll enjoy it more if he knows what to expect."

"The other Clans will know he used to be a kittypet," Squirrelflight pointed out.

"Yes," Bramblestar responded. "But he's not anymore."

Squirrelflight's eyes gleamed. "I'll go let Sandstorm and Graystripe know about the Gathering," she meowed, rising to her paws.

"Squirrelflight . . ." Bramblestar called as she turned away.

His deputy swung around, an inquiring look in her eyes. "Yes?"

"I just wanted to say . . ." Bramblestar struggled to find the right words. "I wanted to thank you for everything. For supporting me over the badger battle. For welcoming the kittypets I brought back. For—for raising three wonderful cats that I'm so proud of."

Squirrelflight stepped closer and her scent swept over him. "We did it together."

"Maybe," Bramblestar murmured. "I wouldn't have wanted to do it with any other cat."

Moving as one they stretched their necks forward; for a heartbeat their noses touched, and their muzzles brushed together. Then Squirrelflight stepped backward, looking ruffled. "I must tell the others about the Gathering."

"Okay." Bramblestar blinked at her affectionately and flicked her shoulder with his tail. "I'll see you later."

The moon was floating in a clear indigo sky when Bramblestar led his cats down toward the lake. In spite of the good omen, his belly was churning. He was dreading what Rowanstar might say about the battle with the badgers.

He's sure to mention it, to warn the other Clans that ThunderClan is interfering once again.

Squirrelflight, who had been padding along beside Jayfeather, quickened her pace until she reached Bramblestar's side. "I know what you're thinking," she meowed. "You're worrying about Rowanstar. Ignore him," she added with a sniff. "He couldn't have fought that battle without us. He might learn to be grateful eventually, even if he is a ShadowClan cat."

Excitement was bubbling up inside the ThunderClan cats as they headed for the lakeshore, and they darted back and forth with their tails bushed up when they saw the debris that the flood had left behind it. The pebbles had been completely covered by branches and all kinds of things that didn't belong.

"Look at all the rubbish that's been washed up!" Amberpaw exclaimed. "There's Twoleg stuff in there, too!"

"Yes, Amberpaw, we can all see it," Spiderleg snapped. "So leave it alone!"

"And dead fish," Lilyheart added. "Yuck!"

But as they crossed WindClan territory and drew closer to the island, every cat grew quieter. Two moons had passed since the last Gathering, a long time in the life of the Clans, and so much had happened since their last visit to the island. Bramblestar guessed that all his warriors were a bit daunted at the thought of meeting the other Clans again.

"I wonder how many cats didn't survive the storm and the flood?" Sandstorm murmured to Graystripe.

"I don't know." Graystripe shook his head sadly. "And what about RiverClan? They had to move so far away. Will they even be here tonight?"

To Bramblestar's relief, the tree-bridge was clear of the water, though the waves lapped against it, sucking greedily in the darkness. *I don't want a repeat of walking on that sunken tree trunk!* A pang shook him as he thought about Jessy. *I hope she's safe, wherever she is.*

The ThunderClan cats bristled as they crossed the bridge with the water gurgling close beneath their paws. Stormpaw in particular looked terrified, though he kept moving across the slippery, mud-smeared trunk. Squirrelflight gave him a word of praise as he jumped down at the other end.

While Bramblestar was waiting for his turn to cross, One-star and the WindClan cats came up behind him. Onestar greeted him with a frosty nod, but did not speak. Bramble-star felt his pelt tingling. He was glad when he could cross the tree-bridge and head through the bushes to the clearing in the center of the island. Relief flooded over him as he emerged from the bushes and saw Mistystar already there with her

RiverClan cats near the foot of the Great Oak. Her gray-blue fur shimmered in the moonlight and her eyes lit up with welcome when she saw Bramblestar.

"How are you?" he called, trotting over to her. "Have you managed to come home?"

"There's been a lot of damage to our camp," Mistystar mewed. "But we're working to rebuild it, and some of our warriors are already staying there overnight." She paused, then added sadly, "We lost Pebblefoot and Grasspelt in the storm, but the rest of our cats are well."

Bramblestar brushed his tail along her side. "I know how it feels to lose cats," he mewed. "We lost an apprentice, Seedpaw."

As the moon rose higher, the RiverClan and ThunderClan cats mingled together, exchanging news, but Onestar kept the WindClan cats aloof, clustered tightly together at one side of the clearing.

I wonder what his problem is, Bramblestar thought. *This is supposed to be a time of truce!*

Eventually Onestar raised his voice to be heard above the chatter. "It looks like ShadowClan isn't coming. We should begin."

Apprehension began to rise up inside Bramblestar. *It's true: ShadowClan should be here by now. Has something bad happened to them? Please, StarClan, don't say that the badgers have come back!*

Turning toward the Great Oak, Bramblestar realized that some of the younger cats had wandered off to check the flood damage on the far side of the island. He could hear them slipping and clambering over the rocks and fallen trees, and their voices rose excitedly.

"There's a dead fox here. Does any cat want it?"

"Yuck, no! That's crow-food!"

"Stop splashing me! Now I've got mud all over my pelt."

Suddenly a loud screech sounded from the shore. Bramble-star recognized Cherryfall's voice. Every hair on his pelt stood on end.

Then her voice came again in a triumphant yowl. "I've found the stick!"

Shocked exclamations rose from the other cats, and they pressed around Cherryfall as she stumbled into the clearing, dragging a long, smooth stick marked with neat scratches.

It's the ThunderClan memorial stick! A shiver went through Bramblestar from ears to tail-tip. *The stick that Seedpaw died for.*

Jayfeather wriggled his way to the front of the throng. His blind eyes blazed with joy as he crouched at one end of the stick and dug his claws into it as if he thought it was going to escape. Standing beside him, Bramblestar ran his paw over the marks, and thought about his lost Clanmates. *We owe them so much.* Yet somehow he felt oddly comforted. Finding the stick again seemed to promise that their memory would never be lost.

Mistystar peered down at the stick, her blue eyes curious. "What is it?" she mewed. "Why is it important?"

Cherryfall explained to her the meaning of the marks on the stick. "And this way," she finished, "we never forget the cats who died in the Great Battle."

There was a pause; Bramblestar could feel the memories weighing on every cat in the clearing.

It was Onestar who broke the silence. "We remember our fallen warriors with a pile of stones at the top of the moor, one stone for each cat. One patrol goes there every day, to remember and be thankful."

Mothwing, the RiverClan medicine cat, stepped forward with a glance at Mistystar. "Willowshine and I created a circle of ferns in which we can each remember our lost Clanmates," she mewed. "The flood damaged them, of course, but they will grow again."

A somber quiet fell across the clearing again, the cats of all three Clans united in grief.

"And we list the names of the dead at the first owl call each night."

Bramblestar whirled around. *Rowanstar!* The ShadowClan leader stood at the far side of the clearing with his warriors around him.

They padded forward to stand with the rest of the Clans, and for a few heartbeats they all remained silent with their heads bowed. Thankful that every Clan was there at last, Bramblestar felt their shared emotions wreathing around him like powerful scent. *We all feel it: the sorrow amid our victory over the Dark Forest. The Great Battle has saved us all, as well as shaping our future. But we paid the highest price we could.*

Raising his head, Bramblestar was suddenly confused. The clearing was packed with cats. *How many did Rowanstar bring with him?* Then Bramblestar saw that these cats were silver-furred with starlight, with a frosty glitter at their paws and their eyes shining with the icy light of the full moon. One by one he felt their gaze rest on him, and he recognized them with growing joy.

The cats who were lost in the Great Battle! They are here: Sorreltail and Ferncloud, Hollyleaf and Mousefur and Foxleap . . . oh, and Firestar!

Bramblestar gazed around and saw cats from the other Clans: Applefur and Cedarheart from ShadowClan; Ashfoot and Tornear from WindClan; Robinwing and Dapplenose from RiverClan; and many, many more.

As cries of astonishment arose from the living cats, Firestar stepped forward and spoke to Bramblestar "There is a way to honor all these cats who gave their lives to save the Clans by the lake. Remember SkyClan? You have the chance to make sure that it never happens again. . . ."

As he finished speaking the starry cats faded away, leaving the living cats gaping. Graystripe spoke for them all. "Did we really see that?"

Bramblestar gave his pelt a shake. With an effort he bounded across the clearing and leaped up into the Great Oak. The other leaders followed him to take their place in the branches.

"I'll begin," Onestar announced, stepping forward. "Wind-Clan has—"

"Wait," Bramblestar interrupted him. "I've got something important to say."

Onestar glared at him, but after a moment he gave an ill-tempered snort and stepped back to let Bramblestar speak.

"Cats of all Clans," Bramblestar began, forcing his voice to ring out confidently over the assembled cats. "We cannot let the fallen go unrecognized, and that includes ensuring the future of all four Clans together. In times of peace, we stand alone, hunt alone, fight with one another over our boundaries. But more than that, StarClan has shown us that there must always be four Clans beside the lake, and in times of trouble, Clan borders are meaningless."

He paused, aware of the momentous suggestion he was about to make that would change the life of the Clans for season upon season. "I wish to create a new rule for the warrior code: that each Clan has the right to be proud and independent, but in times of trouble they must forget their boundaries and fight side by side to protect the four. Each Clan must help the others so that no Clan will fall."

Rowanstar stepped forward to Bramblestar's side, his neck fur bristling. "It's always ThunderClan who decides to interfere," he hissed. "Any cat would think Firestar wasn't dead."

Bramblestar raised a paw to silence him, mighty and imperious. "Firestar *is* dead. I am leader of ThunderClan now. And I am proud to uphold his legacy of preserving all the Clans in the forest. No Clan was left behind on the Great Journey to find the lake. No Clan was abandoned to fight alone against the Dark Forest. No Clan will be allowed to fall now, not if the rest of us can protect them."

Looking down, Bramblestar saw Squirrelflight sitting in her place on the roots of the Great Oak. She was gazing up at him, and the love and warmth in her eyes sank into the depths of him, supporting him. "The strength of many preserves all!" he finished.

"Yes!" Mistystar's cry rang out as soon as Bramblestar had finished speaking. "We should do as Bramblestar says. It's for the good of every cat."

Onestar was working his claws into the bark of the branch where he stood. "You don't leave me much choice," he muttered grudgingly. "Okay, I agree."

"Rowanstar?" Bramblestar prompted. His pads burned with tension: Would the ShadowClan leader be able to put his pride aside and accept a change that would help preserve the Clans into the far future?

"I suppose I'm outvoted," Rowanstar growled. "Let it be so. . . ."

Enthusiastic yowls broke out from the cats in the clearing below. Listening to them, Bramblestar looked up to see the stars glittering more fiercely above his head. He wondered if he was imagining things, but it seemed to him that they had drawn closer together, sending an even brighter light down onto the island. With StarClan's help, the Clans had survived the flood, survived badgers, sought out new hunting grounds. The warrior code was even stronger than before with this new law. This would be Bramblestar's legacy to all the cats who came after him.

Under StarClan, four Clans will be one, to preserve the four.

TURN THE PAGE TO SEE WHAT HAPPENS NEXT
IN AN EXCLUSIVE MANGA ADVENTURE. . . .

CREATED BY
ERIN HUNTER

WRITTEN BY
DAN JOLLEY

ART BY
JAMES L. BARRY

PERHAPS NOT, BUT WE STAND A GOOD CHANCE OF EXHAUSTING OUR WARRIORS IF WE KEEP THIS UP.

DO WHAT YOU NEED TO DO. I'M GOING TO ORGANIZE THE PATROLS.

I DON'T KNOW WHAT'S WRONG WITH ME.

I'VE NEVER FELT LIKE THIS BEFORE.

THUNDERCLAN CANNOT HAVE A WEAK DEPUTY.

SQUIRRELFLIGHT? YOU AWAKE?

HRRMM...

I ALREADY TOOK THE FIRST DAWN PATROL OUT.

WHAT? HOW LONG-- THE SUN'S UP!

WELL, I FIGURED YOU MUST HAVE NEEDED TO SLEEP.

THE WARRIORS! THE APPRENTICES!

THEY'RE IN THE HOLLOW. THEY'RE WAITING FOR YOU.

TAKING IN THOSE KITS AS MY OWN WAS THE RIGHT THING TO DO. I KNOW THAT. LIONBLAZE, JAYFEATHER, HOLLYLEAF...

IT WAS AN HONOR TO RAISE THEM. STILL... KNOWING I COULD NEVER BEAR KITS OF MY OWN...

WHAT'S WRONG? CAN'T SLEEP?

HERE. SNUGGLE UP TO ME.

I CAN STILL FEEL THAT PAIN.

I'M NOT SURE HOW MUCH TIME HAS PASSED WHEN I WAKE AGAIN.

I'VE NEVER FELT LIKE THIS BEFORE.

...AND I FEEL SICK. SICKER THAN EVER.

I'VE GOT TO GET AWAY...

...GET SOMEWHERE I CAN THINK.

I LOVE THUNDERCLAN. I'M SO THANKFUL FOR IT...THANKFUL THAT WE SURVIVED THE FLOOD. THAT WE'RE AS STRONG AS EVER.

BUT STARCLAN HELP ME...

I'M SO SCARED!

SQUIRRELFLIGHT...

THE END.

Warriors: The New Prophecy

Follow the next generation of heroic cats as they set off
on a quest to save the Clans from destruction.

Warriors: Power of Three

Firestar's grandchildren begin their training as warrior cats.
Prophecy foretells that they will hold more power than any cats before them.

Warriors: Omen of the Stars

Which ThunderClan apprentice will complete the prophecy that
foretells that three Clanmates hold the future of the Clans in their paws?

HARPER
An Imprint of HarperCollinsPublishers

All Warriors, Seekers, and Survivors books are available
as ebooks from HarperCollins.

Visit www.warriorcats.com for the free Warriors app, games, Clan lore, and much more!

Warriors Stories

Download the separate ebook novellas or read them in two paperback bind-ups!

Don't Miss the Stand-Alone Adventures

Delve Deeper into the Clans

HARPER
An Imprint of HarperCollinsPublishers

Visit www.warriorcats.com for the free Warriors app, games, Clan lore, and much more!

Warrior Cats Come to Life in Manga!